LADY *of* LIGHT

Other books by Kathleen Morgan

Brides of Culdee Creek Series
Daughter of Joy
Woman of Grace
Lady of Light
Child of Promise

Guardians of Gadiel Series
Giver of Roses

These Highland Hills Series
Child of the Mist
Wings of Morning

LADY *of* LIGHT

BRIDES OF CULDEE CREEK • BOOK THREE

KATHLEEN
MORGAN

Revell
Grand Rapids, Michigan

© 2001 by Kathleen Morgan

Published by Revell
a division of Baker Publishing Group
P.O. Box 6287, Grand Rapids, MI 49516-6287

New paperback edition published 2007

Printed in the United States of America

Library of Congress Cataloging-in-Publication Data
Morgan, Kathleen
    Lady of light / Kathleen Morgan.
        p.   cm. – (Brides of Culdee Creek : bk. 3)
      ISBN 10: 0-8007-5755-6
      ISBN 978-0-8007-5755-7
      1. Scottish-Americans–Fiction. 2. Women pioneers–Fiction.
3. Married women–Fiction. 4. Colorado–Fiction. I. Title.
PS3563.08647 L3   2001
813'.54–dc21   00-067351

Scripture is taken from the King James Version of the Bible.

13   14   15   16   17   18   19   9   8   7   6   5   4   3

For my mother

CLAIRE
"Bright, illustrious, source of light"

No man, when he hath lighted a candle, putteth it in a secret place . . . but on a candlestick, that they which come in may see the light.

Luke 11:33

Prologue

Highlands of Sutherland, Scotland, March 1898

He fell after the second blow, to lie in an ever widening pool of blood.

Clutching her torn blouse to her, Claire Sutherland stared down at her uncle for the longest time, then glanced up to meet her brother's angry gaze. "Mother of God, Ian," she whispered, nearly retching from the renewed swell of stark, vivid fear, and stench of whiskey and sweat that engulfed her yet again. "What have you done? Och, what have you done?"

"Naught that you wouldn't have done, if I was the one being attacked," the fourteen-year-old muttered. He lifted the bloody, stout wooden stick, stared at it as if seeing it for the first time, then flung it aside. "Fergus is a foul-hearted drunk and lecher. He went too far this time, though, in laying a hand on you."

As a fierce spring wind howled in from the ocean, shaking the wooden rafters and battering the stone house, Claire hesitantly walked to where her uncle lay, squatted, and turned him over. After a horrified moment, she looked up. "Och, Ian. There's so much blood. Did you have to hit him so hard?"

"And what would you've had me do?" Ian's face mottled in his fear and frustration. "Politely ask him to stop ravishing my sister?" He laughed harshly. "Och, aye. As drunk as he was, Fergus would've made short work of tossing me out the window, or worse."

Claire's gaze lowered to her blouse. At the sight of the shredded fabric and marks of grubby hands, an image of her uncle attacking her but a few minutes before filled her.

Once more she saw his beard-stubbled face lowering to hers, felt his fat, thick lips slobbering over her neck and cheeks before claiming her mouth. Then there were his filthy hands, touching her, tearing at her clothes as he pressed her backward onto the rough-hewn table.

A freshened panic flooded Claire, as it had during those horrible, panic-stricken moments when she had fought frantically to protect herself. Her breath came again in short, painful gulps. Her heart pounded wildly in her chest.

"Still, I don't know who'll believe us, when we tell them what Uncle Fergus tried to do," Claire finally forced herself to reply. "After all, we aren't from these parts, and he was born and raised here."

"He isn't thought verra highly of. Mayhap the constable—"

"Fergus Ross has kin aplenty!" A little too sharply, Claire cut him off. "They'll stand by him, and the constable will soon be gone at any rate. Then who'll protect us? Nay"—she shook her head in fierce denial—"we can't risk it. We'll have to devise some other plan."

"The blame is mine, not yours," her brother protested. "They wouldn't harm you."

Claire straightened. "And do you think I'd let them lay one hand on you, brother? Nay, not while I draw breath."

"Then what shall we do?"

Almost of its own accord, Claire's gaze swung back to their uncle. "There's no way around it. We'll have to leave, find sanctuary elsewhere. After tonight, it'll only go the worse for us."

Ian chewed on his lower lip, his youthful brow furrowed in thought. Finally, he nodded. "Aye, it's the best plan. And it'll suit me fine. I never cared much for this place at any rate."

Mayhap not, his sister thought as she hurried to her small, enclosed boxbed in the single-roomed croft house to change. What lay ahead, though, might not be any better.

She crawled inside, pulled the shabby, woolen curtains to, and shivering in revulsion, quickly stripped off her ruined blouse. As much as she hated to face it, Ian was right. They'd never be able to return to this house. It was tainted beyond hope of ever being clean again.

Tainted, Claire thought with a sudden swell of despair. As were she and Ian . . . and their vain dream of ever finding a safe haven, or a place to call home again.

1

The Village of Culdee, Highlands of Strathnaver, Scotland, May 1899

For nothing is secret, that shall not be made manifest; neither any thing hid, that shall not be known. . . .

Luke 8:17

"Hie yourself out of bed this instant, Ian Sutherland, or your teacher won't be the only one who'll lay the tawse across your hands this day!"

Claire sent one final, narrow-eyed look across the crofter's cottage toward the boxbed holding her fifteen-year-old brother, then turned back to the rough-hewn table and the two carved, wooden bowls filled with uncooked oatmeal. She poured a portion of boiling water from the kettle into each bowl, then set the kettle

13

aside. Without further ado, Claire pulled up a small stool and sat. After sprinkling some salt over the now rapidly softening porridge and stirring it in, she poured a generous serving of milk atop it all.

Behind her, Ian groaned, kicked off his feather tick comforter, and shoved from bed. "I don't see what it matters if I'm late to school or not," the lanky, chestnut-haired boy grumbled as he padded barefoot across the packed dirt floor to the pitcher and wash basin. "Old man Cromartie will find some excuse before the day's out to lay the strap to me. He always does."

"Then mayhap you should devote a bit more time each eve to your studies." Claire stirred the milk into her oatmeal, then scooped up a helping of the Scots' staple food in a horn spoon. "He means only to encourage you to excel, after all."

"Och, aye." Her brother gave a snort of disgust. "The day Archibald Cromartie cares a whit for my success will be the day I choke down an entire haggis without complaint!"

Claire smiled at Ian's scathing reference to the traditional dish of ground ox or sheep organ meats mixed with oatmeal, suet, onions, and seasonings that was then stuffed in the animal's scraped stomach and boiled. "Well, *I* care, and that's all that matters. One of us must make it out of this village and accomplish something with his life. I can always wed, if need be. You, though, my fine lad, will need schooling to make your way in the world."

"Aye," Ian agreed with yet another disdainful snort. "As if *you're* of a mind ever to wed. I can't see you as a fishwife, or working the fields beside a big lout of a husband for some master." He paused to splash water onto his face and wash his hands, before glancing back up at her. "But then, mayhap you won't even have a choice, if Dougal MacKay has any say in it. He means to make you his wife, you know."

At the mention of the biggest, loudest, most arrogant Highlander between Loch Naver and the towering heights of Ben Loyal, Claire rolled her eyes. "Och, and that day will be a long time in coming, if *I* have any say in it! I can't bear the man. He's ruthless, crude, and I don't like the way he looks at me."

She shivered at the memory of the last time Dougal had waylaid her at the market. He'd had the audacity to grab her arm when she had made a move to evade him. His rough, possessive touch had made her skin crawl.

"Then if you won't wed the most well-to-do farmer in all of Culdee, mayhap it'd be best you finish your own schooling." As he spoke, Ian pulled on a pair of thread-bare, brown trousers and tucked in his nightshirt. "Nowadays, a lass can attend university same as the lads."

"*If* I was ever to further my education," Claire retorted tartly, "it wouldn't just be for some token certificate. I'd instead hie myself to America, where a woman can study *and* win the same degree as a man." She paused to shovel another bite of porridge into her mouth. "But it doesn't matter, at any rate. We both can't afford to attend university, and so it must be you."

"Nay, it doesn't *have* to be me." Her brother walked over to gaze solemnly down at her. "You can't go on the rest of your life sacrificing for me, Claire. It won't make what happened go away, or atone for what we did. Besides, I'm nearly a man now. It's past time I stop wast-ing my life with useless things like conjugating Latin verbs and plowing through Virgil and Horace. What's needed nowadays is a strong back and stout pair of arms, not a mess of useless tales and fancy words."

His sister slammed down her spoon and turned to glare at him. Enough was enough, she thought, her always volatile temper brimming to the breaking point. She didn't need to be reminded yet again of that horrible night just a year past now, or the miserable years leading up to it. They had come to Culdee to forget and start anew.

"What's needed, Ian Sutherland," she hissed, "is that you finish your porridge before it gets cold, then hie yourself to school. Father MacLaren and St. Columba's are waiting on me. Meantime, I'm the only family you've left, and as the eldest, I mean to be obeyed. The time will come when you'll make your own decisions about your life. When it does, I want you to make them with all the information at hand. So, until that day arrives, it's off to school with you."

He shot her a disgruntled look. Then, with a huge exhalation of martyred resignation, Ian plopped down onto his stool. "Och, and haven't *we* become the harridan this morn?" he grumbled.

"Aye, mayhap I have." Claire sighed. Ah, she thought, how swiftly the regrets could rush back to drown one in a floodtide of broken dreams, if only one let them! "Still, someone has to put her shoulder to the plow and finish what she so boldly if foolishly set out to do five years ago. But I make my vow, before you and the Lord above, that I won't have you ruining your life, as well, in the bargain."

ɞ

Even before he opened his mouth, Claire could tell the tall, dark-haired stranger with the unusually wide-brimmed, black hat wasn't a Scotsman. Something about him had caught her eye as she swept the parish church steps later that afternoon. Something she noted even halfway down the hill, as she watched him climb the winding road leading through Culdee to where the old, dry stone church had perched for the past seven hundred years.

Perhaps it was his fine, dark suit, dust-coated after the long walk from the coach stop just outside the village—and how well that suit accentuated his broad shoulders and long, lithe legs. Then again, perhaps it was the way he moved, his stride smooth, effortless, powerful. Or perhaps, just perhaps, Claire thought as the stranger finally reached the base of the church steps and paused to squint up at her, it was his sheer masculine beauty, from his tanned face and strong jaw to his straight nose and striking, smoky blue eyes.

One thing was certain. She had never seen a more handsome, physically impressive man.

"Do ye think, lass," a rusty, old voice rose unexpectedly from behind her, "ye might do well to greet our guest? 'Twouldna speak well o' our fine village to gape and stare overlong at every stranger who comes our way."

"Och, Father MacLaren! I didn't hear you come up," Claire cried, losing her grip on the broom as she wheeled about to face him. In that same instant, she realized her error. With a gasp, she spun back around and grabbed for the broom, just missing the wooden, wheat straw implement. End over end, the broom tumbled down the long course of steps to land at the stranger's feet.

With a grin he set down his canvas travel bag, stooped, and picked up the broom. Climbing halfway to meet Claire, he offered it back to her. "Have a care, ma'am, or you might be the next thing landing at my feet."

She could feel the heat flood her face. This was daft, the way she was acting, Claire scolded herself. It wasn't as if she had never met a fine-looking man before. It wasn't as if she had never seen a masculine glint of admiration directed at her, either.

Claire managed a taut smile. "You're from America, aren't you? I can tell by your accent."

His gaze never wavered from her face. "Yes, I'm from America. Colorado to be exact. Funny thing is, though, where I come from it's you who'd be branded with having the accent."

Claire laughed. Despite the stranger's attempt at bravado, she could now see a deeper glimmer of uncertainty in his eyes. Her strange unease dissipated. She felt confident and in control again.

"Well, you're in the Highlands now, my braw lad, and you're the foreigner, not I." She glanced over her shoulder at the old priest. "If you haven't further chores for me, Father, I'll be on my way. Ian should be heading home soon. I've a fine pot of colcannon simmering and a loaf of bread yet to bake for supper."

"And havena ye a wee moment more to spare for our new friend, lass?" The gray-haired cleric cocked his head and arched a shaggy brow. "Dinna ye wish to hear what his needs might be?"

If the truth were told, Claire wished she were as fast and far away from the tall American as she could get. Pleasant and well mannered as he seemed, there was just something about him . . . something disturbing that she couldn't quite put her finger on. But she couldn't very well admit that to his face now, could she?

"I didn't wish to pry," she forced herself to reply. "It appears he came to see—"

"Reckon you might as well stay, ma'am," the stranger interrupted just then. "In fact, you may be as much help as the padre here. I'm looking for some kinfolk, and I haven't any idea where to begin."

Reluctantly, Claire turned back to face him. He *was* a stranger in their land, after all, and no true Highlander would deny anyone hospitality. "Well, if you could tell us the names of your kin, mayhap that would be the best

18

way to begin. It would be nigh impossible, even for a man as knowledgeable as Father MacLaren, to help you without names."

The American pulled off his hat and ran a hand roughly through what Claire now realized was black, wavy hair in dire need of a trim. "That's just the problem, ma'am. The last kin of mine who lived in Culdee left here in 1825. His name was Sean MacKay, and he was my great grandfather."

"That was seventy-four years ago, lad." The priest's glance skittered off Claire's. He scratched his jaw. "'Twill be a challenge to find yer true kin, though if ye be a MacKay, in a sense these hills are filled with yer kin, for these are MacKay lands."

"I've got time," the American muttered cryptically, and with what Claire almost imagined was an edge of bitterness. "It's why I came all this way north from Glasgow."

"Did ye, now?" Father MacLaren grasped his cane and climbed awkwardly down the steps to stand beside Claire. "And who be ye, then?"

"I'm Evan MacKay, son of Conor MacKay, the owner of Culdee Creek Ranch, east of Colorado Springs, Colorado." He held out his hand.

"Well, I've heard o' Colorado, but not o' this Colorado Springs." The priest accepted the American's proffered hand, and gave it a hearty shake. "I'm Father William MacLaren of St. Columba's Kirk. And this bonnie lassie," he added, turning to Claire, "is Claire Sutherland, my wee housekeeper."

The man named Evan rendered her a quick nod. It wasn't quick enough, though, Claire realized with a twinge of irritation, to hide a freshened gleam of appreciation.

"Pleased to meet you, ma'am." He shoved his hat back on his head, lifted his face to the sun that was even now dipping toward the distant mountains, then frowned.

19

"Well, as you say, the search for my kin might be a challenge. And it certainly isn't one I care to take on today."

"Nay, I'd imagine not," the priest agreed amiably. "The morrow will be soon enough. If ye wish, ye can then begin with our church records. Mayhap a wee look into the baptismal and wedding register will provide ye with additional clues to solve yer mystery."

"I'd be much obliged, Padre."

Father MacLaren stroked his chin and eyed him speculatively. "Have ye lodging then, already arranged for the night?"

"No." Evan MacKay gave a swift shake of his head. "But if you could direct me to an inn or boarding house . . ."

"There's no inn, leastwise not in Culdee." The old priest's brow furrowed in thought. "Indeed, the closest inn's in Tongue, a good sixty miles north o' here.

He turned to Claire. "Doesna yer landlord have another small croft to let?"

"Aye," she replied slowly, not liking where the conversation seemed suddenly to be heading. "But the dwelling is shabby indeed, and no fit place for such a fine man as Mr. MacKay."

"It's Evan. Please, call me Evan." He gave a low, husky laugh. "And believe me, Miss Sutherland. I'm not all that fine. I can handle just about anything that provides me with a roof over my head."

"This isn't America, you know," Claire protested, not at all pleased with the idea of the tall man residing so near to her. "The winds blow bitter off the sea and when it rains, the chill can sink deep into your bones."

Once more, Evan laughed. "And you, pretty lady, haven't lived through a Colorado winter. As bad as your Highland weather might be, it's no worse in comparison."

"Ye see, lass?" Father MacLaren offered just a little too eagerly. "'Tis the perfect solution. If Mr. MacKay . . . Evan . . . lives nearby, he might even be willing to earn a bit o' his board by helping ye and Ian in the garden plot and caring for Angus's sheep and chickens. 'Twould take a load from yer shoulders, wouldna it?"

"Aye, I suppose so," Claire admitted. "Just as long as Angus doesn't raise our rent in the doing."

"Och, dinna fash yerself. I'll have a talk with the mon. He's a MacKay, after all. 'Twouldna hurt him to extend a wee bit o' hospitality to kin, now wouldna it?"

"Nay," she muttered. Angus MacKay was as tightfisted as any Scotsman could get. Odds were, though, he just might lower the rent for one of his blood, even if he surely had never seen fit to do so for her and Ian. But then they were Sutherlands, she reminded herself with a twinge of resentment, and not even from these parts.

"Then get on with ye, lass. Escort Evan here to Angus's." The old priest gave her a gentle nudge. "As ye said, ye'd best be on yer way. There's that pot simmering, and the bread ye've yet to bake."

She stared at him in disbelief. Did he really expect her to lead this stranger—this *American*—through Culdee and all the way home? Why, she'd be the talk of the village for weeks to come!

Yet what else could she do? It wouldn't be polite to refuse. Indeed, what plausible excuse could she give?

She exhaled a frustrated breath, then turned to the American. "Well, shall we be on our way, Mr. MacKay?"

He grinned at her. "Evan. Please, call me Evan."

"I prefer Mr. MacKay, if you don't mind." Claire rendered the priest a curt nod. "I'll see you on the morrow then, Father."

"Och, nay." The priest held up a silencing hand. "Take the next day or two off. Assist Evan in discerning who his true blood kin are. 'Tis the hospitable thing to do."

Once more the heat warmed Claire's cheeks, but this time it was fueled by rising irritation. She'd swear Father MacLaren was playing the matchmaker. Well, his well-meant efforts would fail yet again. She didn't want a man in her life. Not now, and not ever.

"As you wish, Father," she gritted out her reply. Someday soon she'd have to have a wee talk with the priest about his marital interference. But not just now. Her first priority must be for her totally unexpected and unwanted guest. The sooner she helped him ascertain who his true kin in Culdee were, the sooner she could be rid of him.

If all went well, she wouldn't have to endure him for long. And it wasn't as if she had to spend time alone with the American or worry about him causing problems. There were neighbors aplenty about, and Ian would be near at night.

Aye, Claire reassured herself. One way or another, the ordeal would soon be over.

ɘ

Evan retrieved his travel bag at the bottom of the hill, and they soon reentered Culdee. They walked so long in silence, he began to wonder why the pretty girl at his side had seemingly taken such a strong and instant dislike to him. Maybe he just didn't have the right touch with the ladies. It wouldn't surprise him much, not after how miserably he had failed with Hannah.

He had hoped coming to Scotland might finally help him get his mind off her. Nothing else had seemed to work. Not leaving the ranch when it became clear what her feelings were for his cousin Devlin, nor a two-month stint driving herds of beef to Kansas, nor the following four months working fishing boats off the coast of Florida. Even the offer to sign on as a ship's crewman on a transatlantic cruise to England three months ago—a trip he had seen as a grand adventure—had failed to ease the heavy ache in his heart.

He had searched for answers the whole time—turned to God, even. Oh, how he had searched, asking himself repeatedly: What had he done wrong to drive Hannah from him? Why didn't he seem to be man enough to stay on and tough it out? Why, once again, had he run when things got too hard to bear? Searched and asked . . . futilely, fruitlessly. If anyone had stormed the gates of heaven for answers, Evan felt certain he had.

Worst of all, he knew he had disappointed his father, failing him yet again. For that he was ashamed and sorry. It seemed, atop all his other deficiencies, he couldn't even be a good son.

Claire Sutherland, however, didn't need to know about any of that. Or leastwise, he added grimly, not until he found his own answers, answers that would finally give him the peace he so dearly sought.

"You don't care much for me, do you, ma'am?"

From the corner of his eye, Evan watched and waited as the auburn-haired girl considered his startling query. Good, he *had* managed to stump her, he thought, when no reply was forthcoming. He could tell she had a quick mind. Those dancing green eyes of hers did little to hide her every thought and inclination.

From the start he had been powerfully attracted to her. What red-blooded man wouldn't be? She was absolutely breathtaking, even dressed in a plain, dark blue, woolen skirt and long-sleeved white blouse with a tartan plaid of green, blue, and black wool. Worn as a shawl, the plaid crisscrossed her breast and was fastened with a round, flat silver brooch worked with intricate scrolling. Her bare feet and ankles, peeking out beneath the hem of her skirt, only lent an additional endearing air.

He had never seen quite that shade of dark, rich auburn hair either. When the setting sun caught it just right, the long, curly mane, falling unbound to the mid-

23

dle of Claire's back, seemed afire with glinting shards of copper and gold. Even the term "crowning glory" seemed an inadequate description of her hair, not that she needed much at all to crown that lovely face or form of hers. Gazing at it, he felt a nearly overwhelming compulsion to reach out and run his fingers through the silky, shimmering strands.

Such behavior, though, wasn't proper in well-bred American society. Evan doubted it would be acceptable here either. On the contrary, he sensed he'd have to step lightly around this particular young lady. She appeared as skittish as a mustang about to be saddled for the first time. If a man wasn't careful, he could get his teeth kicked in.

"Well, do you or don't you like me?" Evan prodded when all the response he seemed to stir from her was a narrowing of eyes and a setting of tightly clamped lips. "Don't hold back your true feelings, ma'am. We're well out of the padre's earshot. And I'm man enough to take it."

With an exasperated exhalation of breath, Claire slid to a halt and turned to glare up at him. "Why do you persist in goading me?" she demanded, her fists rising to settle on her hips. "If you'd any respect for Highland ways, you'd know how hard we strive to treat strangers with respect and cordiality. But I warn you, Mr. MacKay. You've nearly gone and pushed me past the point of good manners."

"So, you *don't* like me!" To further needle her, Evan grinned in triumph.

"I didn't say that." Claire huffed in frustration. "Why, I hardly know you!"

"Then why are you stalking through Culdee so fast and furious? Seems pretty clear to me that you can't wait to be rid of me."

She eyed him for so long, Evan was tempted to ask if some horn or other strange growth had suddenly sprouted from the middle of his forehead. Then she sighed.

"I beg pardon if I gave you such an impression. It was neither kind nor Christian to treat you in such a fashion." A tittering arose from the doorway of a croft house they had just passed. Claire wheeled about and shot the offending pair of girls a quelling look, then turned back to him. "Come. The longer we stand here, the more the tongues will wag."

"And you don't particularly like being the subject of gossip and endless speculation."

As if she was now fighting back a grin, one corner of her mouth twitched. "Nay, not particularly."

"I can well understand," Evan said, striding out once more. "Culdee Creek's a small community in itself, what with my cousin and his family living not a hundred feet from the main house, and a bunkhouse full of ranch hands just down the hill. Then there's our nearest town of Grand View, which is only a bit larger than this village. Folk in our neck of the woods don't seem to have much better to do with their time than stick their noses into other folk's business."

Scrambling to keep up with him, she shot Evan a curious glance. "You spoke of Culdee Creek being a ranch. Are you a cowboy, then?"

He shrugged. "I reckon, if riding a horse, roping and branding steers, and shooting a revolver makes me a cowboy." He arched a speculative brow. "Does being a cowboy elevate a man any in your esteem?"

"I can't say for certain. I've heard cowboys are an uncouth, dangerous lot."

"Kind of like what I've heard about Highlanders. Of course," Evan drawled, "it strains the imagination how any man who runs around in skirts could be all that dangerous."

"They aren't skirts, you silly oaf." Claire shook her head with what Evan could only suppose was a long-suffering forbearance. "They're kilts." She shot him a suspicious glance. "Are you quite certain you're a Mac-Kay? No true Highlander would ever question another Highlander's courage, you know?"

"Aye, I'm a MacKay, and no mistake," he replied, mimicking her soft burr. "Just never ask me to wear that skirt . . . er, kilt."

"Dinna fash yerself. If you don't think it an honor to do so, then you don't deserve to wear one."

Evan frowned. "What does that mean? 'Dinna fash yerself'?"

"Och, naught more than don't let yourself be annoyed or bothered," she said, leading him across a sturdy, curving stone bridge spanning a small stream. "It's mayhap an old way of talking, but there are some phrases that just seem to hang on."

"I suppose every country has its old favorites."

Claire chuckled. "Right you are. Mayhap you can tell me some of your favorites, when we've—"

The sound of childish voices, lifted in excitement, rose on the air. As they drew nearer, sporadic, angry shouts, interspersed by rising cries urging on someone to fight, grew louder. Then, as Evan and Claire moved past a stand of beeches blocking the gathering from view, two boys, slugging away at each other, could be seen.

"Ian," Claire whispered hoarsely. She broke into a run.

Evan stared after her for an instant longer, then followed swiftly in her wake.

2

Let us search and try our ways, and turn again to the LORD.

Lamentations 3:40

His features contorted in rage, Ian slugged Malcolm MacKay squarely in the face. Blood spurted from the taller boy's nose. The pain and taste of blood, however, only seemed to spur Malcolm on. With a roar, he flung himself onto Ian, toppling them both to the ground.

Girls squealed in terror. Boys shouted their approval. Then both pushed even closer around the two combatants now battling in the grass. It took all Claire's strength to elbow her way through the crowd and reach the front. Her stomach clenched in despair at the sight of her brother yet again, in less than a month, engaged in a fight.

"Stop it!" she cried. "Ian. Malcolm. Stop it now, I say!"

Oblivious to her frantic pleas, the two lads fought on. Claire glanced around, gauging which boy, standing about avidly watching, might be strong enough to help her pull them apart and hold them. Just then, a hand settled on her shoulder.

"Let me take care of this."

She turned and looked up into Evan MacKay's dark blue eyes. At the compassion she saw there, gratitude filled Claire.

He paused only to set down his canvas traveling bag and remove his hat and jacket before stepping into the fray. First he grasped the back of Ian's belt and lifted him bodily off Malcolm. As Ian gained his balance and whirled around, fists high in outrage, Evan's booted foot shot out and neatly tripped him. Malcolm, halfway to his feet by then, apparently decided to seize the advantage.

As he went for Ian, now sprawled flat with the wind knocked out of him, Evan grabbed Malcolm by the collar and jerked him back. Howling in anger, the big, red-haired boy lifted a fist toward Evan.

"Don't try it, son," Evan warned, his voice gone hard and low, his gaze narrowed. "You aren't yet man enough to take on the likes of me."

His chest heaving, his fair face beet red, Malcolm paused to eye his new opponent. "Let me go," he finally snarled. "I havena any grudge with you. 'Tis Ian who's the thief. And, this time, he's going to pay."

"Lying swine!" his opponent countered furiously, scrambling to his feet. "Take it back, I say, before I whip you some more!"

He advanced on Malcolm, but before Evan could make a move to halt him, Claire stepped between them. "It's over, Ian." Her steely glance met and locked with her brother's. "You know I don't hold with fighting."

"Then you should've been here to smack Malcolm's smart mouth," her brother retorted, still flushed with anger and the thrill of battle. "I won't abide anyone calling me a thief!"

"Mayhap you should stop your thieving then!" the other boy cried. He made no move, however, to escape Evan's clasp. "Jamie here was to take that money to the seamstress to pay his mither's debt. He's sure to get a thrashing now, when his mither learns he was robbed by the likes of you."

"If he's lost the money, he deserves a thrashing." Ian's lip curled in derision. "That's no reason to blame it on me, though."

"It is if you've taken the money," Claire interjected, gripping her brother's shoulder. "Have you, Ian? Tell me true, lad."

Suddenly, if almost imperceptibly, Ian couldn't quite meet Claire's gaze. Her heart sank. He *had* stolen the money.

She had hoped her brother had finally outgrown his thieving habits in the past year since they had come to Culdee. Though he had continued to engage in periodic brawls with his schoolmates, Ian had always insisted they had been the result of some bully like Malcolm MacKay picking on him, or of some younger child whose aid he had come to. But now . . . Claire had to wonder how much else of what Ian told her had also been lies.

"I didn't take Jamie's money," her brother muttered, still refusing to look directly at her. "Jamie's lying, and Malcolm was just looking for an excuse to fight me. That's all there is to it."

"Ian . . ." Claire warned. "Don't tell me a falsehood."

"It isn't a falsehood!" He stepped back, his expression now indignant, accusatory. "It's a fine day indeed, when your own kin won't believe you!"

"How much did you lose, son?" Evan turned to Jamie.

The small, towheaded boy dressed in shabby trousers that barely passed his knees, gazed up at the tall American. "A pound sixpence, sir."

Evan dug into his pocket and pulled out a handful of silver and gold coins. "Well, how about I make you a loan until we find the lost money? Just so your mama doesn't have to whup you, okay?"

29

Jamie's head bobbed in eager agreement. "Aye, that'd be fine, sir. Just until we find the lost money."

"You willna find the money," Malcolm growled under his breath. "Leastwise not unless you search Ian Sutherland's person."

With an obvious show of ignoring the other boy, Evan counted out the money and handed it to Jamie. Then he turned to Malcolm. "Where I come from, son, we take a man at his word until it's proven otherwise. If the money was stolen, the truth will come out sooner or later. And if it wasn't, well, I reckon we'll find that out, too."

The red-haired boy glared at Evan for a long moment. Then, with a final, quelling look at Ian, he turned on his heel and stalked off. The rest of the children, apparently robbed of their evening's entertainment, soon followed.

Wordlessly, Claire handed Evan back his hat, jacket, and traveling bag. Then, her hurt and disappointment at her brother's lie still smarting, she turned and strode away. Evan and Ian stared fleetingly after her, before hurrying to follow. Eventually Evan caught up with her, even as her brother seemingly decided it wise to continue lagging behind.

Coward, Claire thought sourly, noting Ian's hesitation. *He doesn't wish to endure my wrath.* Then she turned her attention back to her dark-haired companion. "Thank you for your assistance." She forced a smile of gratitude. "I don't know what I would've done without you. Both Malcolm and Ian are fast growing into such great beasties, I doubt I could easily have stopped them."

Without breaking stride, Evan doffed his hat to her. "My pleasure, ma'am."

"He isn't always like that, you know?" For some reason, Claire felt compelled to explain her brother's actions. "Ian just has a hard time fitting in well with his schoolmates. To make matters worse, he has a temper the equal of mine."

"Surely you're joshing, ma'am. I've never met a more sweet, gentle lady than yourself."

Not certain if he was serious or just teasing her, Claire sent Evan a quick, searching glance. One corner of his mouth twitched—a mouth, she noted with a sudden and most disconcerting ripple of feminine awareness—that was full, firm, and most delectably masculine.

Inexplicably, irritation filled her. "Well, Mr. MacKay," she gritted out the words, "keep needling me, and you may well discover how truly sweet and gentle I can be. After all, this is a serious matter, my brother fighting and being accused of thievery."

As if assessing whether Ian might overhear their conversation, Evan glanced behind him. "You mentioned he gets into a lot of fights," he then continued, apparently satisfied that Ian had dropped even farther behind and wouldn't be a party to what was being said. "Does he often get accused of stealing too?"

She was tempted to tell him the truth, then caught herself. Truly, she must be a bit addled in the head, Claire decided, to confide in a total stranger—and foreigner—no less!

Fiercely, she shook her head. "Nay. Hardly ever."

At the deception, guilt surged through her. Though she hadn't really lied, she had bent the truth a bit. Ian didn't get accused frequently of stealing, leastwise not as often as he seemed to get into fights. Indeed, this was only the second time since they had come to Culdee that Ian had ever been named a thief.

Compared to all the thieving he had done prior to that just so they could survive, Ian hardly stole at all anymore. *If* he truly had stolen, Claire corrected herself.

She had no proof, save the guilt she thought she had seen just a short while ago in her brother's eyes.

"Well, that's good to hear," Evan's deep voice drew her back from her troubled musings. "Maybe there's a chance then that Jamie's money will turn up."

"You think he stole Jamie's money, don't you?" Claire's pent-up fears exploded in a white-hot burst of anger. "Why not just come out and say it?"

Evan stopped dead in his tracks. "Don't you?"

His simple, direct query blindsided her. "N-nay," she stammered, all at once at a loss for words. "I just told you–"

"Miss Sutherland, I'm sorry," he said, his gaze full of understanding. "I admire your loyalty to your brother, and I didn't mean to put you on the spot. Besides, it's really none of my concern."

"Aye, you're right. It isn't your concern." His smoky blue eyes bore into hers. She found her mouth going dry and her palms damp. "Still," she finally forced herself to say, "I'm beholden to you for paying Jamie. After that, Malcolm hadn't a thing further to say or prove."

"It seemed the best way to settle things, at least temporarily."

"If Jamie's money doesn't turn up after a time, I'll repay you."

"That won't be necessary. If you help me for the next couple of days, as Father MacLaren suggested, it'll be money well spent." Evan chuckled. "In addition to your kindness in setting me up with a roof over my head, of course."

Och, aye, Claire thought in belated remembrance. Angus MacKay's extra croft house. In all the excitement, she had nearly forgotten her primary mission.

She glanced around. In the interim of their journey and the breaking up of the fight, twilight had settled over the land. Already, the light of candles and fish oil lamps gleamed from windows—bright beacons in the rapidly dimming gloaming. It was past time to reach home, Claire decided, if they were to see to Mr. Mac-Kay's basic necessities before dark.

"Well," she muttered, quickening her pace, "we'll just have to see about that. Meantime, we've still a good half-league walk before we reach my landlord's holdings. It would be best if you stepped out a bit."

Evan laughed then, a deep, rich, full-bodied sound. "Yes, ma'am," he said, lengthening his stride. "I reckon it would."

ど

Angus MacKay and his wife, Flora, had apparently just sat down to supper, when Claire drew up with Evan and Ian at his door. A few brisk raps on the wooden portal drew a grumbling, burly Scotsman who jerked open the door to glare down at them.

"Well, what is it, lass?" he immediately demanded. "Ye know 'tis past rude to interrupt a man at his supper."

"I beg pardon, Angus." She stepped aside and indicated Evan, standing just behind her. "I brought you a tenant for your other croft house. Since he hasn't anywhere to reside, I thought—"

"He's welcome to it, but he canna stay in that house this eve," Angus snapped. "'Tis filthy from disuse. 'Twill most likely take a day o' cleaning to make it fit for humans. He'll have to stay elsewhere 'til the morrow."

"But I told you, Angus," Claire protested. "He has nowhere else to go."

"Then let him stay wi' ye and Ian fer the night, or send him back to Culdee. I'm certain Father MacLaren would put him up."

"But Angus—"

33

The tawny-haired man's face reddened, and he held up a warning hand. "'Tis the best I can do fer him on short notice." He finally looked to Evan. "See me on the morrow and we'll talk." With that, Angus MacKay slammed the door in their faces.

"He didn't even give you a chance to tell him Evan was kin," Ian muttered in disgust. "By mountain and sea, but Angus hasn't a kindly bone in his body!"

"Och, he's a good man in his own way," Claire said in their landlord's defense. "He just gets a wee bit grumpy when his meals are disturbed." Then, knowing she had little other choice, she turned to Evan. "If you don't mind a pallet on the floor, you can stay with us this eve. It hardly makes sense to send you back to Culdee in the dark. Odds are you'd lose your way and fall into a burn and drown, or be set upon by one of our Highland beasties."

"Your concern for my welfare is most flattering, ma'am." A wry humor gleamed in his eyes. "I wouldn't want to put you out, though, or impose further on your hospitality."

Claire made an impatient sound. "And isn't that an expectation when requesting hospitality? That you'll be imposing on someone?" She tugged on his jacket sleeve. "Well, dinna fash yourself. It can't be helped, and it's only for one night. On the morrow, I'll help you set your house aright. Then you'll have your peace and privacy for as long as you wish to remain in Culdee."

"Well, if you're certain you don't mind . . ."

"I don't mind. Now, come along. Our own supper's ready, and I'm famished."

Even as she denied them, though, second thoughts did assail Claire. At every turn, circumstances seemingly contrived to thrust Evan MacKay into her path. It was bad enough Father MacLaren had suggested Angus's croft house for Evan, a house not fifty feet from

34

hers. But then to be forced to nursemaid him in his quest to discover his true kinfolk, and now even to put him up for a night in her own house . . .

It wasn't fair. It wasn't fair at all!

ᶜ

Claire and Ian's little croft house, though small, appeared quite clean and cozy. The simple rectangular building was constructed of mortar and stone, the roof thatched with sod divots stuffed with barley straw. It possessed but a single entrance, and two small, glass-paned windows situated on either side of the door. At both ends of the cottage, a chimney protruded.

Inside, the house opened onto two rooms joined between by a long vestibule off the front door. Claire led Evan into the larger chamber on the right, which was most evidently the living area and kitchen. As she hurried to light the oil in several cast-iron contraptions she called cruisies, Evan glanced leisurely around.

The walls were lime-washed, the two windows decorated by lace curtains and pots of bright red geraniums. The floors were hard-packed clay, covered in places by mats of plaited straw and bent grass interspersed with several colorful rag rugs. On the far wall was the fireplace. Simmering over a now smoldering peat fire was a cast-iron pot hanging from a chain. Nearby, stacked on both sides of the hearth, were a variety of pots and pans plus several ladles, and what looked to be some sort of griddle.

Against the adjoining wall sat a tall, enclosed wooden box with doors that contained a bed. In the center of the room stood a rough-hewn table set with stools. Two low chests, a wickerwork cabinet, and a tall cupboard laden with an assortment of pottery and wooden dinnerware completed the room's décor.

"That's Ian's bed." Claire indicated the boxbed. "You can sleep near the fire, if you wish."

"Sounds good, ma'am. Sure beats the cold, hard ground out of doors."

As if she felt her hospitality still lacking, she nodded curtly, took down a bowl from the cupboard, then paused. "Are you thirsty, Mr. MacKay? We've a jug of ale. Or I can make you a pot of tea."

"The ale sounds right fine, ma'am."

"Ian, why don't you show Mr. MacKay where to wash up," Claire said, glancing pointedly at her brother, "then fetch him a cup of ale? Meanwhile, I'll make us some bannocks to go with the colcannon. There isn't enough time now to bake bread."

Ian looked to Evan, then motioned toward a corner near the cupboard. On a small table sat a red and white-striped pottery pitcher and basin. Evan put his traveling case on a stool and removed his jacket. After unbuttoning his shirt cuffs and rolling up the sleeves to his elbows, he headed toward the wash basin. For good measure, before he even washed his hands, he splashed some water on his face and scrubbed it.

It felt good to be inside the snug little cottage. Evan had to admit, though, that he was surprised at how the day had turned out. Never, in his wildest flights of imagination, had he ever dreamed he'd end up in the house of a beautiful, if outspoken and hot-tempered, Scottish girl. Still, what surprised him more than anything was that, despite the foreignness of his situation, he felt strangely at home.

Perhaps it was his Scot's blood rising to the surface. Perhaps it was the fact that, despite their superficial differences, people were all essentially the same at heart. Or perhaps, just perhaps, he had always been called here. Called here to find the answers his often lonely, frequently confused, and always searching heart sought.

36

Immediately Evan shook off that last consideration. His weariness, combined with the wild, romantic Highland setting, must be putting some strange ideas into his head. Besides, what mattered most right now was getting a hot meal under his belt and a good night's sleep. Tomorrow was time enough to deal with tomorrow.

He dried his hands on a small piece of cloth hanging beside the wash basin, then ambled over to where Claire stood mixing a dough of some sort. "Need any help?" he asked.

She glanced up in surprise. "Nay," she replied slowly. "I don't think you'd know how to make bannocks at any rate."

He shrugged. "I've served a turn or two as trail cook. No one ever complained about my cooking, or took sick from it."

"Well, then, watch me carefully." She dumped the dough out onto a floured cloth she had set on the table. "You pat this into a circle until it's about the thickness of the width of your fingernail. Then neaten the edges by pressing inwards with the flat of a knife." Claire paused in the task to point toward the fireplace. "Could you bring me the girdle propped up beside the hearth?"

"Girdle?" Evan walked to the fireplace and picked up the open, iron-worked griddle by its arched handle. "Do you mean this?"

"Aye. The girdle. It's what we use to bake our bannocks—and scones, for that matter—on. You grease the girdle, put it over the fire, and then brown both sides. It usually takes ten minutes on the first side, and about five on the other. Much faster then baking bread in a cast iron pot. Next you slice the bannock into wedges. It's verra tasty with butter, or even cheese."

"Sounds like a handy implement to have—a girdle, I mean." He grinned. "And what, by the way, is colcannon? A kind of stew?"

"Nay. It's finely mashed potatoes mixed with cooked cabbage, cream, and leeks."

Evan's grin faded. "No meat?"

"Not this eve. Meat's verra costly. We can't afford it too often."

"Oh."

Claire cocked her head at him. "Do cowboys eat a lot of meat, then?"

"Yes, as a matter of fact they do. Remember, I grew up on a cattle ranch."

Ian ambled over. "Every night? Do you eat beef every night?"

Evan nodded. "If we want. Sometimes we eat a chicken, or some fish, or pork, or even venison or game birds in season. We always raise a few pigs, plus have a henhouse full of chickens for meat and eggs."

Their astonishment almost palpable, Claire and Ian looked at each other. Embarrassment filled Evan. Had he overstepped his bounds, or appeared the braggart?

"Look, I didn't mean to imply the bannocks and colcannon wouldn't be plumb delicious," he hurried to explain. "We all have our favorite foods. That doesn't mean, though, a man shouldn't be open to something new and different."

He glanced at the girdle where Claire had placed the rounded bannock dough. "Er, shouldn't you be putting that on to brown? I don't know about you, but my belly's about as empty as a schoolhouse in the middle of summer."

"Och, aye," she said with a laugh, reaching over to grab the girdle. "You aren't shy, are you, Mr. MacKay, about making your needs known?"

Evan paused to think on that unexpected observation, then chuckled softly. "No, ma'am, I reckon I'm not."

3

*Be not forgetful to entertain strangers: for thereby some
have entertained angels unawares.*

Hebrews 13:2

The next morning, as the first fingers of sunlight stroked the land, Claire rose from her own boxbed in the room across the entry hall. She said her morning prayers, then washed, dressed, and after a brief, longing look at the curved wooden clarsach sitting in the corner, left her room.

The day ahead was already busy enough. Much as Claire wished it otherwise, she didn't dare squander even a few minutes playing her beloved, bogwood harp. She also didn't wish to wake their guest prematurely.

Evan MacKay's journey to Culdee, which Claire knew had been on one of the old coaches still running to the farthest limits of Scotland, must have been exhausting. The tall American slept on, she noted as she entered the living room, cozily ensconced before the hearth in his

39

snug little nest of blankets and an old quilt. He lay on his side facing her, his dark hair tousled, his expression peaceful.

Claire tied a long white apron about her waist, then tiptoed over and reached across him to appropriate the teakettle sitting to one side of the hearth. Just then Evan stirred, rolling onto his back and throwing off the blanket that had previously covered him to his neck. With a soft gasp, she jumped back.

At the very least, he was barechested. Claire didn't linger to discover anything more. A death grip on the teakettle, she bolted from the room and out the front door.

Her heart still pounded so hard when she finally reached the farm's well that it took a minute or two to realize she had carried the teakettle with her. Heat flooded her face. She gave a wry laugh. Her intent had been to leave the kettle on the table, then gently stir the coals and add a few sticks of wood to get the fire going before heading to the well to fill a bucket of fresh water. The sight of Evan MacKay's impressive chest, however, had dashed all her plans.

In but a moment of fascinated perusal, Claire had noted the breadth of his shoulders. His arms were strong and well muscled, too, his chest lushly covered with a dark thatch of hair that arrowed down his rippling belly before disappearing beneath the blanket. Gazing at him, a surprising, shameful rush of desire had filled her.

Claire exhaled an unsteady breath. It wasn't decent that a man possess such unsettling good looks and such an equally unsettling body. Yet it was even more improper still that the sight of him just then should stir such feelings within her. She hardly knew the man! Not that he'd even stay in Culdee long enough, Claire was quick to remind herself, for *anyone* to get to know him properly.

As she grasped the handle of the well windlass and began to turn it, she lifted a fervent prayer of thanks that Evan MacKay would be sleeping in his own house this eve. It would be even better if he didn't decide to linger overlong in Culdee, once he discovered and met with his kin. Claire didn't need anyone or anything disrupting the peaceful, settled life she and Ian had finally managed to build here. Especially not some cowboy with the most outlandish outlooks and ideas.

"Need any help with that, ma'am?"

Claire's grip slipped from the windlass handle. The handle spun and, with a groan of metal and wood, the bucketful of water she had nearly cranked to the top of the well plummeted back down, striking the water with a resounding splash. She wheeled about.

"By mountain and sea! Must you sneak up on a body so?" With a snort of disgust, Claire lifted her fists to rest on her hips. "Do you know you're one of the most unsettling of men? Do you, Evan MacKay?"

"To tell you the truth, ma'am, you're the first woman who's ever told me that." He managed a lopsided grin and held out an empty bucket. "Reckon I kind of like it."

Claire glared back at him. And wasn't he the cocky one, she thought, standing there barefoot and clad only in his black trousers and hastily tucked in shirt, the early morning sun catching in his tousled, ebony hair and glinting off his strong, highbred features? Did he realize how handsome he was? Or how the sight of him made her heart flutter as wildly as some bird's wings?

Most likely he did, Claire realized sourly as she finally accepted the bucket. A man like him surely had the lasses swooning at his feet. She'd not be joining, however, the swarm of avid little bees sure to buzz about this particular honey pot. No good would come of it.

"Well, don't let your pride get the best of you," she muttered. "Anyone in Culdee could tell you I'm not the sort easily swayed by sweet words or empty compliments. Best you save them for the other lasses."

Evan's grin faded. Blast, but the woman could get her dander up in the blink of an eye! He supposed he shouldn't be surprised. Anyone with such red hair most likely couldn't help having a temper. And it wasn't as if he didn't find her feisty nature appealing. He always liked a challenge, whether it be an unbroken filly with fear in her eyes or a maverick steer ready to cut and run.

Problem was, the last thing Evan wanted was for Claire to be afraid of him, or mistrust his intentions. He meant her no harm or dishonor. On the contrary. When he looked into her deep green eyes, all he felt was admiration, attraction, and a fierce protectiveness.

The reason for his sense of admiration and attraction was obvious. Claire Sutherland was like some beautiful doe with those big eyes and long dark, lashes, her lithe, slender, but wonderfully feminine body, and delicate features. For the life of him, though, he didn't know why he felt so protective of her.

Perhaps it sprang from the realization that, just like some wild thing of the forest, there was an air of vulnerability about her that belied all her attempts at a fierce independence. There was also a pain glimmering deep in her eyes, a haunted anguish that plucked at him more strongly than her beauty and grace ever could. It touched something in Evan, something familiar that spoke to him of his own pain and unrequited needs.

But how to reassure Claire he only wanted to get to know her better, be her friend? With a sigh, Evan walked to the well and leaned against its stony bulk.

"So what would you have me say and do, Miss Sutherland?" he asked, shooting her an inquiring glance. "I'm trying to be friendly and honest. Can't you just accept my comments at face value, until I prove myself otherwise?"

His blunt query seemed to take her momentarily aback. She stared at him, narrow of eye, as if she were trying to probe his mind. Then she shook her head.

"I don't know how to answer you." Claire set down the bucket, once more grasped the windlass, and began to turn the handle.

"Why not just say what comes to mind? Treat me as a friend, rather than as the enemy. It's as good a place to start as any."

She gave a shrill laugh. "Aye, and how about you treating me the same way then—as a friend—rather than as some lass to tease and goad for the sheer sport of it?"

Evan straightened and turned to her. "It's not just me, is it? You don't really like men at all, do you?"

Claire couldn't quite meet his gaze. "Not most men," she admitted reluctantly at long last. "I haven't had much reason to trust them."

He smiled, inordinately pleased she had been willing to confide even that much. "Nor should you, especially not me, who you met just yesterday. All I'm asking, though, is that you give me a chance." At her look of surprise, he laughed. "Do you have any inkling how enchanting you are, one moment the fierce and fiery warrior and, the next, the startled, naïve little girl? You really shouldn't fault a man for finding you so appealing."

"Och, aye, and if I don't, next you'll be thinking I'm playing the flirt!" Coloring fiercely, she lifted the bucket from the well. "You mustn't imagine this is all some game, you know?"

Evan stepped up, took the bucket from her, and poured the contents into the bucket he had brought. "I don't. Can you at least begin by believing that?"

Chewing on her lower lip, she studied him for a long moment before replying "Mayhap." Then Claire picked up the teakettle, and fell into stride beside him as he next headed back toward the cottage. "It would be the hospitable, Christian thing to do, I'd imagine."

"Yes, it would." Deciding it best not to press his luck, Evan changed the subject. "So, what's the plan for the day? Our landlord did say I could move into my quarters, didn't he?"

"Aye. After breakfast, I thought we might spend the morn cleaning up the bulk of the mess and fixing you a bed to sleep in for tonight. Then, after the midday meal, we could return to St. Columba's and see what we could discover about your kin."

"I can't think of a more pleasant way to spend the day, in the company of such a bonnie lassie."

Claire rolled her eyes. "You can't stop yourself, can you? From the rich and honeyed words that flow constantly from your tongue, I mean? Are all cowboys, then, so quick with the compliments?"

"I couldn't say, ma'am." Evan laughed. "Perhaps it's just my rich and honeyed Scots' blood rising to the surface. Who wouldn't wax eloquent in such a wild, glorious land?"

"And *I* say, have a care, Mr. MacKay," she replied with a husky chuckle, "or you'll surely toss all sense and caution to the four winds, and soon take to wearing a kilt."

"Heaven forbid!" he said in mock horror, then laughed again.

He was such a happy, easygoing man, Claire thought as she walked back into the house. Nothing appeared to darken his mood for long. And, for all the teasing he seemed to enjoy at her expense, he could just as quickly turn it on himself.

There was something disarming about Evan MacKay, something that could, bit by bit, undermine the hard-won fortress guarding a woman's heart. If a woman wasn't careful, she could fall under a certain cowboy's

44

spell before she even knew it. Even a woman, Claire realized with a sudden ripple of unease, who had made a solemn vow, that horrible night now a year past, never to trust anything but her own motives and efforts ever again.

ç

Breakfast, as always, was milk and porridge. After sending Ian off to school and washing the dishes, Claire gathered an assortment of rags, buckets, brooms, and brushes, and promptly headed for the second crofter's cottage. Evan, a bemused smile on his lips, followed close behind.

The smaller house was in an even filthier state than Claire had imagined. She took one look at it, heaved a big sigh, and handed two wooden buckets to Evan. "Fill them both, if you please," she said. "We'll be needing plenty of water to get this dwelling fit for human habitation."

Evan, buckets in hand, promptly departed. With a narrowed gaze, Claire once more surveyed the cottage. Thick cobwebs filled every corner, the silken strands festooning the roof beams before spanning downward to adorn a scrawny chest, a somewhat tilted cupboard, a rickety dining table, and two chairs. The empty void within the boxbed hadn't been spared, either, and appeared draped in gossamer shrouds of white, as did the three meager windows of the single-room house.

"Well, best be getting to it," Claire muttered as she grabbed up a broom and tied a large rag around the wheat straw bristles. "At this rate, aught I do this day will be a decided improvement."

By the time Evan returned with the two buckets of water, she had cleaned the ceiling and its corners, and was now attacking the windows. After gracing the tall American with a sidling glance, Claire gestured toward the windows. "You can start washing them, if you will. Might as well work our way down to the floor as we go."

"Sure thing, ma'am." He brushed away the cobwebs clinging to one end of the table, and set a bucket on it. Then, after grabbing two rags, Evan flung one over his shoulder and dipped the other into the bucket he carried to the first window. He was soon scrubbing away at the thick grime coating the panes.

For a long while, both worked in silence. At last, though, as they joined forces to clean out the sooty, ash-filled hearth, Claire ventured a glance at the man kneeling beside her. "You're a strange one, even for a man, I mean."

Evan turned and arched a dark brow. "How so?"

"Most men would be grabbing their kilts and dashing for the hills by now, rather than shame themselves with woman's work."

He chuckled, the deep, rich sound reverberating most pleasantly around Claire. "Would you rather I pay you for this work and leave it all to you?"

Her eyes widened in horror. "Nay, I wouldn't. I'm already in your debt for the money you gave to help Ian yestreen. But if you'd consider that debt paid if I finished cleaning your croft for you . . ."

"That debt was paid long ago, in the hospitality you showed me last night, in your willingness to help me with this cottage, and in tracking down my kin. In fact"—Evan grinned—"if I'm not careful, it'll soon be *me* deep in your debt once again."

Claire eyed him skeptically, then gave an incredulous snort. "Indeed, you really are a strange one."

"But a strange one you might eventually come to like?" He cocked his head and wagged his brows. "Maybe even call friend?"

She pulled the ash bucket, brimming over now with chunks of charred wood and cinders, closer to her. "You can't stop while you're ahead, can you?" Then, in spite of her best efforts to keep a straight face, she laughed. "Och, you *are* strange, but strangely likeable, too."

"Then I'm definitely making progress. First with the brother, and now, the sister."

His statement gave Claire pause. The cowboy was certainly correct in his assessment of Ian's feelings for him. From the start, Claire had seen how quickly—and most surprisingly—her brother had warmed to him. Perhaps it was the fact that Evan was a stranger, or because he was an American cowboy. Or perhaps it was just Evan's engaging, friendly manner.

Whatever it was, Evan MacKay was the first man, aside from Father MacLaren, whom her brother had shown any warmth toward or interest in. The realization both heartened and disturbed her. It was good Ian was, at long last, beginning to open himself to another in trust. But it was also unfortunate he did so with a man who would soon be gone from his life.

Still, Claire couldn't deny the bond already beginning to form between her brother and Evan MacKay. "I can't thank you enough for your kindness and interest in Ian," she managed to choke out past the sudden tightness in her throat. "He hasn't had . . . well, he doesn't make friends verra easily these days. Yet I know the lad's lonely and hurting."

"And confused," Evan offered softly. "It's to be expected at his age." As if recalling some poignant memory, he smiled sadly. "I had my share of problems with my pa when I was Ian's age, and finally ran away from Culdee Creek at seventeen. Took a year of hard living and near starving to death, though, to make me swallow my pride and come home. Even so, we had a lot of fence mending to do, my pa and me, before we finally made our peace."

47

He sighed and shook his head. "Still, if it hadn't been for Abby, I don't reckon we would've ever made up."

"And who is Abby?" Claire couldn't help it. She needed to know. "Your mother, sister, or wife?"

"My stepmother." Evan grinned. "In case you're ever interested, I'm not and never have been married."

"Well, if the truth be told," she muttered, her cheeks flaming, "I'm not. I just wished to understand the relationships in your family better, that's all."

"Abby wasn't my stepmother at the time, only my pa's housekeeper and tutor to my half-sister, Elizabeth. But even then she'd begun to have an effect on my pa, softening his heart."

"She sounds like a fine woman."

He nodded. "Oh, she is. She is." Evan hesitated, his forehead wrinkling in thought. "Back to Ian, though, I reckon my point was he's going through some difficult times just growing up. The best you can do is love him and stand by him."

"I try." Claire exhaled a long breath and looked away. "Surely I do. But there are times when it's verra hard to stand by him."

"Like yesterday, when that other boy accused him of stealing?"

Horrified that Evan seemed to have read her mind, Claire jerked her gaze up to his. "I didn't mean—"

"I saw how you looked at him, heard the doubt in your voice," he offered quietly. "And I don't tell you that to reproach you, Claire. I can see how much you love your brother. You wouldn't doubt him unless you'd good cause."

"No, I wouldn't."

She met his steady, searching gaze, inexplicably soothed—rather than incensed—by his sudden use of her given name. A barrier had been broached and, as surprising as that revelation was, Claire suddenly didn't care. Though she was loath to betray Ian or speak ill of him to another, there was something in Evan's eyes that made the words come–something warm, compassionate, strong, and compelling.

Evan would do more than understand and commiserate. Though she wasn't sure from whence the certainty came, Claire sensed he would be there for her, stand by her, and help her as best as he could. Oh, how she needed someone strong to walk beside her, to bolster her when her strength failed! She hadn't known that kind of comfort in a long, long time.

And it had been *such* a very, very hard year.

"It's my fault, but all Ian knows is stealing," she forced herself to say. "Our father died, drowning in a storm while fishing at sea, when I was just five and Ian two. Three years later, however, our vain, beautiful mother wed an Englishman while on holiday near our home in Sutherland. Most reluctantly, we were soon ensconced in England with my mother and new stepfather."

Claire turned back to scraping ashes from the back of the hearth. "I hated it in England–my cold, distant stepfather, the ridicule and taunts of the local children, and the way my mother slowly pulled away from us, preferring to pretend she was far too young to have children as old as Ian and me. By the time I was thirteen, I'd had all I could bear. With the money I had hidden away over the years, I bought passage back to Scotland, to my aunt's home. At the last minute Ian begged to come with me and I, arrogantly imagining I was returning him to a far better life, agreed."

"So, he was only ten when he ran away with you back to Scotland." Evan shook his head in wonderment. "What a plucky pair you two were."

At the memory of the years to come, hot tears stung Claire's eyes. "Foolish and foolhardy would be more to the point," she countered bitterly. "Once back in Scot-

49

land, I begged my aunt, who had married in the ensuing years, to take us in. She was hesitant at first, but finally did so. That was when the trouble really began.

"My uncle was a cruel, physically abusive man who drank too much. Eventually, he was in his cups so much he couldn't work. We lived in squalor." She laid aside the little shovel. "It was then that Ian first began to steal, just so we'd have food to eat. And, when I thought it could get no worse, my aunt died, supposedly from a fall while out foraging the nearby sea cliffs with her husband."

"Which placed you totally at the mercy of your uncle."

Terror shot through her. Did he know? Claire wondered, her pulse accelerating. But how *could* he know?

She looked at him, searching Evan's eyes for any sign he suspected what was next to come. All she saw, though, was that same warm compassion. The fear faded; the pounding of her heart subsided.

"Aye," Claire agreed. "Ian and I were totally at our uncle's mercy. I became so desperate I seriously considered taking Ian and returning to our mother in England." She paused to drag in an unsteady breath. "Before I could carry out my plan, though, my uncle died. I felt there was naught left for Ian and I then but to move on, which we did. We finally found sanctuary and a home here in Culdee, where Father MacLaren offered me work cleaning the rectory and church."

"Claire, how old were you when you came to Culdee? And how old are you now?"

"I was seventeen. I'm now eighteen."

"Just a year ago then." Evan reached out and covered her hand with his. "As I said before, you two were a plucky pair."

For a moment suspended in time, Claire stared down at the hand covering hers. It was a beautiful hand, broad of span, long-fingered, and powerfully supported by

50

thick, strong tendons. The nails were short, if rather grimy right now from the hours of cleaning. A sprinkling of dark hairs covered the back of it. A strong hand, she mused. A hand meant to protect, to hold, to caress . . .

Abruptly, Claire jerked away. She grabbed the ash can and climbed to her feet.

"What's wrong?" Evan stared up at her in concern.

"W-we've squandered far too much time chatting away," she mumbled as she turned to walk from the house. "Sweep out the hearth now with the broom, while I dump this bucket outside. Then it'll be time to clean the floor and finish up by bringing you some bedding, or we'll never get to Culdee this day."

Not even pausing to await a reply, Claire spun about and bolted from the cottage. Only when she had reached the farm's refuse pile did she finally halt. Her breath coming in great gulps, Claire stood there, gazing numbly down at the garbage, the ash bucket still clenched in her hand.

Stood there and stared as the sheer, unmitigated terror of that night engulfed her once again. This time, however, the old fears traveled with a new companion. If anyone ever guessed what had really happened to her uncle that night, it would all be over.

And she, simple, silly girl that she was, had almost betrayed everything in an unguarded moment with a charming stranger.

4

Show mercy and compassions every man to his brother.
Zechariah 7:9

Ever so carefully, Claire turned yet another yellowed page of St. Columba's parish baptismal book, scanning the faded, feathery script for some mention of a Sean MacKay, born in the mid-1780s. Beside her, Evan sat deeply absorbed in the parish marriage records. However, even with Father MacLaren's eager assistance for the first hour that afternoon, they were finally left to their own devices when he was called away by a young couple wishing to arrange their upcoming marriage.

"Any luck yet?" Evan asked, glancing up at her. "So far, I've found three Sean MacKays, and two of them were wed to a Rose." He shook his head and sighed. "I didn't realize how popular a name Sean and Rose were in those days. What I really need are the names of my great-grandfather's parents or brothers and sisters.

Surely at least one of them would have stood as witness to their marriage."

"Well, if you'd been a wee bit more knowledgeable before you came to Culdee," Claire muttered, gingerly turning yet another page, "we might have made quicker work of searching them out."

Evan sighed and shook his head. "All I remember is my great-great-grandfather's name started with an *L*." He grinned. "Or, leastwise, I think it began with an *L*."

"Och, and aren't you a big help?" Claire made a sound of disgust and rolled her eyes. Then, as her gaze lowered once more to a fresh page, she gave a start. "Here's something·verra interesting." As Evan rose and leaned over her shoulder, she pointed to the date of March 5, 1786.

"Sean MacKay . . . son of Lachlan and Sheena Mac-Kay, nee Ross . . ." He paused, his brow wrinkling. "Hmmm . . . this is very interesting indeed. Lachlan MacKay . . ." He nodded slowly. "Now that I think about it, that *was* my great-great-grandfather's name."

Evan grinned. "I've found him, Claire! I've found him!"

"Aye, it seems you have," Claire said as she flipped back a few pages and paused. "Especially considering the other Sean who wed a Rose didn't have a Lachlan as his sire. It'll be far easier to identify the sisters and brothers now, and then find any of their ancestors who stayed behind when he emmigrated."

The next half hour passed in far more fruitful investigation. By midafternoon, Claire and Evan walked from the rectory library with a list of several potential Mac-Kay relatives. Father MacLaren, finished with the young couple by then, met them in the hallway a short distance from his office.

Evan, a triumphant smile on his face, waved the sheet of paper before him. "We've found eleven people who might be relatives of mine. Can you help in narrowing the list down a bit?"

The old priest nodded. "Aye, mayhap I can. Why dinna ye join me in my office? Mrs. Fraser was just about to serve tea, and she always prepares far more than any one man could hope to eat."

"Sounds like a fine plan to me, Padre." Evan turned to Claire. "Is that all right with you?"

"Aye." She smiled. "We can't tarry overlong, though. I need to purchase fresh fruit and vegetables for supper, not to mention bake bread before the day is out. You'll dine again with us, will you not?"

"If you'll have me again, I'd be honored."

"Well, I can't see any other way for you to eat," Claire said as she followed Father MacLaren into his office. "It isn't as if you have aught to cook with, nor any food to cook."

The priest cut her a sly look over his shoulder. "Mayhap Evan would prefer to pay ye for yer meals, and save himself the added expense of buying a cook pot and such that he willna wish to take home to Colorado at any rate. Had either of ye thought of that?"

Claire sat in the small chair she had pulled up before Father MacLaren's desk. "That's a consideration, to be sure." She glanced up at Evan. "Would that be agreeable to you?"

"I've no complaint with your meals." He paused, then grinned. "That is, if you have no complaint with occasionally cooking any meat I might be able to buy or hunt down."

"Och, to be sure you'd never hear a complaint from me, and most certainly not from Ian, about any meat you'd bring to our cook pot."

"Good. Then it's settled." Evan turned back to the priest, who had finished settling himself behind his desk, and slid the sheet of paper containing the fruits of their hours of research toward him. "Here, Padre. Are there any folk on the list still living around these parts? Some or all might well be my kin."

As Father MacLaren studied the list, Mrs. Fraser bustled in, a loaded tray in her hands. Evan immediately jumped up to help the elderly woman, taking the tray and carrying it to the little table sitting ready beside the priest's desk.

Stacked around a white, porcelain teapot painted with bright purple thistles were four teacups and saucers, four plates and silverware, and four cloth napkins. A large plate was filled with scones, and sugarcoated shortbreads shaped into thin, triangular "petticoat tails." A plate of cream-filled buns, which Claire soon informed Evan were actually called cream cookies, appropriated the remainder of the tray. Accompanying the fare were small, cut-glass bowls of honey, butter, raspberry jam, and orange marmalade.

"Looks like a fine feast, ma'am," Evan observed as he graced the rotund, white-haired woman with his most appreciative smile.

Mrs. Fraser blushed prettily. "'Tis hardly aught to crow about. If I'd known earlier Father would be having guests, I'd have really given ye a taste o' my culinary skills. But as 'tis,"—she made a dismissing wave over the tray of luscious bakery goods—"I canna claim to any great pride this day. Ye must return another time, when I can serve ye a tea worthy o' guests."

Father MacLaren chuckled. "Och, aye, that ye must. Just be certain, though, ye havena eaten all day and mayhap the day 'afore, too, or ye willna do such a fine tea justice."

Once more, Evan smiled his most charming smile. "I'd be right honored, ma'am." He pulled up a chair and indicated that Mrs. Fraser should sit. "But for now, why don't you rest up a bit while I serve you?"

The older woman sent the priest an uncertain look.

"Aye, sit, Mrs. Fraser," Father MacLaren urged. "If Evan wishes to wait on ye, then 'tis best ye enjoy it to yer heart's content. Claire and I can see to ourselves."

With one final, half-hearted protest, the elderly housekeeper did just that, basking in the attention Evan proceeded to lavish upon her.

Claire couldn't believe her eyes. Never in her wildest flights of fantasy could she have imagined a cowboy capable of such fine manners or knowledgeable of the proper way to serve tea. But then, when it came to a certain American, she was learning quickly not to limit her expectations.

By the time tea was finished and Mrs. Fraser had whisked away a far lighter tray, Father MacLaren had narrowed their painstakingly researched list to just two people still living in the area. "Old Donall and his wife Lainie MacKay are yer best bets. They're well into their eighties, yet their minds remain as sharp and clear as a Highland burn running fresh from the mountains. They're also the kindest, wisest folk ye'd ever hope to meet."

Claire cocked her head. "They don't live in Culdee, though, do they? I would know of them."

"Nay, they dinna," the priest agreed, leaning back with a satiated smile. "They live out near the glen between Ben Loyal and Loch Naver. On foot, 'twould take ye a good hour's walk."

She turned to Evan. "It's best, then, we plan to visit them on the morrow."

"We?" The tall American arched a brow. "I don't expect you to come, Claire. You've already sacrificed enough of your time on my behalf."

"And do you seriously think you can find your way out to the glen all by yourself?" She gave a laugh. "I think not. Besides, Father bade me take a day or two to help you, and this is but the first full day. However you

56

look at it, I owe you yet one more day before my obligation is fulfilled."

"Well, since you put it that way, I reckon I'd be a fool to refuse."

The wry twist of Evan's lips belied his mild response, and Claire immediately felt ashamed. She hadn't meant to convey the impression that the rendering of her assistance had been a burden. That would've been inhospitable. And it also would've been far from the truth.

But honesty and common sense weren't always agreeable bedfellows, especially when it came to a certain cowboy. So Claire chose to ignore the message inherent in his words, and respond only to his statement.

"Aye, you would be a fool to refuse my offer of escort," she retorted briskly, "and since it's apparent you're not a fool, the matter's settled." Claire rose and brushed a few lingering crumbs from her skirt. "I'll be happy to be of assistance."

She smiled then at Father MacLaren. "Thank you for your aid in finding some of Evan's kin. And thank you, as well, for the fine tea."

"Och, dinna fash yerself, lass." He gave a merry laugh. "'Twas my pleasure, and no mistake. My pleasure," he added with a twinkle in his eyes as his glance swung to Evan's, "in more ways than one."

&

By this time of day, Claire noted wryly as she scanned the few remaining turnips, potatoes, and onions, the vegetable stands were always sparse pickings. There was no making up for it, though, after all the time they had spent at St. Columba's. The sparse pickings would just have to do for this eve's meal.

"Could you perhaps fit some poultry into your cooking plans tonight?" Evan asked from beside her. "I see a few still available over there in that butcher's window."

Her glance lifted in the direction of his hand. Sure enough two plump, pale pink chicken carcasses hung in Robbie Stewart's butcher shop window. She nodded, her mood brightening. "Aye, it would be a most welcome addition to the meal. We could have stoved chicken with potatoes tonight, then use the rest on the morrow for another meal."

"Stoved chicken?" Evan asked with an arch of a dark brow.

"It isn't as dreadful a concoction as you might think," Claire said with a laugh, noting the wary look in his eye. "It's but a layer of seasoned potatoes and onions in a cook pot, then some chicken joints, then another layer of seasoned potatoes and onions, then the rest of the joints and some water. I cook it all up in a pot over the fire. It's verra tasty."

Relief slowly brightened his eyes. "Sounds like it. I'll get the chicken then, while you buy the potatoes and onions."

"That's a fine plan," Claire agreed before turning back to the vegetable stand.

Five minutes later, her purchases wrapped snugly in brown paper, she wandered over to another stand containing fresh herbs. Her stash of rosemary and sage was running low, she mused, and it would be best to replenish it.

A hand settled on her arm. "So, lass, have ye been purposely avoiding me o' late?" a deep voice demanded. "I havena seen ye the past two days, though I looked for ye daily at the kirk."

At the sound of Dougal MacKay's thick burr, Claire winced in dismay. The burly farmer's timing couldn't have been worse. For the past few months, he had

58

made it known about Culdee that Claire was his—even though she had yet to give her consent or ever would, for that matter. With the help of his tavern-drinking cronies, however, Dougal had managed by either verbal or physical intimidation to eliminate further potential suitors for her hand. He wouldn't be pleased now to see her with Evan, who was bound to appear at any minute.

"I've been busy helping a kinsman of Donall and Lainie MacKay," she replied, gracing him with one of her sweetest smiles. Though they had yet to unequivocally confirm that Evan and the old couple were truly related, the odds were in their favor, which didn't really make what she had just said an untruth. "Mayhap you've heard of him—the American—Evan MacKay?"

"Aye, I've heard o' him," the reddish-blond-haired man growled. "All the lasses are nigh unto swooning over his braw form and fine looks. But ye're not a Mac-Kay. How is it ye're spending so much time with him?"

"He came to the kirk to ask Father MacLaren's help in finding his kin. I was there, and Father asked me to assist him for a few days."

"And those few days are over then?"

Claire shrugged out of his grip. "Nearly so." Tiring at last of the man's questions, she cocked her head and fixed him with a hard stare. "And what's it to you, Dougal MacKay, if they aren't? You aren't, and never will be, my keeper."

Once more, Dougal took her by the arm. "I am if I say I am." His gaze narrowed. "Ye havena gone and gotten any fool ideas, have ye, that ye'd rather set yer cap for the likes o' him than me?"

"Och, and aren't you the big fool?" Claire pulled back, attempting to free herself of the farmer's grip, but in response Dougal only held her tighter. "I've told you before I've no wish ever to wed. Why would I now be daft enough to set my sights on some stranger, and a foreigner to boot?"

"Who knows?" He pulled her so close the paperwrapped vegetables pressed hard now between them. "Mayhap because ye imagine a better life awaits ye in America, and that ye can run from yer people and responsibilities by doing so? Or mayhap because ye hope yer precious brother would stop his fighting and thieving there, and suddenly become the little angel ye've always hoped he'd become."

Claire gave a disparaging laugh. "Have you been in your cups again, Dougal? You talk as if you're whiskey besotted."

"Ye canna run from me or yer people, lass. Ye belong here. I willna allow any man to take ye from me!"

"And I say, let me go and let me be!" Placing a hand on his broad chest, Claire shoved back hard, breaking at last his hold on her arm. "I'm not your wife, and never will be. You've no right to tell me what I can and can't do!"

"I think the lady has a point there, mister."

As one Claire and Dougal swung to face Evan, who had joined them at last. He, too, now had a wrapped parcel tucked beneath his arm. Standing there, his dark hair windblown, his stance loose, a slight smile quirked one corner of his mouth. It was all a ruse, however, Claire realized. The light glinting in Evan's smoky blue eyes was hard, and rife with warning.

Dougal paused to look him up and down, then snickered. "So, ye're the bonny lad all the lasses are talking about. Meeting you at last, I canna say as how I see the reason for all the clash ma claver."

"They weren't idle tales, Dougal MacKay!" Claire countered hotly, angered now for Evan's sake if not for her own. "He's a real cowboy. He wrestles steers and can hit a rat with his six-shooter half a mile away, and—"

60

"Whoa, hold on, hold on." Hand upraised in protest, Evan grinned down at her. "Though I'm flattered you suddenly seem to hold me in such high regard, I doubt Dougal here is interested in any of my particular talents."

"Hardly," the big Scotsman muttered.

"Well, in case you mayhap failed to realize it," Claire said, glaring now at Evan, "he just all but insulted you."

"Did he?" Evan appeared to consider that statement, then shrugged. "Well, no matter. I've been insulted before, and by better men than him. All I care is that we be on our way. Ever since you explained how you make stoved chicken, my mouth's been watering thinking about our supper." He stepped up and offered her his arm. "Shall we be heading for home, then?"

Claire hesitated but an instant, then took his arm and stepped out with Evan down the street. He was right in not allowing Dougal to drag him into a shouting match, then a fistfight. Far better to leave the big farmer standing there, still struggling to muddle through the implications of Evan's words. When he finally did, the impact would be greater than any blow to the face or body could ever be.

Mayhap, just mayhap, Dougal MacKay had finally met his match, Claire mused as she walked along. Mayhap he would finally leave her be. If such a miracle were to occur, she'd be ever so grateful that Evan MacKay had come into her life. Why, she might even have to throw common sense to the four winds, and take back her ill-chosen words about him being a burden!

Claire smiled. With each passing day, he really *was* becoming quite a handy person to have around.

ॐ

The next morning dawned clear, bright, and warm—a perfect day for a walk into the rolling hills outside

Culdee. Though Saturday, Ian still had several hours of schooling to attend. Despite his heartfelt entreaties to be allowed to accompany them to visit Donall and Lainie MacKay, Claire was adamant. School must always come before pleasure.

After packing the remains of last night's meal, a half-loaf of the bread she had baked, and a flagon of cider into a small basket, Claire removed her apron, flung a light shawl across her shoulders, and set out with Evan toward the distant peak of Ben Loyal. For a time they walked along in a companionable silence. Finally, though, Claire could contain her growing curiosity about Evan's life in Colorado no longer.

"So, have you ever faced down a gunslinger or fought Indians?" she asked.

With a jerk of surprise, Evan slid to a halt and eyed her. "No," he answered carefully. "Gunfights aren't all that common anymore. And nowadays the Indians around Colorado Springs are pretty peaceable."

She gave a disappointed sniff. "Sounds verra tame to me. I can't say as how the tales, then, justify the truth."

He laughed. "Well, times change, I reckon. If you ever want to take a trip out to Colorado someday, though, I'd be happy to round up a few Indians and retired gunslingers for you."

Evan's laughter was so infectious Claire couldn't help herself. She chuckled. "Och, and wouldn't you have to eat those fine words, if I was ever to take you up on such an offer! I can see it now, the look on your face."

"Can you really, Claire?" he asked softly, his expression suddenly sober. "I think I'd be very happy to see you. I know I'd be plumb proud to squire you around on my arm." Evan grinned and shook his head. "The looks I'd get from all the hands would be a sight worth seeing."

There was something in his words, and gleaming deep in his eyes, that gave her pause. What she had initially intended as teasing banter had taken an unexpected turn. Claire cursed her foolish tongue, even as she knew she had been casting her net to see what she could catch.

"Well, it was a silly thought at any rate." She stepped out once more. "I can't ever see myself traveling to America."

With a few quick strides, Evan caught up with her. "And why not? Are you so bound to Scotland and this village, then?"

Claire shot him an irritated look. "Nay, but I haven't any reason to leave here. Besides, I've responsibilities–to my brother and to Father MacLaren. As do you," she added. "You can't remain here either. Your father depends on you."

At the mention of his father, a fleeting look of pain crossed Evan's face. "Yes, in many ways I suppose he does," he admitted reluctantly. "And no, I can't remain here. I have responsibilities–responsibilities I haven't always faced up to as best I should."

She glanced at him as they walked to the end of the worn, dirt path and turned toward the verdant hills that lay before Ben Loyal. "Did you come here, then, to escape those responsibilities?"

Evan's jaw tightened. "Partly. I had hoped that some time away would help me sort things out . . . come to terms with . . ." His voice faded.

"Go on," Claire urged, even as she knew she ventured once more where it was best not to go. But what choice had she? Evan needed to talk–badly, so it seemed–and she couldn't pretend to ignore his pain. "You needn't worry that your tale will ever get back to your home. And Father MacLaren will vouch that I'm not a gossip."

"It's not that, Claire. I just . . . I don't want you to think badly of me."

"Did you kill a man, then, or rob a bank?"

At the eager tone in her voice, Evan's glum mood appeared suddenly to lift. He laughed. "Nothing quite so dramatic."

"Och, then how bad could it be?"

Evan sighed and pulled her to a stop. He gestured toward a tumble of boulders beneath some birches growing beside a small, gurgling brook. "Could we sit there for a few minutes?"

She nodded. "If you wish." Without awaiting his reply, Claire walked over and took a seat.

He joined her, set down their lunch basket, and hopped up on a nearby boulder. For a long while Evan just stared at the little stream. "I was in love with a girl," he finally said, "and she fell in love with someone else. It shattered something in me when I lost her. A confidence, a sense of my self-worth, a trust that I would ever again be worthy of another woman's love. I couldn't bear to see them both together, couldn't handle the pain, so I ran out on my pa."

"Aye," Claire agreed, finding in Evan's tale some unnerving similarities to her own life. "And when that trust is shattered, it's so verra hard to regain that old sense of hope and joy in life again. It's so verra hard to open yourself to others."

"Yet we must. To do otherwise is to live as half a person, to deny oneself the wondrous opportunities—and people—still out there waiting for us." He paused, a thoughtful furrow forming between his brows. "And, worst of all, it's cowardly and dishonorable."

Evan's mouth twitched sadly. "It was cowardly and dishonorable, leaving Culdee Creek. I'm not proud of it. But I just couldn't go back until I worked out my feelings for this girl."

"How will you know when you've done that? Worked out your feelings, I mean?"

64

He shrugged. "I'm hoping I finally have." He looked up then, his dark gaze enigmatic. "Maybe I'll find what I've always been seeking here, in the land of my ancestors. Stranger things have happened, you know."

"Aye, they have. There's something about the Highlands that speaks to the soul—especially to one of the blood as you are, Evan."

Climbing to his feet, he offered his hand. "Thank you, Claire."

She hesitated for a brief moment, then took his hand and slid off the boulder. "I didn't do much."

"You listened. You cared. Then you finally called me Evan. That in itself means more to me than you may realize."

They stood there, gazing at each other, for what seemed a very long while. A strange warmth filled Claire, sweet, melting, and so very unnerving. She felt drawn to Evan, felt an irresistible pull that compelled her to move toward him.

He must have felt something similar. He moved toward her. The hand grasping hers slid up her arm; he took her other arm, too. Some emotion flared in his eyes—a chaotic mix of tenderness, desire, and excitement.

Evan wanted to kiss her. Claire suddenly knew that with an instinct strong and sure. A part of her wanted to kiss him, too, a part she had never before permitted to gain a foothold. Claire knew she didn't dare allow it to do so now either. No good would come of them growing closer. Evan had responsibilities that would call him away soon enough.

She inhaled a ragged breath and stepped back, breaking the gentle hold he had on her. "We must be on our way," she said, struggling to mask the uneven timbre of her voice. "The day draws on, and we've still half the distance to go to Donall and Lainie's."

Evan gazed down at her with thoughtful eyes. Then he smiled. "Yes, I suppose you're right. We've done about all we could here, at any rate."

With that, he stooped, retrieved the basket, and set out. For a time Claire stared after him, wondering what he had meant by that cryptic statement. Then, with an exasperated toss of her head, she muttered "Men!" and hurried to catch up with him.

ত

She was coming to trust him, Evan thought with a joyous exultation as he walked along. Coming to trust and like him. There was something more, though, beginning to build between them: an attraction, a need that pulled at them as inexorably as two magnets or as flames to tinder.

All the same, Evan knew she was still wary. The first untoward move could still send her fleeing, never to trust or approach again. Beneath that proud, resourceful facade, Claire was so exquisitely vulnerable. He must use the utmost caution and the greatest of care.

But the effort, Evan knew, would be well worth it. Claire was a prize beyond his wildest dreams. The longer he was with her, the more she made him forget Hannah. She intrigued him, challenged him, and renewed his hope in life and loving. She was everything he had ever been looking for in a woman.

All it would take was the patience to unlock that door guarding the wall Claire had placed about her heart.

5

Walk in love, as Christ also hath loved us. . . .
                                        Ephesians 5:2

Girdled by sparse stands of birch and alder, the small, drystone croft house of Lainie and Donall MacKay lay in a cozy little dip between two verdant hills. The walls of stacked stones and clay rose to about six feet high before meeting a low-hanging roof of sod divots covered with barley straw thatch. Despite its long, rectangular shape, the house possessed what seemed the more common two small windows on either side of the door.

Approaching the croft house, Evan surveyed it dubiously. As simple as Claire and Ian's dwelling may have been, this structure looked downright primitive. If he didn't miss his guess, a century old was a meager estimation of its age.

As they neared, a scrawny, gray, wiry-haired dog ran from the house, barking at the top of his lungs. Evan pulled Claire to a halt. "Why don't you stay back while I see if friends can be made with that dog?" he suggested, eyeing the little animal with ill-disguised distaste.

She laughed. "Och, so you think you must now protect me from four-legged animals, too, do you?" Claire twisted free of his grasp and walked forward, flipping the end of her skirt toward the barking canine. "Wheesht, wheesht!" she hissed shrilly.

Startled, the dog halted. Stiff-legged but silent, he stood there, hackles on the rise. As they passed, giving him a wide berth, the dog remained frozen in place, snarling softly. By the time they reached the stone stoop outside the door, however, the animal apparently decided to relinquish his defense of hearth and home. Tail tucked between his legs, he slunk off to the rickety cattle byre standing not far away.

Evan turned to her. "What did you say to shut up that mangy cur? Whatever the words, they sure had a magical effect."

Claire grinned. "Och, I did naught more than tell him to be quiet. I took that dog's measure a ways back, and knew he didn't mean any harm."

His mouth quirked. "Did you now? And is there no end to your talents, Claire Sutherland?"

"Nay, there isn't," she replied with a laugh. "And it's past time you realized that, too." Claire paused to incline her head toward the door. "Shouldn't you, as the long-lost kin, be announcing our arrival?"

At that moment the door swung open. "So, what have we here?" a wizened old man demanded gruffly, sticking out his head. He waved a gnarled wooden cane in their direction. "Have ye come to rob us, then?"

"Och, nay." Claire held up a hand in friendship. "If you're Donall MacKay, we've come to pay you a call."

Watery blue eyes narrowed beneath a pair of wild, bushy white brows. "And why would ye wish to call on the likes o' me? Who be ye, anyways?"

"My name's Claire Sutherland," she replied calmly, "and this"—she indicated Evan—"is Evan MacKay, one of your kin from America. Father MacLaren sent us."

At mention of the priest's name, the old man opened the door a bit wider. "Did he now?" He riveted the full force of his piercing appraisal on Evan. "And ye say ye're kin o' mine, do ye? From America, no less?"

After his recent failure with the dog, Evan decided it was past time he showed Claire he could stand up for himself. "Yes on both counts, sir." He stepped forward and doffed his hat. "My great-grandfather was Sean MacKay of Culdee. I'm hoping you might have heard of him."

Donall squinted up at him. "Lachlan and Sheena's eldest, do ye mean?"

Evan nodded. "Yes. He wed Rose Fraser and emigrated to America in 1825."

"Aye, I know o' him. I was but a lad o' ten when he left Culdee, never to return agin'. And ye say ye're his great-grandson?"

Once more, Evan nodded. "Yes, sir. That I am."

The old Scotsman swung open his door and stepped aside. "Well then, come in. Come in. Our poor home and all that we have are at yer disposal. Come in, I say!"

Joyous relief filled Evan. Though the trip to Culdee had begun on a lark, now it seemed as if everything since he had left Culdee Creek Ranch had been leading him to this very moment. Far from his own home, he had found family once again—family whose roots were far more ancient than his, but of his blood nonetheless.

He turned to Claire. "Do you mind visiting a bit with them before we head back to Culdee?"

"Nay, I don't mind," she said. "I expected no less. It's the hospitable thing to do."

Evan indicated Claire should precede him, then followed in her wake. His first impression, as he walked inside, was one of darkness and smoke. The source of the smoke was soon evident. A small peat fire burned in a circular hearth in the middle of the second and largest room. The hearth was surrounded by flat stones with a higher rock to one side where Evan knew the fire could be banked. Above the fire, suspended from an iron chain, hung a fat, cast-iron cook pot.

On closer inspection, he noted the walls and rafters were covered with a thick coating of soot. The main room was sparsely furnished. Two wooden chairs, their frames formed from bent tree branches, sat beside the fire. Nearby were a scarred wooden table, a chest, and two stools. Along one stone wall, several shelves protruding from iron brackets were filled with an assortment of chipped pottery jugs, mugs, plates, and wooden cooking utensils. In one corner were a wooden washtub and several barrels. Baskets hung overhead from the rafters, keeping company with three fat hens that, at their arrival, clucked loudly in disapproval.

An old woman, her arms full of blankets, walked in from the other room. "Well, well," she croaked in a voice gone rusty with age, "what have we here?" She paused to peer first at Claire, then Evan. "I canna recall invitin' anyone to come callin'. Can ye, Donall?"

"They're kin, Lainie," her husband offered, raising his voice a notch. "Or, leastwise, so the young lad claims. What did ye say yer name was, laddie?" he asked, glancing back at Evan.

"Evan MacKay. Sean MacKay's great-grandson." He turned to the old woman. "I'm pleased to meet you, ma'am."

"Ehhhy?" Lainie said, cupping her right ear. "What did ye say?"

"Sean MacKay," Donall repeated even more loudly. "He's the great-grandson o' my mither's brother. Dinna ye recall that braw, strapping young MacKay who left here when ye were a wee lassie, headed for America?"

He hobbled to one of the chairs, sat, then looked up at Evan. "Och, but there was some weepin' and wailin' over his departure. The finest flower o' Scotland left the Highlands in those sad days o' the Clearances, ne'er to be seen in these parts agin'. "

"He's kin, ye say?" Lainie queried. "Well, put on a kettle o' water, will ye, Donall? I must get these blankets aired 'afore the day's gone. We can all sit then, have a spot o' tea, and chat a bit."

Claire hurried over and held out her arms. "Here, let me help you. We'll be done in the wink of an eye. Then we can all chat together."

"Och, and aren't ye a kind lassie?" Lainie laid the blankets in Claire's arms. "Are ye wife to the laddie then, and a part o' our family by marriage?"

At the old woman's question, Evan straightened and shot the auburn-haired girl a quick look. To her credit, Claire managed to hide her discomfiture well, the only hint of her embarrassment the becoming rosy tint that suddenly washed her cheeks.

"Nay, I'm not wed to Evan," she all but choked out. "He's but a friend."

"Too bad," Lainie observed matter-of-factly. "Ye'd make a bonnie couple."

If Claire responded to that blunt statement, Evan didn't hear. She hurried from the house, Lainie stiffly bringing up the rear. He stared after them for a long moment, then turned back to Donall who sat by the fire watching him.

"Ye care for the lass, dinna ye?"

Evan's breath caught in his throat. Blast, he thought. The last thing he needed was that kind of information getting back to Claire. She'd bolt and run for sure.

Still, there was no purpose served denying what Evan knew the old man had so easily ascertained. "Yes, I do,"

71

he admitted reluctantly. "I'd be much obliged, though, if you didn't say anything to her about it."

"And why all the hudge-mudge?" Donall rose and walked to the water bucket. "A lass was never won by keepin' yer feelin's for her a secret."

"It's not as simple as it may seem." Though he had only met the old Scotsman a few minutes ago, Evan felt as if he had known him for years. Funny, he mused, how neither time, distance, nor culture had blurred the sense of family he so quickly felt with this old couple.

"Love's always simple. 'Tis the people who make it complicated." Donall struggled to balance himself with one hand on his cane, while he attempted to pour water into the old, porcelain teakettle sitting on the shelf.

Evan strode over. He took the water bucket from his host, quickly filled the teakettle, then wheeled about and headed back to the fire. After removing the iron cook pot from its chain, he hung up the kettle.

"I'm just visiting here," he began again when Donall once more claimed his seat at the fire. "Sooner or later, I need to head back home to America."

"So, wed the lass and take her with ye. She'll not be the first lass who followed her man to another land."

Evan gave a wry laugh. "Claire's got a mind of her own. She's hardly the kind to run after a man."

"Aye, few Scotswomen are, leastwise not unless they love the man. Ye'll jist have to win her heart then, willna ye?"

He stared down at the old man in stunned disbelief. "And what makes you think—"

"Och, ye do."

Nonplussed that Donall had so easily read his mind, Evan switched tack. "Well, then what about Claire? What makes you think she—"

"She has feelin's for ye, and no mistake."

That statement drew Evan up short. Even the remotest consideration that Claire might feel something for him filled him with a fierce joy. "I-I don't know what to say about that," he muttered awkwardly.

"Ye dinna need to say aught, lad. Ye must jist *do* somethin' about it!"

He considered Donall's words for a moment, then nodded. "Yes, I suppose I should, shouldn't I?"

The sound of female voices drifting ever nearer put an abrupt end to their conversation. The topic, however, continued to linger in Evan's mind the rest of the afternoon as they shared tea and talked, then combined the contents of their lunch basket with the old couple's meager meal, then talked some more.

By the time the sun began its languorous descent toward the mountains, Evan could see that Donall and Lainie were beginning to tire. He stood, brushed the crumbs from his black serge trousers, and looked to Claire.

"Probably time we were heading back, don't you think?"

She climbed to her feet. "Och, aye. We'll have to hurry as it is to reach Culdee before dusk." Claire smiled down at their host and hostess. "It was a wonderful day, visiting with you. I'd heard of you before from Father Mac-Laren, and I must say I'm verra sorry never to have visited until today."

"Dinna fash yerself, lass." Donall awkwardly pushed to his feet. "'Twas our pleasure to have ye and yer young man in our house. Especially a young man who is also kin."

Once again a becoming blush stole up Claire's neck and face. "Er, Evan isn't my—"

Evan took her by the arm. "I'd like to visit again sometime soon, if that wouldn't be an imposition. There's still so much more I want to learn about my Scots family."

"Ehhhy?" Lainie queried, cupping her right ear. "What did ye say?"

"He said, wife, that he'd like to visit us agin'." her husband shouted.

Her expression brightened. "Och, aye. Come agin'. We'd find that most pleasin'." Her dark-eyed gaze swung to Claire. "And ye, lass. Pray, come with the laddie, will ye? I find yer company most pleasin' as well."

Claire smiled and nodded. "If I can, I will." She stooped and picked up her now empty basket.

"Good-bye for now, then." Evan turned and, with Claire at his side, headed for the door.

"Fare ye well," Donall called.

"Until next time," his wife joined in.

After the darkness of the little croft house and the heavy peat smoke, outside seemed overly bright. The fresh air, however, was a welcome relief. As he walked along, Evan dragged in lungful after lungful of the sweet Highland air.

Everything, he noted with heightened senses, seemed fresh and new. The stark mountains looming behind them. The vibrant hue of the green grass on the hills. The intensely blue sky that was already beginning to soften with shades of lavender, slate, and indigo at its edges.

He found himself most profoundly aware, however, of the woman at his side. She was exquisite; at that particular moment, he couldn't recall ever having seen a more beautiful woman. She walked with the grace of a deer, her movements smooth, effortless, supple. The sweet nearness of her, as they strolled along, made his heart ache.

If Donall hadn't so casually pointed out the obvious only a short while ago, the truth would've most forcefully struck home now. He was falling in love with Claire Sutherland.

The realization filled Evan with an odd mix of happiness and fear. Happiness that he had surely, and at long last, found the woman of his dreams. And fear that

74

she would—just like Hannah—ultimately spurn him and his love.

He felt fairly certain Claire's feelings for him were more than those of disinterested friendship. Even Donall had said he could see she cared for him. But could Claire's affection for him ever grow into love?

Frustration welled in Evan. He had been such a blundering idiot when it had come to Hannah. He had forced the pace of their relationship far too fast and had finally driven her away. Somehow, some way, he must not make the same mistake with Claire. If he had to go slowly with her, then so be it.

Still, it took all Evan's self-control to contain the almost constant urge to stop right there on the road and take Claire into his arms. It wasn't in his nature to play games, or to restrain emotions he honestly and deeply felt. But sometimes, Evan reminded himself, a man had to pay a mighty big price if he was to win his heart's desire.

"You're certainly quiet," Claire observed just then, casting him a quizzical glance. "Are you unhappy about your visit with Donall and Lainie?"

Evan shook his head. "No, not at all. They're good, kind folk. The things they told me about my ancestors made me even prouder to be of Scot's blood then I already was. I was just mulling over what they'd said. And besides," he added, shooting her a roguish grin, "I figured you might, after the past three days, be getting a little weary of my company. Didn't see any sense in talking you to death."

"Och, I'm not weary of your company." Claire smiled. "You're a most entertaining man, you are, Evan MacKay."

"Am I now?" He laughed, thoroughly disarmed. "Well, I must say you're the first woman who has ever told me that."

An impish dimple danced in both her cheeks. "Well, don't let it go to your head."

"Not much chance of that. Leastwise, not with a girl like you. You'd be the first to put me firmly back in my place."

"Aye, that I would," she concurred. Claire paused then. "The morrow's Sunday. Would you like to accompany Ian and me to Mass at St. Columba's?"

Evan considered her offer briefly. He hadn't been to church since he had left Culdee Creek last August. And, even before that, his religious faith had been little better than lukewarm. But Claire seemed to set a good store on churchgoing, and the opportunity to spend any and every moment he could with her was sufficient incentive to attend church.

"I'd be much obliged," Evan replied. "Haven't had much opportunity to keep holy the Sabbath, what with all the traveling I've been doing, but I'd be glad to take you up on the offer. What time's Mass?"

"We like the morning services that begin at eight. Is that too early for you?"

He shook his head. "No. I'm an early riser. That suits me just fine."

"I'll call for you a half hour earlier then. That'll give us time to make the walk to St. Columba's and say our private prayers before Mass."

Watching an errant breeze dance in her gloriously shimmering curls, Evan knew exactly what his prayers would be. If God would only give him Claire Sutherland for his wife, he'd promise to serve the Lord the rest of his days. In fact, Evan decided, as he strode along in the ever deepening beauty of the waning day, he might as well get started on those prayers right here and now.

2

Monday morning, Claire settled back into her usual routine. After rousting Ian out of bed and feeding him his breakfast, she soon sent him heading out to school. The little cottage was then quickly put to rights and, after an all-too-short time spent practicing her clarsach, Claire headed out to her daily duties at St. Columba's.

It felt strange not to have Evan at her side, she mused as she made her way down the dirt road leading to Culdee. As surprising a thought as it was, Claire realized she actually missed him. The day just didn't seem quite the same, nor did it possess the heady sense of excitement and interest without Evan.

That particular revelation gave her pause. She couldn't recall ever in her life missing some boy, or feeling such a heart-deep need for his presence. Long ago, Claire had ceased allowing herself to either depend upon or need someone. If you let a body get too close, she well knew, they were bound, at the very least, to end up disappointing you.

Besides, except for Ian, she hadn't let another person matter that much to her since her aunt died. Well, no one, she quickly amended as St. Columba's tall steeple came into view, except Father MacLaren. But he was a priest. Everyone loved and trusted him.

Still, the inescapable truth remained. She did miss Evan, and he *did* matter. She almost wondered if she weren't beginning to fall in love with him.

With a savage shake of her head, Claire flung the terrifying consideration aside. Fall in love with Evan Mac-Kay? Why, she'd be daft even to contemplate such a thing! She was just imagining—well, dreaming would be closer to the truth—that he might care for her. He was a kind, warm, generous man who treated everyone well. Still, it was past time she return to reality—a reality that must not, and couldn't ever, include a certain handsome cowboy.

As Claire climbed the last of the steps leading to the church entrance, Father MacLaren was just finishing his morning constitutional around St. Columba's shady grounds. He ambled over.

"Och, but 'tis good to see ye, lass. I must admit the sacristy is in sore need o' a cleaning after Jamie MacNeal set fire to one o' the altar linens after this morn's Mass. I dinna know how many times I've warned the lad to have a care with the candles." He smiled ruefully. "There's still soot and ash all over the sacristy, though I did try to tidy it up as best I could."

She chuckled and shook her head. "Well, I hate to see such beautiful linens ruined, but Jamie's no worse than Ian. Do you recall that baptism when he first knocked your holy oils into the baptismal font, then in his eagerness to retrieve them, ended up tipping over the entire font?"

"Aye, I remember that day all too well," the priest said, nodding. "He drenched my feet so thoroughly, I feared my shoes would never dry out agin'. " Father MacLaren paused then. "Would ye join me for a spot o' tea 'afore ye see to the sacristy, lass? There's something I've been meaning to talk with ye about."

Claire arched a brow. "Indeed? And what might that be, Father?"

"Och, naught to worry yerself over," he said as he took her by the arm and led her into the church. "'Twas but a wee question or two I had for ye . . ." His voice faded, and his forehead wrinkled in what appeared to be deep thought. "Hmmm, I wonder if Mrs. Fraser has any o' those tasty scones left from yesterday's tea?"

She smiled. The old priest seemed to be doing that more and more often of late—jumping from one subject to another without logic or warning. She supposed it was a prerogative of age and increased responsibility. Probably, Claire thought wryly, it had a lot to do with the care and training of a new crop of altar boys each year. Ian was only one lad, and he was enough of a handful. She could only imagine what a troop of eight or nine lads would be like.

Ten minutes later, both were comfortably ensconced in Father MacLaren's office, sipping steaming cups of tea laced with milk and nibbling on yesterday's scones spread with a generous smattering of orange marmalade. Just as Claire was beginning to wonder if the old priest had forgotten the reason he had invited her in for tea, he suddenly launched into the topic.

"I saw Evan with ye at Mass yestreen," he said, eyeing her over a fresh cup of tea he had just poured and lifted to his lips. Father MacLaren took a careful sip, lowered the cup back to its saucer, and stared at her expectantly.

Totally bemused, Claire nodded. "Aye. I invited him to come with us. Like all MacKays, he was born and bred a Catholic. I can't say, though, he strictly practices the faith, but he seemed no worse for the experience."

The priest set down his cup and added a spoonful of sugar. "I'd imagine not. He was so taken with ye, I doubt he hardly remembers aught o' what transpired. And ye,"–he finally met her gaze–"ye didna seem overly occupied with aught going on around ye, either, so big were yer eyes for the likes o' him."

Hot blood flooded Claire's face. Holy Mother Mary, had her fascination with Evan MacKay been that evident? "I knew he'd been away from church for a time and I . . . I was just attempting to ease his way."

"Och, and was that the way o' things, was it?" The priest gave a disbelieving snort. "Rather, I'd say ye're smitten with each other. And I'd say ye both need to hie yerselves post haste to see me about when to begin announcing yer marriage banns."

6

As the man is, so is his strength. . . .
Judges 8:21

For the longest time, Claire could do little more than stare back at Father MacLaren. Her brain failed to formulate a response. Her throat went so tight she could barely swallow, much less force sound through it. And her tongue just sat there, unable to articulate a word.

But then, what would've been the point? Gazing into the priest's kindly brown eyes, she knew she could never lie. Yet to admit to feelings for Evan, much less seriously contemplate he might actually have similar feelings for her . . .

"Come, come, lass," Father MacLaren finally urged. "I've never known ye to be so short on words. Spit out what ye wish to say and be done with it."

"I . . . I don't want to wed Evan MacKay," Claire finally croaked out the admission. "Why, I hardly know the man! Besides, he hasn't told me he even cares for me, much less asked for my hand in marriage."

"Och, and why doesna that surprise me?" The old priest chuckled softly. "I canna as yet say why Evan hesitates, but I certainly know why ye do. And that, sweet lass, is why I wished to talk with ye."

Claire shook her head in denial. "It's far too soon to talk of marriage. That's the only reason I hesitate."

He pushed his teacup aside and leaned forward, resting his arms on his desk. "Be truthful with yerself, lass. 'Tisna the only reason. Nay, far from it."

She looked away, finding sudden fascination with the scene outside the window. An ancient Scots pine grew there. In its branches was a red squirrel industriously dining on a young, green pinecone. His summer coat had come in and was bright chestnut. His feet and lower legs were orange-brown. As he gnawed away at his meal, his long, red-tufted ears moved and twitched.

He was so dear, with big, dark eyes and a luxuriant tail. Claire could've gazed at him for hours—and would've far preferred to do so. But such a luxury was not to be. Father MacLaren sat but a few feet away, watching, waiting.

With a sigh, she turned back to face the priest. "I don't wish ever to wed, and well you know it. It's enough that I have Ian."

"Ian willna always be with ye. He'll grow, make a life o' his own, and leave. Then what will ye have, lass?"

"I'll have myself. I'll have the freedom at last to do what I wish with my life." Her chin lifted defensively. "And that will do me fine."

"Ye were created to be so much more than that, lass." He smiled. "Ye shouldna squander the gifts the Lord has given ye, or clasp them tightly to yerself. Gifts never given stagnate and shrivel, but gifts shared with others are constantly replenished and deepened. How else can the good Lord work His miracles, or shine His healing light, if not through us?"

"Truly, I haven't all that much to offer." Firmly, Claire shook her head. "What little I do have, I must save for Ian. You know how I've ruined his life, taking him with me when I ran away from home all those years ago. I owe him so much. I don't have time for aught else."

"Ye've far, far more to offer than ye may yet realize, lass." The priest's smile gentled. "Ye must finally let go of yer guilt, ye know, over what ye imagine ye've done to Ian. 'Twillna do either of ye any good to carry such a burden yer whole life long. Nay, on the contrary. 'Twill close yer heart to yer true calling, and destroy any chance ye may have to find a God-filled, lasting happiness."

Claire didn't know how to respond. Father MacLaren surely had a much closer relationship with God than she had. Why, save for her morning and bedtime prayers and her faithful attendance at Sunday mass, she hardly even thought of God. Well, Claire quickly amended, she at least didn't think of God as much as she *should* anyway. She loved the Lord, though. That she did. And if the old priest seemed to think the good Lord's hand was somehow involved in her growing affection for Evan . . .

"What purpose would be served in me wedding him and leaving Ian and my home here?" she wailed, confusion now beginning to stir her emotions into a chaotic jumble. "Ian needs me, Father!"

"Aye, that he does." He nodded in solemn agreement. "But mayhap God isna asking ye to give him up, but only to open yerself more fully to life—and love."

She frowned. "I don't understand."

"Think on it, lass. Mayhap Ian would thrive in a new land where he could start afresh. He seems to like Evan, and Evan, him. A strong man in his life wouldna be such a bad idea, would it? Indeed, how many times have ye mayhap wished for the same thing?" His mouth quirked wryly. "Too many to count, if I dinna miss my guess."

It was true. Claire *had* wished, even prayed, for some help and guidance for Ian. More than anything she had ever wanted, she wanted her brother to grow up and make something of himself. It would make up for so much that he had lost in following her all those years ago—and for the damaging effect it still seemed to have on him.

Evan had talked of his father's fine cattle ranch in Colorado. He had said he would eventually inherit that ranch. Surely she and Ian would have a much better life there. They'd certainly eat well. She remembered Evan talking about all the beef and other meat they consumed.

Suddenly, at the realization of the direction her thoughts were taking her, shame filled Claire. What kind of woman was she, she railed at herself, to mentally tick off all the practical reasons she should be marrying Evan? What had become of her heart, her human decency? Even for as short a time as she had known Evan, Claire knew he deserved better than that.

But she also recalled him speaking of his broken heart. Though he claimed he was over the girl he had left behind in Colorado, one brief discussion of the subject was hardly enough to convince her. He just didn't sound like a man ready to get married. And that was reason enough, among so many others, not to precipitously open her heart to him just yet.

"There's wisdom in all that you say, Father," Claire finally admitted. "But Evan is still getting over a girl who fell in love with someone else. Indeed, it's the reason he left America, why he eventually came to Culdee. He's still looking for answers and an easing of that pain."

"Hmmm." The priest cradled his chin in his hand. "I wondered what the true reason for his journey was. Still, I know what I saw. The lad's quite taken with ye, lass. If he wasna gazing at ye yestreen with the eyes o' love, then I've gone and outlived my days o' useful service at St. Columba's."

"Och, Father, you've many years of useful service left in you," Claire said with an unsteady laugh. Then her smile faded. "I just don't know if I'm the right woman for Evan. Mayhap I do have gifts within me that God intends for me to share. But are they the gifts that Evan needs? And have I the courage it would take to open my heart to him, to make his home mine, and his people my own?"

"Well spoken, lass. Ye're beginning to face the real issues at last. And leastwise," the priest offered with a chuckle, "his family *are* Scotsmen. Ye'd be with folk o' yer own kind."

"Aye, but life is different in America. As wonderful as it might be, it isn't Scotland."

"True enough. Sometimes, though, ye must sacrifice to gain a greater reward."

She sighed. "If only I could be certain it was truly God's will that I should wed Evan. It would make it all so much easier."

"Pray on it, lass. Ye've been a wee bit amiss in that of late, as we both know. Pray and trust. The Lord will answer ye when the time is right."

Claire managed a wan smile. "Aye, I suppose so. And it isn't as if Evan has even asked me to wed him. Or mayhap ever will."

"Nay, he hasna, has he?" Even as Father MacLaren solemnly agreed, laughter danced in his eyes. "Somehow, though, I dinna think that will remain much of an obstacle. Not for verra long, at any rate."

ॐ

Claire finished brushing up one side of her hair, then slid a pretty, tortoiseshell comb in place high on her crown to anchor it. After doing the same with the other side, she tied the remainder of the long, curly length at the nape of her neck with an emerald green ribbon. Critically yet also very nervously, Claire then examined her image in the small wall mirror beside her bed.

Her hair looked passable, she supposed. Her face was scrubbed until it was clean and pink. Her one good linen blouse had seen better days, as had most of her clothing, but at least it had been washed until it was snowy white, then crisply pressed. She wore her best woolen skirt and shawl, both in a Sutherland plaid of blue, green, white, and red. A belt, her plain silver brooch, stockings, and leather shoes completed her ensemble.

She hoped Evan would find her attractive and only have eyes for her this eve at the *ceilidh.* The traditional, periodic gathering of neighbors in the village center for storytelling and songs, a celebration that usually went on until the wee hours, seemed like the perfect way to spend time with Evan and not appear as if she was fawning over him. Still, if a beautiful June night under the stars didn't finally bring out the romantic in him, Claire figured nothing would.

Three weeks had passed since Father MacLaren's talk with her, and Claire had yet to discern any sign of Evan's purported affection. He remained friendly, helping her each night with the evening meal. He went to mass with her each Sunday, had long talks with Ian, and the time he didn't spend doing chores for Angus or visiting with Lainie and Donall, he spent making small repairs to her croft.

But never once had Evan tried to hasten the progress of their friendship or spoken like a man intent on courtship. If there had ever been a spark of love growing in Evan MacKay's breast for her, Claire was convinced it had all but died away. Problem was, the more she was with Evan, the deeper her own feelings for him grew. Och, but he was the most maddening of men!

She made a face at herself in the mirror, then turned away. "Serves you right," she muttered disgustedly. "When you first came to Culdee, you spurned the advances of all the eligible young men. And now you finally understand how much pain your coldheartedness must have caused."

A sudden restlessness assailed her. Claire paced the confines of her small room until her glance snagged on the old wooden clarsach lying on its soundboard atop her clothes chest. Mayhap its sweet voice would calm her jangled nerves. There was time yet, before Evan came to fetch her. Time enough to spend with her beloved harp.

She walked over, picked up the little clarsach, and carried it to the room's single chair. Sitting, Claire nestled the instrument in the curve of her left shoulder. With her fingernails, she lightly stroked its brass wire strings, eliciting a melodious, bell-like tone. Then, with a sigh, she positioned her hands and started to play.

After a time, as it always did, the music began to soothe and uplift her soul. Claire played several ancient ballads; then a lively jig, plucking the strings then dampening them with strong, sure fingers. When she finally paused, a knock sounded at the front door.

"Claire? It's Evan. May I come in?"

She quickly laid aside the clarsach, straightened her shawl, and checked her appearance once more in the mirror. Then she turned and hurried from her bedroom. "Aye, come in, Evan." As she spoke, Claire pulled open the front door. "Have you been waiting long? I must have forgotten the time. I do that frequently when I play my . . ."

At the sight of the bouquet of flowers Evan held in his hand, her voice faded. He grinned and thrust them at her.

"I saw these at the market today, and I couldn't resist buying them for you. A pretty lady deserves pretty things."

"Why, thank you, Evan." Claire knew her face must be turning several shades of crimson as she accepted the bouquet. It was a mix of pink and red rose buds, lacy fern fronds, and sprigs of white heather. It was also, she thought, the most beautiful gift she had ever received. "Thank you ever so much."

They stood there for a long moment, suddenly shy and awkward with each other. Then Claire remembered her manners.

"I'd best be putting them in some water before we leave for the *ceilidh*," she mumbled, wheeling about and striding into the main room. "I wouldn't want them to wilt while we were gone."

Wordlessly, Evan followed her into the room and watched as she found a pottery vase, filled it with water, and placed the flowers into it. "There, that'll brighten the room, don't you think?" she asked as she placed the bouquet in the middle of the big table.

At her query, Evan appeared to finally find his tongue. He jerked, then nodded. "Yes, it does look right fine there." As he spoke, though, he never once considered the flowers, but stared at her. Ever so slowly, a smile lifted his lips. "I must say, as pretty as they are, they can't begin to compare to how beautiful you look tonight, Claire."

At Evan's words, and the undisguised look of admiration in his eyes, a thrill vibrated through her. She managed an unsteady grin. "You don't look so bad yourself."

And, indeed, he didn't. Since she had seen him last, Evan had had his dark hair trimmed. In the cruisie's flickering illumination, the glossy waves glinted with highlights of ebony and midnight. His skin was tanned from all the time spent outdoors, a most attractive contrast to the white shirt he wore unbuttoned at his throat and rolled up at the sleeves, and his navy blue flannel vest. His black trousers skimmed long legs and slim hips, accentuating even more the width of his shoulders and breadth of his chest. In his hand Evan clutched his everpresent black cowboy hat, a "Stetson," he had called it.

She thought him a most handsome man, even more so than when she had first met him. It was strange indeed, Claire thought, how coming to know the heart of someone only made him look the better. A month ago, she would've laughed such a statement to scorn but now . . . now she knew how wrong she would've been.

"Well, shall we be on our way?" Evan extended his arm to her. "After all you and Ian have told me about these *ceilidhs*, I don't want to miss a minute of it."

"Och, aye," Claire agreed, stepping up to take his arm, "they *are* great fun. Haven't you any such celebrations in America?"

As Evan led her from the house, his brow furrowed in thought. "Well, there's quite a bit of excitement and celebrating on the Fourth of July, our nation's birthday. And the little town near the ranch, Grand View, periodically has a town dance and social. All the single ladies make a box dinner that's auctioned off to the single men. Then the lady whose box you've bought gets to eat the meal with you." He grinned. "It works out very well, if you're of a mind to court the lady."

She shot him an arch look as they walked along. "And how many box dinners have you bought?"

"Not too many. And none of any lady I was ever of a mind to court."

"That's a most intriguing custom. Mayhap I'll have to suggest we give it a try."

"If you did, I'd be first in line to buy your dinner."

Her heart gave a leap, then began a faster rhythm. "But only because you know and trust my cooking, I'm sure."

"No." Evan pulled her to a halt. "Not only because I know and trust your cooking, Claire. Far from it. I'd buy your dinner because it'd be yet another excuse to spend time with you. And because I'd like to court you, if you'd be of a mind to consider it."

Claire inhaled a sharp, shallow breath. Now that Evan had finally uttered the first words signaling his intent to change the pace of their relationship—an intent she had been dreaming about since Father MacLaren's talk—her sudden surge of joy was swiftly replaced by one of fear. What had once been but a pleasant dream had become reality. A reality she must now face and commit to, one way or another.

As she gazed up into his warm, wonderful eyes, however, one by one all of Claire's fears melted away. She felt as if she had known Evan for a long while now. She trusted him. And she knew, with a woman's instinct strong and sure, that he was worth the risk, if any man was.

Then the sound of rough, male voices, raised in laughter, drifted down the tree-lined road leading from Culdee. Claire frowned. If she wasn't mistaken, one of those voices sounded suspiciously like Dougal MacKay's.

"Is that ye, Claire?" his deep voice boomed of a sudden, rising from the shadows. "I told the lads ye'd be on yer way to the *ceilidh* by now, but they insisted we come fetch ye nonetheless."

As he spoke, he and a group of four other men moved toward them. Dougal and his gang of thugs. Unease rippled through Claire. If it had just been her alone tonight, she would've soon set Dougal straight. He'd back down quickly enough, rather than risk the full force of her temper.

Things, though, wouldn't go so well for Evan if Dougal found her with him. She knew that from bitter experience, the few times she had walked to some other village social with one of the local lads. Dougal would never back down from anyone he suspected was trying to court her. Especially with all his friends behind him.

Claire looked to Evan. "Mayhap it would be best if you went on without me. I could walk the rest of the way with Dougal and the others, and rejoin you once I reach Culdee."

His face an inscrutable mask, Evan stared down at her. "And why's that, Claire? Have you suddenly decided to throw me over for Dougal?"

"Nay." She shook her head, even as a sick feeling twined and twisted in her belly. "But Dougal won't take kindly to you escorting me to the *ceilidh* instead of him. He has been known to resort to violence—he and his friends." She grasped him by the arm. "Please, Evan. Go now, before it's too late—"

"Well, well, what have we here?" Dougal MacKay growled as he and his cronies at last drew up before them.

"I think it's pretty obvious, mister," Evan said, meeting the other man's narrow-eyed gaze with a steady one of his own. "Claire and I are on our way to the *ceilidh*. You're welcome to join us if you'd like."

Dougal looked him up and down. "And what if I say instead, hie yerself along and leave Claire to me? What would ye do then?"

"I think I'd leave it up to the lady in question." Evan turned to her. "Do you want to go to the *ceilidh* with Dougal or with me, Claire?"

Though her heart cried out the opposite, she forced herself to give the answer for Dougal. "For your sake, it would be best if I went with him, Evan."

The burly Scotsman gave a hoot of triumph. "Jist as I supposed! Claire wants to go with me!"

Evan smiled with grim resolve. "That's not what I asked you," he said softly, never taking his gaze from hers. "Do you *want* to go with Dougal instead of me?"

"Nay," Claire whispered, her whole heart in her reply. "You know I don't."

"Well, then it's settled." Evan took her by the arm and turned to face the men. "You heard her, Dougal. Now, let us by."

As Evan stepped forward with Claire, the big farmer moved to stand before them. "And *I* say, let her go and be on yer way while ye're still able. Claire's mine. 'Tis past time ye acknowledged that."

"Claire's no man's unless she chooses to be."

Evan's bold statement was finally enough to stir Claire to action. It seemed there was no way to avoid a confrontation now, at any rate. "Aye, Dougal," she said, glaring up at him. "It's true. I've never once encouraged you in your determination to take me as wife." She scanned the others. "Have any of you ever seen me once cozy up to Dougal, or heard me speak tender words of love to him? Have you?"

Two of the men standing behind Dougal, John Cameron and Henry MacDuff, actually looked away and shuffled their feet, but, like their compatriots, they refused to reply. With a sinking heart, Claire shook her head. None of them, she realized, would go against their leader—no matter how wrong he was.

Dougal smirked. "Well, enough o' this." He glanced over his shoulder. "Lads, help me out here, will ye?"

As if on cue, all four men strode up to Evan. For a split second, Claire thought Evan meant finally to passively acquiesce. Then, he released her arm and flung himself at his opponents.

"Run, Claire!" he yelled, falling into the press of bodies.

In the next instant, Dougal had grabbed her about the waist and pulled her out of harm's way. Fury swelled in her. Claire twisted and fought in the big farmer's grip. "Let me go!" she screamed. "Let me go!"

To add further emphasis to her demand, Claire dug her elbow into Dougal's side. His grip on her momentarily loosened, then tightened once more. He slid his other arm across her chest, pinning her tightly to him.

"Stop yer brattlin'," he snarled in her ear. "'Twill do ye no good to struggle and squirm. The fight will be over in but a moment as 'tis."

Yet even as Claire slumped against him, panting for breath, she saw that Dougal's prediction was far from accurate. Already Henry lay on the ground, senseless. Blood streaming from his nose, Georgie Sinclair flailed wildly and ineffectually at Evan's head. And John Cameron and Donald MacKay, Dougal's older brother, though still two-to-one against Evan, seemed to be the recipients of far more blows then they were landing.

When Georgie finally got too close and went down with a quick jab to the jaw, Dougal seemed to have had enough. With an oath, he flung Claire aside and stalked up to Evan. Evan's back was turned to Dougal as he battled with the man's two cronies. He didn't see or hear Dougal coming.

Claire, climbing hastily to her feet, however, guessed Dougal's intent. "Evan, behind you!" she cried.

At her call Evan wheeled about, but it was too late. Dougal's huge fist slammed into his jaw. Evan staggered back, right into the arms of Donald and John, who grabbed him and held him tightly.

"Enough o' this, I say!" Dougal shouted. He pulled back his arm, then thrust it square into Evan's middle.

With a grunt, Evan doubled over. Dougal, however, wasn't finished. Over and over he hit Evan, landing blow after blow wherever he could.

"Nay! Stop it! Stop it!" Claire screamed, grabbing hold of Dougal's right arm and hanging on with all her strength. "You'll kill him!"

"And what if I do kill him? He's been naught but trouble since the first day he came here." His face contorted in rage, the farmer finally paused. "Ye belong here in Culdee with me. The sooner ye see that, the better off ye'll be."

"You pig-headed oaf!" Claire cried in reply. "Killing Evan won't change my mind about you. Nay, far from it. And all you'll get for your efforts is prison!"

The mention of prison finally seemed to penetrate the big Scotsman's rage. Turning, Dougal looked back at Evan. Slumped over, breathing heavily, Evan appeared barely conscious. The Scotsman gave a snort of satisfaction.

"Well, he's learned his lesson," he muttered. "And what o' ye, lass?" Dougal glanced now to her. "Have ye learned yer lesson at last, too?"

Claire gazed up at him, fury—and a fierce, fresh resolve—swelling within her. "Aye, that I have, Dougal. That I have."

"Will ye accompany me to the *ceilidh* then?"

She shook her head. "Nay. I need to see Evan home. Thanks to you, he isn't in any condition to attend the *ceilidh* now."

"Dinna fash yerself. The lads can see him home."

"Nay, *I'll* see him home, and that's that!"

He must have caught the hard, angry edge of determination in her voice at last. After a moment more of indecision, the farmer nodded his consent. "Have it yer way then. Jist as long as we finally understand each other. Jist as long as ye finally face the fact whose woman ye are, and what ye must do aboot it."

Claire met his stern look with an unflinching one of her own. "Och, I do, Dougal. I understand everything." She paused to add even greater emphasis to her final word. *"Everything."*

7

My sins are not hid from Thee.
Psalm 69:5

"Here, let me have a look at you now," Claire said twenty minutes later as she helped Evan reenter her house and take a seat in a chair at the table.

The trek back had been arduous. Evan was in pain and had to halt frequently to catch his breath. Though he hadn't said much, she knew it had taken all his strength not to give up and just lay down right there on the road. It had taken all her strength, as well, not to break into tears, so moved was she at his courage in standing up to Dougal and his thugs, then uncomplainingly making his way back home.

No man had ever before dared confront Dougal MacKay when he was backed up by his friends, much less fight against such unfair odds. No man in Culdee had ever had the courage to try.

But Evan was a man who stood up for those he cared about. She could depend on him. For the first time in a long while, Claire felt safe and protected. She had finally found a helpmate.

In the brighter light of the cruisies, Claire made a quick survey of Evan. A jagged slash above his left eyebrow oozed blood, as did his split upper lip. His right cheekbone sported a rapidly purpling bruise. His shirt was torn in several places, some small patches of drying blood stained his sleeves and numerous grass stains now marred its once snowy whiteness.

It was the uneven way Evan breathed, however, that caused Claire the most concern. She made quick work of treating his eyebrow and cut lip, then pulled off his vest and began unbuttoning his shirt.

"What do you think you're doing?" he rasped, grabbing her hand to halt her.

"You've hurt your chest, haven't you?"

He waved away her concern. "It's nothing more than bruised ribs. No need to worry."

"I'll cease my worrying once I have a look at you." Ever so gently, Claire pulled her hand free. "Now, if you don't mind, I need to get your shirt off."

Evan eyed her for a moment, then managed a lopsided grin, which only made him wince when the action caused a tug at his split lip. "Have at it then. It's been one of my favorite daydreams, you know, the thought of you undressing me. If I'd realized sooner what the secret to that was, I'd have gotten myself beaten up a long time ago."

She shot him a disgusted look, then began unbuttoning his shirt. "As if you're in any condition to do aught about it, even if I was undressing you for other than medicinal reasons. When it comes to women, you men have a verra rich, if misguided, fantasy life."

"Well, wishing and dreaming can be helpful in mustering the courage needed for action. How do you think I ever found the guts to ask you to allow me to court you?" Evan sighed. "But I reckon I'm too late, aren't I?"

Her hands stilled in the act of opening his shirt and sliding it from his shoulders. "Whatever do you mean?" Claire glanced up to meet his piercing gaze. "I didn't have the chance to answer you earlier."

"Then why did you tell Dougal you understood everything at last? I knew you weren't agreeing to marry him, even if he did seem mollified by your response. But I also didn't get the impression, at that moment, that you were any too pleased with men in general."

Totally flabbergasted, Claire stared down at Evan. "Well, it's reassuring that you at least had the sense to trust my judgment when it came to Dougal," she finally found voice to reply. "Of course I in no way meant I intended to wed him."

"Well, you didn't sound like you wanted ever to wed any other man, either." He cocked his head, studying her. "Me included."

She sighed and rolled her eyes. "Och, I didn't mean you, you silly man! When I said I understood everything, I meant I finally realized it was you I had given my heart to. That now that I'd met you, there wasn't anything to keep me here anymore. And that I finally knew what I must do about it."

Evan's expression of utter amazement was downright comical. Claire would've laughed if she hadn't been afraid of hurting his feelings. But beneath that look of incredulity lay an unguarded vulnerability and a wild, joyous hope. They were precious, tender emotions. Claire had no intention of dashing them, especially when they mirrored so closely her own feelings.

"Aye," she said, smiling as she gently slid Evan's shirt off his shoulders and down his arms. "If we'd had the

97

time before Dougal had come,"–Claire set his shirt aside–"I was ready to accept your offer to court me. And then, when I had to watch them beating up on you . . ."

Overcome by the memory of that brutal fight, she swallowed hard and fought back tears. "Well, it drove home even more forcefully my true feelings for you."

"You said you realized you'd given your heart to me." Evan's voice deepened to a rich, husky timbre. "Are you saying you love me, Claire?"

As she gazed down at him, bare of chest and bruised of body, his eyes dark with ardent affection, a wave of knee-weakening desire washed over her. It was all Claire could do not to throw herself into his arms. Indeed, only the extent of his injuries and consideration for his battered condition held her back.

So, instead, she glanced away. If she looked at Evan another instant, Claire thought, she'd surely say something she'd long regret. There was time enough to go slowly with each other, if only she maintained a level head and controlled the pace of the courtship. If only she had the strength . . .

Evan took her hand, kissed it tenderly, and pressed it to his chest. "Would it make it easier for you to tell me, if I first admitted I love you and want you to be my wife? Because it's true, you know. Looking back now, I realize I fell in love with you from the first moment I met you, and have just been too afraid to tell you, for fear I'd drive you away."

With those words, tears flooded her eyes and spilled down her cheeks. Claire wrenched her gaze back to his. It was true, she realized, seeing the unmistakable proof shining in Evan's eyes. He really did love her.

A warm, sweet surety filled her, and she yielded at last. She loved him so much. In that love, Claire suddenly knew there was no obstacle in life that they couldn't surmount together. At long last she had found her other half, the man to complete and sustain her. God was so good!

"Aye, it would help indeed," she whispered. "For I love you, too, Evan MacKay, and would be honored to become your wife."

"And would you also be willing to go to Colorado and live there with me?"

She nodded, knowing it would have come to that if she agreed to wed him. "It would seem the best for all. I can't vouch that Dougal would cease his beating up on you just because we were wed. He's never been a verra good loser."

Evan chuckled. "And *I've* never been one to back down from a fight, especially if I happened to find Dougal alone someday."

They both paused then, gazing at each other with eyes brimming with love. How wonderful, Claire thought, to feel so comfortable, so free with another person. She had never realized such emotions were possible, especially with a man. Especially a man from another land, who was raised so differently from her.

The consideration of leaving Culdee and Scotland did unsettle her, though. She would have to depend heavily on Evan—especially at first—to support her and ease her way. And how would his family feel about him bringing home a wife from abroad?

"Are you certain," Claire began, choosing her words with care, "that your family will approve of you wedding a Scotswoman? Mayhap they had some other lass already in mind for you? A lass with wealth or great land holdings to her name. I can bring you naught, Evan, save myself."

"You're all I want, Claire." He smiled. "They'll love you just as much as I do. You'll see. And as far as having another girl in mind for me, my pa knows that'd be a lost cause anyway. I'm too much like him when it comes to having things my way."

Claire chewed on her lower lip. Evan wasn't the only person who needed his way–at least in one other thing. The issue of Ian was a subject on which she couldn't compromise. Sooner or later, she'd need to broach the issue of what to do about him. No matter how much she loved Evan, Claire couldn't–and wouldn't–leave Ian behind.

"And would your father mind if you not only brought home a wife, but her brother, too?"

His smile faded to one of solemn regard. "Did you really think I'd ask you to desert Ian, Claire?"

"I . . . I didn't know." With heart pounding, she met his searching scrutiny. "Most times, a man doesn't expect to be saddled with additional kin when he takes a woman to wife."

"Well, maybe most times that's true, but not this time. I know how important Ian is to you. Now, I'm not saying," he hurried to add, "that I don't have concerns about him, but I also know he wouldn't fare well here if left all to himself." Evan shook his head. "No, I know it won't be easy taking Ian with us, but it's got to be done."

Relief, so intense it made her dizzy, flooded Claire. "But will there be room for all of us at your ranch?"

"If there isn't, we'll either build an extra house at Culdee Creek, or find a place to live in Grand View." Once again Evan lifted her hand to his swollen lips, then lowered it to clasp it close. "Don't worry about a thing. Leastwise not about what'll happen once we get to Culdee Creek. Right now, the only issue that matters, since you've agreed to marry me, is do I still have to court you? Or can we see Father MacLaren tomorrow about making wedding arrangements?"

Taken aback by his sudden change in tack, Claire laughed aloud. "By mountain and sea, Evan MacKay, but you're not a man who wastes any time, are you?"

"Well," he admitted with a shrug, that immediately elicited a wince, "all this talk about the ranch and my family has gotten me homesick. I've been gone almost nine months now. Reckon it's time I think about heading home. I've got some unfinished business to clear up."

At his mention of unfinished business, Claire's gut twisted. She hid her rising dread by lowering her gaze to examine Evan's ribs. "With the girl you once loved, you mean?"

"Yes, with her," he answered honestly, wincing yet again when she gently touched his side. "And with the man she is most likely married to by now. But I've also got unfinished business with my pa and Abby, and my little sister Beth. I owe them all a big apology. I need to ask their forgiveness for running out on them like I did. I made some big mistakes. It's past time I was man enough to own up to them."

Gazing down on him, Claire thought Evan the most brave, wonderful man she had ever known. It took great honesty to recognize when you had done wrong, and great courage to own up to it. She only wished she possessed that same courage when it came to telling Evan the real truth about her past.

It was a secret that could well jeopardize their future together. Indeed, it might well change how Evan felt about her. And she was far from ready to risk that—no matter how great the sin in keeping the truth from him.

❦

The first banns, announcing their impending marriage in a month's time, were read in St. Columba's that Sunday. No legitimate protests against their upcoming wedding were filed, even if the announcement stirred a passing ruckus in the back of the church, where Dougal sat. That afternoon, Claire and Evan made a trip to Donall and Lainie's to share the good news with them and request that the old couple stand as witnesses to their marriage.

Once Lainie finally understood the reason for the excitement—after much shouting and many explanations from her husband—she tearfully accepted for the both of them. Next, she promptly took down the MacKay clan harp and offered it to Claire as a wedding present. "Our line will die with us," she insisted when Claire protested. "But if I pass it on to ye and Evan, the harp will remain with true kin. Ye must take it, lass. Besides, who else but a fellow harper would treasure it as much?"

After much hesitation, Claire finally agreed to exchange her clarsach for Lainie's, knowing full well that she had gained a far greater heirloom in the trade. On the way home she clutched the beautiful harp to her, feeling as if, even before she wed Evan, she already belonged to his family.

Twice more, in successive Sundays, the banns were read. Twice more, Dougal mumbled and grumbled, but never once could he be found after Mass or in Evan's near vicinity to "discuss" his complaints. Several times in the ensuing weeks, Claire and Evan also met with Father MacLaren to discuss their impending marriage and the realities of wedded life. Claire bought fabric and hand-stitched a long, white wedding gown. Plans were made to hold an early evening wedding Mass in St. Columba's, followed by a sumptuous supper cooked and served by Mrs. Fraser in the rectory. And, finally, in the midst of all the excitement and preparations, the morning of their wedding arrived.

"Drat! Drat! Drat!" Claire exclaimed for the umpteenth time that morning. She stomped about the cottage searching for yet another item to pack in the big steamer trunk holding all of her and Ian's earthly possessions for the trip to America. "Now where did I put my sewing basket? And where's my good winter shawl?"

From their vantage on the stoop outside the front door, Evan and Ian shared a commiserating grin. As Claire worked herself into an ever-worsening frenzy, both males had finally decided the wisest course was to beat a hasty retreat. And there they had remained for the past hour, with little hope things would soon calm enough to venture back inside.

"She rarely gets this way," the boy spoke up at last. "In case you were beginning to wonder if wedding her was such a grand notion after all."

Evan chuckled. "Well, that's reassuring."

"I think Claire's just verra nervous, what with a wedding this eve, then us all leaving Culdee on the morrow's coach. She's had a lot on her mind of late, you know?"

"Yes," Evan agreed solemnly, "I know. I just wish there was something I could do to ease her anxiety. In the end, I *am* the cause of it all."

Ian nodded. "Aye, that you are. I suppose, though, it can't be helped."

Evan grinned at the boy. "So, you're not having second thoughts about leaving Culdee then?"

"Nary a one!" Ian laughed. "Why, I can't believe my good fortune. I'm going to be a cowboy! Do you know how jealous all the lads at school are because of that? Suddenly, I'm no longer the outcast or source of ridicule. Not that I ever gave a fig for what any of them thought of me," he muttered as an afterthought. "They all looked down on me—and Claire, too—just because we weren't from these parts. But now they have to stay, while we leave for the land of cowboys and Indians. And *we* can look down on *them!*"

103

"There's a lot to be said for Scotland and Scottish ways," Evan offered gently, unwilling for Ian to speak poorly of his own land. "You shouldn't think ill of this place. In many ways it has helped form you into the person you are. Why, even in the short time I've been here, I've found much to inspire me. I'm grateful for the friendships made, kinfolk rediscovered, and the life I've had the good fortune to live. But, most of all, I'm grateful for you and Claire. You both mean so much to me."

As if he were struggling to contain a smile, Ian's mouth twitched at the corners. "I thank you for saying that. We haven't had verra many friends except each other, and Claire has given up a lot for me. I want her to be happy, too. . . ."

Inside the house, something fell to the floor. From the loud crash and clatter, Evan gathered it was something breakable. His supposition was quickly confirmed when Claire gave a wail of anguish, then began to weep. Evan glanced at Ian, who shrugged sympathetically.

"I'd say," the lad commented smugly, "it's past time *you* were heading back into the house. Claire's not one much given to weeping. Something must truly be twisting her insides to make her cry. And, since you're her intended, I'd say the honor now falls to you. Just one thing more, though." He pulled out a small, cloth bag and offered it to Evan.

"What's this?" Evan asked.

"The money I owe you for Jamie's debt. Consider it my wedding gift."

Wordlessly, Evan accepted the bag. Ian blushed, shrugged, and climbed to his feet. For a fleeting moment more he gazed down at Evan, then turned and sauntered away.

Mixed feelings assailed Evan. He was happy Ian trusted him enough to admit a wrongdoing, that the boy was man enough to finally attempt to set things right.

But the confirmation that Ian was a thief wasn't all that comforting, especially now, on the eve of leaving for the States. He could only hope that things would be different once they got to Colorado.

Inside the little croft house, the sound of Claire's weeping continued. Ian glanced back over his shoulder, his mouth quirking in commiseration.

"Coward," Evan muttered affectionately, eyeing the boy's retreating form with envy. Then, with a deep exhalation of breath, he pocketed the money, climbed to his feet, and reentered the croft house.

Claire sat on the hearth, her face in her hands, weeping inconsolably. At her feet lay the scattered remains of a clay pot that had once held barley meal, now lying wasted on the floor. Evan hesitated but a moment, then walked over and took a seat beside Claire on the hearth.

"It was only an old jar, sweetheart. You couldn't have taken it with you anyway."

"I-I know," she sobbed.

Perplexed now, he slid closer and slipped an arm around her shoulders. "Then what's the matter? This isn't like you, Claire."

With a soft moan, she leaned into him and laid her head on his shoulder. "I-I don't kn-know! This should b-be the happiest day of my life, and I've never f-felt so out of sorts or confused." She wept all the harder. "Och, Evan. What's wr-wrong with me?"

Unease gripped him. The worst possibility of all assailed him. What if Claire was having second thoughts about getting married? What could he say to ease her doubts? And what if nothing helped? What would he do then?

"Maybe it's just a case of pre-marital jitters," he finally ventured. "I've heard it can affect folks in different ways."

"N-nay, it isn't th-that. It's far, far w-worse!"

This time, fear clamped hard around Evan's heart. Please, God, he fervently prayed. Don't let it end here. I don't know what I'll do if I lose Claire, too.

Yet, even as he lifted the prayer, Evan also knew he didn't want Claire to enter into their marriage with doubts, or reluctantly. He loved her too much to purposely risk hurting her. So, with a sinking heart, he held her close and asked the one question he dreaded asking above all others.

"Are you regretting having agreed to marry me, then? Do you want to postpone the wedding?"

With a cry, Claire jerked back. "Och, nay. Never!" The terror in her eyes, however, gave lie to her words.

"You don't really love me, do you?" Evan forced himself to ask. "Tell me the truth, Claire. You owe me that much at least."

She nodded, averting her gaze. "Aye, that I do. But the truth . . . may turn you against me . . . once and for all."

"You shouldn't marry a man you don't love."

At that, she lifted her tear-filled gaze back to his. "It isn't my love I'm worried about, but yours, once I tell you . . ."

With a sob, Claire clutched at him, clenching the fabric of the white shirt he wore in her hands. "I love you, Evan, with my whole heart, but I fear . . . I fear . . ."

"What? What do you fear? Tell me, sweetheart. Nothing can be so terrible that, together, we can't overcome it."

"I love you, but . . . but I fear I may be using you in the bargain. That day you first met Dougal, he said some things to me. Things that hurt because I wondered if they weren't true."

"And what were those things he said, Claire?"

"Dougal accused me of setting my sights on you because I imagined a better life awaited me in America. He said I wanted a better life for Ian there, too, that I

106

hoped my brother would finally change and become a good lad away from here. Then he said I was only using you as an excuse to run away from my people and responsibilities here."

"It doesn't matter what Dougal said." Relief washed through Evan. "What matters is what *you* believe. Do you think you're marrying me just to use me?"

"Och, nay, Evan. I love you. Truly I do. But it's also true that I stand to gain so verra much in wedding you. Yet what do you really gain in the bargain?"

He chuckled, the sound vibrating through his chest to sink deeply and reassuringly into hers. "I gain a wonderful, brave, intelligent, loving woman. And, though I might have more materially to offer you than what you have here, life on a ranch isn't what anyone would call an easy living. The land is hard, the work backbreaking for men and women alike, and there are never any guarantees about anything. You'll be expected to carry your fair share, and sometimes even more. So will Ian, for that matter."

He smiled, his gaze full of love. "But what matters now isn't what might happen, but what *will* happen. I love you, Claire. More than anything I've ever wanted, I want you to be my wife. The only question remaining is, do you still want to marry me?"

Once more tears filled her eyes and coursed down her cheeks. "Aye, Evan," she whispered hoarsely. "More than anything, I still want to marry you."

❧

The light from the wall cruisie bathed the room in a soft, golden glow. Fresh-cut flowers scented the air with their sweet fragrance. Clean sheets, plump pillows, and a fluffy comforter beckoned invitingly.

Though everything was prepared–including Ian spending the night at St. Columba's rectory–Claire paced the room nervously, one moment nearly striding to the door to call Evan to her, then the next wheeling about and hurrying to the opposite end of the room to clasp her arms about her protectively. If she had known how panic-stricken she would have been tonight–her wedding night–she was certain she'd have never had the courage to go through with the marriage.

But she *had* made her vows in the sight of God, Father MacLaren, Ian, and Lainie and Donall MacKay. There was no going back. No going back . . . no matter how desperately she now questioned what she had done.

Evan, bless his kind, patient soul, waited still, out there in the living area. He had told her to take all the time she needed to prepare herself. If he had realized, though, that Claire doubted now she'd ever be ready, he might not have been quite so generous with his offer.

Best to just call him in and have it done with, she thought. The marital union surely wasn't half as bad as she was fearing. Indeed, she had heard some of the wives giggling about it from time to time at the village well. Despite their embarrassment at speaking of the marriage bed, they seemed to actually find pleasure in the act.

Claire sensed it would be the same with Evan. Indeed, it was almost a relief to finally think of him in that way and not feel guilty about it. He was her husband now, after all. And she did want him.

But still the doubts and fears assailed her, whirling about in her mind until she couldn't make any sense of anything. She knew she wasn't in a proper frame of mind right now to receive anyone, much less a husband intent on consummating their marriage.

Her glance fell on her clarsach, the one Lainie had given her. It symbolized, in so many ways, the abrupt transition her life had made today. A MacKay family heirloom, the harp was now rightfully hers as a MacKay wife. An exquisitely wrought instrument, it held the promise of music beyond any she had known before. Yet only with its playing would the songs flow forth. Only within her hands, and heart, would it reveal the depths of its beauty—and its secrets.

Claire walked to her clothes chest and picked up the harp. She pulled over the chair, sat, and placed the instrument on her lap. It felt right there, like it had always been meant for her, nestling so naturally in the curve of her shoulder. Lightly, she stroked its strings. The most ethereal notes rose into the air, drenching her in rich bass and bright, high trebles.

She placed her ear on the sound box and plucked the strings again. A wonderful resonance reverberated against her face, filling her head with the most beautiful, vibrant tones. In that moment, it was almost as if the harp spoke to her, became a living being.

A song, a haunting tale of love lost and found, of misty, Highland meadows, of towering, craggy mountains, and icy, rushing burns, began to flow from her fingers. Claire closed her eyes, forgot everything but the music, and played. On and on her nimble fingers plucked and stroked, coaxing out everything the little clarsach possessed. And, as the song finally ended, she felt at peace once more.

"That was so very, very lovely," Evan said.

With a gasp, Claire's eyes flew open. He stood there, smiling and so heartbreakingly handsome, in the doorway.

"I-I'm sorry," she stammered. "I forgot you were waiting."

"It doesn't matter. I very much enjoyed listening to you play. In your music, I see so much of you. Your kindness, your courage, the depths of your feelings, and your love." He leaned against the doorjamb, and shoved his hands in his trouser pockets. "Hearing you play, you inspire me. You make me proud you chose me for your husband."

Och, but Evan was such a wonderful man, Claire thought. If only he knew that the honor was far more hers than his, in his choosing her to be his wife. She stood, walked to her clothes chest, and carefully laid the clarsach down.

"You can come in, you know," she murmured then. "This is as much your bedroom now as it is mine."

Evan straightened, removed his hands from his pockets. "Still, I didn't want to presume. . . . " His voice faded as he suddenly seemed to notice what she was wearing, and how she looked.

Claire's throat went dry. The nightgown she wore was the same one she wore every night. What with the impending trip to America, there had been no extra money to spare on a new, and perhaps prettier, nightgown for her wedding night. Yet, as Evan continued to stare at her, she felt as if she were dressed in some regal robe—or nothing at all.

"Do you know how beautiful you look?" he said just then, his voice gone low and husky. "It makes me almost afraid to touch you."

"Och, aye." Claire managed a shaky laugh. "And me, little more than a poor lass without a penny to her name."

He moved to stand before her then, and took her into his arms. At his touch, Claire shivered in an odd mix of fear and anticipation.

Evan must have noted her reaction. "Don't be afraid," he said, his tone now soothing. "I'll go slowly, as slow as you want. We've got all the time in the world."

She hid her face on his shoulder, basking in the warmth of his body and the heady scent of him. "I'm sorry," she whispered. "It isn't you, but me. It has all

110

gone so verra fast—meeting you, falling in love with you, wedding you. And now, on the morrow, leaving Scotland for another land."

"I know." Evan began to stroke her head. "I'm asking so much of you."

"Nay, you're asking no more than many husbands would ask. I . . . I just don't know if I can be the kind of wife you need."

Evan laughed then. "And don't you think I have the same doubts, that I can be the kind of husband you need? All we can do is love each other, try our very best, and trust. Trust in each other, in our love, and in the holy vows we made today before God." He bent and began feathering soft little kisses across her forehead, down her face, moving ever closer to her mouth. "And that, I think, will get us through everything life can put in our way."

"Truly, Evan?"

"Yes, sweetheart. Truly."

With that, he pulled her even closer, his hands caressing her head, his fingers threading through her long hair, his mouth capturing hers. And, like the music Claire had performed just a short while ago on her harp, Evan soon caught her up, body and soul, into that sweet, ardent song played from time immemorial between a husband and a wife.

8

One month later

He that wavereth is like a wave of the sea driven with the wind and tossed.

James 1:6

As the Colorado and Southern Railroad locomotive wound its sinuous way through the hills of the Colorado high plains, its whistle shrilled a series of sharp blasts. At the sound, Claire glanced up from her reading of Mrs. Hannah Cobb's *Home Cook Book and Family Medical Adviser,* a gift from Evan while they waited in New York City's Grand Central Station for the first of their many railway adventures. For her efforts, she was rewarded with a fresh dose of soot and ash from the locomotive's smokestack as it blew in through the open window.

"The train's signaling Grand View's depot," Evan explained to Ian, who stood on the opposite side of the car, gazing out the window. "In a few minutes we'll top that next hill, and you'll see the town."

The assurance they were finally at the end of their journey was music to Claire's ears. If she never traveled on a train again, it would be too soon. The journey across the Atlantic on that steamship had been difficult enough. She had been seasick nearly the whole time. But the train trip across over half the United States had been even worse.

They hadn't been able to afford first-class accommodations, and had ridden during the day on stiff-backed seats. They had slept at night on shelves for beds. Her seasickness had also returned, thanks to the car's incessant rocking. Stops to take on more fuel or water for the steam engine were frequent, and the jerks from the train's starts and halts were enough to nearly snap Claire's head from her neck. To add to the misery, the early August weather had been blisteringly hot, far hotter than anything she had ever experienced in Scotland. Thankfully, the train's speed, once it started moving, blew a cooling breeze into the compartment. But whenever the train stopped for refueling . . .

The views outside, at least, had been fascinating and frequently even awe-inspiring. Nothing Claire had ever read about America had prepared her for its immense size and geographical diversity. She had stared out the windows for many hours at a stretch, mesmerized by the ever-changing scenes passing before her.

This was her new home, her land now. She wanted to absorb all she could about it as quickly as possible. Besides, the more she kept her mind occupied and her hopes up, the less time Claire had to think about the journey's discomforts, or about Scotland . . . and how homesick she was already.

That deep, empty ache would eventually subside. Claire had to believe that. It was all just so new, so foreign, and she felt so out of place. Not that Evan, bless his heart, hadn't done everything he could to ease her way.

He hardly ever left her side, patiently explaining everything as many times as she and Ian needed to hear it. She was so grateful to have such a wonderful husband.

"There, there it is," he exclaimed at that moment, casting Ian an excited look. "That's Grand View. We're home, Ian. Home at last!"

Watching him, his handsome, chiseled face alight with such simple joy, Claire's love for Evan swelled anew. Och, but he was so proud of his country, and most especially of Colorado. Some of his enthusiasm couldn't help but rub off on her and Ian. And it was a beautiful land. A beautiful, if so very different, land than what she had always known.

Though the grassy hills were green, they lacked the deep, verdant richness that only frequent, Highland rains could bring. This far east of the Rocky Mountains, which Claire could see looming in the distance, the trees were sparse. Only random, isolated stands of pine trees growing near rocky outcroppings or leaning precariously from towering bluffs dotted the open, hilly land. And where the Highland's broad glens and craggy mountains had boasted a wealth of rivers and rushing burns, here the watercourses were few and far between. Indeed, many of them, this late in the summer, were dry.

An occasional hawk or falcon soared overhead. Herds of small, brown-and-white deerlike animals with short, jagged horns on their heads–pronghorn antelope, Evan called them–grazed placidly not far from the railroad bed. From time to time they'd "spook" and race off, the rhythmic pounding of their hooves barely audible over the creaking, clanging, and rumbling of the train.

From time to time, they'd also pass a solitary ranch or farm. That kind of isolation Claire understood, for it wasn't much different from life in the Highlands. The difference in the scarcity of people, though, lay in the fact that Scotland's rugged lands failed to support very many, while here it was obvious Colorado was still but an essentially unsettled land.

As their speed began to slow, the train's whistle tooted once more. Claire closed her book, bent, and shoved it into the carpetbag on the floor. Then she pulled out her handbag, extracted a mirror, and examined her face.

Aside from a smudge of soot on her cheek and a few errant, windblown curls, Claire supposed she looked presentable. She had quickly noticed that married women in America wore their hair up, unlike Scotswomen, who marked that life passage by turning to the wearing of the little white, frilled caps called mutches. When she had reached America, she had soon put her mutch away and twisted her hair up onto the back of her head. The sooner she began to look like an American, Claire reasoned, the sooner she'd be accepted and feel like one.

"Look, Claire," Evan said, joining Ian at the window. "There's Pa, and Abby, and Beth. They got the wire I sent them from Denver in time, and they've come to meet us."

At mention of Evan's family, Claire's stomach clenched. She had dreaded this moment, even as she knew the meeting was the culmination of their long journey. What if they didn't like her, or were displeased that their son had wed so precipitously and without their approval? She and Ian had come too far to risk being rejected again.

No good was served, though, Claire reminded herself, worrying about what might not ever happen. Besides, Evan had assured her his father and stepmother were good Christians. Even if she hadn't been his wife, they'd surely welcome her out of Christ's love.

The train finally lurched to a halt. Claire gathered her rapidly shredding courage, pinned on her little, dark blue sailor hat trimmed with a band of white grosgrain ribbon, and, picking up her two bags, joined Evan. He paused in his waving to shoot her a loving glance.

115

"Have I told you yet today," he asked, scanning her from head to toe with a heated look, "how beautiful you are?"

"Only about ten or eleven times so far," Ian muttered disgustedly beside him. "You've been married a month now. Aren't you ever going to quit cooing at each other like a pair of turtledoves?"

"I certainly hope not," his brother-in-law said, grinning. He slid his arm about Claire's waist and pulled her close. "And, for the eleventh or twelfth time today, let me tell you how beautiful you are, Mrs. MacKay."

His happiness was infectious. In spite of the nervous fluttering in her stomach, Claire smiled. "Thank you, Mr. MacKay. A woman, even one already wed a full month"—she shot her brother a quelling look—"never tires of hearing such sweet words. Now, if only your family finds me even half so appealing . . ."

As the other train passengers filed from the car, Evan turned her around and guided her down the aisle. "Well, we're about to find out, aren't we?"

Though he smiled when he spoke the words, and his eyes shone with a deep conviction that everyone would love Claire, her heart nonetheless began a frantic pounding. Her first glimpse of the MacKays was fuzzy, the bright sunshine outside momentarily blinding her. Then Evan was releasing his hold on her waist, jumping down from the train, and raising his hand to her.

"Come on, Claire. Come and meet my parents."

She pasted on a wobbly smile, took his hand, and climbed down the steps. Before Ian even had a chance to follow, Abigail and Conor MacKay, accompanied by a suddenly shy, dark-haired and dark-skinned girl, hurried up to them.

Father and son stared at each other for a long, emotion-laden moment, then hugged each other. "It's good to have you home again, Son," Conor said, his voice husky. "We've missed you."

116

Evan leaned back in his father's embrace. "It's good to be home, Pa. Home to stay, this time for good."

Abby moved up to offer her own greetings, and finally so did the girl who Claire surmised must be Evan's sister, Beth. Evan grabbed Beth and picked her up, whirling her around. Her shyness forgotten, his sister squealed.

"Put me down this minute, Evan MacKay," she demanded, suddenly all propriety and indignation. "I'm not just your kid sister anymore. I'm a young lady. I'm thirteen now, you know."

He laughed and set her down. "Why, you are, aren't you, Bethie? You really *are* starting to grow up."

"Er, Son." Conor's glance strayed to Claire and Ian. "Maybe you'd better hurry up the introductions a mite, so we don't keep your wife and her brother standing out here in the hot sun any longer than need be."

"Yes, you're right, Pa." Evan wheeled about, held out his hand to Claire who took it, and pulled her to him. "Abby. Pa. Beth. This is my wife, Claire, and her brother, Ian." He turned to Claire and Ian. "And this is my father, Conor MacKay, his wife Abby, and my sister Beth."

There was a fleeting instant of awkwardness. Then Abby stepped up to Claire and embraced her. "Welcome, Claire. We're so happy to have you. So happy that Evan has finally found the woman of his dreams."

Claire smiled and returned the embrace. Abby was a pretty woman who looked to be in her late twenties, with rich, chestnut-colored hair, hazel eyes, high cheekbones, and a short, pert nose. Though Abby was of medium height, Claire still felt like she towered over her new mother-in-law.

"Thank you, Mrs. MacKay," she mumbled, feeling coarse and gangly next to such an elegant woman. "I'm happy to be here at last."

117

"Please, call me Abby," her mother-in-law urged. "We'll be spending a lot of time together at Culdee Creek, and I'd like to think we'll be fast friends."

Claire nodded, forcing a smile. "It would be most appreciated . . . Abby. I'm sure there'll be much to learn in the days and weeks to come."

Her hand still on Claire's arm, Abby turned to her husband. "Well, it's your turn now, Conor, to greet your new daughter-in-law."

Conor MacKay nodded. "I've been looking forward to it, but thought I'd let you two women have at it first." He moved close, took Claire in his arms, and gave her a quick hug before releasing her. "Welcome, Claire. Culdee Creek's your home now, and I hope you'll soon come to look upon us as family."

He was a big man, broad-shouldered and nearly as tall as Evan, in his late thirties by her guess. His strong, chiseled features reminded her of an older, more weathered version of his son. His own black, wavy hair was just as unruly as Evan's, too, with a touch of gray frosting his temples. His smoky blue eyes were the exact shade of Evan's, and far too piercing for comfort as he quietly assessed her.

She smiled and nodded. "Thank you, Mr. MacKay. I'll need the support of a new family, as far afield as I now am from my own people."

"Conor. Please, call me Conor."

Claire nodded once more. "Conor it is, then." She turned to Ian, who all the while had been standing back watching everything–particularly Beth. "This is my brother, Ian Sutherland," she said, catching hold of his hand and dragging him up to stand beside her. "He's verra interested in learning to break mustangs and rope a steer. Aren't you, Ian?"

He flushed, then shot her an offended look. "Och, and I'm sure they're caring about such things right now,

Claire." He did render them all a quick inclination of the head, though. "I'm pleased to meet you." His glance lingered finally on Beth.

Claire nudged him in the side. Ian flushed even redder, and dragged his gaze from the girl's.

"Well, it's probably time we were heading on home," Conor said. He looked to Evan. "Why don't you and I see to the luggage, while Abby shows Claire and Ian where the carriage is. I figure the ladies can all ride together in the buggy since it has a top, and we men can follow in the buckboard."

Evan nodded. "Sounds good to me, Pa." He turned to Claire. "I'll meet you at the buggy."

She smiled wanly and rendered a nod of her own, then followed Abby around to the front of the train depot. The whitewashed building stood beside a dirt road. Not far away, Claire could see the first wooden buildings lined up on both sides of a street that soon intersected with an even longer one. Grand View wasn't a big town, but it easily seemed larger than Culdee. It also, thanks to the rolling hills and flat stretches of plains surrounding it, seemed stuck out in the middle of nowhere.

"We'll drive down Winona, the main street, as we leave town," Abby said as she drew up before a large, black buggy with iron spoke wheels and a black top. "That way you'll get a better look at what Grand View offers. It's not a large town, but there's enough here to meet our basic needs. And sometime, after you're all settled in, we can take a trip to Colorado Springs."

"Where's that?" Claire asked, shading her eyes and glancing around.

Abby pointed west, toward the mountains. "Colorado Springs is situated at the base of the Rockies, and is becoming quite the resort. Though it can't rival Denver, our state capital, it possesses many amenities, including first-class hotels, many fine homes, and a wide assortment of stores."

Claire smiled. "To be sure, *that* would be a sight to see."

"Well, why don't we all climb into the buggy?" Abby asked, waving in its direction. "I see the men coming with the trunk, and the buckboard's parked here, just behind the buggy." She glanced at Beth. "Go ahead and take the backseat, will you? I'd like Claire to sit up front with me, so we can visit along the way."

Beth eyed Ian, who stood beside her watching Evan and Conor reach the buckboard and load the trunk in the back. "Maybe Ian would like to ride with us," the girl suggested. "There's plenty of room in the backseat."

"If he'd like, that would be fine." Abby looked at him. "Well, would you, Ian? Like to ride with us, I mean?"

Ian started to chew on his bottom lip. "Hmmm . . ."

Claire knew that look, and knew he was searching for some polite way to back out of the offer. She supposed he felt as uncomfortable as she, and the thought of sitting next to a girl who was most prettily eyeing him wasn't exactly his cup of tea. Mayhap in another year or so, anyway, but apparently not just now.

"I'm thinking Ian might prefer the company of men," she whispered, leaning close to Abby. "He isn't overly versed with young ladies as yet, if you get my meaning?"

Abby chuckled. "Yes, I think I do." She motioned toward Conor and Evan. "You know, Ian, I'd imagine the men might need some help with that trunk. Would you mind riding in the buckboard instead, and keeping an eye on the trunk so it doesn't get too banged up?"

A look of relief flashed in the boy's eyes before he quickly masked it. "Och, aye, ma'am. I'd be glad to help."

Before Beth, whose expression brightened eagerly, could offer to join him, Abby grasped her by the shoulders and gave her a gentle push toward the buggy. "Now, up with you then. It's time we were heading for home."

The girl shot Abby a disgruntled look, but silently complied. Claire and Abby soon joined her, settling themselves on the front seat. After the sun's heat, Claire was grateful for the ample shade the buggy top provided. Even so, she pulled a handkerchief from her handbag and dabbed at her face.

"It does take a bit of getting used to," Abby offered, smiling in sympathy. "To the heat out here on the plains, I mean. I'm originally from New England, which I imagine is a lot closer to Scotland's weather, and I recall my first summer in Colorado as being stifling at times. But you'll adjust after a while."

"I'm certain I will," Claire mumbled as Abby took up the reins, then clucked at the horses to set out.

Behind them, Evan slapped the reins over the backs of the team pulling the buckboard. "Giddyap now!" he cried.

At the joyous excitement in his voice, Claire turned around. His eyes bright, Evan grinned back at her. He looked so happy, so much in his element with his dark jacket off and his shirt sleeves rolled up past the corded strength of his forearms, that Claire couldn't help but wave and grin back.

As the buggy lurched forward, a stiff breeze swooped down, ruffling her husband's dark, wavy hair. Her heart swelled with pride and love. She was so very, very fortunate to have married him. Surely everything would work out. It couldn't help but do so, with a man such as Evan MacKay at her side.

"This store on the left," Abby explained, drawing Claire from her musings, "is Gates' Mercantile. We do the majority of our shopping there, for whatever food we can't raise ourselves, for fabric to make clothes, and for all sorts of odds and ends." As they passed the big building, she turned the horses to the left. "And now we're on Winona Street, which is the main street into town."

121

Claire saw a long row of false-fronted buildings, most with signs proclaiming the purpose of each establishment: The Crown Hotel, Town Hall, Edgerton's Butcher Shop, Mrs. Lombardy's Rooming House, Nealy's Livery. Before the buildings ran a long, wooden boardwalk, which Claire surmised helped keep one out of the dirt streets.

"We also have a town doctor–Doc Childress–an icehouse, a feed lot, a school, and two churches," Abby continued.

At the mention of churches, Claire's ears perked up. "Two churches? Is one, mayhap, of the Roman Catholic faith?"

"No." Abby shook her head, softening the action with a smile. "The closest Catholic church–St. Mary's–is in Colorado Springs. Grand View's two churches are Presbyterian and Episcopal. We attend the Episcopal church. The Reverend Noah Starr is pastor there." She shot Claire an uncertain glance. "Will that be a problem for you? Attending Sunday services with us?"

Claire frowned. She hadn't even thought to ask Evan about the available churches in the area. She could only wonder what Father MacLaren would say if he had known.

For a fleeting instant, the old priest's kindly face flashed through her mind's eye. His parting words came again, strong and clear. "Put aside yer doubts and go with God, lass," he had said that morning they had visited him for a final blessing before the coach came. "He'll be with ye, no matter how far ye travel or how strange the land and people. He'll be with ye, as long as ye carry Him always in yer heart."

At the memory, rife as it was with a renewed swell of homesickness, Claire's eyes filled with tears. She needn't worry what Father MacLaren would think about her not being able to attend Mass, just as long as she worshiped the Lord in some church whenever possible, and carried Him always in her heart.

"No, it won't be a problem," she replied at long last. "There'll be many things I'll have to adapt to, I suppose. If you'll just be patient with me . . ."

Abby reached over and patted her hand. "Take all the time and ask all the questions you want, Claire. I don't offend easily. I want to do whatever I can to ease your way in these first few months. After all, you're family now."

She shot Evan's stepmother a grateful glance. "I thank you for that. My fondest wish is to make Evan proud of me."

"Well," Abby said with a laugh, "I think you've already accomplished that and more. I don't recall ever seeing Evan quite so happy as when he first introduced you to his father." She paused, licked her lips, then cocked her head. "If you don't mind me asking, how *did* you and Evan meet?"

"Och, one afternoon I was sweeping the steps outside St. Columba's kirk, where I worked as housekeeper, when he walks up all tall, dark, and so verra handsome and asks for help in finding his kinfolk."

"Was this anywhere near Culdee, Scotland? The last letter we received from Evan mentioned his decision to visit Culdee."

"Aye," Claire agreed with a nod. "It's the verra same place. And Father MacLaren, our parish priest, seemed to think it'd be a most excellent idea for me to help Evan in his search. He always did have a matchmaker's heart."

Encouraged by Abby at all the appropriate places in her tale, Claire made quick work of the retelling of her and Evan's courtship. And, when she finally brought the story to an end with their arrival in New York City, Abby silently drove for a few minutes more before asking one final question.

"So, how long was this courtship of yours, then? It doesn't sound like you knew each other all that long."

Claire could feel her face growing warm. She had known that the brevity of their courtship might well be a sore spot with Evan's parents. Indeed, several folk in Culdee had wasted little time speculating as to the reason for the short time elapsing between when they had first met and when they wed. But none of them understood. Evan was different from the other lads she had known. He was so good, kind, so very, very special. And he offered so much more—for her and for her brother.

"I met him near the first of May, and we were wed in St. Columba's on Fourth of July," she said, deciding the sooner all the facts about their courtship were out in the open, the sooner they could move past them. "It was your country's Independence Day," Claire added. "Evan said it was a perfect day for us to do so. We'd never forget our anniversary, and the whole of America would help us celebrate it each year."

Abby laughed. "Yes, I suppose it *was* a perfect day, wasn't it?"

"You aren't angry or disappointed, are you, that we didn't wait to wed until we arrived here? I know it might seem selfish of us, but we were so in love. Besides, Evan was verra eager to return home, and I didn't think it'd be proper for us to travel so far unless we were man and wife . . ."

"No. No," the older woman was quick to assure her, even as a tiny furrow formed between her brows. "As you say; it wouldn't have been proper. What matters in the end is that you and Evan are happy. We've all the time in the world now to get to know each other, don't we?"

"Aye, that we do," Claire agreed with a firm resolve, totally certain her and Evan's love was, and would always be, strong enough to weather any storm.

All they had to do now was prove it to everyone else.

9

Hate stirreth up strifes: but love covereth all sins.
                              Proverbs 10:12

"So, Pa," Evan said as he guided the team down the road behind the buggy, "what's happened at Culdee Creek since I left last August?"

Conor sent his son a slanting look. "A lot's happened. Anything specific you'd like to hear about first?"

Evan hesitated, then cast a glance behind him. Ian sat at the back of the long buckboard, one hand on the steamer trunk to steady it, the other on the tailgate, gazing out at the scenery with avid interest. There was little chance, what with the creaking and groaning of the wooden wagon and pounding of horses' hooves, that he'd be able to overhear their conversation.

With a sigh, Evan turned back to stare at his father. "Might as well just get it over with, I reckon." He looked down. "What happened between Hannah and Devlin? Did they end up getting married?"

It took several seconds for Conor to answer. "Yeah, they got married—at Thanksgiving—and are very happy. How do you feel about that?"

125

Evan wasn't sure how he felt about that bit of news, but he also wasn't fool enough to admit it. Besides, it didn't matter anymore anyway. Hannah was married. So was he. And he loved Claire. That was all that counted.

"I figured as much," he admitted finally, glancing up at his father. "I only hope they're as happy as Claire and I."

"She seems like a lovely girl. Claire, I mean. You're both so young, though."

"Ma was fifteen when she married you. Claire's eighteen." Evan's mouth tightened with passing irritation. "How old were you when you wed Ma? Seventeen? Eighteen?"

"I was seventeen."

"Well, I'm twenty-one. That makes both Claire and I older than you and Ma were when you got hitched."

"True enough," his father admitted. "And you can see how well our marriage worked out, too."

He had known this issue would eventually come up, but Evan was surprised it had been broached so soon. "So what are you trying to say, Pa? That we made a mistake? That we were too young to get married?"

"How long have you known Claire, Evan? You didn't leave for England until January. That was the last letter I got anyway, postmarked in the United States. Then, the end of April, we got your letter telling us you were headed to Culdee."

"I met Claire the beginning of May," Evan muttered.

"So you knew Claire how many months? Two, three?"

"Two." There was an edge of rising anger in Evan's voice now, and he couldn't quite hide it. But then, why should he? He had been home less than an hour, and already his pa was lecturing him like some school kid. "I don't think this is such a good subject, though, to be discussing right now. I can't—I won't—undo what I did. I love Claire, and you need to respect us and our marriage."

126

"Yeah, I reckon I do." Conor scratched his jaw. "It's just with you leaving here, all upset about losing Hannah, and then suddenly showing up again with a wife on your arm . . . well, I'm concerned. You two have a lot of adjustments ahead of you. Never too soon to recognize the potential pitfalls."

"I know we'll have to work at our marriage." Evan sighed. "And I'm well aware both Claire and Ian might have a hard time learning to adapt to our way of life. Still, love should be enough to get us past all the rough spots."

"Yes, it should," his father said. "But sometimes, no matter how hard you try or how badly you want it, it just plain isn't."

෬

As they topped one last hill, Culdee Creek at last came into view. A long road led down to the ranch from a tall, log gate. Atop the gate was a wooden sign etched with the ranch's name, and the wagon-wheel-rutted path was a dusty, brown rift cleaving acres of green grass and wildflowers. As Abby expertly directed the horses to turn into the open gate, Claire leaned forward with interest.

Culdee Creek Ranch was nestled in a small valley flanked on the north by a pine-tree-studded hillside. To the south and east, some sort of deciduous trees lined a creek flowing down to a large pond. Up ahead was an impressive, two-story wooden house painted white and trimmed with dark green. Behind that building, Claire could barely make out another, smaller house set off in the trees.

They passed two, tall, dark green barns built on high, rock and mortar foundations; several corrals, a pigpen, and a storage cellar of some sort attached to one of the

127

barns. An additional long building–also another dwelling place, if the smokestack sticking out of the roof on one end was any indication–completed the ranch structures. Ranging in every direction as far as Claire could see, were barbed-wire-enclosed pastures wherein grazed fat, brown-and-white Herefords.

"So, what do you think of Culdee Creek?" Abby asked, shooting her an inquiring glance. "Does it measure up to what Evan may have told you about it?"

"It's quite large, isn't it?" Claire observed, turning in her seat to make sure she hadn't missed anything. "Evan said it was a big ranch, but I had no idea . . ." She scooted back around. "Does your husband truly own all this land?"

"Yes, he does. It *is* quite impressive, isn't it? There are ranchers in these parts who own even more land than Conor, though. Most years Colorado's grasslands aren't particularly lush, and cattle need a lot of grazing land to fatten for market."

Up ahead a slender, blonde woman, a toddler in her arms and two small children clutching her skirts, walked onto the front porch of the big house. As the buggy drew near, Claire could see she was young–most likely only a year or two older than herself–and very beautiful. The woman smiled and waved, then walked down the front porch steps to meet them.

Abby reined in the horses, tied the lines to the brake arm, and jumped down. Claire and Beth followed.

"Well, how has my big man been?" Abby asked, walking up to the blonde woman and holding out her arms for the little boy. "Mama has missed you."

Black-haired and blue-eyed, the toddler looked close to two years old. With a wide grin, he reached for her. "Mama. Mama!"

Abby took him and hugged him close. "Was Sean any trouble, Hannah?"

The woman called Hannah shook her head. "He was just fine. Jackson and Bonnie and Sean all played together." Her gaze drifted to Claire. "My name's Hannah MacKay," she said, offering her hand in greeting. "I'm Devlin's wife."

"Devlin?" Claire took her hand and shook it. "Let me see if I can recall correctly. He's Evan's . . . second cousin?"

"Yes," Abby cut in. "Devlin and Conor are first cousins. Their fathers were brothers, the sons of Sean Mac-Kay. Sean emigrated from Culdee."

"Och, that's right," Claire laughed. "You'll have to excuse me if I take some time to properly sort out all the kinfolk."

"Well, if it's any consolation"—Abby, her son snugly on her hip, turned to Claire—"aside from a few more assorted children and Devlin, you've just about met all the kinfolk." She gestured to the two children still standing beside Hannah. "The little boy there is Jackson, and the little girl Bonnie. They're Devlin and Hannah's children . . . as are two more children I don't see right now. Devlin Jr.'s the oldest and is eight, and Mary is the next oldest at age five."

"You all seem a verra fruitful family," Claire observed with a smile.

The buckboard pulled up just then. Evan leaped down and strode to his wife's side. He slipped an arm about her waist and gave her a quick kiss.

"I see you're already busy meeting more of the family."

"Aye," Claire nodded. "I've met Hannah, Sean, Jackson, and Bonnie. Aside from a few others, I believe I've met everyone."

For some reason Claire couldn't quite fathom, an uncomfortable silence seemed to settle over them then. She glanced up at Evan. A strange expression on his face, he was staring at Hannah.

Claire looked to Hannah. She smiled back at Evan, her serene gaze warm and welcoming. An uneasy feeling twined in Claire's gut. There was something amiss here, she realized, but it was something she couldn't quite put her finger on.

"You look well, Evan," the blonde woman finally said. "And it seems your journeys were very productive this time. Not only did you return with a lovely wife, but a handsome young man, too."

Evan turned to Ian, who had halted at his side. "This is Ian, Claire's brother. Ian, I'd like you to meet Hannah, my cousin Devlin's wife."

Ian rendered her a half bow. "I'm verra pleased to make your acquaintance, ma'am." He straightened and grinned. "Truly, you're the most beautiful woman I've ever laid eyes on."

Hannah flushed. "Why, thank you, Ian. I don't know when I've received a more gallant compliment."

Evan shot Ian a skeptical look. "You're becoming quite the charmer, aren't you? It won't be long, I'm afraid, before we'll have to be warning Grand View's fathers to lock up their daughters when you come to town."

For an instant, Claire could've almost sworn she heard a tinge of irritation in her husband's voice. She shook it off. No purpose was served imagining things, she scolded herself, especially when she was so tired.

"Well, shall we all go inside?" Abby asked as her husband walked up. "It looks like the hands will take care of the trunk, and after such a hot, dusty trip, I thought we all might enjoy tall glasses of cold lemonade."

"Yes, let's do that," Conor said, taking his wife by the arm. "I'm sure Claire and Ian are most likely parched by now. I know I am."

Hannah turned and, with Jackson and Bonnie, reentered the house. Abby and Conor, followed by Beth and Ian, brought up the rear. Evan, however, remained standing beside Claire, his head turned to the right, staring toward one of the barns. Puzzled, Claire glanced in the direction of his gaze.

There, partly shadowed by the barn doorway, stood a tall, dark-haired man watching them.

ॐ

The small bunkhouse behind the main house had been hastily prepared for Claire, Evan, and Ian. The building consisted of a parlor room in front, replete with a cast iron potbellied stove, a long table and four chairs, and two rocking chairs set near the stove. Bright, red-and-white gingham curtains fluttered at the two open windows, a red, hooked rug graced the floor, and several colorful, floral prints hung on the walls. Off the parlor were two bedrooms, one with a white-painted, full-sized iron bed, and the other with a single bed.

Claire scanned the little house. "It's more than adequate," she pronounced at last. "In fact, it's wonderful!"

Joining Evan at the steamer trunk he had just opened, she next began pulling out the meager linens she had brought with her. Buried beneath the linens was the MacKay family clarsach, and beneath that were her and Ian's clothes. At the bottom of the trunk lay a few books, some cooking items, and a carved, wooden box containing Claire's hair combs, ribbons, and some special mementos.

She soon had everything put to rights. Evan glanced up at her from one of the rockers. "Come, sit for a spell, Claire." He extended a hand toward her. "It won't be suppertime for another couple of hours, and I know you must be tired."

131

From the smaller bedroom, Claire could hear Ian snoring softly. He was the wise one, she thought. But now that she was finally here, she found she couldn't sit still.

"Nay," Claire said, shaking her head. "Suddenly, I find I'm no longer weary. Do you think Abby needs some help with the meal? Might as well begin learning about American cooking."

He studied her thoughtfully, and a gleam of desire slowly ignited in his eyes. "I'm sure Abby has everything under control. But, if you're feeling so energetic, I suppose we could test out our new bed. I haven't had a moment's privacy with you since our wedding night and, since we've the time . . ."

At his words, Claire drew up short. Suddenly, their bedroom took on a special appeal. "Aye, that's a fine idea, Evan MacKay. You've indeed been sadly neglecting me."

A grin on his lips, Evan rose. "You're not a shy girl, are you? About what you want, I mean?" He walked toward her.

With a gay laugh, Claire danced from his clutches and hurried over to close Ian's bedroom door. Then, with a twirl of her skirts, she wheeled about and scampered off to their bedroom. Grinning, Evan quickly followed in her wake.

❦

An hour later Claire lay in Evan's arms, contentedly watching the slow, rhythmic rise and fall of his chest. Their loving had been passionate but now, in its tranquil aftermath, she marveled at how totally fulfilled she felt. Until she had wed Evan, she had never known what it was to feel so close, so united with another. It was truly one of God's most wondrous gifts, Claire mused, this physical and spiritual joining of a woman and man.

With her fingers she drew random circles on her husband's hair-whorled chest, but Evan slept on. His face was relaxed, peaceful. It filled her with such satisfaction to know she was part of that peace, that she could give joy and completion to such a kind, wonderful man. And here, in the isolation of their little bedroom, Claire almost imagined they were the only two people left in the world.

It would've been far simpler if they had been. But most times when one married, one accepted not only one's spouse into one's life, but his family, too. Not that Conor and Abby didn't seem like wonderful people, Claire hastened to add to herself. It was just that she'd had so little time with Evan since they were wed. There was still so much to discover about him, and about herself, as his wife.

Well, Claire thought with a soft sigh, there wasn't anything she could do about his family. And, no matter how difficult the days and weeks to come might be, they would always have this room. This room and this bed where no one could ever intrude.

A knock sounded at the front door. Claire frowned. Had they overslept? Were they late for supper?

She slipped from bed and quickly dressed. Evan dozed on. Quietly closing the door behind her, Claire hurried across the parlor, all the while patting her errant curls into place.

A tall man with dark brown hair, a long, lush mustache dipping well past the corners of his mouth, stood there. He wore boots, blue denims, and a white-and-blue striped shirt. In his hands, he held a Stetson.

"Good evening, ma'am," the man said. "I'm Devlin MacKay, Evan's cousin."

He looked quite attractive in a rugged sort of way, his features craggy, his nose slightly irregular, as if it had once been broken. Though nearly as tall as Conor Mac-

Kay, he appeared to carry a few more pounds of muscled bulk. As imposing as he was, though, his rich, warm brown eyes were kind as they gazed down at her.

"Aye, that you are," she replied with a grin. "I immediately noted the strong family resemblance."

"And you must be Claire, Evan's wife. Is he about? I'd like to talk with him, if I could."

"Aye." She stepped aside, indicating he was to enter. "Evan's asleep. Why don't you have a seat while I wake him?"

Devlin hesitated. "I could come back some other time."

"Nay." Claire shook her head. "It's past time he began to stir. Abby invited us for supper"—her glance snagged on the small clock sitting on the table—"and we need to be joining them in a half hour's time."

He took a chair at the table. "Then I'd be much obliged, ma'am."

"Claire. Please, call me Claire. After all, we're kin now."

A tentative smile lifted the corners of Devlin's mouth. "Claire it is, then," he said softly, as she turned and headed for the bedroom.

Evan was still asleep. For a brief moment more, she watched him, a sweet sense of loving possession flooding her. Then Claire walked to the side of the bed he was closest to, and laid a hand on his shoulder.

"Evan? It's time you were waking." She shook him gently. "Evan? Wake up."

He smiled and captured her hand in the big, warm clasp of his own. "I must be dreaming." He inched open one eye. "A beautiful, fiery-haired woman is in my bedroom."

Pulling her down until she leaned across his chest, Evan scanned her face. "Why don't you climb back in bed with your husband? I can think of all sorts of pleasant things we can do."

Claire laughed, placed a quick kiss on his mouth, then reared back. "Nay, there isn't time for such 'pleasant things' right now. Your cousin Devlin has come to see you, and he awaits in the parlor."

Evan went very still. His mouth tightened; his eyes narrowed. "Devlin, you say?"

Before she could answer, he pushed her gently away and shoved up in bed. "Well, reckon there's no time like the present to have it out with him."

"What's wrong, Evan?" Claire watched him slide from bed and begin to dress. "Are there problems between you and Devlin?"

"You could say that." He gave a humorless laugh. "There have always been problems between me and Devlin."

"And exactly what kind of problems might those be?"

Evan finally met her glance. "It's a long story, and not the time to go into it, what with Devlin waiting on me."

"Well, don't you think it's past time you and he were settling those problems? You're kin, after all."

"Yeah, I know." Evan, clad only in a pair of clean denims he had taken from the room's small chest of drawers, sat back on the bed and pulled on socks, then his boots. "It's not that easy, though."

"It's easy enough, if you forgive him and he forgives you."

He donned a red cotton shirt, buttoned it, then tucked it into his denims. "Maybe that'll come someday. I just don't know if it'll be anytime soon."

"He seems nice enough."

Her husband shot her a quizzical look. "And you could tell that from just a few minutes of talking to him?"

She shrugged. "Father MacLaren always said I was quick about such things."

135

"Well," Evan drawled, his mouth softening into a grin, "I can't recall you being that quick when it came to me. If I remember correctly, you didn't seem to like me at all when you first met me."

"On the contrary, I liked you far *too* much, and that frightened me. Hence, I tried to keep you at arm's length."

Evan walked to the door, then paused. "Well, be that as it may, I'd advise you not to make any snap judgments about Devlin. He can be mean and unpredictable." With that, her husband opened the door and strode into the parlor.

Claire rose from the bed and walked to the doorway. She saw Evan draw up before his cousin. For a long moment both stared at each other, their expressions inscrutable, the tension fairly crackling between them. Then Devlin smiled and held out his hand.

"Welcome home, Evan. It's good to see you again."

Evan didn't return the smile or accept the proffered hand. "Is it really, Devlin? Good to see me, I mean?"

"I don't hold any grudges." Devlin's hand fell back to his side. "Why not put the past behind us and start fresh?"

"No, I don't imagine you *do* hold any grudges," his cousin ground out. "After all, you got what you wanted."

Devlin's gaze skittered to Claire, still standing in the bedroom doorway. "Maybe it'd be best if we took this outside."

At his words, Evan seemed to remember Claire's presence. He turned, glanced at her, and reddened. "Yeah, maybe we'd better." He grabbed up his Stetson from the hook by the door. "I'm going outside to talk with Devlin, Claire," he announced. "I'll be back in a few minutes."

With that, the two men turned and headed out the front door. Claire stood there for a time. Then, with a rising sense of uneasiness, she walked back into the bedroom.

10

A brother offended is harder to be won than a strong city.
Proverbs 18:19

Evan set out for the old cottonwood growing off to one side between the bunkhouse
and Devlin's ranch house. He could hear his cousin's
footsteps behind him, but he refused to slow his pace to
allow him to catch up. Only when he finally halted
beneath the tree's shady cover did Evan turn to face
Devlin.

"Well, spit out what you came to say, and be done
with it," Evan growled. "I've got a new bride waiting on
me, and I'd rather spend my time with her than on the
likes of you."

Devlin pulled up before him. He smiled faintly. "Yes,
you do, and a right pretty little lady she is. Congratula-
tions on your marriage, Evan."

With a curt nod, he barely acknowledged the friendly
overture. "Heard you and Hannah finally got hitched.
Don't expect me to congratulate you on that."

His cousin's gaze never wavered, though Evan knew
his own expression must have been hot enough to scald

the feathers off a chicken. However, before he could follow his scathing retort with another harsh comment, Devlin sighed, removed his Stetson, and ran a hand roughly through his hair.

"I was hoping you'd have made your peace about what happened with Hannah, before you came back. I was also hoping you'd gotten over her, especially when Conor told me you were bringing a wife home."

Evan could feel the blood warm his face. "I *have* gotten over Hannah," he snapped. "I wouldn't have married Claire if I hadn't. But that doesn't mean I've forgotten the underhanded way you stole Hannah from me." Bitterly, he shook his head. "No, a man doesn't forget something like that, especially from his own kin."

"So, it's me you're still mad at, and not Hannah? Is that how it is, Evan?"

"Yeah, something like that."

Devlin rubbed his jaw. "Well, that's good to know. Can't say as how I care much for your hard feelings for me, but it would've near to broken Hannah's heart if you were still mad at her, too."

"Well, she made her choice, didn't she?" In spite of himself, Evan couldn't quite hide the acrimonious edge to his words. Shame filled him. He bit his lip and looked away.

When had he become such a hard-hearted, vindictive man? Evan wondered. Hannah had always treated him with caring and compassion. And Devlin was his cousin.

Still, the wound Hannah had inflicted when she had chosen Devlin over him wasn't as well healed as he first imagined. And Devlin . . . well, they had never seen eye-to-eye on anything. He couldn't ever recall a time when they weren't butting heads over one thing or another.

"I told you before, and I meant it, Evan. I want us to start fresh."

The sound of Devlin's voice, rich with entreaty, pulled him from his embittered musings. Evan swung his gaze back to his cousin's. "Why's it so all-fired important to you now? It never seemed to matter much before if we got along."

"Things have changed. My life's changed." For a moment Devlin looked down, rolled the brim of his hat between his hands, then lifted his glance back to Evan. "Hannah's come into my life, and so has the Lord. I'm trying to see things differently now, and treat folk better."

Evan stepped back and shook his head. "Fine words, Devlin, but I think I'll just hold off a bit and see how well you live up to them. Can't say as I much trust you, not after all we've been through."

"Just give me a chance, Evan. Culdee Creek's too small a place for men to carry grudges. Especially men who are kin. Especially men who have wives and family who can't help but come into close contact mighty often."

Inexplicably, renewed anger filled Evan. Things hadn't changed as much as Devlin might like to think they had. "I don't need you lecturing me about my responsibilities to Claire," he snarled. "And I don't need you talking down to me like I'm some snot-nosed kid either!"

Devlin's mouth quirked in wry apology. "Sorry. You're right. It's past time I started treating you like the man you are. I just don't want our women dragged into this, that's all. I'd like Hannah to feel comfortable with Claire. To feel welcome in your home."

"Hannah's welcome anytime she wants to come over," Evan muttered, knowing, at least in this instance, Devlin was right. "In fact, I'd be much obliged. I want Claire to make friends, to feel like she fits in here."

"Good." Devlin smiled then. "Reckon that's what matters most right now. You and me, well, in time we can work things out. Just as long as you're willing to give it a try."

"For the sake of the women," Evan said through gritted teeth, "I'll give it a try."

Devlin held out his hand. "Then let's shake on it, and be done."

He eyed his cousin's outstretched hand for a long, emotion-laden moment, then took it and shook it. "Yeah, let's be done with it. I need to get back to Claire."

"Thanks, Evan." Devlin released his hand. "You don't know how much this means to me."

Evan stared at his cousin's now smiling face, his gut clenching with a crazed mix of feelings. If he didn't know Devlin better, he'd almost be willing–

"I've got to get back to Claire," he muttered instead. Turning on his heel, Evan abruptly stalked back to the bunkhouse.

ॐ

"What's going on, Evan?" Claire asked when he finally reentered the house. "What happened between you and Devlin to cause such hard feelings?"

He paused to hang his Stetson on its hook before turning to face her. "I don't want to talk about it."

Apprehension curling within her, Claire walked up to stand before him. The look of pained confusion she saw in his eyes, though, filled her with compassion. "You don't need to feel you must protect me from the truth, whatever it might be," she said, reaching up to stroke his face. "I'm your wife. I'll stand beside you no matter what."

Evan smiled then, though the action never went further than his mouth. "I know that, Claire. And I treasure your loyalty and concern. But it's more than protecting you, or keeping the truth from you. It's me." He sighed. "I need to sort it all out for myself first, before I can share it with you. Will you trust me in this, give me the time I need to do so?"

She wrapped her arms about his neck and leaned her head on his chest, wanting to offer him whatever comfort she could. "Aye, that I will, husband. Just don't ever feel you can't tell me what's ailing you. If we can't depend on each other, then who can we depend upon?"

"No one, I reckon," Evan replied with a heavy sigh, encircling her in the strong, warm haven of his arms. "No one."

They stood there for a time, drawing solace from each other. Finally, though, Claire leaned back and gazed up at him. "Considering your problems with Devlin, do you wish me to keep my distance with Hannah?"

"If you want to make friends with her, go right ahead. Devlin and I both agreed we didn't want our personal difficulties affecting you women." For a moment, Evan looked as if his thoughts were elsewhere. Then he seemed to remember himself. "I'd just appreciate it if you wouldn't discuss Devlin's and my problem with her. I know how you women are when it comes to your men, but you both need to let us work things out ourselves. Okay?"

Claire nodded. "Okay."

He released her, stepped back, and glanced at the clock. "Er, don't you think it's time you were waking Ian? We're supposed to join my parents for supper in ten minutes."

"Och, aye. Ian." Claire laughed. "Truly, Evan MacKay, when I'm with you I seem to forget everything but you." She cocked her head. "Do you think it will ever get better?"

Evan grinned, and this time the action was heartfelt. "I certainly hope not, Mrs. MacKay. It'll be a sorry day in our marriage if that ever happens."

"Then we'll have to take great care that it doesn't," she said as she wheeled about and headed for Ian's room. "Just not right now, of course."

"Of course," he called softly. "There's always tonight, though, isn't there?"

"Aye." Claire giggled, the delight swelling within. "There is indeed."

❧

After a delicious supper of braised beef with brown sauce, roasted carrots, turnips, onions, and potatoes, they all adjourned to Abby and Conor's parlor for coffee and chocolate nougat cake. Eager to sample all of the culinary bounty offered her, Claire even tried her first cup of coffee—heavily laced with cream and sugar. She soon pronounced the hot beverage suprisingly palatable, if not quite on a par with a good cup of tea.

Talk gradually turned to the state of this year's hay crop and the cost of feed. Beth and Ian quickly adjourned to the kitchen, where she promised to teach him the game of checkers. Claire's attention began to wander as well, and she entertained herself studying the room in more detail.

The parlor was ornately furnished with a fine Turkish rug covering the hardwood floor, heavy, dark blue oriental tapestry curtains at the two windows, and a massive, carved oak combination bookcase and cupboard against the far wall. The settee that she and Abby occupied was covered in a blue-and-green velvet, and trimmed in rosewood. Conor and Evan sat in the two dark leather armchairs before the moss rock fireplace. Over the mantel hung a portrait of an older Scotsman dressed in a blue, green, and black tartan kilt that Claire knew to be the MacKay plaid, a basket-hilted sword hanging at his side.

142

"That's Conor's grandfather, Sean MacKay," Abby quietly offered. "He was a handsome man, wasn't he?"

"Aye," Claire agreed with a nod, "that he was. It makes me feel a wee less homesick, seeing his picture, knowing some part of him is here."

"Like a part of Scotland is here, too, even this far away?"

She turned to Abby, appreciation for the woman's insight filling her. "Aye, something like that."

Abby laid a hand over hers. "You're very brave, you know, to come all this way."

"I wouldn't have done it if it wasn't for Evan."

The chestnut-haired woman smiled. "I know."

Across the room by the fireplace, Conor cleared his throat. "Well, Abby, do you think it's time we tell them about our little surprise?"

Abby shot Claire an impish grin, gave her hand a reassuring squeeze, then turned to her husband. "Yes, I think it is."

All eyes riveted on Culdee Creek's owner. "We wanted to give you and Claire a fitting wedding present to welcome you home," he said, meeting his son's inquiring gaze, "and Abby and I decided that the best present we could give you was a real house of your own. So, just as soon as we can get the lumber delivered from the Pinery, we're going to start building you two a nice house out back near the edge of the pines. It'll still be close enough to walk down anytime you want to visit, but far enough away that you'll have some privacy when you want it, too."

"Pa," Evan began, "I don't know what to say. It's too much. We can—"

"You can help us build it, that's what you can do." Conor held up a silencing hand when Evan tried once more to protest. "I want you home to stay, Son, where you belong. And that means keeping your wife happy with a place of her own."

"Truly," Claire lifted her voice to object, "I find the bunkhouse more than adequate. My needs are little, and I'm used to far plainer accommodations."

"Let us do this for you and Evan, Claire," Abby cut in just then. "It'll give us as much pleasure as it'll give you. To have Evan back home, to be a complete family once again . . . well, it has been Conor's and my dearest wish. Besides," she added with a smile, "sooner or later you'd need a bigger home anyway, once you and Evan decide to start your own family. And, rather than have to build then in haste, why not start the house now at everyone's leisure?"

There was no getting around Abby's logic or Conor's sincere wish to do something special to celebrate his son's homecoming. Glancing from one parent to the other, Claire knew to refuse, or even protest further, would be ungracious. Besides, if the truth were told, the thought of her very own house held an enormous appeal. As did, for that matter, the consideration of someday filling the home with her own bairns.

"I don't know what to say," she murmured, meeting Evan's questioning gaze, "save that it's a wonderful gift, a gift, if Evan agrees, I'd accept most gratefully."

"And I'll accept it, too, Pa," Evan said, "because Claire wants it. Thank you. Thank you for everything."

"It's our pleasure, Son."

"Still, I want to do most of the work myself, Pa," Evan then hastened to add. "After I finish whatever ranch chores that need doing each day, of course. And, as much as I can, I want to help pay for the supplies out of what I earn. Gift or no, it's not fair you carry the whole expense."

Conor held up his hand. "Evan, we can afford it. Culdee Creek's seen some mighty good years of late. I'd rather you save your money to buy things for the house. You'll need a lot to set up housekeeping, you know."

At Evan's look of surprise, Abby and Claire both laughed.

"I know you men generally think a house comes fully furnished," his stepmother said, "but let me tell you a bit about what you'll be needing. There's bed linens, curtains, towels, rugs. Then there'll be dishes, pots and pans, glasses, and silverware for the kitchen. And I haven't even mentioned the furniture to sit upon, a table to eat on, and cupboards and chests to store things in."

At the stricken look on Evan's face, Abby paused. "Shall I go on, or are you finally beginning to grasp some of the needs?"

He swallowed convulsively and nodded. "I think so." Evan turned back to his father. "Well, maybe you're right, Pa. Maybe I *do* need to save my money for other things."

"Setting up a household *can* run into a few dollars," his father gravely acceded. "The marrying is always the easiest part. And it's certainly the cheapest."

Evan grinned. "So I'm beginning to see." He cast Claire a teasing glance, before meeting his father's gaze once more. "I just didn't realize how much work it took to properly care for a wife, leastwise not until this moment. Problem is, Pa, by the time a man realizes it, it's too late to do anything about it."

As both women scowled in mock indignation, Conor threw back his head and laughed. "It sure is, Son. It sure is."

❦

Two days later, work on Evan and Claire's house began. At Conor's insistence, several of the ranch hands were enlisted to help with the initial labor. The site was cleared and leveled, then batter boards were erected to mark building lines and excavation boundaries. After

145

the cellar was dug, a rock and mortar foundation was laid. Then work on the framing and floor joists began.

Claire couldn't believe the speed with which the building was progressing. The plans called for a similar design to the main house, if on a slightly smaller scale. In addition to a cellar, the first floor would offer a large kitchen complete with plumbing for a kitchen pitcher pump, a parlor, a study, and a small laundry room off the enclosed back porch. Upstairs were three bedrooms, and above them was an attic for storage and space to hang laundry during cold or rainy days.

Never in her wildest dreams of coming to America had she envisioned a big, brand-new home of her own. Time and again, Claire had to pinch herself to see if she was dreaming as she visited the construction site several times each day. She only wished there was more she could personally do to help with the house.

"Oh, your work will come soon enough," Abby laughingly commiserated with her as they drove to Grand View that first Sunday after Claire and Evan's arrival. "Just wait until you move into your new home. The men most conveniently disappear whenever you need help moving a piece of furniture or hanging curtains. Luckily, you've got Hannah and me to help you."

"I can't wait." Claire glanced over her shoulder at the small caravan trailing behind them. Besides her and Abby in the carriage, there was Beth with Sean in her arms. Alongside her sat Ian. Devlin, Hannah at his side and Bonnie and Jackson between them, followed in the buckboard, with Devlin Jr. and Mary sitting in the back. Evan and Conor brought up the rear on horseback.

Luckily, it had rained last night and the roads were still damp. After the dusty trip from Grand View that day they had arrived on the train, Claire was grateful for small favors. She imagined, though, that she'd sooner or later be eating her share of dirt out here on these dry plains.

As they topped the last hill separating them from the sight of Grand View, the bell of the Episcopal church began to ring. The sound filled her with anticipation. It would surely seem more like home, once she had again worshiped in the Lord's house.

Not that the plain wooden structure with the gabled, clear glass windows and tall steeple looked at all similar to the old, moss- and ivy-covered stone church of St. Columba. But then, not much out here in this windswept grasslands looked like home. Still, the people seemed kind and generous, and they did speak essentially the same language.

Eight buggies and four buckboards were already stationed around the church. Abby halted the horses, set the brake, and climbed down. Claire soon followed her, taking Sean from Beth. As they waited for the rest of the Culdee Creek clan to join them, Claire looked around her in fascination.

Women dressed in their Sunday best, feathered, flowered, and beribboned hats on their heads, strolled up to the house of worship on the arms of black- or brown-suited men, calling out to one another in greeting as they went. Children scampered around them with frenzied glee, seemingly in pursuit of their last opportunity for freedom before settling down into their church manners. To Claire, the happy, chaotic scene was heartening. The pastor, whoever he was, was evidently a wise, tolerant, paternal man.

Just then, a dark blond-haired man who looked to be in his mid-twenties and an older woman stepped out onto the landing before the church's front door. Attired in long robes, he began to greet each person by name as they paused briefly before entering the church. Realizing that this must be the wise, tolerant, paternal pastor—

147

who she had assumed would be markedly older—Claire could only gape in astonishment.

"That's Noah Starr, our pastor, and his aunt, Mildred Starr," Abby offered, noting Claire's look of surprise. "Noah's only been pastor a little less than two years, since his uncle died unexpectedly of a heart seizure. He's done a wonderful job, though. Everyone loves him."

She could well imagine all the young women of Grand View loved him, Claire thought, if for less than properly reverent reasons. The Reverend Noah Starr was quite attractive, with his wavy hair, well-molded mouth, and finely hewn features. Though only of moderate height, even the voluminous robes failed to hide his powerful body and aura of physical strength.

Claire could only hope the Reverend Starr might someday fill even a portion of the role Father MacLaren had so skillfully and lovingly occupied as spiritual advisor. She prayed that it would be so, for her journey back to the arms of a loving God had only recently commenced. Not until the day she had told the old priest about that awful night, had Claire finally caught a glimpse of the miracle of God's mercy and forgiveness. Not until that day had the terrible wounds even begun to heal. And now, though she admittedly fell by the wayside from time to time in her weakness, she tried so much harder to follow the Lord.

Evan, Conor, Devlin, Hannah, and their children soon joined them. As Culdee Creek's owner stepped up to take his wife by the arm, Evan moved to Claire's side. "Are you ready for church, Mrs. MacKay?" he asked, smiling down at her with husbandly pride and possession.

She smiled. "Aye. It will be the first time, though, that I've set foot in a church other than Catholic, so you'll have to help me with the prayers, and all the proper times to sit and stand."

As they headed up the church steps behind the rest of the congregation, Conor glanced over his shoulder at her. "Once you get used to it, I think you'll find more similarities than differences. After all, we all serve the same God."

"Aye, that we do," Claire murmured in fervent agreement. "That we do."

11

Acquaint now thyself with Him, and be at peace: thereby good shall come unto thee.

Job 22:21

The Reverend Noah Starr was a surprisingly good preacher. Despite the occasional whispers and curious stares slanted in her direction by some of the congregation's female persuasion, Claire soon found herself both transfixed and inspired by his words. Words full of God's love that inflamed her heart, just as had those of Father MacLaren's.

By the time the organ's final bass notes faded and everyone began putting away their hymnals, Claire's joy was complete. She was in a foreign land, but already she felt welcome. She had found a new church, a church where truly the spirit of God dwelt.

The Reverend Starr and his aunt awaited them outside. Sparing no time on social niceties, Mildred Starr immediately walked up and took Claire's hand. A matronly older woman, her heavily silvered brown hair plaited into a single braid and twisted at the top of her head to form a neat, tight bun. Her eyes were a bright blue, her cheeks plump and rosy, and what seemed an almost perpetual smile was on her lips. She reminded Claire so strongly of her and Ian's beloved old English nanny, Janie Hampton, that Claire couldn't help but feel an instant bonding with her.

"Welcome, welcome," the woman said, patting her hand. "I've been so eager to meet you ever since Conor told us you were coming, that I near to forgot myself and rode out to the ranch several times in the past few days. But my nephew here," she added with a wry glance in the priest's direction, "insisted I give you some breathing room."

"Not that the breathing room lasted very long," Noah Starr good-naturedly observed from behind her. "I'm surprised you didn't come equipped today with a cake in one hand and a plate of cookies in the other."

Mildred laughed. "Oh, that'll commence soon enough." She turned back to Claire. "In fact, if everyone has time, I'd like to invite you all over for some coffee and cake right now. So as how I–and Noah, too, of course–can get to know Claire and her brother a little better and catch up with all that's happened with Evan, too."

Claire cast her husband a hesitant look. "Well, it would be most hospitable of you, Mrs. Starr, but I don't know if–"

"Millie," the woman was quick to correct her. "Call me Millie. Most folk do."

"Well, Millie," Claire tried again, "I don't know what plans all the MacKays have for today. Mayhap it would be best–"

"Oh, pshaw," Millie again cut her off, this time with a laugh. "The MacKays always have time for a visit and some sweets. Don't they, children?" As she spoke, she glanced for confirmation from Devlin Jr. to Mary and then to Beth.

An eager expression on his freckled face, Devlin Jr. nodded so hard a lock of carrot red hair fell onto his forehead. "Sure do, ma'am," he replied. Then, as if remembering himself, he glanced up at his father. "If it's all right with you and Hannah, Pa."

Devlin studied his son for a moment, tugged at his long, dark mustache, then turned to Hannah, who nodded her permission. "It's fine with me if we stay on a bit and visit with Millie and Noah. That is," he quickly amended, "if it's all right with Conor and Abby."

Abby laughed. "Oh, we can stay for an hour or so, I'd imagine."

"Then it's settled." Millie took Claire by the arm and began to escort her down the church steps. "Noah can catch up with us just as soon as he puts away his ceremonial frocks. And, in the meanwhile," she continued, glancing at Claire, "tell me all about your trip to Colorado, and about how you met Evan, and your home in Scotland."

For an instant, all Claire could do was gape at her. She had never known anyone quite like the gregarious, take-charge Millie Starr. Gazing down in the older woman's bright blue eyes, however, she could see the true friendliness and caring compassion that already seemed such an integral part of Millie's character. Claire sensed that Millie's only intention was to ease her way, and make her feel at home here as soon as humanly possible.

"Well," Claire began as they walked along, "the journey here was quite an experience. New York harbor was a sight to behold and—"

"Oh, I just thought of something!" As if in amusement at her own forgetfulness, Millie laughed. "Do you sew?"

"Aye," Claire cautiously replied. "I can sew, though I haven't had much time of late to do so."

"Next Wednesday." She nodded firmly. "The Grand View Ladies Quilting Society meets in the town hall. We always work on someone's quilt and visit and, of course, have refreshments. Can you come? It'd be a perfect way to meet most of Grand View's ladies and make some new friends."

Misgiving, mixed with a sudden attack of shyness, filled Claire. "But I don't know aught about quilting. Mayhap another time . . ."

"Oh, pshaw!" Her companion gave a disbelieving snort. "There's not much more to it than the fine stitchery that goes into most things. And we'll teach you what else you need to know. Besides, you'll soon find a need for some warm quilts. Colorado winters can be brutally harsh."

Somehow, Claire knew it was next to pointless to argue with Millie when she had her mind already made. "Well, if you don't think I'll be in the way. . . ."

"In the way!" The older woman gave her hand a squeeze. "Why, missy, you'll be a breath of fresh air, that's what you'll be. And, to welcome you to the quilting society, I know just what I'll make to celebrate the occasion."

The children scampered before them, as the adults followed behind. They walked through the open gate of a white-picket-fenced front yard, past flower beds brimming with hollyhocks, delphiniums, daisies, and rose bushes, and up to a single-story wooden house. In the corner of the yard a huge, gnarled tree towered like some gentle despot. Such a pretty place, Claire thought. Welcoming, cheery, and overflowing with bounty. Just like Millie, she realized, the consideration heartening her.

"Yes, a nice apple spice cake and a sour cherry pie will do for starters," Millie murmured half to herself. "And I'll get Sarah Dalton to cook up some of her delicious peanut brittle. And Maisie Wilkins makes a delicious fruit punch . . . ."

As she followed her hostess up to the front door and walked inside, Claire couldn't help but smile to herself. Aye, Millie was indeed a lot like Janie Hampton. And

Janie had been more a mother to her and Ian than their own had ever been.

❦

"I might as well warn you right now about Old Bess," Abby informed Claire two hours later, after returning to the ranch. "She's a good cookstove, but she has a mind of her own. Get too flippant or in a hurry with her, and she's sure to teach you a lesson."

A bemused smile on her face, Claire squatted beside Abby in the kitchen before the big, cast-iron cookstove. She had to admit she had never heard of a stove being addressed as if it had a personality, much less a temperamental one. But then, she had never cooked on such a magnificent, if monstrous, piece of black iron before either. A simple hearth fire and an iron kettle or girdle had been the extent of her cooking aids.

"To start a fire," Abby explained, tugging open several doors on the cookstove, "you first have to fill the firebox with some nice, dry wood. Then, after starting it, you have to get all these doors and regulators adjusted for the proper airflow into the stove. This little door here"– she indicated a long, narrow door below and to the left of the firebox–"is the main draft regulator. This is the one that'll give you problems on Old Bess, if anything does. There are times when I wonder if I'll ever get it open just right to make the fire burn hot."

"It looks simple enough."

"Well, looks can be deceiving, as you're bound to discover sooner or later." Abby shoved to her feet. "How about I put on a kettle of water? By the time we've got the pork roast in the oven and the potatoes peeled and starting to cook, I'll bet the water will be hot enough for a cup of tea."

Claire stood. "That's a fine idea. Now, what would you like me to do? Peel the potatoes or prepare the roast?"

Abby shrugged. "Peel the potatoes, if you don't mind."

The next half hour was spent readying the food for cooking and, just as Abby had predicted, by then the tea water was simmering nicely. She took down two pottery mugs from one of the kitchen's two cupboards; filled a silver tea strainer with tea leaves, then held it first over one cup, then the other as she poured boiling water through it. A few minutes later, both women were sitting at the cloth-covered table sipping their tea.

For a time they sat in companionable silence, Claire savoring the sounds of the kitchen. Sap from the pine logs in the firebox snapped and crackled, seared by the flames of the now vigorously burning fire. Within the stove, a thick pork roast—seasoned with salt, pepper, and rosemary—sizzled, releasing the most mouth-watering aroma. The large pot of potatoes began to steam, and foamy layers of starch floated to the water's surface. On a sideboard, the remaining stash of last fall's dried apples had been made into a crusty cobbler.

It was a cozy, cheerful kitchen, Claire thought. The creature comforts it afforded boggled the mind. In addition to the huge cookstove that offered both an oven for baking and a surface for cooking, the big sink was equipped with a gadget Abby called a pitcher pump. All Claire knew was that vigorously raising and lowering the handle soon delivered a steady stream of fresh, clean water. The floor was of hardwood rather than the packed earth she had always known. There was a place to store smoked meat in the cellar, and not far from the house was a springhouse with a natural spring running through it that kept cool milk, cheese, and butter.

It was all most assuredly the height of luxury.

The sound of feet on the back porch jerked Claire from her contented musings. The door swung open, and a laughing Ian and Beth hurried in.

"When's supper?" her brother demanded, glancing from Claire to Abby.

Claire rolled her eyes and shook her head. "Supper won't be ready for another hour or so. And, generally, one offers a greeting before launching into one's questions. That's far more polite, to say the verra least."

Ian colored in embarrassment. "I beg pardon, ma'am," he muttered, barely managing an apologetic glance at Abby.

The chestnut-haired woman chuckled. "Your apology's accepted. And to answer your next question, we'll be having roast pork, boiled potatoes, green beans, and an apple cobbler for dessert."

The young man's eyes lit with anticipation. "Truly, it sounds verra delicious." He looked to Beth, who had stood there the whole time gazing at him. "It appears that we've time for a wee round of checkers. What do you say, Elizabeth?"

She grinned and grabbed his hand. "I think that sounds quite fine. Come on,"–she tugged on Ian's hand–"let's go. I need to even the score for you beating me the last time we played."

With that, they dashed from the kitchen and into the parlor, leaving a trail of laughter.

Abby arched a brow at Claire. "Elizabeth, is it? No one calls her Elizabeth."

Claire shrugged and smiled.

ɕ

"They're getting along quite nicely, don't you think?" Abby paused to take another sip of her tea. "Ian seems to be settling into life here with great alacrity. Is he always so quick to adapt?"

Claire tensed. Was there more to Abby's casually couched question than met the eye? Surely Evan hadn't told her about Ian's checkered past?

"He seems quite happy to me," she hedged, not quite meeting Abby's inquiring gaze. "Evan keeps him well occupied each day with riding lessons and ranch chores, and then, in the afternoons, with working on the house. I don't see how Ian couldn't help but be 'settling in,' as you say."

"Oh, I didn't mean to imply that I had any problems with him." Despite Claire's best attempts to hide her unease, Abby must have sensed something was amiss. "Ian's a dear, sweet boy. It's just that school will be starting in another month, and I was wondering if he'd be feeling comfortable enough by then to attend classes."

Relief filled Claire. Abby's questions had indeed been as innocent as they seemed. "Most likely he will. Does Beth plan to begin school then, too?"

Abby hesitated, then resolutely met her gaze. "I don't know. She hasn't attended school in Grand View for years. But she's come such a long way in the past four years, and maybe if Ian was there . . ." She inhaled a deep breath. "Well, I thought maybe this time I could convince her to give it a try."

"What happened for Beth not to like school?" Claire leaned forward. "If you don't mind telling me, that is."

"No, I don't mind telling you. You're family, after all." Abby sighed. "Before I came to Culdee Creek, or even knew Conor or Beth, a former housekeeper caused Beth to be accused by her schoolteacher of stealing his prized pocket watch. He locked her in the closet beside the wood stove to punish her, and she nearly died from the heat. It took months for Beth to recover from the incident, and Conor vowed not ever to send her back to school again."

"How old was Beth at the time?"

"Eight. She was just eight years old."

"That was exceedingly cruel of the man," Claire murmured, even as she recalled some of the cruelties she and Ian had also suffered in their young lives.

"Yes, it was. There's more, though. Even before Beth was punished so harshly, she'd been having problems with her classmates. Beth's mother, you see, was a Cheyenne Indian woman whom Conor had hired for his housekeeper and nanny to Evan, after Evan's mother ran off with another man. And, though Conor loved this Indian woman, he never wed her."

The enormity of Beth's plight slowly filtered through Claire's mind. Not only was the girl a half-breed, but she was illegitimate, too. "I suppose the other children knew all this, about Beth, I mean?"

Abby nodded. "Yes. It's hard to keep much secret from such a small, tight-knit community out here. And some folk less tolerant or forgiving chose to punish Beth for her father's actions. Unfortunately, their children figured it gave them free rein to torment Beth."

Claire pushed her mug back and forth between her hands. "Do you think much will have changed, just because Beth's older now?"

"I'd like to hope so. Beth's a lot more confident and assertive than she used to be. Conor's status in the community has improved, and he's once more considered a respected citizen. And, considering the fast friends Beth and Ian have become . . ."

"Ian's verra loyal to his friends, and will stand up for them." Claire lifted her gaze to Abby's. "I don't think he'll long tolerate anyone harming Beth. But I must also tell you that he had problems at school in Culdee, and was

158

frequently in fights. I don't wish for him to begin so poorly again."

"He seems a good-hearted, bright young man. Perhaps he'll be able to make a fresh start here."

"Aye," Claire murmured, "I pray that it'll be so. I couldn't bear it if he failed yet again."

Abby reached over and placed her hand on Claire's. "As I couldn't, if Beth failed. Sometimes, though, the Lord sends a helpmate when someone most needs it. I'm praying that's what Ian will be for Beth, and Beth, for Ian."

Like sunlight breaking through a cloud-shrouded day, hope flooded Claire. After all the pain and horror her brother had been through, he deserved a chance to redeem himself and build a new, better life. It would make up, if only in some small way, for what her pride and thoughtlessness so many years ago had caused him.

"Aye, mayhap it is indeed the Lord's plan," Claire agreed softly. "It would be a blessing if it was. A grand and glorious blessing."

 c

The Wednesday of the Grand View Ladies Quilting Society meeting dawned bright and warm. With a mix of nervousness and eager anticipation, Claire hurried to help Abby with the breakfast and morning chores, then joined Evan and Ian for the trip to Grand View. The plan was to drop her off at Millie and Noah Starr's house, pick up cattle feed and deliver it back to the ranch, then return for her four hours later when the quilting society adjourned.

Though the terrain hadn't changed much in the two weeks since they had first arrived, Claire was already beginning to view the land with new, more appreciative eyes. Where once she had seen only sparse, rather scraggly green grass, she now saw bright wildflowers among the waving blades. Where once she had found the wide, rolling hills austerely barren, now she noticed what a marvelous, unobstructed backdrop they provided for the startlingly blue sky. And where once she had mourned the lack of rain and the dry, dusty land, she now rejoiced in the abundance of clear, sunny days.

"It's amazing," she said to Evan as he drove along, "what a difference but two weeks can make."

Dark blue eyes crinkled in a lean, tanned face. "Colorado does grow on you, if you give it even half a chance. I can't tell you, though, how happy it makes me that you're coming to like my home." With his free hand, Evan took her hand and lifted it to his lips. "I love you so much, Claire."

"And I love—"

A loud groan rose from behind them. "Will you two ever cease your love talk?" Ian sighed. "You're both far too old to be carrying on like this, you know? Even Elizabeth talks about your behavior."

Claire gave an exasperated snort, pulled her hand from Evan's, and turned in the seat to eye her brother. His continued harping on her and Evan's relationship was beginning to wear a bit thin. "Elizabeth, is it?" she shot back at him. "Well, I find it passing strange that no one at Culdee Creek save you calls her that. One would almost think you're beginning to carry on a bit yourself."

Evan cast a sharp look over his shoulder. "Is that so? What's going on, Ian? Do you have feelings for my sister?"

"Och, it isn't like that!" Ian graced Claire with a withering glare. "Elizabeth's just special. She's not like most girls. She's more like . . . like a sister. She listens to me, and when she has something to say, well, it's about important things, not dresses and hair ribbons and kissing boys."

160

Glancing from her brother to her husband, Claire wished she had bitten off her tongue rather than have teased Ian like she had. If looks could've translated into action, her brother would have already trussed, skewered, and roasted her over a blazing fire. Evan looked none too pleased, either, if the taut lips and muscle twitching in his jaw were any indication of his true feelings.

"Och," she said with an uneasy little laugh, "I didn't mean aught by that, Ian. I know you and Beth are but good friends. I was teasing you to get back at you for what you're constantly saying about Evan and me. But I gather this time I may have gone too far."

"Aye, that you did," Ian muttered.

Claire sighed and shook her head. "Well, then I'm sorry for it, that I am. And sorry if I upset you, too, Evan."

"It's okay," he bit out the words. "I guess I'm just being a bit overprotective of my sister. She's grown up a lot in the past year. She's getting to be a young woman—and a very pretty one at that—and it has all happened so fast I haven't had a chance to catch up to it yet."

Claire patted his hand. "It's quite understandable, Evan." She looked back at Ian once more. "Isn't it, Ian?"

"Aye, I suppose so," the young man replied, even as he shot Evan one of those old, wary looks that always pierced clear to the depths of Claire's heart. "No harm done."

ፊ

As Evan and Ian drove off in the buckboard, heading for Grand View's feedlot, Claire paused to wave, then turned and headed up the gravel-strewn path leading to the rectory. At her knock, the Reverend Noah Starr answered.

For an instant Claire just stared, then finally found her tongue. "Er, I'm sorry to disturb you, Father Starr, but Millie's expecting me."

"Come in. Come in." He stepped aside and swung open the door. "My aunt's just finishing up icing her cake for the quilting society get-together. Why don't we wait for her in the parlor?"

She was tempted to tell him she'd join Millie in the kitchen, or even wait outside. As much as she already admired the Reverend Starr, Claire felt at a complete loss in speaking to him alone. Indeed, what could a simple country girl such as she have to say to such a gifted, brilliant man?

Still, good manners demanded she acquiesce to his request, so Claire reluctantly followed Noah Starr into the parlor. He took a seat in a burgundy, damask-covered wing chair, and indicated she should sit on the flowered settee.

"Nice day," the Reverend Starr commented mildly. "Too fine a day to spend indoors making endlessly tiny stitches on some quilt." He laughed, the sound rich and warm. "But then, I cherish whatever free time I have to spend out of doors, so I can hardly call myself a neutral observer."

Claire settled herself, smoothing the green-and-white calico skirts of the summer dress Abby had lent her, then glanced up. "Aye, it *is* a glorious day," she managed to croak out, "but I've been so looking forward to meeting more of the town's ladies, that I'm willing to sacrifice a wee bit for the opportunity."

"I think you'll find most of the ladies quite pleasant. We're very fortunate in Grand View to have so many good Christian women."

"Aye, so it seems."

Silence fell between them then, and Claire found sudden fascination in twisting the small, heart-shaped locket Evan had recently given her.

"So, how do you like your new home so far?" the young priest finally asked. "It must have been very hard, leaving Scotland behind, no matter how much you love Evan."

The concern in the Reverend Starr's voice resonated with her. Claire jerked her startled gaze back to his and, for some inexplicable reason, tears filled her eyes. Frantically, she blinked them away.

"It was indeed hard to leave Scotland," she rasped, "but everyone—yourself included—has tried to make me feel welcome. In time, all will be well with me."

"It was hard for me at first, too, moving out here after living all my life in New England. I tried in every way I could to find some excuse not to come. But my uncle needed me, and I finally faced the fact this was where the Lord wished me to be. Still, there were times in the early months when I hated this place. I feared it would swallow me up, that I'd never amount to anything if I stayed here."

Noah Starr smiled sadly. "In those days, I had imagined that I'd a brilliant career ahead of me in some wealthy old church in some large city. But you know something, Claire? I would've lost myself in such a place. But here . . . here in this small, simple town, I now see everything so much more clearly. I believe this is where the Lord wishes me to make manifest His glory."

He blushed then. "I'm sorry. I didn't mean to go on so long, or presume to tell you this at such short acquaintance. I tend to get a little ahead of myself at times. Please forgive me if I've offended you."

So shocked she didn't know how to respond, it was all Claire could do not to stare. "You didn't offend me, Father," she finally managed to reply. "Indeed, it's most heartening to hear you speak so freely of things that touched you, and of experiences we might well share. You've given me much to think on, about God's will for me and how I might best manifest it here."

"That's truly what I intended to do, even if I tripped all over myself in the doing."

The young priest smiled then, and the act only lent his already handsome features an even more radiant beauty. Claire inhaled a sharp breath.

"Well, I see Noah is handling his duties as host quite admirably," Millie Starr observed with a laugh from the parlor doorway. A colorful, padded box in her hands, she walked into the room. "Here, this is a welcome gift from Noah and me." She held the box out to Claire.

"Och, you didn't have to give me aught," she said, coloring fiercely as she accepted the box. "Your kindness and friendship were quite–"

"Hush, child," Millie chided. "Open it and see what's inside."

A twisted, blue twine latch closed the box, covered in a green-and-blue floral pattern. Claire flipped the latch and opened the lid. Inside was a sewing kit consisting of a little red velvet pin cushion, a brass box of black pins set with bright beads, two papers of various sized sewing needles, two silver-plated thimbles, several spools of thread, and a tiny pair of gold-plated scissors.

"I-I've never had anything so grand," Claire whispered, looking up at Millie and Noah's smiling faces. "I don't know what to say."

"No need to say anything, child," the older woman replied briskly. "You'll need those things to do your quilting, and any other sort of mending that your two menfolk are bound to bring you sooner or later. It was a practical gift, and that's all there is to it."

"Well, nonetheless, I thank you from the bottom of my heart. I'll cherish it always."

Millie looked to Noah. "Well, if you're still of a mind to help out, the cake and sour cherry pie are ready to carry to the town hall."

Noah stood. "I'll be glad to. Do you have everything else you'll need?"

She nodded. "My sewing basket's by the front door." Millie turned to Claire. "Come along then, child. It's past time you were meeting the other ladies."

Claire stood, clutching her sewing basket to her. "Aye," she replied, her heart so full of gratitude for a friend like Millie—and Noah, too, she realized—that she thought it might burst. "So it is."

12

Is anything too hard for the LORD?
Genesis 18:14

The ride back home to Culdee Creek was strained and silent. Several times, as they headed out of town after picking up the load of corn from the feedlot, Evan tried to initiate some sort of conversation with Ian. The attempts, however, always died on his lips. The young man's expression and physical demeanor presented as much an obstacle to pleasant conversation as any words ever could.

Ian sat there on the buckboard seat, a tight, shuttered look on his face. His arms clasped across his chest as if to protect himself and ward off any physical trespass. His legs were crossed, his body facing away from Evan.

Never, from the first day he had met the lad, had Evan seen Ian act like this. And he wouldn't be now, Evan well knew, if *he* hadn't said what he had said earlier. In an unthinking, almost reflexive response, he had all but accused Ian of having improper thoughts about Beth. In his belated attempt to finally become the brother his sister had always needed, Evan knew he had jeopardized–and probably unfairly–his relationship with Ian.

It was bad enough he had hurt Ian's feelings in the doing. Then he had compounded the injury by upsetting Claire, too. She had quickly picked up on the undercurrent of masculine hostility. Her efforts to smooth over the raw feelings between her brother and husband had been painfully apparent. Thinking on it now, Evan was surprised she hadn't immediately insisted on canceling her day with the quilting society to accompany them back home.

But maybe it was better that she hadn't. This was a matter best settled between men, and, like it or not, Ian was fast approaching manhood. Problem was, how did one broach such a sensitive subject with an already sensitive boy?

Evan dragged in a deep breath, then exhaled slowly. He reined in the team at the side of the road. "Ian, turn around. Look at me. We need to talk."

Most reluctantly, the lad turned to face him. Though he uncrossed his legs to do so, his arms remained folded across his chest. "What do you want to talk about?" he asked warily.

"I was out of line a while ago, when I all but jumped down your throat about Beth." Evan sighed again, and shook his head. "I didn't think. I just reacted like some dumb old lummox of a brother. I didn't give you the benefit of the doubt, or even care to do so. For that I was wrong. For that I'm sorry."

Ian eyed him cautiously. "I can understand your need to protect your sister. I can even accept that you might have wondered about my intentions. But still, you should've given me a chance. I did so with you, when it came to Claire."

Remorse lanced through Evan. "Yes, you did, and that, I think, makes you the better man. There's not much more I can say, though, except I'm sorry. That, and I hope you'll find it in your heart to forgive me, give *me* another chance."

"I do like Elizabeth, you know." Ian bit his lip, glanced briefly away, then forced his gaze back to Evan's. "In more than just a brotherly way. And I think she likes me in more than a sisterly way, too."

Once more the anger swelled, and it took all of Evan's self-control not to react negatively. When he had married Claire, he had tacitly if not legally also taken on responsibility for her brother. Ian was family now. If he didn't tread carefully here, he might irreparably damage their relationship and turn the boy against him.

"So, you didn't tell me the full truth back there, did you?" he asked with all the gentleness he could muster.

"Nay." Ian hung his head. "I didn't. I was afraid."

Evan chuckled. "Well, I don't know many men who would've, faced as they were with an irate brother. But you did tell the truth now, and I'm much obliged."

"What will you do?" He looked up, searching Evan's face. "Tell your father? Forbid Elizabeth to be with me?"

"Culdee Creek's an awfully small place. I reckon it'd be mighty hard keeping you two apart."

"It would be verra unfair, too. Elizabeth and I haven't done aught wrong. We just like each other verra much."

"I know." Evan glanced down at the reins he held, studying the leather lines with great deliberation. His heart went out to the lad. Ian was entering a potentially turbulent and confusing, yet glorious time in his life.

It was a big responsibility—this chance to be a brother, if not actually a father to Ian. Yet such a charge required qualities Evan feared he might be insufficient in rendering, if indeed he didn't totally lack them. It wasn't as if his own father had been the perfect parent. Only since

Abby had come into his life had Conor MacKay finally allowed the frozen block of his heart to thaw.

Still, surely the caring and effort involved would count for something.

"There's a proper way to act around ladies," Evan said. "An honorable, respectful way." He paused to eye the boy intently. "Do you get my meaning here, Ian?"

"Aye." He nodded. "You're speaking of not taking improper liberties with Elizabeth. But I'd never do that. I swear it!"

"And I believe you, Ian. Still, if you're willing, I'd like you to come to me, talk with me, whenever you're confused or unsure what to do next."

"I'd like to feel I *could* talk with you about aught," Ian began carefully. "When we were in Culdee, I felt that way."

"And now?" Evan prodded gently. "Now that you're here?"

"Well, until today, I felt certain I could come to you—and I still wish to, mind you," he hurried to say, "but if there were ever problems between Elizabeth and me, whose side would you take?"

"I'd try not to take sides, Ian," Evan answered as honestly as he could. "I'd try to point out the possible consequences of your actions and the effects they could have on the rest of your life. A man should carefully consider these things, especially when it involves more than just himself. And a man needs to do what's honorable, and be willing to take responsibility, too."

"I want to make Claire proud of me. She's suffered enough because of me."

"I don't think she counts it as suffering, Ian. Claire loves you and will do most anything to help you."

A pensive look darkened Ian's face. "I love her, too."

169

"As do I. And that's why, above everything else, we must talk to each other and try to be friends. Because we both love Claire."

The young man smiled then. "Thank you, Evan. For everything."

Evan grinned. "Dinna fash yerself, laddie." Then, with a smart slap of the reins, he signaled the horses to set out once more, heading for home.

"Hello, I'm Mary Sue Edgerton," an attractive, raven-haired girl said as she slid into the chair next to Claire. She smiled at Claire, then took a short, thin sewing needle and piece of thread from her bag, threaded the needle, and scooted her chair closer to the big quilting frame. After burying the thread's end in a spot near where the quilt pattern began, she slipped on a little gold thimble and began to make tiny, evenly spaced stitches.

Claire watched, transfixed by the precise sewing. Then, finally remembering her manners, she greeted Mary Sue in turn. "And my name's Claire MacKay. I'm Evan's—"

"Oh, I know who you are," the other girl was quick to interrupt her. "News about the MacKay clan travels fast around these parts. You came from Scotland and you're Evan's new wife."

"Aye, that I am." She smiled. "And are you wed, or do you work at some trade?"

An indefinable emotion flickered in Mary Sue's eyes and was gone. "No, I've yet to wed, and I have no special trade, save my training to someday be a wife and mother. I live at home with my parents, here in Grand View. My father's the town butcher, and that's my mother, sitting over there."

She pointed toward a stern-faced, rail-thin woman who was even then taking a seat beside Millie Starr. Claire couldn't help but wonder if Mrs. Edgerton was truly as unpleasant as her visage seemed to indicate. She supposed she'd find out sooner or later.

"With all the cattle ranches in this region, I'd imagine your father must be most prosperous, butchering all that meat," Claire observed. "It's a great blessing, it is, to have such wonderful beef to feast upon as oft as one likes."

Mary Sue shot her a puzzled glance. "Well, I'd never thought of it quite like that, but I suppose you're right." She paused in her quilting. "Why don't you get started on that rose pattern?" She indicated a lightly penciled floral motif on the quilt square lying before Claire. "We can just as easily talk and sew. This *is* a quilting bee, after all."

"A quilting bee?"

"Yes." Mary Sue nodded, then, as if suddenly realizing Claire might not know what that term meant, she chuckled and hurried to explain. "A 'bee' is a gathering of people for a specific purpose, in this case to work on a quilt. A well-made quilt takes a lot of time and effort for one woman to sew all by herself, but if the work's shared, then the quilt's finished in no time. We're working on a wedding quilt today for Lacy Nealy, the blacksmith's daughter. She's to be married next month to one of Culdee Creek's hands. You might know him; his name's Henry Watson."

Claire recalled a short, heavily muscled man in his late twenties of that name. His hair was sun-streaked brown, his eyes blue, and he sported a carefully waxed, long handlebar mustache. Aside from that, however, she knew nothing about him save that he had worked at Culdee Creek for the past six years.

"Well, then this quilt will have even greater meaning for me," she said, "being as how it's for someone from

171

Culdee Creek. Problem is, I don't know aught about quilting. Could you explain how you make the stitches?"

Mary Sue studied her for a moment, then nodded as if making up her mind. "Sure, I'll show you. There's nothing to it, really. It just takes a bit of practice to get the stitches small and evenly spaced, but once you do . . ."

The next three hours, save for a half-hour break to socialize and eat the various desserts the ladies had brought, were spent working on Lacy Nealy's wedding quilt. By the time the meeting drew to a close, Claire was actually beginning to develop some skill with the quilting needle. As she gathered up her equipment and began to put them away in her new sewing basket, Mary Sue touched her on the arm.

"Aye?" Claire glanced up.

"I'm going to step outside for a breath of air," the dark-haired girl said. "When you're finished, would you care to join me?"

Flattered that a pretty, friendly girl like Mary Sue seemed to have taken such an interest in her, Claire nodded eagerly. "I'll join you in a few minutes."

The midafternoon sky had taken on a cloud-strewn appearance while they had all been inside, Claire noted when she finally joined the other girl outside the hall. To the west, high over Pikes Peak, thunderheads formed.

"Looks like we might be in for a rain storm," Mary Sue commented, casually scanning the long stretch of Winona Street. "Is someone on his way from Culdee Creek to fetch you? If so, they'd better get here soon, or you might not make it home before the storm breaks."

"Evan should be arriving any time now." Claire glanced down at the gold watch pinned to her chest. "He's supposed to be here at three."

"So, how have things gone between him and Hannah and Devlin since he came home?"

Claire frowned. What a strange question to ask, she thought, out of the blue and all. She looked at Mary Sue, trying to catch some hint of her expression, but the girl's head was turned to the right, as if something in that direction had suddenly caught her eye.

"There's problems between him and Devlin, you know," Mary Sue chose that moment to elaborate, "and all because of Hannah."

"Indeed?" Claire's mouth went dry, and a small tendril of caution curled within. "I didn't realize the MacKay family squabbles were such common knowledge in Grand View."

"This one about Hannah sure is." Ever so slowly, Mary Sue turned back to her. "If you don't know anything about it, though, I'm not going to be the one to tell you. It's not my place. But have a care, Claire. Hannah isn't all the sweetness and light she tries to let on she is."

"She's been quite kind to me," Claire said, unwilling to stand there and allow someone who was now her kinswoman to be maligned. "And, after all, I can only judge someone based on how that someone treats me."

"True enough," Mary Sue agreed quite amicably. "I didn't mean to stir up trouble between you and Hannah, after all. All I'm saying is, have a care. Just have a care."

∂

On September 5, Ian turned sixteen and was feted with a grand birthday party. Two days later Ian and Beth, accompanied by Devlin Jr., started school in Grand View. Though Beth was far more apprehensive than Ian, their other classmates seemed to accept them both without hesitation. The one-room schoolhouse, with grades ranging from first through high school, soon became a place both eagerly anticipated attending each day.

"Of course," Abby said with a chuckle, almost a month after Claire's first introduction to the Ladies Quilting Society, "I'd imagine a lot of Ian and Beth's pleasure in school of late has to do with being together." She paused to pour out three mugs of tea, then placed a plate of sliced Boston brown bread on the table between her, Claire, and Hannah. "They've become all but inseparable."

"Aye, that they have," Claire agreed as she served herself a slice of the fragrant, molasses-sweetened bread. "I'm so verra pleased with how well Ian seems to be fitting in, and with all the friends he's made."

"He's a kind, friendly boy," Hannah added her own assessment. "Devlin Jr. all but worships the ground he walks upon, and Mary, Jackson, and Bonnie like him just fine, too."

Claire beamed, basking in the praise of her brother. At last. At long last everything seemed to be coming right for them. She laughed. "I think Ian near to sees your children as the younger brothers and sisters he always wished he'd had. You bore your husband some bonny bairns, that you did, Hannah, though I can't for the life of me understand where Devlin Jr. and Bonnie's fine red hair came from. I'd wager there's a proud Scots ancestor back there somewhere."

Hannah and Abby exchanged a thoughtful glance. Then the blonde-haired woman sighed. "Devlin and I only share one child in common—Jackson. His other three children were born to his first wife who died almost two and a half years ago." She smiled. "That's where Bonnie and Devlin Jr.'s red hair came from—their mother, Ella."

Surprise filled Claire. "Och, and I thought you and Devlin had been married for a long while. I beg your pardon."

"You don't need to apologize, Claire." Hannah paused to sip her tea. "You didn't know, and perhaps I was remiss in not telling you. Devlin and I married this past Thanksgiving. Before that, Devlin was wed to Ella, who died of the influenza shortly after Bonnie's birth."

Gradually, Claire's surprise transformed to shock. Bonnie was two years old; Jackson was three. Could it be that Hannah had all but admitted she had conceived her son outside the bonds of holy matrimony? Indeed, she realized as she made some swift calculations, Jackson had been conceived while Devlin's wife Ella still lived. Hot color flooded her face.

Her sudden embarrassment wasn't lost on either Hannah or Abby. "Hannah first came to Culdee Creek three years ago," Abby hastened to explain, "after she escaped from Sadie Fleming's bordello in Grand View. She was pregnant with Jackson and begged me to help her, which, with Conor's agreement, I did. After Ella nearly died bearing Bonnie, Hannah helped out with Devlin and Ella's children and in caring for their house. Unfortunately, then the influenza took Ella. In time, Hannah became Devlin's permanent housekeeper and caretaker of his children. Their relationship grew until, finally, Hannah and Devlin fell in love."

Claire chewed on her lower lip, loath to ask the next question on her mind, but at last she threw all caution to the wind and did so. "What was Hannah doing in a bordello?"

"I was a prostitute, Claire," came Hannah's gentle reply. "I was forced into the life as a girl and, though I tried repeatedly to escape, until Abby came, they always brought me back."

"But how did Devlin become Jackson's . . . ?" It was too embarrassing to go on. Claire let the question die.

"How did Devlin become Jackson's father, if he was still wed to Ella?" Hannah finished for her. "Well, during

175

a difficult time in his and Ella's marriage, Devlin called on me at the brothel."

"Oh." Once more, Claire blushed. "I see."

Evan's stepmother reached over and laid her hand on Claire's. "We thought it best you hear the truth from us rather than from someone else, Claire." Deep concern darkened her eyes. "Still, what is past is past, and forgiven in the sight of God."

Inexplicably, Mary Sue Edgerton's words that day of the quilting society meeting rushed back now, filling Claire's head with wild, disjointed phrases. *Problems . . . and all because of Hannah . . . Have a care . . . Hannah isn't all . . . sweetness and light . . . Have a care. . . .*

Was there mayhap some truth in Mary Sue's words? Claire now wondered. Or were the young woman's motives less than altruistic, shielding a more rancorous intent? There was no way of knowing, save with further insights and experience that only time could give.

In the meanwhile, however, Hannah was now family. No matter how unsettling the truth about Hannah's past was, Claire would honor her Scottish heritage with its fierce clan loyalty, and do her best to give the other woman the benefit of the doubt.

"Aye," Claire agreed softly, first meeting Abby's then Hannah's now wary gaze, "what is past is indeed past, and doesn't concern me. I didn't know you before, Hannah. I only know you now. And, as Devlin's wife, you and I are kin. I'll stand by you as best I can."

A smile of relief lifted the corner of the young woman's mouth. "That's good to know, Claire. I value your friendship deeply. But I also didn't feel it was right to withhold the truth about my past from you. Especially when what I was is common knowledge."

Claire opened her mouth to reassure her she understood, when Conor strode in from the parlor.

"Abby, I just got back from town," he said, his voice unsteady, his expression one of extreme gravity. "Seth Harris at the telegraph office flagged me down just as I pulled up in front of Gates' Mercantile. He gave me this."

Culdee Creek's owner held out a folded piece of paper. Hesitantly, Abby took it, opened the telegram, and began to read. The color drained from her face.

"What is it, Abby?" Hannah asked, her voice now taut with worry. "What does the telegram say?"

The paper in the chestnut-haired woman's hands fell to the tabletop. "My father," she whispered finally. "My father's very ill, and not expected to live."

ॐ

"What will you do, Pa?" Evan asked that evening, after riding in from a day of fence mending to hear the news. "Claire said Abby intends to go home to be with her father. Are you planning on letting her travel all the way back East by herself?"

"No." Conor shook his head with grim resolve. He shifted restlessly in the wicker rocker on the main house's front porch. "I've got to go with her. There's no telling how bad it'll be back there, and I can't let Abby go through it alone. I *won't* let her go through it alone."

"I understand, Pa." Evan leaned forward in his own chair, rested his forearms on his thighs, and laced his fingers together. "We can handle Culdee Creek—Devlin and I—while you're gone. In fact," he added with a wry grin, "it's about time I try my hand at running the ranch. It's not fair that you have to carry all the responsibility anymore."

"I appreciate that, Son."

At his father's words, pleasure filled Evan. "I just want to pull my weight, Pa. That's all."

"We'll have a meeting real soon, you, me, and Devlin, and divvy up the duties."

177

Evan leaned back and nodded, firmly squelching the unpleasant realization that, with his father gone, he'd have to work even more closely with his cousin than before. Still, though his feelings for Devlin hadn't changed much in the past month, he couldn't burden his father with those concerns right now. Some how, some way, Evan vowed to work it out, even if it meant gritting his teeth and pretending a friendship he didn't feel. His pa deserved that much—and more—from him.

"Fair enough," he said instead, then paused. "Have you and Abby decided when you'll be heading out?"

Conor sighed and shoved a hand raggedly through his dark hair. "Most likely the day after tomorrow. We'll take Sean with us. He's too young to be separated from his mother. I'd like to leave Beth here, though, if you don't mind. She's just finally started back to school, seems to be enjoying it, and I'd hate to ruin the positive beginning she's finally made."

Evan frowned. "If Beth stays, she'll be all alone in the big house. Maybe Claire, Ian, and I should move in with her until you and Abby return."

"Yes." As if warming to the suggestion, Conor nodded. "That's a fine idea. You and Claire can take our room, and Ian can have your old room. It'll be easier for Claire that way, having a kitchen of her own and all." He grinned apologetically. "Don't see as how your house will be ready anytime soon anyways. We've made a good start, but what with the extra ranch work you'll have to take on in my absence . . ."

"Don't worry about a thing, Pa. The bunkhouse will do us just fine when you get back, even if it means spending the winter there if need be. In the end, it'll all work out for the best."

"Yeah," his father agreed softly, "it always does, doesn't it?"

13

It was not an enemy that reproached me; then I could
have borne it.

Psalm 55:12

The next evening, Conor called Evan and
Devlin together for a meeting. Full of
eager anticipation, Evan arrived early. At last, he thought
as he took a seat by the parlor hearth, he'd begin to
repay a little of all that he owed his father. At last, the
satisfied realization thrumming through him, he'd stand
head-to-head with his sire as he shouldered full responsibility for Culdee Creek in his father's absence. And, at
last, even if the consideration was perhaps far sweeter
than he cared to admit, Devlin would finally be forced
to acknowledge his coming to power and maturity as
the mantle of running the ranch was placed, if only
temporarily, on Evan's shoulders.

Conor, a steaming mug of coffee in his hand, soon
joined Evan in the parlor. He settled into the leather
chair opposite his son and took a tentative sip. "Devlin
should be here any minute," he then said. "Before he
arrives, though, there's something I need to talk with
you about."

Expectation swelling, Evan leaned forward. "About the ranch, Pa?"

"Yeah, about the ranch." Conor rose, turned to the mantle, and set his mug on it. "I've given a lot of thought to the arrangements needing to be made while I'm gone." He gripped the thick, walnut-stained mantle for a long moment, then turned back to face Evan. "I know you probably figured you'd be the one to run Culdee Creek, and someday you will, but Devlin knows this ranch and all its working nearly as well as me. You, on the other hand, between growing up and being gone twice for extended periods, are just starting to get a handle on it."

His father met Evan's stunned gaze with an apologetic yet steadfast one of his own. "Right now, Son, Devlin's the man to run Culdee Creek, and that's the way I want it."

Horror and total disbelief engulfed Evan. Then bitter resentment surged up, boiling within. *Devlin.* Once more Devlin had emerged victorious. Once more, he'd have the right to lord it over him, to order him about, to be the favored one. It was almost . . . almost as if his father was trying to punish him, that he thought more of Devlin than he did his own son!

At the consideration, Evan felt a wrenching stab of pain. His gut clenched and twisted. More than anything he had ever wanted, he suddenly wanted to get up and storm from the room. Angry words formed, fighting to break free and spew forth at his father.

But Evan wouldn't, couldn't, allow either to happen. Staring up into his father's eyes, he saw the anguish the difficult decision had caused him. If his father could've had it any other way, Evan sensed he would have. Besides, the fault didn't lie with his father. It lay with him.

He was the one who had robbed him and run off with enough of the ranch's money that the theft had set

Culdee Creek back for several years. *He* was the one who had again run away a year ago, just because his heart had been broken and he couldn't handle losing Hannah to Devlin.

It didn't matter that, this time, he was home for good. It didn't matter that he intended to become, at long last, the son and heir his father had always hoped he would be. His father couldn't know that yet. How could he, after all the fool things his son had done in the past? Only time, unswerving loyalty, and hard work would prove the rock-solid sincerity of Evan's intent.

In the end, Evan admitted bitterly, he deserved this. He deserved it and would accept it, no matter how hard it might be to swallow.

"If that's the way you want it, Pa," he forced out, nearly choking on words tasting as caustic as bile, "then that's how it'll be. I told you I'd pull my weight in any way I could, and I meant it."

A guarded look of relief flared in Conor's eyes. "I'm glad to hear you take the news so well, Son. I'll admit I was worried."

"I didn't say I liked it, Pa," Evan muttered. He glanced away. "I just said I'd accept it."

"Even though Devlin's boss, I want you to work closely with him. Start learning the business end of running this ranch." His father paused, took a deep swallow of his coffee, then eyed him. "Do you think you can do that, Son? Work closely with Devlin?"

Evan knew what his father was asking. He wanted reassurance that Evan could put aside his still-unresolved anger and hard feelings toward his cousin. He wanted to know if his son was man enough to forgive, move past the youthful antagonism Evan had always felt toward Devlin. Problem was, Evan wasn't sure he *was* man enough to do that, leastwise not just yet.

The realization shamed him. He couldn't fail his father, no matter how strong his personal antipathy for Devlin still ran. "I'll do my best, Pa," he finally ground out. "I give you my word. I'll do my best."

A knock sounded at the parlor's front door. Conor's gaze locked for an instant more with his son's, then he climbed to his feet. "Reckon that's all any man could ask of another. Reckon that's all any man can do."

With that, he turned and strode toward the door. Evan stood, squared his shoulders, and waited. Conor opened the door and welcomed Culdee Creek's foreman inside. After a brief greeting, the two men turned. Devlin's glance met Evan's.

Schooling his features into an expressionless mask, Evan nodded in welcome. "Glad to see you," he said, walking over to stand before his father and cousin. He hesitated for an instant, steeling himself for what he must next do, then held out his hand. "Pa's going to depend on the both of us until he returns," he said, "so I reckon it's time I take you up on your offer to let bygones be bygones."

A fleeting surprise widened Devlin's eyes, then was gone. He nodded in turn, and accepted Evan's proffered hand. "That's fine by me," he drawled with a slow grin. "That's *right* fine by me."

❧

The next day, Abby, Conor, and Sean caught the train out of Grand View. The entire MacKay clan saw them off in fine fashion. Then, as Hannah, Devlin, and their brood headed home, Evan, accompanied by Ian and Beth, dropped off Claire at the town hall for her monthly Ladies Quilting Society meeting.

"By the time I come back for you," he said, his hands lingering at her waist even after the quick kiss they had shared, "I'll have our clothes and things moved into the upstairs bedroom. And there's plenty of food left over from last night's supper, so you won't have much to do when you get home but warm things up."

Claire eyed him with misgiving. "Mayhap, but I still don't feel right spending so many hours in town today, what with Conor and Abby just leaving. I could just as easily pass on this month's meeting, and—"

"Hush." Evan pressed a gentle finger to her lips. "A few hours for yourself once a month isn't too much to ask. I want you to take this time. It's good for you to make some friends outside Culdee Creek, not to mention socialize with them a bit."

"Och, but aren't you the dear lad?" Knowing by now that look of unshakeable conviction when she saw it, Claire gave up her protests with a laugh. When he chose to be, Evan was as stubborn as any Scotsman born and bred.

"Yes," her husband admitted with a nod and cocky grin, "I am indeed, and best you never forget it." He pulled her sewing basket out from behind the seat, handed it to her, then climbed into the buckboard. "I'll be back at three o'clock. Will you be waiting here, or at the Starrs'?"

"At the Starrs'. Millie has a new book she wants to lend me, and I'll walk back with her to pick it up."

Evan tugged on his hat brim in farewell. "See you at three, then."

Beth waved from her seat beside Ian. "Good-bye, Claire."

Claire watched as the three of them drove off and headed out of town, though her gaze was really focused on her husband. The bright, sunny day and blue sky provided a perfect backdrop for Evan's broad-shouldered, narrow-waisted, and trim-hipped physique. He sat on the buckboard seat with a relaxed grace, one forearm resting on a denim-covered thigh propped higher than

183

the other, and leaning slightly forward, both hands gripping the reins.

She didn't think she'd ever tire of watching him. With his dark Stetson, scuffed, dusty boots, and long, lean-muscled legs encased in those well-worn denims, Evan looked every bit the cowboy she always imagined. Claire had to admit that, as much as she liked a man in a kilt, she equally liked one well-clad in snug-fitting denims, wearing boots and a Stetson.

"Lusting after your husband, are you?" a familiar feminine voice intruded just then on Claire's affectionate musings. Mary Sue Edgerton stepped from the shadows beyond the town hall's open doorway and sauntered over. "Tsk, tsk. Here I thought that little act we play to win a man became superfluous, once we got a wedding ring on our finger."

Fleetingly, Mary Sue's calculating observation gave Claire pause. Then she decided, as she turned and caught a glimpse of the other girl's smiling face, that Mary Sue was surely jesting. "Well, I can't say I know or understand all of your American customs as yet," she replied laughingly, "but I haven't observed any lack of fondness between husband and wife since I've been in America. Abby certainly continues to have a great affection for her husband, and though Hannah has been wed to Devlin nearly a year, her continued devotion toward him is also still most pleasantly apparent."

"Hannah!" The ebony-haired girl gave a disdainful sniff. "One has to wonder how much of her devotion is sincere, and how much is false. She used to make her living playing to men's egos, you know, not to mention all those additional male parts a properly bred lady would never put name to. But then, what else would you expect of a former prostitute?"

At the sarcasm, tinged with glee, in the other girl's voice, Claire's temper flared. "It doesn't matter what

Hannah used to be!" she said through gritted teeth. "What's past is past. Hannah's been good to me. She's also family. I'll thank you not to speak ill of her."

A long silence ensued. Something akin to anger flickered in Mary Sue's eyes, then, as she stepped back and smiled again, it was gone. "Claire, you have my sincerest apology. You're right to reprimand me for my unkind words. What is past *is* past. I just hate to see someone use someone—like Hannah did Evan. You know he followed her around for the longest time like some adoring puppy. But, in the end, it didn't matter to Hannah when she finally tossed him aside and set her cap instead for Devlin. After all Evan did for her, after how deeply and devotedly he seemed to love her, he deserved better than that."

Claire, who at that moment had been casting about for some excuse to end the conversation and head inside, did a double take. An adoring puppy indeed! "What do you mean, Hannah tossed Evan aside for Devlin? I don't recall Evan ever speaking of Hannah in such a way."

"Don't you?" Mary Sue shot her an arch look. "Well, maybe it slipped his mind? Or maybe he just didn't want to cause any problems between you and Hannah, knowing he'd be bringing you back to Culdee Creek? Or, though I hate even to bring this up—yet as your friend I feel I must—maybe he still isn't over her? If there's even half the truth in all the rumors, she *is* the reason he left here over a year ago, you know?"

The revelation that Hannah was the cause for Evan leaving Culdee Creek sent a shard of jealousy plunging through Claire. That pain, however, was nothing compared to the searing sense of betrayal that followed in its wake. Why hadn't Evan ever told her Hannah was the woman who had broken his heart? Why was she

185

forced to first learn about it from the likes of Mary Sue?

It was all too much to fathom, much less deal with right now. One thing, however, was certain. Evan had put her in a decidedly embarrassing position, one she was inadequately prepared to defend. Suddenly, Claire was as furious with her husband as she was with the smug-faced girl standing before her.

"And mayhap all of this is none of your business," Claire snapped, at the end of her tether. She met Mary Sue's now innocent gaze with a challenging one of her own. "Well," she demanded hotly, when no reply was forthcoming, "what do you think? Is aught of this any of your business?"

"Most likely not." The girl flushed scarlet and took a step back. "It's the truth, though, whether or not you care to believe it."

"The truth as best as *you* see it, anyway!"

This time, Mary Sue's eyes widened in shock. "Well, I never! Here I am, trying to be a good and true friend to you, and this is the thanks I get!" With that she turned and, with an injured sniff, stomped back inside.

From within the hall, Claire could hear feet shuffling and chairs scraping across the wooden floor as the members of the Ladies Quilting Society began to take their seats around the large quilting frame. Suddenly, however, she was loath to join them. If Mary Sue knew about Hannah and Evan, how many more in there knew, too? she wondered. Did they laugh and talk about her behind her back when she wasn't around, pitying her ignorance over what must well be common knowledge? Frustration swelled anew. Why, oh why, hadn't Evan told her about Hannah?

Suddenly, Claire felt dizzy, sick to her stomach. She glanced frantically around. A short, wooden bench, painted an incongruous shade of bright red, snugged up beneath a window just a few feet away. She stumbled over to it and sat, her sewing basket still clenched in her hands.

Hannah . . . Hannah, who had tossed Evan aside for Devlin . . . Perhaps, as Mary Sue had warned the first day they had met, Hannah wasn't all that she seemed.

I was in love with a girl, and she fell in love with someone else . . .

Unbidden, Evan's words that day they had first gone to visit Lainie and Donall MacKay crept back into her mind. Claire hadn't given his admission much thought then, beyond trying to comfort Evan in his grief. And by the time she might have begun to consider the tale further, Evan had seemed so taken with her that Claire felt certain the mysterious girl was no longer a problem for either of them.

But now . . . now she wasn't so certain. Evan hardly talked to Hannah. Evan still held a grudge against Devlin. And, worst of all, Evan had never once admitted to Claire that Hannah was the girl who had broken his heart.

Had Evan truly ever gotten over losing Hannah, even now that they were both married to others?

Doubt engulfed her, then fear, then scalding rage. She went hot, cold, then hot again. "Och, Evan, Evan," Claire moaned, clenching her eyes shut, digging her nails into her palms.

Perfect love casteth out fear . . . a tiny voice, sounding suspiciously like Father MacLaren's, whispered of a sudden in her mind.

As quickly as the turbulent emotions had visited her, they were gone. Claire gave a shaky laugh. "Fool," she scolded herself. "Will you, then, suspect your husband on the word of some girl who obviously has a grudge against Hannah? Evan loves you, and Hannah is now a godly woman, no matter the sins of her past. Don't condemn them out of hand. Give them both a chance to defend themselves."

Aye, Claire resolved, that was exactly what she would do—give them both a chance to defend themselves. Problem was, how in heaven's name was she ever to tactfully broach such a delicate subject? And what, she thought as a shiver of dread rippled through her, would she do if the truth wasn't all she hoped it would be?

❦

"Well, I'm *still* not so certain your father did right by you in setting your cousin over you," Claire observed that evening, as she and Evan put fresh sheets on the bed they would now share in Abby and Conor's bedroom. "I am happy, though, that you and Devlin are trying to work out your problems at long last. It'll make the mood around here a sight better for everyone, especially now, with your parents gone."

"Pa did the best he could," Evan muttered as he tried, and failed, to properly miter the top sheet corner on his side like he had seen Claire do. He gave up and just stuffed it beneath the mattress. "And if the mood between Devlin and me was bothering you, you should've said something a long time ago."

"Och, aye," his wife said with an exasperated snort. "A lot of good that would've done me. I don't like to be the one to mention this, but has anyone ever pointed out that you can sometimes work yourself into a black humor?" She opened the blanket and tossed it into the air so that his half floated over to him.

Evan shot her a narrow look. Though Claire had an easy day, he hadn't. He was bone-tired. He and Devlin had already had a few tense moments over what cattle to cull from the herd for market, and the finger he had burned restarting Old Bess for Claire, so she could fin-

188

ish warming up their supper, was throbbing fiercely. Now, on top of everything else, he really wasn't in the mood for any snide comments on his behavior.

"Look, I've been working some mighty long hours lately, even before Pa decided to leave." Evan knew his tone could've been gentler, that he could've softened his words with a smile, but he just didn't have the energy. He took his side of the blanket, smoothed it out, then unceremoniously shoved the foot end of it under the mattress. "Can't we postpone this discussion regarding the sorry state of my attitude until tomorrow? About all I can handle right now is some shut-eye."

The teasing light faded from Claire's eyes. A strange look crossed her face. "Aye, I suppose we can. Of course, we won't talk about it tomorrow either. You'll surely have too many chores to attend to before breakfast, and then you'll be out of the kitchen even before you swallow down your last spoonful of porridge."

At the mention of the oatmeal mush she insisted on serving every morning, Evan grimaced. "Well, since we're now on the subject of porridge, do you think we might be able to have something else for a change? It's one thing for me to eat it every morning. But the hands you'll now have to cook for in Abby's absence aren't going to be as tolerant. You do know how to make flapjacks, don't you? Or how to fry up some bacon and eggs? If not, I'm sure Hannah would be glad to show you."

A rosy hue washed her face. She clamped her lips tightly and averted her gaze. "Aye, I know how to make flapjacks and fry eggs," Claire replied softly. "Mayhap not half so well as Hannah, mind you, but I do know how. I just didn't think they were proper food to begin the day with. Porridge, on the other hand–"

"I haven't anything against porridge, Claire," Evan interrupted her before she launched into yet another lecture. "But I'd just like a good old, stick-to-your-ribs,

American breakfast on occasion, too. I don't think that's too much to ask, is it?"

She turned from picking up the colorful, log cabin style quilt that went atop the blanket and stared at him long and hard. Evan could see the hurt seep into her eyes, the way her pretty mouth began to tug down ever so slightly at the corners. He knew it was his fault. His words had been harsh, derogatory even.

He sighed. "Look, Claire, I didn't mean that the way it sounded. It's just that I'm—"

"I know." She held up a hand to silence him. "You're tired." She quickly unfurled the quilt and let it also float down onto the bed. "Like you said before. Tomorrow's soon enough to talk."

Walking to the commode, she took up the large, porcelain pitcher and pulled it close to her. "Get on with you. Begin your preparations for bed. I'll soon be back with some hot water for you to wash with." In a flurry of skirt and petticoat, Claire was gone from the room.

Evan stared at the closed door for a few seconds, then began unbuttoning his shirt. Things were bad enough with his father gone, he thought in exasperation as he tugged his shirttails free of his denims, without now upsetting his wife. He had never fully comprehended, though, how draining the day-to-day responsibility of running a ranch was. Problem was, from here on out it was only bound to get harder.

He walked to the bed, sat, and tugged off his boots and socks. Just as he was setting them beside the chair, Claire reentered the room, the pitcher in her hands. "Here, let me take that," Evan said, striding over to relieve her of the now full, steaming container. "I wasn't thinking. I should've been the one to go down and fetch this." He paused, a lopsided smile on his lips. "I also want to apologize for my unkind comments earlier. Tired or not, they were uncalled for."

"Och, dinna fash yerself," his wife said, sending him a cautious, slanting look as she turned and closed the bedroom door, then went to stand before the oak dresser with its oval, beveled mirror. "When I'm overly weary, I can be a bit sharp-tongued myself. I'll forgive you, if you promise to forgive me for those times I snip and snap at you."

As she spoke, one by one Claire began to pull the pins from her hair until the rich, auburn bun unfurled and tumbled down her back. Standing there in the middle of the bedroom, the pitcher of water still clutched in his hands, Evan watched, mesmerized, as Claire next finger-combed her long, wavy tresses, then took up a white-bristled hair-brush. With long, languorous strokes, she ran it repeatedly down her hair's glossy length.

His mouth went dry. His hands became damp, and an ardent need to take Claire in his arms and kiss her until she was breathless swelled within him. Heated, loving actions whirled through his head. Evan opened his mouth to share them with her. Then, as if she had suddenly realized he was watching her, Claire's gaze lifted, meeting his in the mirror.

"Aren't you going to wash up?" she asked. "I'll be ready soon for some water myself, but I wanted you to have it first—you being so weary and all."

Evan grinned. He deserved her little dig about him being so tired, especially when all thoughts of sleep had fled in the past few minutes. "Go on and finish with your hair. I'll be done soon." He carried the pitcher to the commode, poured water into the porcelain basin, then set the vessel beside it. He made quick work of washing his face and hands, then vigorously applied a generous dose of Dr. Grave's Unequaled Tooth Powder to his teeth. Finally, his bedtime ablutions completed, Evan shed his denims and climbed into bed.

191

With hooded eyes, he watched as Claire finally undressed and donned a simple, cambric nightdress trimmed with lace, washed her face and brushed her teeth, then padded across the hardwood floor and knelt for her nightly prayers on her side of the bed. Her head bowed. He heard the soft murmur of Claire's fervent entreaties. A tiny twinge of guilt that he wasn't kneeling there beside her assailed him. After all, Evan thought, gazing at his glorious, beautiful young wife, he had even more to be thankful for than she.

He had her. He had returned to Culdee Creek, his home. With each passing day he realized more and more deeply how truly blessed he was to have his family, this ranch, and the promise of a rich, full life that lay before him.

A rich, full life that might someday even include children of his own. Evan smiled at the consideration, and even more at the remembrance of the exquisite pleasure inherent in conceiving those children. He pillowed his hands behind his head, waiting patiently for Claire to finish her prayers and join him.

Yes, indeed, Evan thought, his body warming with a most husbandly anticipation. As hard as the work could sometimes be, there was much to be said for everything that went with being a family man.

14

*And when ye stand praying, forgive, if ye have ought
against any: that your Father also which is in heaven
may forgive you your trespasses.*

Mark 11:25

Her prayers finished, Claire shoved to her
feet, paused to turn down the oil lamp
until the flame extinguished, and climbed into bed. No
sooner had she pulled up the covers, then Evan turned
toward her.

"Do you know how much I love watching you brush
your hair?" he asked, his voice a husky murmur as he
reached over and took a long tress between his thumb
and forefinger. "I think your hair was the first thing that
caught my eye about you, that first day we met. In the
light it's like . . . like molten fire . . . yet when I touch it,
it's as smooth and soft as silk." He lifted the lock, brushed
it against his face, and inhaled. "And the scent is flowers,
and fresh air, and big, blue, open skies."

Claire shifted uneasily, wanting nothing more at that moment than to jerk her hair from Evan's grip and turn away. She was still upset over her confrontation with Mary Sue today, not to mention what she had learned from the gossipy girl. Evan hadn't helped things any when he had attacked her porridge a few minutes ago, then held Hannah's cooking up as a shining example of what he really wanted.

The primary reason, however, for not welcoming her husband's amorous advances was his failure to tell her about his past love affair with Hannah. It angered her that he had purposely withheld that information. What angered her even more, though, was the position it now placed her in of having to confront him about it.

Confrontation, Claire had learned from sad experience, always seemed to put one person on the attack and the other on the defensive. In such situations, the defender's testimony wasn't generally as trustworthy as one would like.

Mayhap it would be better, she tried to reason with herself, to sleep on the matter and give her seething emotions time to cool, before broaching the subject with her husband. The matter had waited long enough as it was. Mayhap when her head was calmer, her heart less torn, she would find the proper words. Words that would set all aright, and heal the breach that had begun to form between them.

"Claire?"

Evan moved closer. His hand slipped across the pillows and beneath her head, to cradle her face in the warm, callused expanse of his palm. He leaned close, his lips touching hers gently, tenderly. In spite of herself, a tremor of desire vibrated through Claire. As much as he had hurt her with his silence, as angry as she was with him, she still loved Evan.

But something was gone—a trust, a sweet innocence. She wasn't so sure she truly knew him or his heart anymore. She couldn't be as certain of his love. And, until she could, she couldn't give herself to him.

"N-nay, Evan," she whispered, pulling back and shaking her head. "Not tonight. I can't . . . I just can't."

For a long moment he was silent. Claire could feel him staring at her, sense his puzzlement. Then he sighed and rolled back over onto his side of the bed.

"Yeah," he muttered, "it *is* a mite strange, making love in my parents' bed. We'll get over it in time, though, I reckon."

"Aye," she agreed hoarsely, the tears welling, then trickling down her cheeks. "We'll get over it in time."

❧

For some reason, it didn't seem any easier to talk to Evan about Hannah the next morning, or that night, or for the next several days. When Evan came to her each night she pleaded the same excuses, adding as well the justifiable reason of exhaustion. If her husband found anything strange in her pretenses, he didn't say. He was soon snoring softly away, while Claire lay there in the dark battling her frustration and pain until she eventually fell into a restless sleep—a sleep that left her tired, irritable, and sick to her stomach each morning.

Cooking three meals a day for the hands soon became a Herculean task as Claire's meager repertoire of American meals began to strain its limits. What little free time she had was consumed in working out new menus, then trying to cook them successfully on the often recalcitrant old cookstove. Too many times to count she found herself restarting the fire and making everyone wait for meals served late.

"That does it!" Evan muttered one morning a week later, when he had been called back to the house to help Claire with the stove for what she knew must seem like the hundredth time. "I'm going to ask Hannah to come help cook lunch and supper. You can watch her children, and maybe pick up some pointers until you're ready to take the job back over."

Her cheeks burning hotly, Claire whirled around from the bread dough she was kneading on the kitchen table. "Nay! I won't impose on Hannah. I won't!"

Her husband closed the firebox door and stood. "She won't mind. She'll even understand. Which is more than the hands are doing, what with late meals and either burnt or half-cooked food."

"I-I'm doing the best I-I can," Claire cried, perilously on the edge of tears.

Evan stared at her, his gaze wary and searching, then finally sighed. "I know you are. But the men work long, hard hours and need their food. They're trying to be understanding, but their patience can only last so long."

"You . . . you think I'm failing you, don't you?" Claire couldn't hold back the tears any longer, and began to weep. "I'm an embarrassment to you, an obstacle to your dream of proving to your father that you can run the ranch in his absence."

"Devlin's running the ranch," he growled, his countenance darkening. "I'll just be blamed for not supporting him like I said I would."

"See? See?" She pointed an accusing finger at him. "I'm right. One way or another, I'll be the cause of your shame." Claire sank onto the nearest chair and buried her face in her flour-covered hands. "Och, I'm so verra sorry, Evan. I'm so sorry!"

"Then help me help you, Claire. Let me fetch Hannah. It'll just be for a while, until you get the hang of all this."

Though frustration now threaded his voice, he made no move to come to her, take her into his arms and comfort her. The realization pierced clear to Claire's soul. He had distanced himself as well; he thought she *was* in the wrong and needed help. And, most painful of all, he was disappointed in her.

Yet how could she explain to him that she didn't want Hannah in the house? That she couldn't bear it right now if Hannah had to come to Evan's aid because his wife had failed him? If Hannah tried to lord it over her in any way—as unlikely as that probably was—Claire didn't know what she'd do, or how she'd react. Or what she'd say—and that worried her most of all.

Yet what other choice had she? she thought miserably. Evan was right. She *didn't* have the hang of cooking on that despicable stove, nor much talent as yet with American food. She did need help. Her confused feelings for Hannah notwithstanding, it wasn't fair that Culdee Creek's ranch hands be the ones to suffer.

"Fine," Claire whispered, pulling out her handkerchief and blowing her nose. "Hannah can help. But only until I can handle things myself. Then she goes back to her house."

"Of course. Hannah has enough work of her own as it is." Evan put on his Stetson, turned toward the back door, then paused. An amused look flared in his eyes. "You know, you might want to go up and wash your face before Hannah gets here. You've got flour all over it."

Claire touched her face. Once more, her cheeks warmed. Then, with a soft cry, she shoved back her chair, turned, and ran upstairs.

❦

Hannah was outside playing with her three youngest children, when Evan walked up. At the sight of her, his heart twisted. In the autumn sunlight, her pale gold hair glowed like a halo. Her skin was soft and smooth, her lips pink and full. When she looked up and saw him approach, her smile of welcome stirred old, painful memories.

But none of that mattered anymore, he fiercely reminded himself. She loved another, and so did he. Still, he had to admit he had missed her and her kind, gentle ways.

"Why, Evan MacKay," Hannah exclaimed, walking toward him and extending both hands, "what a pleasant surprise! Would you like to come in and visit for a spell? I have raisin applesauce cookies cooling, and the coffee's still fresh."

After the tumultuous episode with Claire just a few minutes ago, Evan found Hannah's hospitable offer most appealing. But he had work piling up even as they talked, not to mention he wasn't sure he could handle an extended visit with Hannah just yet. So, with a regretful smile and shake of his head, he declined.

"Best not today," he said, courteously removing his Stetson and taking both of her hands in his one. "Devlin's counting on me to ride the fence line and help repair any barbed wire that's come down."

"Yes, it *is* nearly the middle of October, and getting on toward the end of fall, isn't it?" She pulled her hands free, and rubbed her arms in an unconscious reminder of the winter cold. "There always seems to be so much work needing done in preparation for winter."

"Yeah, there is."

An uncomfortable silence settled then between them.

"So, how are you, Evan?" Hannah finally asked. "Since you left, you've never been far from my thoughts or prayers."

He glanced away, suddenly awkward and tongue-tied. "I'm doing okay." He looked back at her. "How about you?"

She smiled. "I'm very happy, Evan. The Lord has blessed me with a good man and wonderful children."

"Funny thing." Evan gave a sharp, bitter laugh. "I never thought I'd ever hear you speak of Devlin in such terms."

"Nor would I, especially after I first came to Culdee Creek. But he's changed, Evan. Truly he has."

"So he claims." As unwilling as Evan was to admit it, he was beginning to see the changes as well in his cousin. He just wasn't quite ready to put words to that acknowledgment.

Hannah eyed him intently. "I'm glad you finally found the right woman for you." She paused to brush a wind-blown tendril of hair from her face. "I never, ever, was that woman, you know."

He didn't particularly want to acknowledge that truth either, but he did. "No, I reckon you weren't, though it still hurt like the dickens anyway, when I lost you."

"But the pain's better now, isn't it?" she asked, a hopeful look in her eyes. "Now that you're back home? Now that you have Claire?"

"Yeah," he agreed with a smile, "I reckon it is." The intense pain, the seething anger, the aching sense of loss were indeed beginning to subside. The realization surprised—and heartened—him.

Evan hesitated, loath to burden Hannah with what he must next ask, but knowing he must. "Look, I've got to get to work. The reason I came by was to see if you could help Claire with the lunch and supper meals each day. Beth's pretty good helping out with breakfast, but school keeps her busy the rest of the day."

"Is Claire having problems with Old Bess?"

He chuckled. The cookstove was infamous around the ranch. "Yeah, and also with mastering a lot of the kind of stick-to-your-ribs cooking the hands need. She tries real hard, and will be able to do it all in time, but right now . . ."

"I'll be glad to help her." Hannah smiled warmly. "You only had to ask."

"I kind of figured you would." Evan stared down into her striking, turquoise blue eyes and, for an instant, lost himself once more in memories. "I'm much obliged."

"And I'm much obliged," she said, stepping closer, "for all the help you've been to Devlin since Abby and Conor left. He's really grateful for your support, you know?"

"Pa put him in charge, and I told Pa I'd do what had to be done."

"Still, I know it's been hard for you, Evan." Hannah lifted a hand to him, then, as if suddenly remembering herself, slowly let it fall to her side. "I just wanted you to know I'm sorry for all the pain I caused you, and hope you'll forgive me. I'd like to think that we might some-day be friends again."

"You did what you thought was best." He took her hand and gave it a quick squeeze. "In the end, that's all anyone can do."

"Yes," she murmured, stepping back, "that's all any-one can do."

Evan stood there for a moment longer, wanting to say more, but not knowing what to say. Then he shoved his Stetson back on his head. "Well, I'd best be going."

Hannah nodded. "Yes. And I'd best be gathering up the children and heading over to help Claire with lunch."

"Well, thanks again." He backed away, then turned and strode off in the direction of the barns. As he walked along, Evan's emotions roiled crazily. He was pleasantly surprised how well his first real talk with Hannah had gone. There had been no rancor on his part, no defen-siveness on hers. Sure, the confrontation had been tinged with a certain sadness, but overlying it, as well, was a strong sense of mutual caring and concern.

He supposed that caring and concern was what mattered most of all to him. Things would never be as they once were between them, but it was still good to know they might someday again be friends. Above everything else, he had always valued Hannah's friendship.

Yes, things were indeed looking up, he mused as he walked along. Then a sudden movement in the main house's upstairs bedroom caught his eye. He glanced up just in time to catch a glimpse of a lace curtain falling back in place.

Evan frowned. Claire had gone upstairs to wash her face. Had she been standing there the whole time, watching them? A fleeting unease curled within, then he firmly quashed it. Claire didn't know about him and Hannah. If she had been watching them, it was only because she was trying to ascertain Hannah's reaction to being asked to come help her.

He probably *should* tell her about Hannah sometime soon, though, Evan decided, as the already stiff breeze picked up, sending dirt and leaves careening around him. He had put it off too long as it was. Still, it might not be the greatest timing in the world to tell Claire right now. Best he wait a while longer, leastwise until Hannah finished teaching her what she needed to know.

ₑ

Somehow, Claire managed to make it through that long, blustery afternoon. She lost count of how many times she bit her tongue rather than deliver some peevish reply to Hannah's innocent questions or good-hearted comments. It was nothing, however, compared to her feelings of utter inadequacy with the mountain of information the blonde-haired woman offered. She found herself growing increasingly confused and frustrated.

Her fierce Highland pride, however, refused to allow her to admit her shortcomings. She'd understand it all in time, Claire kept telling herself. All she needed was just a little more time.

"Well, I suppose that's enough for one day, don't you think?" Hannah asked as she shoved three big dishes of beefsteak pie into the oven to bake. She straightened, wiped her flour-coated hands on her apron, and pushed a stray lock of hair behind her ear. "What with the boiled carrots and turnips, the fresh bread, and the custard for dessert, there should be enough food to please the men."

Claire, busy filling the sink with hot water to soak all the pots and pans, glanced up. "Aye, it should indeed. Thank you for your help today, Hannah."

Devlin's wife smiled. "Think nothing of it. When I first came to Culdee Creek, I had no cooking skills at all. It took Abby months to teach me enough to be of any help. You, on the other hand, only need a bit of fine tuning."

In spite of her determination to keep an emotional distance from Hannah, Claire brightened. "Do you really think so? I feel like such a dolt, dashing about the kitchen each day, frantically trying to prepare a decent meal on time."

"It just takes experience. Once you work out a schedule and develop some comfort with a variety of recipes, all this will seem easy." A considering look on her pretty face, Hannah untied her apron and removed it. "You know, for the time being, maybe it'd be best if you worked out a weekly menu. That way you can plan better, and incorporate any leftovers into one of the next day's meals."

"Aye," Claire agreed grudgingly, "that might be best."

"See what you can do tonight to plan lunch and supper for the rest of the week," Hannah said as she walked over and hung her apron on a peg near the stove. Behind them, a particularly forceful blast of wind slammed into the house. "In the morning, after breakfast, we'll look over your plan."

"But I don't know enough recipes to devise a whole week's worth of menus!" Claire protested, her frustration swelling anew. "Leastwise, not recipes that would please most of the men anyway."

"Here, use this." Hannah grabbed up a maroon, leather bound book from one of the cupboards and handed it to Claire. "It's the *Fannie Farmer Cookbook.* I can't tell you how many times I borrowed it from Abby when I first took over housekeeping and cooking for Devlin and his family."

Reluctantly, Claire accepted the book from Hannah. She hated feeling beholden to her, especially after the tender scene she had witnessed this morning between her and Evan. Watching them from the upstairs bedroom window, the last vestiges of doubt that the two had once shared some special relationship had vanished.

The truth was painfully clear. Hannah and Evan still cared for each other. All that remained to be discovered was how deeply.

To contain the jealous anger that suddenly flared within her, Claire clutched the book to her chest. "Thank you, Hannah," she managed to grit out the words. "I'll work on the menus this verra night."

Hannah nodded. "Then I'll leave you to finish up here while I head home." She walked over, picked up a chubby Bonnie and settled her on her hip, then took little Jackson's hand. "Come along, Mary," she called to the five-year-old who sat coloring quietly in the parlor. In but a few minute's time, Claire found herself once more alone in the kitchen.

With a sigh, she poured herself a cup of tea and carried it to the table. Wiping away a coating of flour where they had rolled out the piecrust topping for the beef-steak pie, she placed her cup on the table and sat.

Outside, the winds continued to blow, seemingly with even more force and fury now. It had started out such a quiet, peaceful day, Claire mused, her thoughts turning pensive. Yet, just as her feelings had become more turbulent and fitful as the day went on, so, it seemed, had the weather. The winds, however, appeared determined to continue their pounding, howling power, while all Claire wanted now was a bit of peace and quiet.

Confused emotions assailed her. All day Hannah had been patient and kind, tirelessly explaining everything and demonstrating various techniques that simplified the cooking process. She had shown Claire additional tricks to try to get Old Bess working at her best. And never once had she complained, or acted put out to be helping Claire.

It made it hard to harbor any grudges against the woman. If the truth were told, Claire could see why Evan had fallen in love with her. She could see why he might love her still.

That admission, however, was almost more than Claire could bear. She *must* talk to Evan about his past with Hannah. She knew she must. But the longer she put off that confrontation, the worse her fears became. The greater her doubts grew. And it wasn't as if, in the past eleven days since his parents had departed, Evan had been the easiest man to get along with, much less talk to.

What Claire needed was someone to confide in. Someone who could advise her about how best to handle this matter. But Abby was gone, and, considering Hannah was part of the problem, Devlin's wife could hardly serve as a confidante. There was, though, Claire realized in relief, Millie Starr.

But how to find enough time to ride to Grand View and visit the woman? she wondered. By the time she finished cleaning up after breakfast, it was time to start lunch preparations; and by the time she finished serving and cleaning up after lunch, it was time to start supper.

There *had* to be a way, Claire vowed—and she had to see Millie soon. This gnawing uncertainty couldn't go on much longer.

The parlor's front door opened. Two people stomped in, then the door slammed shut. "I told you, Elizabeth," Ian's voice rose, gruff and angry, "it's best you let me handle this. No one need be the wiser—"

A windblown Ian stalked into the kitchen and saw his sister sitting at the table. His next words died on his lips. He paled, and slid to a halt.

Claire gasped. "By mountain and sea, Ian Sutherland!" she cried, noting his black eye, bruised cheekbone, and split lip. "Whatever happened to you?" She pushed back her chair, stood, and hurried to him.

His shirt was torn at the shoulder, his trousers smeared with grass stains and mud, and his hands were scratched and abraded. A trickle of dried blood wound from his collar to the middle of his chest. Claire grabbed his hand to pull him closer. Ian hissed in pain and jerked back.

She eyed him suspiciously. "What's wrong with your hands, Ian? Let me see them."

"Nay." Firmly, her brother shook his head and shoved his hands into his trouser pockets. "There's naught wrong with them, save they're a wee bit bruised from punching some lads in their smug, sneering faces."

"Och, nay, Ian!" Claire rolled her eyes and shook her head. "Don't tell me you were fighting at school again!"

"He only did so to protect me," Beth declared hotly, stepping forward to stand at Ian's side. "Some boys started teasing me about me being half-Indian, and when they refused to heed Ian's warning to stop, he had no choice but to make them stop."

"Well," Claire muttered, eyeing her brother with stern disapproval, "you seem to have gotten on the losing end of the battle this time, lad." She grasped his shoulder and guided him to the chair she had just vacated. "Sit. I'll see what I can do to clean you up a bit."

"I'm fine," he grumbled. "And I didn't lose the battle. If you think *I* look bad, you should see the other three lads."

"Three lads, was it?" Claire took down a bowl, walked to the sink, and pumped it full of water. She grabbed a clean rag and bar of soap, then carried them all back to the table. "Beth, fetch Abby's medicine box, will you, lass?" she asked, casting the girl a look over her shoulder.

As Beth hurried to comply, Claire placed the items she had gathered on the table, then pulled up a chair facing Ian. Sitting, she wet the cloth in the water, rubbed soap on it, and began to gently cleanse her brother's face. "Was there no other way to stand up for Beth," she asked softly, "than to start a fight? You've hardly been in school a month, Ian, and already you're fighting again. This will not do, no matter the reason. Do you hear me, lad?"

"I won't have anyone speak ill of Elizabeth." He winced as she washed his bruised cheekbone. "For myself, they can call me what they will, but they won't speak ill of her!"

"Have the other children been saying things about you then, too?"

"Naught that I can't bear."

"And does your teacher know of all this?"

Ian grimaced, but whether from the discomfort of her ministrations or in disgust at the mention of his teacher, Claire couldn't tell.

"She thinks all the problems are of my doing. She says I have a chip on my shoulder."

"She used a cane on Ian today," Beth declared suddenly from the doorway, the medicine box in her hands. "That's why his hands hurt so."

Claire locked gazes with her brother. "Show me your hands, Ian."

"Och, Claire, it isn't aught to—"

"Show me your hands!"

Reluctantly, Ian lifted his hands. The palms were bright red, swollen, and the imprint of some long, slender object could be seen crisscrossing the flesh in several places. White-hot rage filled her.

"Here,"—she shoved the bowl of water toward him—"put your hands in there. It will help lessen the swelling." Her glance moved back to Beth. "And why did this teacher of yours see fit to whip my brother? Wasn't it enough that he got bruised and beaten fighting?"

"Miss Westerman said Ian was a troublemaker, and she was tired of it, so she aimed to teach him a lesson he wouldn't soon forget." The dark-haired girl's eyes filled with tears. "He could hardly hold his horse's reins on the way back home, it hurt him so." She shot Ian a moisture-bright, adoring look. "He's so brave, isn't he, Claire?"

"Aye," she muttered, "and foolishly impulsive and headstrong, too." She motioned to Beth. "Bring over the medicine box, lass. I need the salve."

Beth did as requested, and Claire soon had most of her brother's scrapes and bruises treated. His hands, however, were a different matter. Each time she looked at them, Claire seethed with renewed anger.

She pushed back her chair and rose. Both young people looked up at her. "Keep your hands in the water," she ordered her brother. "I'm going to the springhouse and bring back a chunk of ice to cool the water even more."

With that, Claire headed from the kitchen. She hadn't lied when she had told them she was going for some ice. First, though, she meant to seek out Evan and tell him what had occurred. Something had to be done about a certain Miss Westerman. Claire figured her husband was just the man for the job.

15

Tribulation worketh patience; And patience, experience; and experience, hope.

Romans 5:3–4

As Claire headed toward the barns, there was shouting. Several men ran toward the second barn farther down the hill. Apprehension filled her. Gathering her skirts, Claire hurried to join the small group forming at the building's far end.

There on the ground lay Devlin, face contorted in pain, right leg bent and twisted behind his left one. "Bl-blast it!" he groaned. "I-I think it's broken."

Claire shoved her way past the ranch hands standing there staring down at him. She knelt beside Devlin. "What happened?"

"I was on the barn roof with Frank"—even as he spoke, Claire glanced up just in time to see the tall, lanky Irishman climb down the ladder propped against the barn and hurry over—"when a really strong gust of wind knocked me off balance. I-I tumbled backward and couldn't stop myself in time. I fell on my right leg and . . . and I heard something snap when I hit."

"Boss, are you all right?" Frank Murphy, black-bearded and skin a tanned leather, knelt beside Devlin and Claire. "I swear I lost ten years from my life when I saw you fall." He pulled off his sweat-stained, brown sombrero and crushed it in his hands. "I tried to grab for you, but it was too late."

"It wasn't your fault." Devlin lifted his left leg and tried to pull his right leg from beneath it. Even the slightest movement of his right leg, however, elicited a grimace.

"Wait, Devlin," Claire ordered, grasping him by the shoulder. "Let me check your leg first before you try moving it again." When he complied, she carefully ran her hands down his leg. Just a few inches below his knee, Claire found the deformity.

"You're right." She glanced up and met his pain-darkened gaze. "It's broken."

Devlin muttered under his breath.

She looked to the Irishman. "We'll need some rags and boards to splint the leg. And you, Henry"–Claire met the young newlywed's gaze–"ride to town and bring the doctor."

"Someone get Hannah," Devlin groaned. "Just be sure to tell her I'm all right. Don't go scaring the wits out of her."

"Aye," Claire agreed. She looked to another hand, Wendell Chapman. "On your way up to get Hannah, stop by the main house and take Beth with you. She can watch the children for Hannah. And have Hannah bring blankets. We can fashion a litter for Devlin with them and some poles. And we need to find Evan, too. Does anyone know where he is?"

"He's out with H. C. and Jonah Goldman in the east pastures mending fences," Frank volunteered, returning with a handful of rags and two narrow boards as Wendell set off toward Devlin and Hannah's house. "I'll ride out and fetch them. It'll only take about twenty minutes to get there and back."

"Well, get on with you then," Claire said. "We'll most likely need all your help to carry Devlin back to his house."

"What about Ian?" the big foreman asked as he gingerly shoved to one elbow. "He's a strong lad. He can help."

Claire shook her head, the unpleasant reminder of why she had come outside in the first place freshly assailing her. "Nay, he can't help. His hands are in a bad way."

Devlin frowned. "What happened?"

"Some problems at school today," she ground out. "But enough of him right now." She took the rags and boards from Frank. "We need to get your leg splinted."

As Claire began to tear the rags into long, thick strips, the Irishman strode off toward a saddled horse tethered nearby. By the time Hannah, face pale, eyes wide, ran back down with Wendell, Claire had Devlin's leg snugly splinted and was tying off the last cloth strip at his ankle.

"Devlin," Hannah cried, sinking to her knees beside him. "What happened?" She slid her hands beneath his head to cradle it in her lap, and brushed the hair from his eyes. "Are you all right?"

Her husband managed a wan smile. "Right enough, considering. Broke my leg, though."

"So I see. And how many times have I warned you to stay off high places when these winds kick up?" she scolded, managing a smile though her eyes filled with tears.

"Too many to count. This time I gambled and lost."

"Are you sure nothing else is broken or damaged?"

He shrugged. "Apart from some sore spots that I'm sure will be black-and-blue tomorrow, I'd say I got off pretty lucky."

"And *I'd* say the Lord was looking out for you this time."
His grin widened. "Yeah, I'd reckon so."

Watching them, Claire knew that, as far as Hannah was concerned, the only man in her life now was her husband. Any continued feelings of love between her and Evan—if there *were* any indeed—were now strictly on Evan's side. Somehow that realization heartened her, if only a little.

To quiet her renewed tumult of emotions, Claire turned to Wendell. "Come, while we wait for Evan and the others, let's prepare the litter. The sooner we get Devlin up to his house and in bed, the better."

They didn't have long to wait once the litter was ready. Ten minutes later, Evan and the two hands rode up. A concerned look on his face, Evan dismounted and strode over. "Decided to see if you could fly today, did you?" he asked, staring down at his cousin.

"Something like that," Devlin drawled, shooting him a wry look from the corner of his eye. "Thought the high winds might just do the trick."

H. C. and Jonah pulled up beside Evan. He gestured toward the litter. "Is that ready?"

Claire nodded. "Aye."

The men soon had Devlin on the litter and were headed up to his house, Hannah and Claire following. After a few anxious moments maneuvering the litter through the front door without dumping out Devlin, he was finally put to bed. The hands then left, leaving Evan and the two women behind.

His Stetson in his hands, Evan lingered at the bedside, looking uncomfortable, but as if he'd like to say something. Claire met Hannah's gaze, who smiled and lifted a finger to her lips.

"What do you want to do about the ranch?" Evan finally asked. "I'll take over all the physical aspects of running it, if you'd like, unless you've someone else in mind for the job . . ."

"You've got enough work of your own to do," Devlin said, shifting his broken leg in an apparent attempt to position it more comfortably on the two pillows Hannah had put beneath it. "But if you think you can also take on the work I was doing, I don't know of a better man for the job."

After a fleeting instant of disbelief, Evan's expression brightened. His chin lifted; his shoulders squared. "I'll do whatever it takes. I won't let Pa, or you, down."

Devlin gazed up at him for a long, considering moment, then nodded. "I know you won't, Evan." He paused to scratch his jaw. "I can take over all the paperwork and ranch accounts you were handling. And we can meet each night after supper and plan things out for the next day."

"Sounds good to me."

Evan glanced at Claire then, and her heart thrilled at the look of excitement gleaming in his eyes. At last, she thought, he'd finally have a chance to prove himself to his father—and to Devlin.

A carriage pulled up outside and, from her vantage near the window, Claire could see an older man climb down and pull his black medical bag from behind the seat. "The doctor's here," she announced.

Hannah hurried from the room, and Evan stepped back.

"Well, best I be going and get everyone back to their chores," he said.

"Yeah, best you do," Devlin replied with a grin.

Evan hesitated. "I just want to thank you for the chance to do this, Devlin. And to tell you I'm much obliged for the trust you're placing in me."

His cousin's smile faded, and he met Evan's gaze eye-to-eye. "It's time, and you and I both know it."

"Yeah," Evan agreed, a slow grin spreading across his face. "Still, it's sure good to hear you say it. Too bad it took a fall off the barn for you to finally give credit where credit's due."

Devlin laughed as Hannah, accompanied by the doctor, entered the room. "Well, never let it be said that we MacKays aren't a bull-headed, hard-nosed lot."

His cousin chuckled softly. "Oh, I don't think there'll ever be much danger of that." Evan then took Claire by the arm and escorted her from the room.

ᘖ

"The ham's all sliced, I've brought a jar of pickles up from the springhouse, the vegetable soup is simmering nicely, and there'll be the cookies for dessert." Claire paused in her litany to make sure she hadn't forgotten anything. "Och, aye, and wait until just before lunch to slice the bread loaves, so they'll have enough time to cool and dry out a bit. I should be back by two o'clock or so. We can get started on supper then."

Beth, sitting at the kitchen table rolling small balls of cookie dough between her hands before placing them on a cookie sheet, nodded for what Claire knew must be the umpteenth time. "I think I can manage. If I run into any problems, there's always Hannah."

"Aye, there's always Hannah, but what with Devlin's freshly broken leg, I'm sure she has her hands verra full right now. I don't want to impose unless absolutely necessary."

The girl gave a long-suffering sigh. "I know, Claire."

Claire grinned. "I'm sorry if I'm blathering on. I suppose I feel rather guilty for keeping you out of school today."

"Well, *I'm* not feeling guilty at all." Beth gave an injured sniff. "After how Miss Westerman treated Ian

213

yesterday, I don't care if I ever set foot in her classroom again! I'm just glad you didn't make Ian go back either, until you have a talk with that woman."

"Aye, but in Ian's case it's because he needs a few days for his hands to heal. And, since today's Friday, what with the weekend he's only missing a day of school."

Claire walked to the bench by the back door, taking up her bonnet beside her handbag and big straw basket. She placed the hat on her head and tied its ribbons snugly beneath her chin. Then, basket and bag in hand, she turned back to Beth.

"Make sure, will you, that Ian soaks his hands in cool water for about fifteen minutes at least once while I'm gone, and that he then puts some of that soothing salve on them. And would you also tell Evan that I've taken the buggy to Grand View? He came to bed so late last night I was already asleep, and left so fast this morning with his breakfast half eaten that I never had a chance to inform him of my plans."

"Sure, I'll tell him." Beth scraped back her chair, stood, and, with the now full cookie sheet in her hands, walked to Old Bess. She paused there to glance back at Claire. "Was there anything else? If not, shouldn't you be on your way? You'll have to hurry if you hope to see Miss Westerman, then get your supplies at Gates' Mercantile, and still be home by two."

"Och, I suppose so," Claire said with a laugh, as she walked across the kitchen into the hallway leading to the parlor. "See you soon, then."

Beth's parting farewell followed her across the parlor and out the front door. One of the hands had brought up the carriage, and a gray mare named Jenny was harnessed in, ready to go. Claire placed her handbag inside the basket, set the basket behind the buggy seat, and, after unfastening the reins tied to the brake arm, climbed in.

Though she really wanted to learn to ride astride one of these days, at this point she was grateful to have finally mastered a horse and buggy. But mayhap, just mayhap, Claire mused as she gently slapped the reins over Jenny's back and the mare set out, after she gained the necessary kitchen expertise she still needed, riding lessons could be her next undertaking. After all, she couldn't call herself a proper western woman, could she, until she learned to ride?

❦

"This isn't quite as simple a matter as you might think, Mrs. MacKay," Alice Westerman explained forty-five minutes later. She paused to gaze out the window near her desk at her pupils playing on the makeshift playground, then turned back to Claire, "This isn't the first fight Ian has been in since school started. In fact, he gets in one nearly twice a week, and school's only been in session a month."

Claire's high pitch of indignant anger dropped a notch. "I didn't know . . . this is the first time he's come home all bruised and bloody . . ."

"Ian's a pretty tough fighter. Until yesterday, he also only took on one boy at a time." The pretty brunette schoolteacher sighed, momentarily averted her gaze, then looked back at Claire. "Yesterday, however, he must have decided it was time to move up to a full-fledged brawl."

"Ian said he was defending Beth's honor, that those boys were calling her names."

"He may well have been. It's obvious he's devoted to her. But that doesn't excuse the fighting, and he knows it. I've warned him about it several times already."

Claire felt sick to her stomach. Not again, she thought. Not here, too, in America. "You were right to cane him,

215

then. I just wish you'd have used his backside, rather than his hands."

"I would've, if I'd thought it would've made an impression." Miss Westerman's brown eyes darkened with regret. "I don't like physical discipline, Mrs. MacKay, but there are rules, and other parents have begun to complain . . ." She paused to rearrange a stack of papers on her desk. "What's going on with Ian, if you don't mind me asking? I know the adjustment to life here must be hard, but he doesn't seem to be settling down at all. His attitude is so wary and brittle . . . well, it's almost as if he expects trouble and is trying to get the jump on it. And his class work isn't up to the level I sense he's capable of either."

Fighting . . . an attitude . . . poor school performance . . . With a sinking heart, Claire realized she had been totally unaware of what had been going on with her brother of late. Since Abby and Conor had left, there hardly seemed a spare minute in the day for Ian, or Evan, or even for herself.

It probably hadn't helped any that things seemed increasingly strained between her and her husband, either. Ian had always been a bellwether, mirroring the direction of her own moods before she even recognized them herself. In some ways they had always been too close, too sensitive to each other.

"I've also had to have some words with Beth and Ian about their unseemly affection for each other." At Claire's shocked expression, Alice Westerman hurried to explain. "Now, before you jump to the wrong conclusions, I want to assure you that they are strictly supervised at all times, so nothing inappropriate has occurred. But the two of them only seem to spend recess time in each other's company, and there's been more than a few occasions when I've seen them holding hands."

"There's naught wrong with a bit of hand-holding," Claire protested, her ire rising again.

"No, there isn't," the young teacher was quick to reply. "But Beth's just thirteen, and back in school for the first time in a long while. She needs to make friends with her classmates, especially other girls her age." She gave a troubled sigh. "The same could be said for Ian, too, if he'd just stop taking offense at every turn and getting into fights. But it's Beth I'm most concerned about, considering her past history. This time, I want school to be a successful experience for her."

Alice Westerman was a kind, concerned teacher. Claire could see that now. She cared about her students—even Ian. It would be wise to enlist her aid in dealing with her brother. The way things were heading, Claire thought glumly, Ian would soon need all the allies he could muster.

"I'll have to have a talk with Ian," she said. "I can't know what is really bothering him until I do. When I find out, though, I'll tell you. I appreciate your concern for him—and for Beth, too—and will do all I can to aid you with them."

"Is Mr. MacKay aware of these problems? Beth is his sister, isn't she?"

"Aye." Claire nodded. "He doesn't know yet, though. We had an emergency at the ranch yesterday, and I haven't had a chance yet to tell him. I'd like to see if you and I couldn't solve this problem between the two of us first. Evan's so burdened just now with worries and extra responsibilities, what with his father and stepmother gone, and now his cousin breaking his leg . . . I'd like to spare him this if it's at all possible."

Miss Westerman eyed her quietly, then nodded. "Well, we'll see if that can be done. It can't hurt to try." She glanced over her shoulder at the clock hanging on the wall. "It's time I call the children in from recess. Is there anything else you wish to discuss, Mrs. MacKay?"

"Nay." Claire climbed to her feet. "You've given me a lot to think on. It'll take me a time to sort through it all." She held out her hand, and the teacher, who had by this time walked around her desk to meet her, accepted it. "I thank you for your time, and for your concern."

"That's my job, Mrs. MacKay."

"Aye," Claire agreed, releasing her hand, "but I don't think every teacher holds to your high standards."

Alice Westerman smiled. "You're very kind to say that."

"I only speak the truth, Miss Westerman." Claire hesitated, then nodded. "I bid you good day, then."

❦

Ten minutes later, Claire entered Gates' Mercantile, where Russell Gates, the general store's proprietor, hurried over to greet her.

"Welcome, Mrs. MacKay," the gray-haired man in his mid-sixties said. "What can I do for you today?"

He was a pleasant sort, Claire decided, of medium height and build, with a pair of spectacles that seemed perpetually smudged and perched on the end of his nose. "I've a few items I need," she replied, as she tugged her bonnet free of her head to hang from her neck by its ribbons. "Those ranch hands eat more food than an army on the march."

"Well, then, we'd better see what we can do for you." He took the list she offered him. "Flour, sugar, lard, beans, coffee, tea, salt, and baking soda. Hmmm, I've got most of what you want here on the shelves, but the sugar, coffee, and tea just arrived this morning, and I've yet to unpack the crates. Give me about ten minutes and I'll have those items out for you."

218

"Take your time, Mr. Gates." Claire set her basket and handbag on the long table holding the bolts of fabric, and began to mosey up and down its length. "I'm sure I can entertain myself looking around."

The older man disappeared through the door at the back of the store, and, for a time, Claire busied herself fingering the colorful calicos, ginghams, and heavier wools and serges stacked up in neat piles on the long cutting table. Her thoughts, however, soon drifted to her earlier discussion with Ian's teacher. How was she ever, she wondered, going to set things aright with her brother? Behind her, the sound of the door opening tugged vaguely at her awareness, but Claire was so engrossed in her troubled musings she didn't bother to look up.

"So, where did you come from?" an unfamiliar male voice rose suddenly from close behind her. "I haven't been back in town long, but I'm certain I wouldn't have missed a pretty little lady like you."

Claire whirled around. Before her stood a tall, swarthy-complexioned man with coal black hair and cold, fathomless eyes. Clad in black boots and trousers, a dark green shirt, and a black leather vest, he was dressed with immaculate care, not a hair out of place, not even a smudge of dust on his spit-shined boots. In his hands he held a black, plantation-style hat.

Still, in spite of his impressive appearance and admiring words, there was something about him that didn't sit right with Claire. She glanced around, belatedly realizing they were the only two people in the store. Would Mr. Gates hear her if she needed help? Indeed, what would the old man be able to do against the far younger, powerfully built stranger?

Then, as swiftly as the apprehension assailed her, it was gone. Silly fool, she chided herself. Your imagination's running away with you. You're in no danger here.

She lifted her chin and held out her hand. "My name's Claire MacKay. Evan MacKay's my husband."

At the mention of the MacKay name, something dark and malevolent scudded across his features. "Well, well," he growled. "Seems in the time I've been unavoidably detained elsewhere, young Evan has gone and found himself a sweet young bride." He cocked his head. "And where are you from, missy? England? Ireland?"

"Scotland. I'm from Scotland. And who might you be?"

"Me?" The man's handsome mouth twisted wryly. "Why, I'm Brody Gerard." He reached out and touched her hair. "That's the most beautiful shade of red I've ever seen. A man could near to lose his mind, running his fingers through it, or watching it tumble down your back."

As he spoke, his hand slid to the bun at the nape of her neck. He pulled a pin free. Shocked at his audacity at even touching her, it took that tug on her hair as he removed the pin to jerk Claire back to action. She gasped, and slapped his hand before leaping back.

"How dare you?" she cried. "I haven't given you leave–"

Brody's hand shot out, grabbed her arm, and pulled her to him. "Now, now, little missy," he drawled, his voice dropping to a low whisper, "don't go and get riled up. I only want to see what your hair looks like, all pretty and wild around your shoulders. Hold still, let me finish, and everything will be just fine."

"It most certainly will *not*, you big lummox!" To punctuate her words, Claire kicked him smartly in the shin.

With a foul string of curses, Brody Gerard released her and jumped back. He bent for an instant, rubbing his injured shin. Then he glanced back up, his gaze incensed, his mouth gone thin and hard.

"That wasn't a very smart thing to do, missy. Especially you being one of the MacKays now, and all."

220

Claire backed away. There was something in his look that sent a tremor of fear through her. One way or another, she decided, she needed to find Mr. Gates, and fast!

At that moment the front door opened. The sound of footsteps, masculine by the tread, carried to Claire. Relief swamped her. She wrenched her gaze from Brody Gerard's. The newest visitor, however, was none other than the Reverend Noah Starr.

Her heart sank. Somehow, she doubted that this man standing before her had any respect for the clergy, or would defer to it in any way. Still, the priest *was* a witness, and maybe just the distraction she needed.

"Good day to you, Reverend Starr," Claire called, even if her voice did come out as little more than a hoarse croak. "I was planning on paying your aunt a wee visit, just as soon as Mr. Gates returns with my supplies."

At her words, Brody Gerard turned slowly to face the Reverend Starr. From her position to one side of the dark-haired man, she could see the expressions change on the priest's face from one of mild surprise, to a dawning awareness of the situation, to a firm, unyielding resolve. Apprehension filled her. What had she drawn Noah Starr into?

"Why, hello, Brody. I'd heard talk you'd returned to Grand View," Noah said quietly. "Just passing through, or looking to find new employment here?"

Brody shrugged. "Can't say as how I've decided just yet. Don't think Sadie will take me back, do you?"

"Miss Fleming isn't known for her kind or forgiving nature, especially toward you since you robbed her." The young priest met the taller man's stare. "But then, after your time in prison, I had hoped you'd have learned your lesson—decided maybe to take up more respectable employment than working as a bodyguard at a bordello."

"So you think a man like me can change his ways, do you, Padre?"

A faint smile touched Noah's lips. "Yes, I do."

"Well, maybe I can, and maybe I can't." Brody leered over his shoulder at Claire. "I don't aim to begin today, though." He turned back to the priest. "I suggest you do the smart thing and leave the way you came. This pretty lady and I have some unfinished business."

"Now what would be the point of that?" Noah quietly demanded. "You heard Mrs. MacKay say she was heading over to the rectory after she was done here. I think I'll just wait on her, and escort her there."

"And what if I tell you I'll walk her there later myself?"

Noah leaned over and met Claire's gaze. "Would you like Mr. Gerard or me to walk you back, Mrs. MacKay?"

"Och, you, of course, Father Starr," she choked out. "As a matter of fact, I had a few things I wished to discuss with you, so it'd be a perfect opportunity to do so."

"Well, I guess it's settled then, isn't it?" The Reverend Starr straightened and looked back at Brody. "The lady would find it more convenient to accompany me."

Claire could see the big man's hands fist at his sides, and his shoulders hunch. For a terrified instant, she feared he meant to attack Noah Starr. Then, with a shuffle of feet and a clatter of metal containers, Mr. Gates emerged from the back room.

"Here's the coffee and tea you asked for, Mrs. MacKay," the store's proprietor said. "I'm still looking for the—" As he caught sight of the three of them standing there, a shaggy gray brow arched in puzzlement. "Well, howdy do, Reverend Starr," he called out as he recognized Noah. "And who's your friend? Can't say as how I—"

Brody Gerard shot him a seething look over his shoulder. Mr. Gates stopped short and blanched. Then, with a vicious curse, Brody strode up to Noah Starr, paused a moment to glare down at him, and stormed from the store.

16

In their mouth was found no guile: for they are without fault before the throne of God.

Revelations 14:5

In the aftermath of Brody Gerard's abrupt departure, tremors wracked Claire's body. She clasped her arms tightly about herself, more frightened by her unnerving reaction than she had ever been with Brody Gerard. Then memories, of a night that now seemed years ago, engulfed her. Memories of her uncle, once again speaking filthy words while he all but undressed her with his eyes, and then the horrible feel of his hands, coarse and dirty as he grabbed her, tearing at her clothes, pulling her close.

"Mrs. MacKay? Claire?" A hand came seemingly out of nowhere to gently touch her arm. "Are you all right?"

With a gasp, she jerked away. "D-don't," she cried, struggling to escape the hideous scene still playing in her mind. "Don't touch me!"

223

"Then I won't," the kind voice came again. From somewhere far away, a chair scraped across a wooden floor. "It might be best, though, if you have a seat. You've been through a pretty upsetting time just now. And you don't look all that well either."

Claire blinked. Her vision cleared, and she was back in Gates' Mercantile. A smiling Noah Starr stood beside her, his hands gripping the top of a well-worn, bent back wooden chair.

"Sit, Mrs. MacKay," he urged again.

Without protest or further hesitation, Claire did as she was told. Gradually, the room stopped spinning. Her breathing slowed, became deeper.

"Feeling any better?" the young priest inquired, leaning over and around to scan her face.

"A-aye." Claire managed a fierce nod, which only sent the room whirling yet again. "Well, almost, anyway."

"Shall I fetch her some water? Or get my wife's smelling salts?" Mr. Gates hurried over to them.

A pair of brown eyes, surprisingly flecked with green and gold, met hers. "Well, Mrs. MacKay?" Noah Starr asked. "Do you need smelling salts, or a glass of water?"

"Claire," she ground out, inexplicably fixing on the priest's continued formal use of her name. Somehow, it irritated her, especially after what he had just done for her in standing up to Brody Gerard. "Please, call me Claire. And nay, I don't need water or smelling salts. All I need is to sit here for a minute more, and I'll be fine."

"Then I'll go on and package up all your supplies, if that's okay with you," Mr. Gates offered. "That way, once you're ready to leave, you won't have to wait on your purchases."

"Aye." She shot him a grateful, if wan, smile. "That'd be most appreciated."

Noah squatted before her. "Did Mr. Gerard harm you, or touch you in any unseemly way? If he did, you could press charges. With his past record, this time Sheriff Whitmore wouldn't hesitate to lock him up."

"His . . . record?" For an instant, Claire couldn't quite grasp the implications of the priest's words. She couldn't seem to grasp anything, save how handsome Noah Starr was with his finely molded mouth and well-hewn features. How his wavy, dark blond hair framed his face and set off his warm, concerned brown eyes . . .

Then she remembered herself. "Aye, I heard you mention he'd been in prison," she choked out. "Whatever did the man do?"

"Kidnapped Hannah, intending to sell her to some madame in Breckenridge. Before that, though, he managed to get himself in plenty of trouble working for Sadie Fleming's bordello right here in Grand View. Had a few run-ins with Conor over Abby, too, before I came here, or so I've been told, and then with Devlin over Hannah." Noah shook his head. "In case you couldn't tell, Brody doesn't feel any too kindly toward the MacKays."

Her mouth twitched with wry humor. "Aye, I gathered that right off."

"Your supplies are ready, Mrs. MacKay, when you're ready to take them," Mr. Gates announced just then from behind the main counter.

"Och, aye." Claire pushed to her feet, where she stood for a few seconds until the freshened wave of dizziness subsided. "Give me a moment, and I'll bring you my basket." She gestured toward the straw basket still sitting where she had left it on the long cutting table.

"Please, permit me . . . Claire." Noah retrieved the basket, then carried it to Mr. Gates. With slow, careful steps, Claire passed by the fabric table, picked up her handbag, and joined the two men. The straw hamper was soon filled, the bill added to the Culdee Creek account.

Noah Starr, however, refused to let her take the now food-laden basket. "Allow me to carry it for you. Is that your buggy tied up out front?"

She nodded. "Aye."

He offered her his free arm, which, after a moment's hesitation, Claire accepted. "Then we're off." Reverend Starr glanced over his shoulder at the store's proprietor. "Thank you, Mr. Gates, and have a blessed day!"

As they stepped outside, the midday sun seemed blindingly bright. Claire blinked and tugged her bonnet back up onto her head to shade her eyes. When they reached her buggy, Noah placed her basket behind the seat, then paused.

"Are you still of a mind to speak with Millie?" he asked.

"Aye," Claire replied. "I can't get much free time for myself these days, and since I don't know when I'll be in town next . . ."

"Fine." He grasped her arm and guided her around to the passenger's side of the buggy. "Then I'll drive you to the rectory. Once you get a good, strong cup of tea and some of Millie's freshly baked crumb cake into you, you'll feel a lot better." With that, Noah helped Claire climb into the carriage, then made his way back around and jumped into the driver's side.

Neither spoke much on the short ride to the rectory. Claire—for some reason that she didn't care just then to examine—felt uncomfortably aware of Noah's presence beside her. Her cheeks hot with embarrassment, she surreptitiously scooted even farther from her companion. Dear Lord, she prayed, deliver me from my foolish thoughts. Quiet my unsettled, bewildered heart. Help me, for I don't understand what is happening to me.

Almost in answer to her prayers, Noah drew up before the rectory. He handed the reins to her, hopped down, and soon had Jenny tethered to the hitching post just outside the white picket fence. Then he walked around to Claire's side.

"Here," he said, lifting his arms to her, "let me help you down."

Claire was tempted to motion him away, rather than risk the feel of his hands on her right now. But she also mistrusted her steadiness. Placing her hands on Noah's broad shoulders, she leaned on him as he grasped her about the waist and helped her from the buggy.

The Reverend Starr was powerful. There was no doubt of that, after the effortless way he swung her to the ground. And he smelled of soap and clean skin, too, she realized, increasingly dismayed over her heightened awareness of him.

"We can leave your basket in the buggy," Noah was saying. "There's nothing perishable in it, is there?"

"What?" Like one rousing from a deep slumber, Claire jerked herself awake. "Och, nay. There's naught perishable in the basket."

"Well, come along then." Once more, Noah offered his arm. "Let's see if Millie's about someplace."

They entered the house, only to realize Millie was nowhere to be found. A note on the kitchen table, however, soon informed the priest that his aunt was out on an errand of mercy, visiting a new mother and her child.

He glanced up at Claire. "Well, she should be back shortly." He smiled in that quiet, unassuming way of his. "In the meantime, there's no reason I can't brew us a pot of tea and serve up a slice or two of crumb cake."

"Och, that won't be necessary, Reverend Starr," Claire immediately protested. "I know you must be busy. Get on with whatever you have to do. I can wait on your aunt by myself."

"Maybe you can, but then again, you and I haven't had much opportunity to talk in quite a while." He walked to a white-painted cupboard decorated with cheery flowers and took down a porcelain teapot and two cups and saucers. "Unless, of course, you'd prefer to be alone with your thoughts?"

"Och, nay." Despite her unsettled feelings for him, Claire refused to appear rude or ungrateful. "I just didn't wish to impose."

Noah placed the teapot and cups on the table, quickly prepared a tea strainer with tea leaves, then took up the kettle of water steaming on the cookstove. "You're not. I can use with a bracing cup of tea myself, after that run-in with Brody. I was beginning to worry there that I might have to resort to fisticuffs to convince him to leave you be."

With disbelieving eyes, Claire stared up at him as he poured the hot water through the tea strainer. "You know how to box?"

He shot her a boyish grin as he walked back to the stove to return the kettle. "One can't study all the time, even in seminary. I used to get out to the local Young Men's Christian Association at least three or four times a week. In addition to my boxing workouts there, I also played on a baseball team. Even now, far from a gymnasium, I still try to keep up with my boxing. Or as best as I can, anyway, without a sparring partner."

No wonder he possessed such a strong, well-toned physique, Claire thought. "It just seems strange, you being a priest and all," she hastened to explain. "Boxing is such a brutal sport."

"Yes, it is," he admitted. "But I didn't see any harm in learning it for the sheer physical training it provided. Besides," he added with a grin, "I figured I might as well, in case I should someday need to rescue a beautiful damsel in distress, as you were today."

Though his mouth was curved into a teasing smile, Claire blushed nonetheless. "Did I ever thank you for that? I can't remember."

"Considering all the confusion, it doesn't matter if you did or didn't. I knew my efforts were appreciated."

"Aye, they were indeed."

Another silence fell, as they both seemed to think it time to take a sip of their tea. The beverage was hot and strong, and just what Claire needed. She found myriad excuses, though, from stirring sugar into her tea, to retasting it, to then fiddling with her spoon, to avoid meeting the young priest's gaze.

"How have things been going for you at Culdee Creek, Claire?" Noah finally asked. "You've been here about two months now, and I've been meaning to ask how you and Ian were doing."

Claire's glance, which had momentarily lifted when he first spoke, fell back to her tea. Maddening tears filled her eyes. Though she fought fiercely to hold them back, they seemed to have a mind of their own, and gushed forth as copiously as the emotions they presaged.

"Och, I don't know how things are going anymore," she sobbed, burying her face in her hands. "Ian's in trouble at school. I-I can't seem to cook a decent meal or hold up my end in supporting Evan s-since his parents left. I can b-barely abide Hannah in my house since I discovered she was Evan's great love, and I feel like E-Evan and I-I are slowly drifting apart."

"Whoa, hold on there." Noah laid a hand on her bent head, caressing it gently. "Let's start from the beginning here, which, if I don't miss my guess, stems mostly from problems with your marriage."

"A-aye, I suppose s-so," she wept.

"How did you find out about Hannah?" He pulled back his hand, paused, then shoved a big, white handkerchief into her line of vision. "Evidently Evan didn't tell you, or you wouldn't be so upset."

"Mary S-Sue." Claire took the handkerchief. Lifting her head, she wiped her eyes, then blew her nose. "She told me all about them one day before the quilting society meeting."

Noah sighed and shook his head. "When *will* that girl cease her vendetta against Hannah? I've yet to understand why Mary Sue hates her so."

"Who wouldn't be jealous of Hannah? She's so beautiful and kind, and I've yet to see a man—no matter the age—who doesn't gaze on her with yearning and admiration." Claire blew her nose again. "I fear Evan may love her still. Why else hasn't he ever told me about her?"

The priest's mouth quirked. "Men, poor sad fools that we sometimes are, can frequently err in how we decide to protect someone we love. I'm willing to bet that's exactly what Evan thought he was doing, especially when he knew you and Hannah would be living so near each other."

"Mayhap," she admitted with a sniffle, "but it was hurtful, nonetheless, what he did. It would've been far more easily accepted if I'd heard the truth from him first, rather than from some gossipy, spiteful girl."

"Yes, it would've." Frowning in thought, Noah leaned back in his chair. "The Lord, though, is offering you an opportunity to grow beyond this, Claire. Love can have no strings on it, but must be given freely through good times and bad. And you and I both know Evan is a good man. He's just new at being a husband."

"Well, I'm new at being a wife," she wailed, "but I haven't betrayed—" She stopped short, as the recollection of her admiring thoughts about Noah Starr flooded her. Heat surged up to warm her cheeks. Claire looked away.

She hadn't exactly *betrayed* her husband, she thought, struggling to justify her earlier actions. She had just been so very grateful to Noah for protecting her from Brody Gerard, that she had overstepped herself. Besides, she had been half-dizzy with fear and relief. That would've made anyone's head spin, and thoughts take surprising turns.

Surely a passing attraction for a kind, handsome man was hardly the same as her husband's secretly, and perhaps still deeply held, affection for an old flame.

"Listen to me, Claire." As if to add emphasis to his next words, the priest leaned across the table and took both of her hands, holding them between his. "You've got to talk to Evan about this right away. Marriage requires more than just love. It requires trust, respect, and a deep, abiding commitment day in and day out. After the first flush of the courtship and honeymoon are over, at times you have to work at the marriage, laying a strong foundation for the years to come."

She gave an unsteady laugh. "And how would you know what a marriage takes? Have you ever been in love, much less wed?"

Noah smiled sadly. "No, I've yet to marry, but I've fancied myself in love a few times. My most enduring relationship, though, has been with that of the greatest Lover of all—the Lord. And I'll tell you true, Claire, it hasn't always been easy. There have been times I wanted to give up, turn my back on Him, because following in His footsteps was so very hard. There were times when I felt as if He had deserted me, even betrayed me to my enemies. And I know there will be times like that again, too. Each day I have to start anew, and hope my love for God will carry me through.

"Don't you see?" he finished, giving her hands a squeeze. "Though I've never been married, I do know something about love and commitment."

Claire gazed at Noah's dear, earnest face and knew he spoke from the heart. There was wisdom in his words, though it would take time for her to sort through it all. But sort through it all she would. It was the very least she owed to Evan—and their marriage.

A smile of dawning hope on her lips, Claire leaned toward him. "Thank you. I'll—"

"Well, there you are, Nephew!" Just then Millie rounded the corner and caught sight of Noah. "I was beginning to wonder—" His aunt's voice faded as she apparently noticed Claire, her hands still clasped in Noah's. "Well, land sakes," she whispered in surprise, glancing from one to the other. "Land sakes . . ."

There was a movement behind her, and another woman stepped quickly into view. Her eyes widened at the scene before her. Then, ever so slowly, a smile lifted her lips.

Meeting Mary Sue Edgerton's avid gaze, Claire's stomach gave a great lurch. Then, noting the direction the girl was staring, Claire glanced back and saw her hands still clasped within Noah's. She blushed furiously and swiftly pulled free.

It was too late, though. A triumphant, calculating gleam had flared to life in Mary Sue's eyes. And, some-how, Claire doubted the girl's assessment of their inno-cent meeting boded well—for either her or the Reverend Noah Starr.

17

Nothing is secret, that shall not be made manifest; neither any thing hid, that shall not be known.

Luke 8:17

That afternoon, once lunch had been served and the dishes washed and put away, Claire sought out Ian. She soon found him on the front porch with Beth. The two made a sweetly innocent pair, sitting with hands clasped together on the white-washed swing, talking softly as they swayed to and fro. Claire was almost tempted to tiptoe away and leave them to their harmless little tryst.

Almost.

There were things, however, that needed to be discussed and hopefully resolved with her brother, things that wouldn't improve with waiting. Some of those things not only involved school, but had to do with Beth.

Claire pushed open the screen door and walked out onto the porch. As the door closed with a sharp snap, two heads swung around. Two pairs of eyes stared at her in surprise. Then Beth blushed and slowly extricated her hand from Ian's.

233

Though Claire noted the guilty action, she chose not to make mention of it. "We need to talk, Ian," she said instead. "Now."

Her brother scowled. "It isn't aught Beth hasn't heard. We can talk out here."

"Nay,"—Claire shook her head—"this is between you and me, brother, and I'm feeling in need of a nice long walk, so come along with you."

For a fleeting moment, as Ian's eyes narrowed and his mouth tightened, Claire almost imagined he was on the verge of refusing. Then Beth rose and gave him a playful shove.

"Get on with you," she said, mimicking his speech and accent. "You hardly see Claire anymore, save for meals. A walk with her might do you a world of good."

At her prompting, Ian's mood dramatically changed. A big smile cracked his taut features. He leaped from the swing.

"Aye, you're right, of course," he said with a laugh. "I *have* been neglecting my sister of late." With a jaunty stride, he walked over to stand before Claire. "Well," he demanded, offering her his arm, "shall we be off, madam?"

She eyed him with wry amusement and took his arm, even as she silently noted how increasingly temperamental her brother had become of late. "You're quite the gallant these days, aren't you?" she muttered instead, holding her tongue on what she was really thinking.

They stepped down off the porch and headed toward the ponderosa pine forest growing on the hills behind Devlin and Hannah's house. "It wouldn't have aught to do with a certain black-haired girl, would it?" Claire queried with an impish grin as they walked along. "Your sudden show of gallant behavior, I mean?"

"It might." Ian's hand slid down her arm to now clasp her hand. "I wouldn't think, though, you'd be complaining about any improvement in my manners."

"Och, I'd never do that." She strolled along for a while longer and, when they finally passed the foreman's house and reached the first of the shaggy pines, Claire halted. "It seems, though, when it comes to school, that your good manners extend only to Beth and no further. Why is that, Ian?"

The now familiar scowl darkened his features once more. "Why is that?" he repeated, meeting her questioning gaze with a defiant one of his own. "Because Elizabeth's the only one at school who treats me with respect. From the first day, there was a group of other students who laughed whenever I talked. They said I sounded funny. It got so bad that I even stopped reciting in class or doing any ciphering up at the blackboard. But no one—*no one*—laughs at me and gets away with it for long."

Claire sighed, recalling that her brother hadn't seemed to mind at all when Beth had so recently teasingly imitated his speech. "Och, Ian, can't you give the others a chance to get used to you? Surely not all the children act so ignorantly?"

He shrugged. "I wouldn't know. The rest of them just sit there and stare."

"Miss Westerman says this wasn't the first time you were caught fighting. She claims you get into fights at least twice a week."

"Mayhap I do. What of it?"

She couldn't believe the sullen tone that had crept into her brother's voice. "*What of it?* Ian, this fighting can't continue! This place is a fresh start for the both of us. Are you so blind you can't see how your fighting threatens that?"

235

He reddened. "And what of you?" Ian countered fiercely. "I can't see how your fresh start is working out all that well for you."

"I-I don't know what you're talking about," Claire stammered, nonplussed as the sudden turn of the conversation now seemed to focus on her. "I have a new husband, a new home—"

"And I've never seen you mope about so, or wear such a long face, save nowadays, since we came to America. Can you truly say you're happy here, Claire? Can you?"

Dear Lord, she thought, her eyes closing for a brief instant, had her distress over her growing distance with her husband, coupled by her yet unanswered questions about him and Hannah, been so evident? But that was a foolish question. If anyone would be the first to notice her changing emotions, it would be Ian. She resolved, no matter what happened, to confront Evan this very night.

"It's a difficult time just now for all." Thinking to hide the truth from him, her glance swung to take in the pine trees with their grayish bark and gnarled branches thick with long, green needles. "I haven't quite mastered cooking for so many folk, and Evan near to works himself to exhaustion each day. And then"—she turned back to face her brother—"there's the adjustment you and I must both learn to make, to this new land and its people."

He gave a snort of disgust. "And what of the problems between you and Evan? When will 'adjustments' be made there to ease your unhappiness?"

A flush of indignation warmed her face. "What's between Evan and me is private, and I'll not be sharing it with you!"

"Aye, as you don't share aught with me anymore! If it wasn't for Elizabeth, I'd have no one to talk to or care about me."

Claire's mouth fell open. Pain twisted her heart. "How can you stand there and accuse me of not caring? You're my brother, my flesh and blood! I'd do aught for you, Ian Sutherland, and you know it!"

"Would you now?" He shoved his hands into his denims and looked away. "I wonder."

She grabbed him by the arm and spun him around. "Just because I've been preoccupied with other things of late, doesn't mean I don't love you just as much as I always have. Is that what all this trouble in school is about, then? That you think I don't love you anymore?"

"Everything you do nowadays is done for Evan!" Ian's eyes blazed with sudden fury. "He's all that matters to you now. But no matter. Just as you've found Evan, I've found Elizabeth."

"Och, aye, and that's yet another subject that needs discussing." Though Claire had been hesitant earlier to broach the topic of Beth, now seemed as good a time as any. "Miss Westerman claims you and Beth spend far too much time together, that you both need to make other friends."

"And do you think I care what Miss Westerman thinks? She's but a mean-spirited spinster who can't abide seeing two people who love–" As if realizing he had said too much, Ian clamped shut his mouth.

Claire, however, was quick to pounce on her brother's slip of the tongue. "Are you saying that you and Beth–"

"Nay." Vehemently, Ian shook his head. "I didn't mean it how it sounded. Forget what I said."

"She's thirteen, Ian, and you've just turned sixteen. You're both too young to be talking of love."

He shot her a seething glance. "I told her you wouldn't understand, and I was right."

"Och, Ian . . . Ian," Claire moaned. She took him by the hand and led him to a fallen tree trunk, where she sat. "Sit," she then ordered, motioning to a spot beside her on the tree. "We both need a few minutes to collect our wits here."

"Naught has happened, nor will happen, Claire," her brother growled as he took his seat. "I know Elizabeth's too young. But I can't help wanting to be with her. Is that so wrong?"

"Nay, it isn't wrong, brother," she softly replied. "But there comes a time in a young person's life when some feelings rise so strongly they can easily overpower good sense. And, though I can't speak for Beth, I'd wager you're now well into that time of your life."

"She makes me feel verra special," he admitted. "And the few times we've kissed . . ."

"Ian, don't you see the complications that your relationship with Beth presents?" She turned to face him, struggling to explain, to warn him before it was too late, even as Claire secretly wondered if it weren't already too late. "Beth's parents are gone for a time, and Evan is now responsible for his sister's welfare. If Beth's and your friendship continues to deepen, as it seems to be doing, Evan might be forced to step between you, forbid you to be with each other. And then what will you do? What will *we* do?"

"Aye, Claire," her brother asked, bitterness now seeping in to darken his voice, "what indeed will *you* do? It's a problem, to be sure, that might well put you in the middle between Evan and me. What would you do then, if you had to make a choice between him and me? What would you do, indeed?"

She stared back at him, a reply—whatever it was—lodging in a throat gone suddenly dry. In truth, Claire didn't know what her answer would have been. All she knew was if she ever had to make such a horrendous choice, it would tear her heart asunder.

And that wasn't anything she cared ever to face, much less consider.

ॐ

"Beth told me you went to Grand View today," Evan said as he undressed for bed that evening. "Something about supplies, and a visit with Miss Westerman."

Claire faltered in her even brushstrokes. She had forgotten she had asked Beth to inform Evan where she was going today. But now, after what the young schoolteacher had shared with her, combined with her own growing concern over Beth and Ian, Claire wasn't so sure she wanted to discuss the reason for her visit at Grand View's school anymore. Yet, short of lying to her husband, which she would never do, there seemed no way to avoid the issue.

At least, though, he had no inkling of her run-in with Brody Gerard. And she meant to keep it that way, even going so far as to ask Noah not to say anything, when he had finally escorted her back to her buggy. There was no telling what Evan would've done if he had ever discovered the liberties the big, dark man had dared try to take. Indeed, after what Noah had told her about Brody Gerard's kidnapping of Hannah, Claire wagered if it hadn't been for his broken leg, even Devlin MacKay wouldn't have been averse to joining Evan in paying Gerard a visit.

"Ian's having some problems at school," she finally forced herself to say. "I'm hoping, between the two of us, though, that Miss Westerman and I can work it all out." She laid her hairbrush on the dresser and walked over to climb into the big brass bed beside her husband. "I didn't think it necessary to burden you with it, unless the problem continues."

Evan, the covers drawn up to his bare chest, stared at her intently. "Why is it I don't think I'm getting the whole story here?"

Claire drew in a slow, deep breath. "Ian was fighting. Miss Westerman disciplined him. I had a talk with Ian today, and I'm hoping that will be the end of it."

"And why was Ian fighting?"

This time, or all the other times? Claire wanted to ask. She chose, however, to assume he was talking about yesterday's brawl. "Some boys were apparently making fun of Beth. Ian took offense and decided to teach them some manners."

"Well, good for him." Evan scooted down in bed. In a most distracting movement of strong, supple muscles, he pillowed his hands behind his head. "Remind me to thank him tomorrow."

"There are better ways of handling most things than fighting. If you don't mind, I'd rather you not encourage Ian to use his fists to solve all his problems."

Evan glanced at her and grinned. "Well, considering Ian's past history, I suppose you're right. But I'm grateful to him, nonetheless, for standing up for Beth."

"Aye, it was a kind and noble thing," Claire admitted. "The intent, leastwise, if not the method."

Her husband continued to stare at her, and his gaze gradually warmed with a decidedly masculine interest. "It's been a while," he finally said, his voice gone low and husky, "since we—"

Before Evan could put words to his thoughts, Claire cut him off. It was past time to broach the subject of Hannah. "There's more, Evan. More we need to talk about."

"About Ian, you mean?"

"Nay." She shook her head, summoning all her courage. "About us."

Evan frowned. Slowly, he lowered his hands to lie on the quilt before him. "And what would you like to talk about regarding us?" he asked with a quiet, deliberate emphasis.

Claire scooted around in bed until she could fully see his face. For a long moment she gazed at him, wrestling with myriad ways to broach the subject of his past relationship with Hannah. Finally, though, as the tension built to unbearable heights, she just blurted it out.

"When exactly were you planning to tell me about you and Hannah?"

Evan's mouth fell open for the briefest instant, before he clamped it shut. His long, strong fingers dug into the bedding, gripping it tightly. Then, with what must have been a supreme effort of will, he suddenly relaxed.

"I assume," he said softly, "you're referring to the fact that I was once in love with Hannah."

"Aye, and what else would it be? She was the lass who you left Culdee Creek for, wasn't she?"

Evan glanced away and nodded. "Yes, she was."

Something in his evasive, almost defiant manner angered Claire. "And I ask again. When were you planning on telling me about her?"

"When I felt the time was right, of course!" He whirled about, a frustrated regret burning in his eyes. "It's not how it seems, Claire. I was just wanting for you to have an easy time of fitting in here, and I didn't want to poison any chance you and Hannah may have had to become friends. None of this is her fault anyways. She's in love with Devlin, and never really hankered after me like I did her."

She met his gaze with a steady one of her own, even as her next words threatened to lodge permanently in her throat and choke her. "And do you still hanker after her, Evan?" Claire finally forced out the dreaded question. "Now that you're back home, and near Hannah, do you mayhap find you regret your hasty courtship and marriage to me?"

241

As her questions unfolded, Evan's expression of incredulity, so comical in its extreme, almost wrenched a strident laugh from her. But Claire wasn't about to settle for anything but the truth, and that truth demanded the spoken word, not suppositions.

"Well, husband?" she prodded, when no reply was forthcoming. "Don't hesitate so, or your silence will in itself give me my answer."

Evan eyed her a moment longer, then exhaled a deep breath. "You've every right to be angry with me, but don't for a minute think that I ever regretted marrying you, Claire. I still care for Hannah, but now just as a friend. She was always so good to me. I can't help but be happy that she's happy. But you're my wife, and I love *you* as a wife."

If his words hadn't been enough to convince her, the ardent look in Evan's eyes did. "Och," she whispered, the tears welling, "if you only kn-knew how hard it's been in the past m-month, wondering, watching, and praying to God each and every night that you l-loved me still. You've just seemed so cold and distant of late, that I began to–"

As Claire's tears flowed, Evan made a sympathetic sound and pulled her to him. "Oh, sweetheart, sweetheart," he crooned. "I'm so sorry. I know I've been preoccupied with the ranch since Pa left, and I know most nights I fall asleep without even holding or loving you, but it was never, *never* because I no longer wished to be married to you. In fact"–he gave a harsh little laugh–"I was beginning to wonder how *you* felt about me. It's not as if we've even made love since we moved into this house, and my parents' bed, you know."

"I-I already knew about you and Hannah by then," Claire said, swiping her eyes. "And then, with you working so hard, us both being so tired, and me feeling like a dolt over not being able to properly cook meals for you

242

and the hands . . . well, I can't say I felt much like making love. But when Noah said I needed to talk with you about this, that we have to work at marriage to lay a strong foundation for the years to come, I decided I must do so—before things got any worse."

Evan went very still, then gently pushed her back from him. "You talked to Noah Starr about our marital problems? When? Today?"

An uneasy presentiment prickled down Claire's spine, and she cursed her rash tongue. "Aye," she admitted slowly. "It's the first chance I've had in a while to take some time for myself. And it wasn't as if I felt comfortable discussing it with you or Hannah. Besides, there surely wasn't anyone else I could talk to, was there?"

"Millie Starr might have been a better choice," her husband gritted out the words. "Or, better still, no one at all, save me."

"I didn't see the harm," she protested, her confusion mounting. "After all, Noah's a man of God, and used to—"

"This is between you and me, Claire," Evan snapped in frustration, "and that's where it should stay!" He glared down at her. "Do you understand? Do you?"

Suddenly, Claire didn't like being close to Evan, much less having his hands on her. She wrenched free and climbed from the bed. "You don't need to lecture me as if I'm some child, Evan MacKay!" she cried, her hands fisting on her hips. "Mayhap you prefer to keep things to yourself and let them fester, but I don't. I tried to be discreet. Noah will understand, keep my confidence. Or would you've preferred I continued to talk with Mary Sue Edgerton, who told me all about you and Hannah to begin with?"

Not allowing him a chance to reply, she laughed shrilly at the consideration. "Och, aye, now *that* would've been a wise choice, wouldn't it? Mary Sue would've gladly listened to all I told her with a most avid ear. Aye, mayhap I should've talked with her instead!"

"I should've known Mary Sue had her spiteful little hand in this," Evan muttered. He shook his head. Then he sighed and threaded an unsteady hand through his hair. "The biggest fool of all, though, was me, in letting it get to this."

"Aye," Claire agreed cautiously, not certain where he was headed with this unexpected new tack. "You should've told me about Hannah straight off."

"Yes, I should've," he admitted wearily, as all the anger and frustration seemed to drain from him in one great rush. "And I reckon I can't blame you for turning to Noah for help. You needed someone to talk to."

"I'd really meant to talk with Millie." Claire's hands fell to her sides. "But she wasn't home, and you know how kind and concerned Noah can be . . ."

"It's all right, Claire. Learning that another man knew more about what was bothering you than I did just stung my pride a bit. I'm sorry I got angry at you for that."

"I suppose, knowing that, your anger was understandable." She managed a tentative smile.

He lifted the covers on her side of the bed. "Come back to bed. You're starting to shiver."

It *was* a bit chilly. Claire wondered, though, how much of her sudden shivering was due to the cool room, and how much was but a delayed reaction to the high emotions of the past few minutes. One way or another, she decided as she hopped back into bed and snuggled up against Evan's long, warm length, she was thankful her worst fears had finally been put to rest.

"Let's not ever again keep secrets from each other," Evan murmured as he pulled her close and kissed the top of her head. "It's just not worth the pain, is it?"

"Nay," Claire whispered. Yet even as she agreed, questions bombarded her, questions that demanded an answer as to why she continued to harbor her own secrets. Secrets like the episode with Brody Gerard today. Secrets about her growing concern over Ian and Beth. Worst of all, the secret of what really happened that stormy night on the seacoast of Sutherland.

Evan was right. Keeping secrets wasn't worth the pain. Yet, just as he had kept the secret of Hannah to avoid hurting her, her secrets also held a similar ability to cause him—and others—more pain. Problem was, how did one know when it was best to keep a secret, and when was it far wiser to reveal it?

18

Bless them which persecute you: bless, and curse not.
Romans 12:14

"So, how did the day go?" Devlin asked two weeks later, as he and Evan met for their daily evening meeting. His leg still immobilized and propped on a stool and two pillows in his kitchen, Culdee Creek's foreman leaned toward Evan with an eagerness surely compounded by his enforced inactivity.

The younger man smiled. He couldn't blame his cousin. Most of their lives had been spent outdoors, engaged year-round in strenuous physical endeavors. Evan could no more stand being cooped up inside for so long, forced to rely on others for help, than he imagined Devlin could.

"Well," he replied, removing his Stetson and hanging it on the hook by the back door, "it's been pretty quiet of late." Evan sauntered to the cupboard, took down a mug, then walked back to the stove, where he poured himself a cup of coffee. "Not that I'm complaining, mind you," he hastened to add with a chuckle. "Lord only knows when we last had a slow day."

"So all the fences are mended, the hay's been put up in the barn, and the cattle going to market separated for shipment to Denver next week?"

"Sure enough." Evan blew on his steaming coffee. "Plus I had the hands put a coat of fresh paint on the two barns and fasten down all the loose boards. Except for moving the remaining cattle into closer feed grounds for the winter, I reckon all the major chores are done."

Devlin took a long swallow of his mug. "Well, unless we get some heavy snow between now and Thanksgiving, we shouldn't have to move the cattle into the feed grounds before December. There's still enough pasture to keep them until then."

"That's what I was thinking." Evan walked to the table, pulled out a chair, and straddled it. "So I was hoping, if it's all right with you, to start working on my house again. The hands can take care of the daily chores, and I'll be sure and check with them at least twice a day–"

"Hey," Devlin said with a laugh and lift of his hand, "I trust you to keep an eye on things. Might as well get as much done on your house as possible while the weather holds."

"Yeah, that's what I figured, too. Now that it's framed, if I can just get the exterior walls up and the roof on before bad weather hits, I'll be able to finish a lot of interior work this winter." He grinned. "After all, Pa and Abby are going to want their house back soon enough."

"Any word when Conor and Abby are planning on coming home?"

"Funny thing." Evan pulled a letter from the back pocket of his denims. "Just got this today when I went to town to order more feed." He handed the letter to his cousin. "Pa wrote this. Says Abby's father is doing poorly, and they

247

don't expect him to last until Thanksgiving. So Pa feels pretty certain they'll be home before Christmas."

Devlin took the letter, opened it, and began to read. "Conor says Sean's growing like a weed." He laughed. "The boy's into everything, now has only one word in his vocabulary, which is 'no,' and shows definite signs of having inherited the MacKay temper."

"Sounds like my little brother's turning into quite a handful. Hope he gets all that wild behavior out of his system before he comes home."

Devlin gave a disparaging snort. "Fat chance of that. The boy won't even be two until the beginning of December. Odds are his 'wild behavior,' as you call it, is only the beginning." He smiled. "Just wait and see. Raising children is what *really* makes you a man."

"Well, I'm hoping children aren't in Claire's and my future until at least we can move into our new house. I want kids someday, but for the time being I'm happy that it's just the two of us. Claire and I first need to work all the kinks out of our marriage, before we take on some babies."

"She seems to be settling down into ranch, and American, life pretty well," Devlin ventured. "Hannah says Claire doesn't need much of her help anymore."

Evan pulled over the sugar bowl, scooped up a generous spoonful, and stirred it into his coffee. "How does Hannah feel about Claire?" he asked, taking care to word his query as casually as possible. "I mean, do they get along okay and seem to be on friendly terms?"

"Reckon so." Devlin paused to scratch his jaw. "Why? Has Claire said something to you about Hannah?" Evan hesitated. In the past, he would have as soon cut out his tongue as confide in his cousin. But things had changed a lot in the past few months.

"No," he said, shaking his head, "it's just that she was pretty upset at first, when she found out about Hannah

248

and me, and I was just wondering if that had since had any effect on her and Hannah's relationship."

Devlin emitted a soft whistle. "Are you telling me Claire didn't know about why you left Culdee Creek when you married her?"

A flush spread up Evan's neck and into his cheeks. "Now don't start on one of your lectures, Devlin, or I'll regret telling you. I told Claire I'd left because of a woman. I just didn't tell her that woman was Hannah."

"Then how did she find out? Did you finally break down and tell her once you got home?"

"No, she found out from Mary Sue Edgerton."

"Blast!" Devlin released a sharp, angry breath. "That girl just won't quit, will she? Makes sense now, the basis for all the rumors."

"Rumors?" Evan straightened in his chair. "What rumors?"

It was now the big foreman's turn to redden. "Oh, nothing much," he mumbled, not quite meeting his cousin's gaze. "Probably just some silly talk, the kind that crops up now and then about any parson, especially one who's unwed."

Evan leaned forward. "And what exactly might that silly talk be?"

For a moment, it didn't look like Devlin wanted to answer. Then, with a shrug and a sigh, he finally did. "There's been things said about Noah and Claire. Seems Mary Sue and Millie caught them alone together a couple of weeks ago, holding hands in the rectory kitchen. Reckon it was Mary Sue, though, who decided there was more afoot than just some innocent comforting going on, and now not only does the entire Ladies Quilting Society know about it, but their husbands as well. I found out from Henry Watson, who found out from his wife, who attends the quilting meetings."

"So, based on one visit Claire made to Noah Starr two weeks ago," Evan muttered disgustedly, "the whole town now thinks there's something going on between them." Angrily, he shoved his coffee aside. "I swear, Devlin, but sometimes I get mighty fed up with all the small town pettiness and gossiping!"

"Well, if it's any consolation, considering the source, I doubt anyone with even a lick of sense is going to make much out of it."

"Nonetheless, now I'm going to have to caution Claire to watch her step, and not pay Noah Starr any private visits for a while."

Devlin scratched his jaw and frowned. "Doesn't seem fair to her, if she's in need of spiritual guidance. Having to forego seeing her pastor, I mean."

"Well, Claire should've thought about it before she was found alone in a compromising situation with another man—an *unmarried* man—even if that man is a priest. They could've just waited outside until Millie came back." Evan cursed softly. "Or she could've waited until someone from the ranch had time to drive her to town and chaperone them properly."

"Yeah, things aren't as safe as they used to be in these parts," his cousin agreed. "Especially with men like Brody Gerard back in town again."

"Brody Gerard?" Evan stared in disbelief. "I thought he was locked up all safe and sound in prison?"

"He served his time," Devlin observed bitterly. "Reckon kidnapping a former prostitute didn't deserve more than a year's sentence. And now he's back in Grand View."

The more he thought about it, the more the news about Brody Gerard didn't set well with Evan. The man had been a burr beneath their saddle since he had first come to town over four years ago, and something

250

warned Evan that they had just begun to see what the cold-hearted, vengeful drifter could do.

"Maybe I ought to go have a talk with Gerard," he growled. "Set him straight on what'll happen if he dares lay a hand on another MacKay, or anyone else associated with Culdee Creek."

"No, not yet." Devlin shook his head. "No sense going out looking for trouble. As far as we know, Gerard has kept his nose clean since he got out of prison. Maybe he finally learned his lesson while he was locked up there. Worse folk than him, you know, have changed their ways."

Evan gave a mocking laugh. "Yeah, and it never snows in Colorado, either!"

"Nonetheless," Devlin urged with a smile, "let's just take a wait-see attitude. If Gerard starts any trouble, we'll hear soon enough. Then we'll come down on him fast and hard."

"Fine," Evan conceded grudgingly. "Still, he's just one more reason for Claire to be careful going out alone anymore. I'll have to warn her about Gerard."

"Yeah," Devlin nodded his agreement. "Best you do."

ò

Claire was just putting away the last of the supper dishes, when Evan returned from his nightly visit with Devlin. She glanced up, a smile of greeting on her lips, and caught sight of her husband's frowning face. Apprehension filled her. Had he and Devlin managed to finally have another falling out?

"What's the matter, Evan?" Laying aside the dishtowel, she walked over to him.

He grabbed her arms before she could lift them to wrap around his neck, and gently pushed them away.

251

"We need to talk." Evan glanced around. "Where are Ian and Beth?"

"Both have gone up to bed." Her anxiety mounting, she tilted her head. "Why?"

"This is between you and me. I don't want them over-hearing." He gestured toward the table. "Why don't you have a seat?"

Increasingly wary with each passing second, Claire did as he asked. Whatever was Evan upset about now? she wondered. Had he discovered Ian's fighting had been going on since school started, or, worse still, found out about Ian and Beth?

Plastering on a pleasant, mildly curious expression, Claire waited until he was seated catty-corner to her. "Whatever do you have to tell me?" she then demanded. "Don't keep me in suspense an instant longer."

"Well,"–Evan leaned on the table–"it seems Devlin heard that Mary Sue Edgerton's been spreading tales about you and Noah. Seems she walked in on some cozy little scene a couple of weeks back, and now has it in her head that you and Noah are friendlier than is proper."

Claire could feel the blood rush from her face. Her heart seemed to double its rate; her mouth went dry, her palms clammy. Dear Lord, she thought, had her tiny transgression against her marriage vows that day already come back to haunt her? If so, it wasn't fair. Her admiring feelings for the priest had been secret and soon forgotten, buried in the deepest recesses of her heart.

Still, her husband expected an answer. Claire decided the best tactic was an offensive one. "And what do *you* think?" she demanded tartly. "If Mary Sue isn't trying to cause problems for Hannah, and indirectly for our marriage, then she now seems to be spreading lies about me, and maligning the good name of our pastor."

"That's kind of what Devlin and I thought."

Relief that her husband evidently thought her and Noah innocent flooded Claire. "And how did Devlin hear about this?"

"From Henry Watson, whose wife attends the Ladies Quilting Society." Evan folded his hands before him on the table. "Talk—be it lies or the truth—spreads like wildfire in a small town and its surrounds."

Anger began a slow burn within Claire. It seemed that Mary Sue not only had a vendetta against Hannah, but now one against her, too. And for what possible reason, save that Claire had refused to allow Hannah to be maligned in her presence, or to feed what seemed Mary Sue's insatiable need for gossip? What a mean, spiteful girl!

"I think, on the morrow, I need to ride to Grand View and pay Mary Sue Edgerton a little visit," she muttered. "Mayhap if the girl learns firsthand the consequences of a wicked tongue, she'll think twice before spreading false tales again."

"Well, I doubt it'd do any good. People like Mary Sue don't learn what they don't care to. And besides, that brings up another thing I wanted to talk with you about. A man has returned to Grand View who I want you to avoid. His name's Brody Gerard, and he hates the MacKays."

Claire shot Evan a startled glance. Luckily for her, at that moment he was looking down. Surely it was a coincidence, she thought, that Brody Gerard had been brought up. Unless . . . unless Noah had mentioned something to Evan after all.

"Well, I don't care to meet any man who hates your family, so I hardly think that'll be a problem." As an excuse to avoid her husband's gaze, she brushed an imaginary crumb off the table. "I won't be deterred, though, from my intent to seek out Mary Sue, or from visiting the Reverend Starr whenever I've a need to. I refuse to hide away out of fear."

"Suit yourself, but I expect that anytime you leave the ranch from now on, you have a hand accompany you. I've already made arrangements for someone to escort Beth, Ian, and Devlin Jr. to and from school each day."

"And will that hand also be required to chaperone me whenever I visit Noah Starr?" Claire demanded, her voice now taut with irritation. Suddenly, life at Culdee Creek seemed constricted and controlled, and she didn't like that. Didn't like that at all.

Evan stared blankly at her. "And why would you . . . ?" Realization dawned, and his mouth tightened in annoyance. "As long as Millie's present somewhere in the near vicinity, I don't see that you'll need to enlist one of the hands to monitor your visits. All I want is for everything to appear completely aboveboard between you and Noah, until all the talk dies down."

"And what if I told you I don't give a fig what everyone thinks? They're all a bunch of silly old fools anyway!"

"Then do it for me, and for the sake of the family." Evan's gaze darkened with anger. "Why are you being so difficult about this?"

"Why?" Claire sighed and shook her head. "Because it's all so ridiculous, and I refuse to play by such petty, mean-spirited rules, that's why! I don't care to slink meekly away when my honor is questioned."

"Oh, yeah, I'd forgotten how proud and headstrong you Highlanders were." With a chuckle, Evan tipped back in his chair. "But this isn't the Highlands, Claire. This is the United States, and the West. Like it or not, people here live by a somewhat different set of rules, and observing propriety is just one of them."

She couldn't believe her ears. Not in all her wildest imaginings had she ever thought Evan would condone such narrow-minded, cowardly conduct! At the realization, a sudden, disagreeable consideration crept into her mind. First, there had been the secret he had long carried about Hannah, and now this prudish, controlling, dishonorable demand. What else didn't she know about the man she had married?

"I can't say I'm happy with you or your foolish little town just now," she said. "Still, I'll abide by what you say so as not to bring shame upon the MacKay family name." Claire shoved to her feet. "Now, if you'll excuse me, I'm verra weary, and wish to head up to bed."

He grasped her arm as she moved past him. "Don't be angry with me. I'm just doing what I think is best."

His gaze was ardently warm and pleading. His firm, sensuous mouth curved up slowly into a most dazzling, heart-stopping smile. For a fleeting instant, as she looked down at her darkly handsome husband, Claire's anger almost dissolved.

Then she remembered the patronizing way he had spoken of her Highland pride, and something hardened within her. No one—not even one's own spouse—disparaged a Highlander's honor. The sooner a certain Mr. Evan MacKay realized that, the better.

Ever so deliberately, Claire twisted free of his grip. "Well, doing what is best has its own price, doesn't it? I only hope, for your sake, that it makes you a warmbedfellow."

❦

The next morning, breakfast didn't go well. The wood was too green, and Old Bess showed her ire by repeatedly firing up, then dying. The biscuits were raw in the middle, the eggs she had been trying to fry sunny-side up—as most of the hands and Evan liked them—ended up having to be scrambled just to get them properly cooked, and then the bacon burned to a crisp.

During the meal the scent of scorched bacon grease hung in the air, the pots and pans piled up in the sink, and though no one said anything, most left their meals half-eaten. By the time Evan finally filed out with all the others, after shooting her an irritated, questioning glance, Claire was on the verge of tears. Muttering to herself in an effort to hold back her teetering emotions, she filled the sink with hot water from a big pot on the stove, sprinkled in some soap, and began to add plates that she first scraped clean in the slop bucket.

"They all act as if it was an infinitely simple thing to cook a meal on that cursed cookstove, and have everything hot and ready all at the same time," she spat furiously. "Well, I'm sick of the lot of them. One would think the fate of the world revolved around their stomachs!"

Behind her, Claire was vaguely aware of the back door opening. At that particular moment, however, she didn't care if anyone heard her or took offense. What did it matter anymore anyway? Besides, it was past time they began, she resolved, to learn a wee bit of what it was like—

"Claire? Is it all right if I come in?"

At the sound of Hannah's voice, the plate Claire was scraping slipped from her fingers and plummeted into the slop bucket with a sickening plop. She whirled around, hastily wiping her hands on her food-stained apron.

"Och, it's you, Hannah," she babbled, embarrassed color flooding her cheeks. "I didn't expect you . . . I thought it was . . ."

At the look of loving concern in the other woman's eyes, something inside Claire crumbled. All the barriers she had erected over the past weeks against Hannah crashed down. A need for understanding, for someone to share all her fears and worries with, swelled with

256

such force Claire was unable to withstand it. She buried her face in her hands and began to sob.

Hannah quickly closed the door and hurried over. "Claire, whatever is the matter?" she asked, slipping an arm about her shoulders to help her rise, then guiding her to the table. "Sit," she said, pulling out a chair, which Claire blindly found and sat upon. "There's nothing so horrible that family and the Lord can't sort it out."

"Och, H-Hannah," Claire wept. "If only you knew the m-muddle I've made of everything since I've come h-here! I can't do a-aught right."

"There, there now." Hannah pressed a finely embroidered lace hanky into Claire's hand. "Surely it's not as bad as all that. Why, I've heard talk that your meals are quite tasty nowadays, and served on time. I know Evan's proud of how well you seemed to have adapted to life here."

"E-Evan! Och, I can't see how he could be proud of me." Claire wiped her eyes and blew her nose. "I near to ruined this morn's breakfast, though I well know it was mainly Old Bess's fault. That and the green wood Ian brought in to start the fire. And then there was the fight Evan and I had last night . . ." She glanced up at the other woman. "I made him sleep elsewhere."

"So you've had your first lovers' spat," Hannah observed mildly. "It was bound to happen. It's not like Devlin and I haven't had a few, as have Abby and Conor."

"He just doesn't understand me," she sniffed, then blew her nose again. "Mary Sue is spreading horrible tales about me and Noah, and now Evan doesn't want me to be alone with Noah for any reason. Och, it's so unfair, not to mention a stain on my honor." Claire laid the hanky on the table. "I know I should avoid any appearance of impropriety, but I suddenly feel as if I have a father, or some taskmaster, rather than a husband."

257

Hannah inhaled a deep, considering breath. "Evan means well. It's just that he's trying so hard to prove himself to his father—and to Devlin, too—that he's trying too hard at times. And, somehow, he has also, in all the confusion, inadvertently lost sight of his proper role as a husband. But he loves you, Claire. Don't doubt that for a second."

At the recollection of her recent doubts about Evan's love and her secret animosity toward Hannah, freshened shame engulfed Claire. "I must ask your forgiveness, Hannah," she whispered. "I've harbored some verra uncharitable thoughts of late about you, too."

The blonde-haired woman leaned back in her chair and tilted her head. "Let me guess. You found out about me and Evan."

"Aye, but it wasn't from Evan that I heard the news. It was from Mary Sue."

"Oh, poor Mary Sue," Hannah said sadly. "She can't seem to ever let go of her hatred of me. But to risk hurting you and Evan to get back at me—well, that's the meanest thing she's ever done."

"Why does she hate you so?"

Slowly, thoughtfully, Hannah shook her head. "I don't know. Maybe because she, a girl from a respectable family, has yet to find herself a husband, while I, a fallen woman from the dregs of society, have. I also think, in some fashion or another, she had set her sights on every MacKay man, then lost each and every one. I'd imagine, deep down, she was none too pleased when you waltzed in with Evan's wedding ring on your finger."

"Yet she seemed, at first, as if she wished to be the best of friends" puzzled Claire.

"Mary Sue's a most unhappy, confused young woman. We must pray for her. Pray that the Lord will open her eyes and touch her heart."

"But she has caused so much trouble, spread so much pain!" Claire protested. "For you, me, Evan, and now the Reverend Starr. When will her cruel lies end?"

"In God's own good time. In the meanwhile, He asks us to be people of great love, and to let that light of love shine for all to see."

Listening to Hannah, seeing the heartfelt truth of her words in her glorious eyes, Claire knew that she spoke from a deep conviction. Admiration for the woman who had endured so much pain in her life filled Claire. Her own troubles seemed to pale in comparison. Even her current troubles with Mary Sue Edgerton.

If Hannah could come through such a fierce testing and find peace and joy, so surely could she. Claire reached out and clasped Hannah's hand, giving it a gentle squeeze. "I don't know if my faith—or courage—is a match for yours, but you've given me renewed hope."

She smiled at Hannah with shy uncertainty. "I'd like to try anew to be friends, if you'll have me."

The blonde-haired woman's lips trembled, and her eyes sparkled now with unshed tears. "I never stopped being your friend, Claire," she said softly. "You're family, after all. A cousin in marriage, but, even more importantly and blessedly, a sister in Christ."

19

See that none render evil for evil unto any man; but ever follow that which is good.

1 Thessalonians 5:15

The retching finally ended. Claire wiped her mouth and damp brow, then climbed unsteadily to her feet beside the chamber pot. Though the episodes of morning vomiting had begun to subside, they had continued far too long—off and on now for almost six weeks. And then there was the matter of her woman's fluxes, which had been absent for over two months.

She was carrying Evan's child.

The consideration filled Claire with joy. A child . . . a wee bairn. She would be a mother, and Evan, a father. Och, but Evan would be so happy when she told him the good news!

The only question remaining was when. Since they'd had their talk a week ago, they had once more been like two newlyweds, stealing quick kisses and loving touches whenever they could throughout the day, and eagerly anticipating each night to come. Claire wanted the announcement of her being in a family way to be equally special.

She had time. She knew from talking to some of the young wives of Culdee that a first babe wouldn't start to show for four or five months. And talk had it that Abby and Conor would be home before Christmas. By her calculations, that would make her not quite four months along by then.

Besides, if she told Evan too soon, the odds were strong he would insist she not work so hard. Yet who else could take over if she didn't cook the meals and run the house? It wasn't fair to continue imposing on Hannah. And it wasn't as if, Claire added, she wasn't strong and healthy. She was a Highlander born and bred, after all.

Nay, Claire resolved, it wouldn't serve any purpose to tell Evan too soon. He had enough to deal with, without adding needless worries about her pregnancy. But, just as soon as Abby and Conor were safely home. . . .

Claire washed up, donned a plain white blouse and dark navy woolen skirt, and made her way downstairs to start breakfast. As was their usual routine, Evan, on his way out to begin a few pre-breakfast chores, had already started a good fire in Old Bess. Claire soon had a large kettle of water on the stove to heat, and she began taking out fry pans to make flapjacks. She quickly discovered, however, that there was barely enough flour left in the pottery canister to make her usual amount of flapjacks.

"Now where did all the flour go?" she muttered to herself. "I distinctly recall . . ." At the memory of Beth's request to bake cookies for a party they were having at school three days ago, Claire's dilemma was solved. Beth had made an inordinately large batch of cookies. She had then

261

shared a generous portion with everyone at that night's supper and the next day's lunch. Unfortunately, Claire hadn't thought to check the supply of flour afterward.

"Well, there's naught to be done for it but make a quick visit to town today," she decided as she donned her jacket, took up a bowl, and headed out first to the chicken coop to gather eggs, then to the springhouse for a jar of milk. Besides, she added as an afterthought, if there was time and Doc Childress was about, it wouldn't be a bad idea to pay him a wee visit, either, just to make certain the babe was all right.

A light frost had fallen last night, and the grass crunched underfoot. In the east, mauve, tinged at its base with rose, faintly washed the horizon. The air was still, but crisp and bracing, reminding her of countless Highland autumns.

It would be dawn soon. The dawn of yet another day of her childbearing, and the first day of the realization of her impending motherhood. It was truly a day that the Lord had made, and she rejoiced in it and was glad.

A mother . . . she was going to be a mother. Clutching the bowl to her, Claire opened the door to the chicken coop and all but skipped in.

ॐ

"Well, and what brings you, all beaming and rosy-cheeked, to Grand View this fine morning?" Noah Starr asked as he walked up four hours later, just as Claire stepped from Doc Childress's office. The priest glanced at the shingle hanging above the door, then met her startled gaze. "Nothing serious in any physical sense, I hope?"

Claire couldn't help it. She blushed, then quickly lowered her head. "Nay, naught serious at all. Just a routine checkup."

262

"I didn't mean to pry, Claire," Noah hurried to say. "Please accept my apologies."

She glanced up then, just in time to note his own embarrassed countenance. "Och, it's naught," she exclaimed, touching his arm. "It's just . . ." At the realization that she most certainly couldn't tell Noah the real reason for her visit to Doc Childress's, leastwise not until she first told her husband, her voice faded.

"So, how are things going at home?" the priest asked with a chuckle, in an obvious attempt to change the subject and avoid further awkwardness. "Had any talks with anyone important?"

At the roguish wag of one brow as he asked, Claire couldn't help but laugh. "Och, aye. In fact, I've had a talk not only with Evan, but Hannah, too, and everything now is just wonderful!" She gave Noah's arm a quick squeeze before releasing it. "Thank you ever so much for your patience and excellent advice the last time I saw you. You were right about everything, of course."

"Was I now?" Noah grinned. "Then I'll have to mark that auspicious date down in my journal. No one will ever believe me otherwise."

"And I," Claire teased, joining in on the fun, "think mayhap you don't give yourself enough credit. Why, I recall last Sunday, you finally managed to get through a complete sermon without having to caution Tommy Dillon not to bang the hymnal on Mr. Hodgen's back even once. Seems to me when you can keep Tommy Dillon mesmerized by a sermon, you've reached the pinnacle of preaching."

"Well, since several other parishioners were equally impressed by that very same accomplishment, I'll tell you a secret. You must promise, though, not to spill the beans."

"Aye? And what would that secret be?" An impish grin on her face, Claire leaned close.

"I promised Tommy a sour-apple candy stick if he could sit through the entire service without once disrupting it." Noah shrugged. "Amazingly enough, it worked!"

Claire cocked her head. "And what if that little secret gets out to the other children? Did you mayhap think to swear Tommy to secrecy as well?"

Fleetingly, the young priest's eyes grew huge, then his face fell. "Oh, my. You're right! I didn't think to ask Tommy not to tell anyone else. If he should mention it to even one or two other children . . ."

"I only hope your priestly stipend is up to affording candy for all the children each and every Sunday."

Noah sighed and hung his head. "And it seemed like such a brilliant solution to Tommy Dillon's antics."

"Mayhap it'd be better to attempt a variation on your plan." Claire pursed her lips and frowned in thought. "Why not offer to throw a small party every few months during children's Bible class, then give out special treats for the most well-behaved in church? It would, I imagine, be a sight less costly for you in the long run."

"What a brilliantly simple plan!" The priest clapped his forehead with the palm of his hand. "And, speaking of parties, have you heard about the town dance being held a week from today? We're calling it the Fall Festival Social, and we'll have music and dancing. In addition, the ladies of the Grand View Quilting Society will be raffling off box suppers to raise money for a new quilting frame, and for supplies to make Christmas quilts for some of the poorer families in town."

Since Claire had purposely missed this month's meeting in order to avoid having to deal with Mary Sue, she hadn't heard about the quilting society's plans. Still, the box supper raffle was for a good cause, and some music and dancing would be fun. "Nay, I hadn't heard about the dance, but I'll share the news with Evan. It sounds so much like a Highland *ceilidh,* that it makes me feel homesick even thinking about it. If there's any way to talk Evan into coming, you can be certain I will."

"Good." He paused. "If you have the time, I'm sure Millie would enjoy a visit. She's a bit under the weather right now, with her lumbago acting up and all. I'm headed back to the rectory. May I tell her you might stop by later?"

"Well, Jonah Goldman is waiting for me in the buggy . . ." She gestured to the black carriage parked just down the street. "After he heard Brody Gerard had returned to town, Evan insisted I now take a ranch hand with me whenever I come to Grand View. But I don't see the harm—"

Just then, the door to the newspaper office directly across the street opened. Mary Sue Edgerton stepped out. As luck would have it, her gaze immediately settled on the two of them standing there on the boardwalk outside the doctor's office. From even across the span of the wide, rutted dirt street, Claire could see the other girl's eyes narrow with keen speculation. Her heart sank.

"I'm sorry, but I have to pass on your request to visit your aunt today," Claire murmured, backing away even as she spoke. "Time is short and I must return to Culdee Creek. But mayhap another time?"

Understanding tinged with regret gleamed in Noah Starr's striking brown eyes, but he nodded and tipped his hat in farewell. "Of course, another time then," he said.

Before she could reconsider her decision and begin to make amends, Claire forced herself to turn and quickly stride to the buggy. Still, though the walk was short, it was one of the hardest journeys she had ever made. Anger seethed within her at the pain she must have caused the kind-hearted priest, and all because of a mean little gossip. It wasn't fair that a person possessed so much power to do so much harm.

It was a power, however, Claire reminded herself as she allowed Jonah to help her into the buggy, that others had given her. But how to wrest that power back? And, even more importantly, what motivated Mary Sue to wield it so cruelly?

❦

The Saturday night of the Fall Festival Social was a perfect autumn eve. The sky was clear; the moon a huge, orange orb hanging low in the heavens. The temperature was cool, but without apparent threat of wind or snow. As Evan helped Claire down from the buggy, the sound of gay fiddle music, clapping hands, and pounding feet floated from the town hall. An eager anticipation filled her. Och, how she wanted to join the others and dance!

Beth and Ian jumped from the backseat. Hand in hand they ran up onto the boardwalk fronting the town hall and entered the building. Evan, occupied with tying the horse to the hitching post, glanced up and scowled.

"You'd think they could've at least offered to help me with the horse, or you with the box suppers," he muttered.

"Och, dinna fash yerself," Claire chided with a laugh. "You're quite capable of tying up the horse, and these four box suppers I prepared aren't that heavy. Let them have their fun. It isn't often there's a dance for all ages to enjoy."

"I suppose you're right." Her husband walked up to take the basket containing the box suppers from her. He tucked it over one arm and held out his other to her. "Come along, Mrs. MacKay. It isn't often *we* get much of a chance to do some dancing either, and I aim to make the most of it."

With a giggle, Claire slipped her arm through his, and together they headed toward the town hall. It was good to walk with your husband, she thought. To spend a night of fun and fellowship with others. In many small ways, life here in Colorado was beginning to take on a comforting patina of familiarity. Though it would never be Scotland, this land possessed its own unique value and significance. It was her husband's home, and hence, now hers. It would be the birthplace of their unborn child and, God willing, of many more to come. She now had friends and family here, a life and purpose that seemed to deepen with each passing day. A life and a purpose she could share with others, and gain so much from them in return. Somehow, she knew that the Lord's hand was in this, had been in it from the beginning, and that it was good.

"I love you, you know, husband," Claire whispered, looking up at him as they walked along.

"Do you now, lass?" Evan replied with a grin and a thick Scottish burr. "And did you know that I love you, too?"

"Och, of course I knew." She giggled. "And do you know what it does to me when you speak to me so? Why, it sends shivers down my back, and makes me want to throw my arms about you and kiss you senseless."

"Weel then," he replied, laying on the accent even thicker, "mayhap we should be turnin' about right now and headin' fer home. Any Scotsman worth his kilt willna e'er turn down such a temptin' offer from such a bonnie lassie."

"Well, this Scotsman will just have to wait until we get back home, which will be much later this eve, by the way," Claire said, nudging him in the side. "For no Scotsman worth his kilt would ever deny his lady a night of dancing and song. Or not, leastwise, if he long valued his kilt."

As they halted before the town hall's main door, Evan threw back his head and laughed. "Not a pretty picture. A Scotsman running about without his kilt, I mean."

"To be sure," Claire agreed, then opened the door and walked in.

The town hall had been cleared of its neat rows of chairs and decorated for the occasion. Tall sheaths of pale gold wheat were stacked in each corner, orange and brown ribbons festooned the rafters, and plump pumpkins perched on the windowsills. Over on the punch and cookies table, a large cornucopia filled with a variety of winter squash and fall leaves served as a colorfully festive centerpiece.

At the far end of the room, a small, makeshift stage had been set up. Upon it were seated two fiddlers, a banjo player, and a man with an elaborately painted, ebony accordion. Beside the stage stood an old upright piano. Claire recognized Russell Gates at the keyboard.

As she followed Evan to the other side of the stage to deliver the box suppers for the raffle, the band struck up a waltz. Claire saw Beth tug a reluctant Ian onto the dance floor and begin to teach him the simple steps. She smiled. They did make an appealing, if albeit overly young, couple.

"Well, would you like to dance, Mrs. MacKay?" her husband asked her just then, distracting Claire from her pensive musings over Ian and Beth. He set the now empty basket beside the raffle table, removed her shawl and placed it in the basket, then took her by the arm and led her out onto the middle of the floor.

"I took your silence as agreement," he explained smilingly as he grasped one of her hands in his and slipped his other hand about her waist. "I hope that wasn't too presumptuous of me?"

Claire chuckled. "Och, it was indeed presumptuous, and no mistake, but seeing as how you *are* my husband, I suppose I won't take offense this time."

"Good." Evan grinned, his dark eyes sparkling. "You'd be the last person I'd ever wish to offend." With that, he swirled her about and, to the four beat music, began to guide her around the dance floor.

As they waltzed around the room, Claire gave herself up to the sheer pleasure of the beautiful music and the heady presence of her husband holding her securely in his arms. Och, it was all so perfect, she thought. This wondrous autumn eve, the gaily decorated room, all the brightly dressed women and their dark-suited escorts, the laughter, the sheer fun. And, to make it all even more special, there was that tiny life growing within her, the miracle that was her and Evan's child.

"You're looking especially radiant tonight," Evan mentioned just then. "Dare I hope I had at least some part in that glow you're wearing?"

"Och, you had a verra large part in it, husband," Claire replied with a laugh and an impish grin. "More than you might ever imagine."

"Good," he said, puffing out his chest in pride, "because I swear you're the most beautiful woman here."

They danced one dance after the other, stopping only for an occasional cup of punch and to catch their breath. People came and went. Sheriff Jake Whitmore, a tall, ruggedly attractive man with chestnut hair and what seemed a perpetually beard-shadowed jaw, finally walked in with Noah and Millie Starr. Mary Sue Edgerton, who until then had been occasionally dancing and frequently ensconced near the punch table with some of her friends, instantly made a beeline toward the sheriff. He politely danced a few waltzes with her, then seemed to find an excuse to head toward the front door.

As Evan finally swung her about to face in that direction, Claire saw the reason for Jake Whitmore's abrupt departure. Brody Gerard had arrived. Her glance met his as he checked his hat and gun with the husband of one of the quilting society members, then turned to scan the room. At the look of frank admiration in his eyes,

Claire stiffened, then deliberately averted her gaze. When she next had opportunity to look his way, Brody Gerard had moved to the punch table, where he had struck up a conversation with Mary Sue.

After that, Claire paid him no further heed. The night was too perfect to let a man like him ruin it. Besides, she had more important—

With a start, Claire realized it had been a while since she had last seen Ian and Beth. Surreptitiously, so as not to alert Evan as they danced, she scrutinized the room. There was no sign of either of the two young people. Unease coiled and twisted within.

"Och," she began when the music momentarily died, "I'd like to take a few minutes for a breath of fresh air." She fanned herself to add emphasis to her words. "With all the people in here now, it has become a bit warm and stuffy."

"Fine." Evan released her waist and started to pull her toward a side door. "I wouldn't mind a short break myself. Especially," he grinned, "in the company of my beautiful wife."

"Och, nay." Claire slid to a halt and tugged her hand from his. "You needn't come. I'll just be a few minutes at any rate. Go. Talk with some of the men. I'm sure you've been wanting to do that, haven't you?"

He eyed her quizzically, then shrugged. "Sure. Just don't be too long, or I'll come looking for you."

"Only a few minutes. I promise." Even as she spoke, Claire began to back away. When she was several feet from her husband, she waved, then turned and hurried out the door.

It was dark and chilly once she moved from the shelter of the town hall. Claire clasped her arms about herself, wishing she had remembered to take her thick, warm shawl. However, in her concern over finding Ian and Beth, she hadn't given much thought to the cold

270

night. Besides, she didn't intend to be outside long–only long enough to find the increasingly troublesome young lovers.

They certainly weren't anywhere on the side of the building where she had exited. Claire walked around to the front, glanced up and down Winona Street, and noted only the various horses and carriages tied to the hitching posts. Then, from somewhere far down the street, a dog howled mournfully and a horse whinnied.

Her concern growing, she made her way back down the side of the town hall. As she neared the end of the building, the sound of voices rose on the night air. Claire slowed, then drew to a halt.

"Please, Reverend Starr," she heard Beth say. "Don't tell my brother. He wouldn't understand. He just wouldn't!"

"How do you know that, Beth?" Noah replied gently. "Evan understands what it's like to care deeply for someone. And you two can't go on like this–am I wrong in assuming this little tryst of yours isn't the first time?–or there's going to be trouble. You both need the help of your family to deal with this before–"

"I agree," Claire announced, forcing herself to turn the corner and join the little gathering. Better to take charge and be quick about it, she decided, or things really *would* get out of hand. "It's past time something be done about this."

Beth and Ian lifted startled gazes to Claire, but Noah only half-turned to render her a nod of greeting. She pulled up at his side. "I must say," she then said, glancing from one youngster to the other, "that I see my trust in you two has been sadly misplaced."

"We weren't doing aught but a little kissing," her brother muttered, casting her a sullen look.

"Indeed." Claire sharply scanned them and found nothing apparently amiss. She relaxed a little. "Well, be that as it may, this is no time to be discussing this now."

271

She took Beth by the arm, then turned to Noah Starr. "I thank you for finding these two for me, Father Starr. I assure you I can handle this from here on out."

For a moment, Noah looked as if he might protest or say more. Then, with a nod and a quiet "Good evening," he turned and walked away.

"So, are you planning on telling Evan?" Ian demanded the instant the priest was out of earshot. "Are you?"

Claire didn't like the surly tone in her brother's voice. "It's his sister that you're taking liberties with," she snapped as she met his gaze once more. "In the absence of their parents, Evan has the right—and duty—to know and to deal with the situation."

"So, you *do* choose him over me then, do you?" Ian cried. "I told you it would come to that sooner or later. And I was right, wasn't I?"

Staring at her brother, who stood there now, shoulders rigid, hands clenched at his sides, challenging her to make a most heartrending choice, it was all Claire could do to keep herself from slapping him. The audacity, the self-centered selfishness! How dare he put her in such a horrible position? *How dare he?*

But now wasn't the time or place for such a confrontation, she cautioned herself. All of them were too upset right now. All of them needed time to calm, think things through a little more clearly.

"It isn't a matter of choosing Evan over you, or vice versa," Claire stated firmly. "It's a matter of right and wrong, and proper—"

"My, my, my," a deep, masculine voice rose unexpectedly from the shadows of a small storage building behind the town hall. "What a most entertaining evening this has been," Brody Gerard observed as he moved toward them. "Too bad that cursed priest showed up when he did. Things were really warming up quite nicely, until he happened by."

272

At his approach, Beth gave a cry and moved closer to Ian. In a protective gesture, he slipped his arm about her shoulders and glared at the older man. "You're a swine, you are," he snarled, "to be spying on us like that!"

Brody Gerard halted. A dark brow arched in warning. "Have a care who you call a swine, boy. I don't take kindly to grown men calling me names, and I don't intend to make any exceptions in your case, either."

"Then why don't you hie yourself out of here?" Ian released Beth and shoved her behind him. "I don't take kindly to Peeping Toms."

Watching them, Claire decided it was past time she put an end to this rapidly worsening little interchange. She stepped between Brody Gerard and her brother. "One way or another, Mr. Gerard, the evening's entertainment out here is over. If you don't mind, we'll just be on our way."

A hand snaked out and grabbed her arm. "Oh, not so fast, missy," he drawled, looking her up and down with that repulsive way of his. "Go on. Send the children back into the dance. You and I, though, still have some unfinished business."

Fear rippled down Claire's spine, and set her skin to crawling. "There's no business I ever care to do with you, Mr. Gerard!" She pulled back, but he held her tight. She jerked harder, but to no avail. "Let me go, please. Now!"

"I'd do what my wife asks, Gerard," Evan said suddenly from behind them. "If it's unfinished business you're looking to settle, I'd be glad to help you out with that right here and now."

Brody Gerard glared down at her, the light in his eyes suddenly flat and hard. "Some other time then, missy," he said softly, releasing her. As Claire hurried to join Beth and Ian at Evan's side, the big drifter's mouth lifted in a feral smile. "Speaking of unfinished business, Mac-Kay, seems like you've got a heap more of it than I do."

"Indeed?" Evan growled. "And what might that be?"

In that moment, Claire knew what Brody Gerard planned to do. She lifted her horrified gaze to his. At the look of malevolent triumph gleaming there, her heart sank. "Nay," she whispered, shaking her head. "Nay . . ."

"Ask your wife why she's standing out back of the town hall with her brother and your sister," the big, swarthy man sneered. "Ask her what those two were doing just before she got here. And then ask her why, though she's apparently known about their shenanigans for a while, she's never bothered to tell you. Ask her, MacKay," Brody Gerard taunted, his smile now brutally victorious. "Because I think once you hear what that boy has been doing with your sweet little sister, things aren't ever going to be the same—"

"Lyin' dog!" Ian roared as, with three strides, he flung himself at the bigger man. His momentum was just enough to knock Brody Gerard off balance, and both tumbled to the ground.

"Ian! Nay!" Claire leaped forward, to be immediately drawn up sharply by Evan's hand on her arm.

"Get some help," he ordered, his face an impassive mask. "Get Sheriff Whitmore!" With that, her husband whirled her about and pushed her in the opposite direction. "And take Beth with you!"

Claire hesitated but an instant, then grabbed Beth's hand and dragged her along. Though she was loath to leave Ian, not knowing what either of the two men might do to him, she also knew she couldn't stop any of them without help. So she ran on, fighting a struggling, crying Beth all the way.

"Let me go," the girl begged. "Let me go! If Brody doesn't kill Ian, Evan will!"

"Nay," Claire ground out, "he won't be that lucky. *Neither* of you will be that lucky. I just hope you're both happy with this particular pot you've stirred."

"We love each other! Can't any of you understand that?"

"Well, it won't mean aught to your father or brother if you and Ian keep on the way you're headed," Claire muttered bluntly, at the end of her patience. "But I doubt either of you have given any thought to that, have you?"

"Oh, just let me go!" the girl sobbed, digging in her heels.

Claire's strength and determination, however, was a match and more for Beth's. She finally pulled her to the hall's side door. "Stay here," she then ordered, "and don't make a scene, or you'll bring even more shame down on your family. Do you understand me, Beth?"

"Y-yes," the girl snuffled, wiping her eyes.

Though it took but a minute or two to locate Sheriff Whitmore in the crowd, quietly explain the situation transpiring out back, then make their way to the site, all three males were bloodied and bruised by the time they arrived. Ian knelt on the ground, his nose broken, spitting out blood. Evan and Brody were locked in brutal combat nearby, neither man giving quarter as they pummeled each other unmercifully.

It required Jake Whitmore and three others to pull the two opponents apart. Even then, Evan and Brody glared at each other with murderous rage, straining at the hands that held them.

"Well, it seems you've finally gone and disturbed the peace one time too many, Gerard," the sheriff said, shaking his head. "I'm afraid that's going to cost you a night or two in jail."

"And what about MacKay?" the big man cried through a lacerated lip, shooting a nervous glance at the crowd slowly forming behind them. "He's disturbing the peace, too!"

"That lowlife was accosting my wife when I showed up," Evan snarled, wiping the blood from his own split lip. "That's grounds enough to lock him up!"

Jake Whitmore turned to Claire. "Is that true, Mrs. MacKay?"

Suddenly, all eyes were on her. Claire swallowed hard and nodded. "Aye, it's true."

"Lock him up, boys," the sheriff then curtly ordered. "Seems pretty cut-and-dried to me."

As the men led Brody Gerard away, though, Ian climbed to his feet. "I'm not finished with you, you lying swine!" he shouted after him, his lean, wiry body stiff with rage. "But when I am, you'll rue this night. You'll rue it to your dying day!"

20

The merciful man doeth good to his own soul: but he that
is cruel troubleth his own flesh.

Proverbs 11:17

After Doc Childress had set Ian's nose, treated Evan's split lip, and taped his cracked rib, the MacKays rode home in a tense silence. Beth and Ian were then summarily sent to their rooms. For a time, as she and Evan washed up and prepared for bed, Claire began to hope nothing more would be said about the evening's unpleasant ending.

Finally, however, Evan, dressed now in only his denims, whirled around as Claire stood at the mirror, brushing her hair. "Well, are you going to explain what Brody Gerard meant by all those accusations?" he demanded. "They're not about to disappear or be forgotten anytime soon, you know."

Claire's hand tightened on the brush handle, her knuckles clenching white. Then, with a weary sigh, she laid aside the brush and turned to face her husband. "He only means to stir up trouble between us—in any way he can. You told me yourself he hates the MacKays."

"So are you saying everything Gerard said was untrue?"

For once in her life, Claire fervently wished not only that she could lie, but lie well. But she couldn't. Evan was her husband, and a marriage built upon lies was no marriage at all.

"Nay, I'm not saying that." She met Evan's hard, searching gaze. "I had more than one reason for going outside last night. I'd noticed that Beth and Ian had disappeared, and I went to look for them."

His mouth went taut with disdain. "Evidently you found them. What were they doing?"

"I wasn't the first to find them. Noah Starr had gotten to Beth and Ian first."

"So you hadn't gone out to meet Noah."

Claire stared up at Evan. "What would ever make you think that?"

He shrugged. "Maybe the fact that just as soon as you left, I happened to notice Noah wasn't around either. And considering the rumors that started up the last time you two were found alone . . ."

There was something in Evan's voice, something that made Claire suspect her husband's intent had sprung from a motive far beyond concern for her reputation. The realization angered her, not only for her own sake, but even more for the sake of the good-hearted, totally innocent priest.

"So, you came out after me because you suspected I might be having an illicit tryst with Noah, did you?" she demanded, refusing to make excuses or back down.

"I didn't exactly say that." Evan had the good grace to blush.

"Aye, you all but did."

He stared at her, and Claire could see his own anger begin to rise.

"Tell me then, Claire, once and for all, that I don't have any reason to suspect you." Evan's voice dropped a notch, became soft and intense. "That's all, just once, and I'll never speak or think about it again."

She could feel the blood drain from her face. Mother Mary, she thought, her panic swelling, did he know about that one day when she had looked upon Noah as more than just her priest and confessor? But how could he? And, even more importantly, how could he doubt her loyalty, her love?

The hurt and sense of betrayal she felt were mirrored in Evan's eyes. She saw it there, shining clear and strong as a starry, Highland night. The realization plucked at a memory. A memory of a day months ago, when she and Evan had first visited Lainie and Donall MacKay.

On the walk to the old couple's croft house, Evan had spoken of Hannah for the first time. Spoken of how the loss of her love had shattered his trust that he'd ever again be worthy of another woman's love.

Recalling that day, Claire understood now how deep her husband's wound still went. How vulnerable he still was, and how he might yet harbor a secret fear of some-day losing even her to another man. But they were unfounded fears.

How, though, to lay those fears forever to rest? How to speak the words he needed to hear?

Mayhap, in withholding her secrets, she had been party to the problem. Mayhap, though she had tried to hide the truth from him, Evan had sensed there had always been a tiny part of herself that she kept from him. And mayhap, just mayhap, that wound would remain and fester until she, at last, fully opened her heart to him and revealed all her secrets.

"You haven't aught to worry about or suspect, Evan," Claire finally said. "You're my husband. I love you."

"And Noah. How do you feel about him?"

She resolutely met his gaze. "I care for Noah. Indeed, the day Noah counseled me about clearing the air with you, I did feel a passing awareness of him as a man. It was an awareness, though, that sprung solely from respect and gratitude for his kindness to me. Aye, the feelings frightened and confused me for a short time, but I soon realized that's all they were—a passing awareness that quickly faded back to the warm friendship we share."

"So, you lusted after Noah, and you expect me to accept that it's over, never to happen again?" He gave a harsh laugh. "Think again, Claire. Don't forget I've been down that road before."

"I didn't actually *lust* after him." Frustration filled her. "I just saw him suddenly as a man as well as a priest. Is that so wrong? Have you never felt that way since we were wed? Have you not even once gazed upon Hannah since we came to Culdee Creek, and not seen her as a woman—the woman you once loved—instead of just a friend and another man's wife?"

"You're my wife now, Claire. I love you, and I'll always be faithful to you." Evan looked away. "That's all that matters."

"Aye, Evan, and it's the same for me. Temptation isn't a sin, unless you give in to it. And I didn't sin in my passing fancy for a man who, by the way, never, ever did aught to suggest or encourage such feelings. Where I did sin, though, was in keeping all the secrets from you. I was wrong to do so, and I'll never do it again."

"Secrets?" He threw back his head in exasperation. "There are *more?*"

Claire dragged in a deep breath. "Well, aye. There's also the tale of my first encounter with Brody Gerard in Gates' Mercantile, the day after Devlin broke his leg."

"Gerard!" he snarled, his expression darkening. "And exactly what happened that day?"

"He wished to see my hair unbound, and proceeded to pull a pin from it. When I slapped him, he grabbed me. Then I kicked him in the shin. That made him verra angry, but luckily Noah happened along at that moment. In that quiet way of his, he finally convinced Mr. Gerard to leave."

"So, tonight wasn't the first time Gerard laid a hand on you." A hard, furious gleam flared in Evan's eyes. "If I had known that when I lit into him . . ."

"That's why I hadn't told you before now. I didn't want to be the cause of you getting into a fight with that man. And I hoped, if mayhap foolishly, that Mr. Gerard would just go away."

"Fat chance! The man's like a vulture, constantly circling its prey, waiting for a sign of weakness to close in for the kill. Best way to deal with a vulture is to shoot him clean out of the sky. You don't give a man like Gerard multiple chances, at least not if you value your life anyway."

At the cold fury in her husband's voice, Claire couldn't help a shiver. She had never seen this ruthless side of him before, and it frightened her. "Well, no matter," she hastened to say. "He's in jail now, and can't harm anyone."

"Yeah," Evan agreed, "and once I tell Jake about this other little incident, maybe it'll be enough to send him back for another stretch in prison." He paused to study her intently. "Well, reckon that only leaves us one last secret to deal with, doesn't it? So how about you finish telling me what happened after you found Beth and Ian with Noah?"

Nay, husband, Claire thought, meeting his gaze. There is *one* more secret besides the problem with Ian and Beth. Some instinct, though, suddenly made her hesitate telling him about that night in Sutherland. Or at least not until the matter of Ian and Beth was resolved first, at any rate. Ian had enough problems right now, without adding even more.

She sighed. "I told Noah I'd deal with Beth and Ian, so he left. That's when Brody Gerard walked out from his hiding place and, not long after, you arrived."

"So Gerard got an eyeful of what went on between Beth and Ian, and then with Noah, and with you."

Claire nodded, her mouth suddenly as dry as cotton. Here it comes now, she thought. "Aye, I suppose he did."

"And what did he see, Claire?"

She knew she could protest that she didn't know, not having been there herself, but she *did* know. Or at least had a pretty good idea anyway. Beth and Ian's guilt had been almost palpable.

"I suppose he saw them kissing," she replied as calmly as she could. "They care deeply for each other, you know?"

"I'd an inkling that might be the case." Evan ran a hand raggedly through his hair, setting the dark, wavy strands awry. "But I'd counted on Ian coming to me before things got out of hand. He'd promised me he would. And then there was also my trust in you, that you'd share any concerns about them with me."

He walked to the room's only chair, a finely wrought oak rocker, and flung himself into it. "Why didn't you come to me, tell me about Ian and Beth before nearly the whole town got involved?"

She licked her lips and swallowed hard. "The whole town doesn't know. Only Noah and Brody Gerard."

"Well, we know Noah won't say anything, but are you willing to bet my sister's reputation on the fact Gerard will keep his big mouth shut?"

Claire didn't reply. Evan knew the answer to that as well as she. Besides, what concerned her now was what

282

Evan planned to do about his sister and Ian. "I was wrong to keep this from you, just as I kept the other secrets, but I thought I could handle it. You were so burdened with all the work and responsibility—"

"That's not really why you tried to keep this a secret, and you know it!" Evan spat. "It was because you were trying to protect your brother. Maybe that's been the problem all along, Claire. You keep making excuses for Ian, trying to solve his problems for him, and he's never had to take responsibility for his own actions." He shoved from the chair and began to pace, shaking his head like some lion parading before his pride. "But not this time, Claire. This time Ian's going to bear the consequences of his actions!"

Fear swelled within her. She clasped her hands to her chest. "And what about Beth? She's as much to blame as—"

"She's thirteen! Ian's sixteen!" Evan swung around and leveled a furious gaze on her. "He's old enough to know better, while Beth is just barely coming into womanhood. Blast it all! Doesn't that boy have a shred of decency or honor in him?"

"Now hold on a wee minute," Claire cried. "You don't know Ian like I do. He has his problems, but he's deep down good and decent. You're talking as if he's some slavering lecher, when he's but a normal lad in love."

"Love!" Her husband gave a snort of disgust. "And pray tell what, at their age, do either of them know about real love?"

"Och, how can you be so thick-skulled, Evan MacKay?" Frustration flooded her. "It doesn't matter what either of them as yet truly knows. What matters is whatever they feel, they feel strongly, with all the power and glory of youth. It'll do no good to punish them for it. We must help them control it, and understand why the fullness of that love must be saved for marriage."

"Well, I don't see any evidence of control or understanding in their behavior tonight!" With that, he took back his seat, closed his eyes, and began to rock.

Claire watched him for a time, knowing full well that Evan was sorting through it all and formulating a plan. The tension built drop by drop, like water leaking through a chink in the roof, until her nerves were strung so tightly Claire thought she might scream. Strung tightly—between her loyalty to her brother and her husband.

If she could have, Claire would have run rather than ever be forced into such an untenable position. But this time there was nowhere to go, no place to hide. Nowhere save here, in this room, and it all—*her* life as well as Ian's—suddenly depended on what Evan would next say.

"He's got to leave Culdee Creek, Claire." The pronouncement, when it finally came, was the most brutal utterance she had ever heard from Evan. "Maybe only for a time, until both he and Beth can get this better under control, but Ian's got to leave."

"Och, nay!" In frantic denial, Claire flung herself at her husband's feet. She laid her hands over his, and felt him clench the chair arms. "Don't send Ian away, Evan! It'd break his heart. Culdee Creek's his home, the first decent home he's had in so verra many years. He needs us all if he's ever to heal."

The tears welled, then spilled down her cheeks. "And I need him. I-I love him."

Evan lifted an anguished face to her. "Do you think I *want* to do this, Claire? Don't you think I feel a responsibility to the boy? And don't you know that I realize how it will hurt you?" He pulled his hands from beneath hers and clasped her face in his palms. "But what choice have I? I'm responsible for my sister while my parents are gone. And, even if they were to come home soon, what kind of position would it put them in, having to weigh Beth's welfare over the impact sending Ian away might have on our marriage? Either way, they'd be forced to choose between one child or another."

"J-just explain all this to B-Beth and Ian," she sobbed. "They're y-young, and haven't the experience yet to understand the p-possible consequences of their actions. But if you t-tell them . . ."

"Oh, I plan to tell them all right. But I also plan to send Ian away for a while, too. It's for his own good. It's past time that boy realize people mean what they say. If he doesn't, he's never going to have a chance in this world."

"H-how can you be so hard-hearted?" Claire wrenched her face free and glared up at him. "He's but a lad, not far from your age when you robbed your father and first ran away from home. Yet your father didn't condemn you or refuse to give you another chance!"

"No, my pa didn't," her husband quietly replied, though his face suddenly had the appearance of one ravaged by painful memories. "First, though, I had to learn a few things the hard way, before I was ready to come home and start over. And that's what I'm thinking Ian needs to do."

"Am I not to have any say in this?" she demanded, her tears drying in the heat of her growing wrath. "He *is* my brother, after all."

"And I'm your husband."

"So you're asking me to choose, are you?"

"I think Ian, when he continually ignored all the warnings you must have given him, made the choice for all of us, Claire," was his simple reply.

She stared up at Evan, so furious she could no longer find words to hurl back at him. As hard as it was to admit, much of what he had said was true. Ian's refusal to heed her warnings *had* brought them to this impasse.

But Ian was young, troubled, and needed their help. Help that Evan had now decided must be withdrawn.

The minutes ticked by, pressing down on her until Claire felt as if she might suffocate. Yet all the while, she yearned for her husband to take her into his arms, soothe away her tears, and promise that somehow, some way they'd work this out. Work it out like they had the other problems this night, like they always had before.

But Evan just sat there, silent, his expression impassive, until Claire thought she'd scream. Finally, she could take the tension no longer. Pushing to her feet, she pulled a pillow and extra blanket from the bed and strode toward the door. As she reached for the door, a soft, sudden scuffle of feet on the other side alerted her to the fact that someone had been listening there.

Claire yanked open the door and stuck her head into the hall. A flurry of feet, a brief glimpse of a nightshirt, and then Ian's bedroom door closed silently. She opened her mouth to call out to her brother, then thought the better of it. Without a backward glance, Claire clutched her pillow and blanket more closely to her and walked from her room.

~

Somewhere deep in the night, Claire was awakened from a fitful sleep on the parlor sofa by the kitchen's back door opening softly, then closing. She lay there for a moment, gathering befuddled thoughts, listening to the heavy tread of footsteps gradually fading away.

It was either Ian or Evan, she realized. An impulse to rise and seek out whoever it was filled her. Then, with an anguished sigh, Claire turned and pulled the pillow over her head. She couldn't deal with any more anger, any more pain this night. The morrow would be soon enough as it was.

ॐ

Breakfast the next morning was so tense for the Mac-Kays that even the hands noticed. The men kept their usual joking and jibes to themselves, then hurriedly finished their meals and left. Evan departed soon thereafter to see to a few chores before church services. Anything, he decided, was better than enduring another minute of the somber atmosphere and the recriminating looks directed at him by both Claire and Beth.

A half hour later, his chores completed, Evan wasn't in any more of a mood to return to the house than he had been when he left. His head ached, his eyes felt like he had rubbed them with grit, and he was bone tired. Another cup of coffee was definitely in order, though, so he headed up to Hannah and Devlin's house.

As he expected, both were in the kitchen, just finishing up their own breakfast. All four of the children were there, too, and their cries of pleasure at his arrival heartened Evan. At least here, he was welcome. At least here, he could relax and bask, if only for a short while, in the warmth of a happy family.

"Well, to what do we owe the honor of this visit?" Devlin asked, lowering his leg from the chair he had it propped on and pushing it over to Evan. "I would've thought, after staying up so late at the town dance, you'd be sleeping in this morning."

"There were some problems,"–he waited until Hannah finished shooing the children out to get them dressed for church–"that cut short our stay in town last night. It's a long story, but Ian and Beth were caught

287

kissing behind the town hall, Noah Starr found them, then Claire. And then, as if things weren't already bad enough, Brody Gerard got in the middle of it. I ended up fighting him, with Ian getting his nose broken–"

"Whoa, hang on a minute!" Devlin cried, holding up his hand. "Sounds like you really *did* have some problems there. Now, start from the beginning, and this time fill in all the important details."

"Yeah, the details," Evan muttered, "like Claire knowing all along that Beth and Ian were getting a mite too friendly, and . . ."

By the time Evan had finished the whole sad, sordid tale, Hannah had returned to the kitchen. "And then I told Claire," he said with a sigh, glancing up at Hannah, "that Ian had to be sent away. She, of course, wasn't at all happy with that, but what else could I do?"

Devlin exchanged a troubled look with his wife. She walked to the back door and took down her jacket.

"I think I'll just take a little walk while you men finish up here," she said. Before Evan could protest that he'd like her to stay, Hannah was gone.

"I see your dilemma," Devlin replied then, turning back to his cousin, "but maybe it's a bit premature making such a harsh decision. Maybe you should think on this a while longer."

"I *have* thought about it." Evan hung his head and rubbed his throbbing temples. "I laid awake all night trying to figure out any other possible solution. But I've got responsibilities now, and one of them is my sister's welfare. Pa trusts me to do the right thing while he's gone. I can't let him down. Not this time, not ever again!"

"The burden of trust and responsibility can be a heavy one at times," the big foreman agreed. "But no one can carry them well without a big measure of compassion."

"I *have* tried to be compassionate," Evan protested, beginning not to like the direction this conversation was headed. "It's just that I can't see any answer other than sending Ian away. I can't trust the two of them together anymore, yet how in the blazes am I going to keep them apart? You tell me that, Devlin."

"But how is sending Ian away any different than running away from a problem, Evan? One way or another, you'll be putting distance between you and it, rather than dealing with it."

Evan's eyes narrowed, and it was all he could do to keep a handle on his temper. "I don't want to run away from anything ever again," he said through gritted teeth. "But this isn't something that'd just affect me, if I made the wrong call. And that scares me, Devlin."

"It'd scare anyone. But no one said taking on the raising of a child, however old and troublesome he might be, was easy."

"And what if Beth gets herself in a family way because of Ian? Then whose fault will it be?"

"We're family, so it'd be all our faults. Most of all, though, it'd be Ian and Beth's." Devlin smiled. "I don't think it'll come to that, though. We've just got to help them, until they can see through it all to what's right. We've got to be there for them, and guide them through it."

Evan stared long and hard at his cousin. When had Devlin begun to deal with everything with such compassion? Compassion . . . what a strange word to use to describe the man sitting across from him. But, after all this time, the description fit him, and fit him well.

Had it been there all along, buried just beneath the pain and anger and frustration? Evan wondered. If so, how much of the man was the result of his finally coming to a peace within himself in loving Hannah, and how much of it was the resultant gift of wholeheartedly turning back to God? Evan suspected the startling change in his cousin was a little of both.

Suddenly, a deep weariness engulfed him. He was so tired of trying to be strong and decisive. Though he still believed sending Ian away was by far the easiest solution to the problem, Evan was no longer certain it was the *best* solution for anyone, himself included.

He leaned back in his chair and closed his eyes. "I need some help with this, Devlin. I'm afraid I'm about to make the biggest mistake of my life."

"I'll help you in any way I can, Cousin. In fact, I'd take it as an honor to help you."

Evan opened his eyes, smiling at last. "Well, I think it'd be the other way around, myself, but one way or another—"

Footsteps sounded on the front porch, and a knocking came at the door. Devlin rose, hobbled the short distance to the door, and opened it. Sheriff Jake Whitmore stood there.

"Come on in, Jake," Devlin said, stepping aside to motion him in. "The coffee's still hot and—"

"Good," the sheriff interrupted brusquely, noting Evan sitting at the kitchen table. "I'm glad you're both together so I can get this unpleasant matter settled all the sooner." His glance locked with Evan's. "There's been some more trouble in town. I thought it best to head out here first thing and see if we could get to the bottom of it, before it really gets out of hand."

c

Beth, red and swollen-eyed, silently helped Claire clean up after breakfast, then immediately headed for her room. Ian never came down from his room at all. Claire gave a passing thought to going upstairs to check on him, then decided to let him sleep. No sense stirring anything up this morn any sooner than need be.

After dressing for church, Claire headed back downstairs for a cup of tea to calm her nerves. A soft knock on the kitchen door, a few minutes after she sat down with her tea, jerked her from her somber thoughts. She looked up just as Hannah's pale blonde head peeked around the door.

"Mind if I join you for a few minutes?" the other woman asked.

Claire forced a smile of welcome. "Sure, come on in. I'm not certain I'll be verra good company this morn, but you're more than welcome to a spot of tea."

Hannah removed her jacket, laid it aside, and quickly made herself a cup. Then she slid into a seat across from Claire. "Evan told us about last night," she announced without any pretense at social conversation. "Is there anything I can do to help?"

"Not that I can think of at this moment, save get Evan to change his mind about sending Ian away." As she spoke, a great lump welled in Claire's throat, and her eyes burned. There were no tears to ease the pain, however. She had cried out all she had last night.

"He's very upset right now," her friend offered. "It's tearing him up to do this to Ian—and to you. But then, there's Beth."

"Aye, then there's Beth," Claire repeated woodenly.

"I also overheard him telling Devlin about Brody accosting you at Gates' Mercantile, and then the fight last night." She sighed and shook her head. "That man can't seem to help creating heartbreak and pain wherever he goes."

Claire nodded her agreement. "He's so full of hate, I can't see how he can stand himself. One would think he finds all his pleasure in other folk's misfortunes, but I can't say that I could imagine him truly happy about aught."

"He isn't," Hannah said. "I think his heart's so wounded he may never find happiness. I keep Brody in my prayers, though. Even if no one has ever been able to touch his heart, I still hold out the hope that God finally will."

Claire stared at her in amazement. She had heard of Hannah's past life from Evan, and the cruel role Brody Gerard had played in it even before Hannah had finally run away to the sanctuary of Culdee Creek. Vicious beatings when she failed to earn enough money some nights, forcing himself on her, and then that first time she had run away and been caught and brought back to the bordello . . . His brutal treatment, when he had later kidnapped Hannah, paled in comparison!

It shamed Claire that she still held such a grudge against Mary Sue Edgerton, who had only harmed her with gossip, while Hannah had not only forgiven a man who had both mentally and physically brutalized her, but now even prayed for his redemption. She still had a very long journey ahead of her, Claire realized, if she were ever to follow the Lord like Hannah already did.

Right now, though, there wasn't time to dwell on the Lord or His ways. All she could deal with was the moment. Nothing else mattered but the growing fear that she would soon lose her brother and, in the process, irreparably imperil her marriage.

"Well, I can't say," Claire muttered, "that I feel any great sense of pity for the man's plight. If it hadn't been for him, Evan wouldn't have found out about Ian and Beth, and I might still have been able—"

The front door slammed open. "Claire, come here," her husband called. "Now!"

Claire and Hannah exchanged a startled look, then rose and hurried into the parlor. Evan, Devlin, and Sheriff Jake Whitmore stood there, troubled expressions on their faces.

"What is it, Evan?" Claire halted before them. "What do you want?"

Evan met her gaze with an unflinching one of his own. "Brody Gerard was killed last night," he informed her, "shot dead while he slept–shot through his jail cell window."

Hannah moved up to grasp Claire's arm. "Dear Lord," she whispered. "Dear Lord."

"That's not the worst of it, Hannah," Evan said. "After the way Ian threatened Gerard last night in front of half the town, he's one of the prime suspects."

The bottom fell from Claire's stomach. The room whirled crazily. She swayed. If not for Hannah's hand on her arm, she knew she would've lost her balance and fallen.

"Come on, Claire." Her friend's voice sounded as if it came from some place far away. "Let's sit you down. Evan, help me, will you?"

The next thing Claire knew, she was seated on the sofa, her head tucked between her knees. Someone was fanning her, and a glass of cool water was soon pressed to her lips.

"Take a sip," Hannah urged. "Breathe deeply and the dizziness will pass."

Claire did as ordered. Eventually, she began to feel better. Still, when she looked up at the three men standing before her, the same, sick sensation immediately returned. With it this time, though, came the horrible memories.

Ian . . . Ian accused of murder. It was a nightmare.

"Evan's a suspect, too," the sheriff said, squatting beside her. "He says you can vouch for his presence here all night, though."

Her glance met Evan's. His expression was flat, unreadable. He wasn't about, Claire realized, to help her in this.

293

"Someone left the house last night," she said slowly, her own words sounding strangely muffled. "I can't say who it was, but it was a male. I don't know what time it was, just that it was verra late."

"But surely you would've known if it was Evan or not. He's your husband, after all."

She could feel the heat rise in her cheeks. "We weren't sleeping together, if that's what you're getting at. I slept downstairs last night in the parlor."

Jake colored in embarrassment. "Oh, I see." He turned to Evan, who stood there, his expression still impassive. "Well, Evan? Did you go somewhere last night?"

"I already told you I never left Culdee Creek after we got home. If Claire heard someone leave the house, it must have been Ian."

The sheriff turned back to Claire. "Well, maybe we need to have a talk with Ian then. Find out why he left the house last night."

Somehow, she had known that would be where the sheriff headed next. The dizziness struck her anew but, this time, Claire fiercely shook it away. This time, she needed a clear head and steady nerves. She needed to be able to think things through and decide what she would next say.

Whoever had left the house last night, there was no reason to assume he had ridden back to Grand View. She cursed herself now for not going after him. At least she would've known who it was and what he was planning to do. But now ... now she didn't know and couldn't protect either one of them.

The recollection of Evan's words last night came back to haunt her. Words about dealing with a vulture by shooting him clean out of the sky. Words about not giving Gerard anymore chances.

Still, it made no sense that Evan would murder Brody Gerard. Evan wasn't that kind of a man. She *had* to believe that. She just had to.

But Ian . . . What if her volatile brother *had* killed Brody Gerard in a misguided fit of temper, after hearing that Evan planned on sending him away? It made no sense to take it out on Gerard, no matter how low-down mean the man was, but her brother's emotions had been running pretty high last night. He might have been so angry and confused that he wasn't–

With an angry, mental slash, Claire cut off her thoughts in midsentence. No matter how upset he might have been, Ian was no cold-blooded killer either. And all this second-guessing about Evan and Ian wasn't getting her anywhere at any rate. What she *did* need to do, though, was say something, and soon, or incriminate Ian just by her silence.

But to all but point an accusing finger at her own brother . . . Claire's stomach clenched, then twisted painfully. For a fleeting moment, she thought she might be sick. Then Evan's words last night filled her head.

Maybe that's been the problem all along, Claire, he had said. *You keep making excuses for Ian, trying to solve his problems for him, and he's never had to take respon-sibility for his own actions.*

Aye, she thought, mayhap she *had* tried too hard all these years to solve his problems, and never given him the chance to do so. But now was certainly not the time to begin. She couldn't–*wouldn't*–betray her brother in such a dastardly manner.

"Aye, Sheriff, mayhap you *should* talk with Ian." Claire forced herself to meet her husband's steely gaze. "But then, exactly what *will* you do, if he, too, claims he wasn't the one who left the house last night?"

21

*Cast thy burden upon the L*ORD*, and he shall sustain thee.*
Psalm 55:22

Ian flatly denied ever leaving the house after going to bed. To his credit, Jake Whitmore handled the situation well, neither accusing nor discounting either Evan or Ian. He finally looked to Claire, shook his head, and sighed.

"Well, reckon I'd best be heading on back. Considering there wasn't much love lost between Brody Gerard and the town of Grand View, I've got a passel of other suspects to question." The sheriff shoved his hat on his head, then paused. "I reckon I don't have to advise either of you"—he looked from Evan to Ian—"not to leave the area until the case is closed or someone's formally charged, do I?"

"I think you've made things clear enough," Evan growled, unable to keep from directing a seething glance at Ian. "Neither of us will be going anywhere. You have my word on it."

"Well, that's good enough for me."

Evan saw Jake Whitmore to the door and stood there, shoulders stiff, stance rigid, until he had ridden off. Then, he turned slowly to face Ian. "Where do you get off, boy, lying to the sheriff like that?" he demanded, his voice gone low and harsh. "You and I both know it wasn't me who left the house last night. And, since Claire would rather die than falsely implicate either one of us, I trust her story that she heard *someone* leave."

"Evan," Claire began, stepping forward, "before you start on Ian, permit me a few minutes to talk with him alone. No good will be served—"

"No. It's past time we deal with Ian together, or not at all." Evan clamped down hard on his fury, knowing that if there was to be any hope of getting through to the boy, he needed Claire on his side. "Can't you see what he's been doing, trying to play us against each other? Well, it's got to stop, Claire, or he'll tear us apart!"

"You'd like that, wouldn't you?" Ian burst out, his face livid. "To win Claire to your side against me? It's what you've been trying to do since the first day you met her, wooing her with your fine words and smooth ways. Never once have you thought of me or my needs."

"That's not true, and you know it!" Evan snapped, rounding back on him. "I've tried to be your friend, to encourage you to come to me when you had a problem or needed something. But, for some reason I can't figure, you persist in seeing me as your enemy." He expelled a long, defeated breath. "Well, I'm tired of it, Ian. And I'm tired of your lying and sneaking around behind my back, too."

"I-I didn't lie. I never rode to Grand View or killed Brody Gerard. I swear it!"

Evan shook his head and held up a warning hand. "Save it for someone who doesn't know you, boy. If you weren't Claire's brother, I wouldn't care what you did, or how much trouble you got into. But you're treading on thin ice when you start dragging the MacKay name through the dirt. Today, you've finally gone too far. Not only have you managed to get yourself implicated in a murder, but you've pulled me into it as well."

"You're only there because you've got reason to be!" Ian taunted. "After all, I don't even know how to use a gun, but I know you do. So who's a more likely suspect because of that, do you think?"

He wasn't getting anywhere with the boy. Evan could see that plainly enough. Indeed, Ian looked almost as if he relished the battle. But, as she had stood there watching them, Claire's face had gone increasingly paler, until she looked as white as a sheet. For her sake, if for nothing else, it was time to put an end to this pointless argument.

"Just go on up to your room, Ian," Evan muttered in disgust. "This is obviously not the time to continue this discussion."

"And what if I don't want to go to my room?" the boy demanded. "What will you do then?"

Had it come to that, then, Evan thought, his fury rising, that now he must be goaded into using physical force? Well, if that cocky kid thought to defy him in his own house—

In a swift move, Claire stepped between him and her brother. "Go to your room, Ian Sutherland," she hissed, rearing up full into her brother's face. "Now!"

The boy stared at her for a long moment, then shrugged. "Fine," he spat. "I'll do that. But only"—he shot Evan a defiant glare—"because you're asking, Claire." With that Ian turned on his heel, stomped from the parlor, and pounded up the stairs.

It took a time for Evan's anger to cool. Finally, however, he found words that were calmer and more considered. "I'm sorry about that, Claire," he said. "I know how it hurts you when Ian and I fight. But I just can't figure out what to do about that boy anymore."

"I know, Evan," was her choked reply. And then, without another word, Claire walked from the room.

ৡ

That day, Claire moved Ian's and her belongings into the bunkhouse. Though it tore at her heart to put such a physical as well as emotional distance between her and her husband, she didn't know what else to do. Both Evan and Ian desperately required some time apart. Of the two, she knew Ian needed the comfort of her presence more than Evan did. Or, leastwise, Evan could handle it better.

In the ensuing days, though the list of possible murder suspects rapidly dwindled, Sheriff Whitmore never returned once to demand further explanations. Nonetheless, emotions at Culdee Creek ran high. Evan could barely bring himself to talk to Ian and, when he did, their confrontations always ended in angry words and accusations. Despair began to hang over everyone like a dark thundercloud, foreboding and ready to burst.

"He hates me, he does," her brother cried one cold, snowy November day as he sat in the kitchen. "He refuses to hear my side of aught. And I think he even suspects that I *did* kill Brody Gerard."

"You must give Evan some time to sort through everything that's happened of late," Claire said as she rolled out dough for a piecrust. "It'll all work out in the end. I just know it will."

"Och, aye," Ian snarled. "And you're the only person who thinks that. Do you see now why I *had* to lie to the sheriff? No one would've believed that I couldn't sleep and just went out for a ride. If I'd admitted to leaving the house that night, I'd either now be in jail or carted off to that reformatory in Buena Vista. You know that, Claire, as well as I."

Hot tears stung her eye. Suddenly, she couldn't even see what she was doing. With a despairing exhalation of breath, Claire set aside her rolling pin. "If the truth be told, I don't know what to think anymore, Brother. All I know is that I see our fine life here crumbling down about our feet."

"It wasn't much of a life at any rate," he grumbled. "I never really liked it here."

"I wonder," she said softly, "if you'll ever really like it anywhere."

"Och, so that's how it is, is it?" With a snarl, Ian leaped from his chair, knocking it over. "Then why don't I just march into town and confess to Gerard's killing? It'll take the heat off you and Evan; I'll be safely out of both of your lives, and everything can go back to the sweet, wee life you imagine you once had here."

"Aye, mayhap it would be best," Claire countered hotly, at the end of her patience. "Why should you ruin my life, as well as your own, in the bargain?"

As if struck by a blow, Ian staggered back, his defiance appearing to dissolve as quickly as it had risen. Tears welled in his eyes, began to trickle down his cheeks. "Y-you'd do that, would you?" he asked, his voice quavering. "You'd t-turn your back on me and walk away, after all we've b-been to each other, after what I-I did for you?"

Like some tiresome, unwanted guest, the gruesome specter of that night so long ago flared in Claire's mind once more. Ian *had* risked everything to save her from their uncle's lewd advances. Yet, as horrible as the experience had been for her, she sensed it had been even

300

worse for him, as he had smashed that stout length of wood repeatedly into their uncle's head, crushing his skull. Though it had taken them a time to realize Uncle Fergus was dead, the horrific reality had struck home soon enough. It was an act that might well haunt them the rest of their lives.

With a soft cry, Claire went to her brother, gathering him into her arms like she had done so many times when he was small. And, like those times, he clung fiercely to her now, sobbing piteously. She thought her heart might break.

"Nay, nay," Claire crooned, stroking his wild tumble of hair, "I won't turn my back on you, or walk away. How could I, after you killed Fergus to protect me? But Ian, och, will we ever, ever be free of that night?" She shuddered. "I still wake up sometimes, the nightmare of watching his body tumble down that steep rock wall into the sea sending me into a cold sweat. Och, but I just want to be free of those memories once and for all!"

"So do I, Claire," her brother whispered. "I can't help it, but I feel like I murdered him. I feel so dirty, so evil. Did we truly do wrong, do you think, pushing his body off the cliff to make it seem as if he'd taken a drunken tumble? Should we have stayed and confessed to what we did?"

"What choice had we?" Claire sighed. "Fergus's kin would've strung you up before a constable could've arrived to take you into custody. Nay," she shook her head with a savage conviction. "There was naught else we could've done. Naught!"

"You must not ever tell Evan." Her brother leaned back to look at her with moisture-bright eyes. "If he was ever to find out what I did, he'd have the final proof he needs to send me to jail. Promise me you'll never tell Evan!"

"Ian," Claire began in protest, "you don't know what you're asking—"

"On the contrary, Claire," a deep voice rose unexpectedly from the hall outside the kitchen, "I think Ian knows exactly what he's asking."

With a gasp, Claire released her brother and spun around. There, standing in the doorway, was her husband. His handsome face taut with rage, Evan glanced from her to Ian, and then back to her.

"I thought there weren't going to be any more secrets between us," he finally said, his voice hoarse with emotion. "Yet now I find that all the other secrets paled in comparison to this one."

"Evan," she began, walking toward him, "I was going to tell you. Indeed, if things hadn't gone so badly that night a week ago, I intended to tell you then. But after you refused to give Ian another chance, well, how could I do it then? Last night just wasn't the right time."

"And how about all those other times *before* then, Claire?" Evan snarled. "How about when we were still in Scotland, before we married? Or after we got to Culdee Creek? What was wrong with all those other times?"

Looking back now, Claire had to ask herself the same thing. Yet, at the time—all those other times—her hesitation had seemed completely justified. Och, but she had been such a fool!

"I was afraid," she forced herself to reply. "Afraid of losing your love. Afraid of changing your feelings for Ian, if you'd learned he had killed a man. Would you have felt safe having him even come to Culdee Creek if you had known? Would you, Evan?"

"That's not the point, Claire, and you know it," he countered angrily. "What matters is that you kept the information from me. You chose Ian over me. What does that say about us, our marriage, and your trust in me? *That's* what really matters in the end."

Hands clenched at her sides, she stared up at him, knowing he spoke true. She *had* kept something from

302

Evan that he'd had a right to know, something that, with Brody Gerard's death, might have cleared him of any charges even as it further implicated Ian. In her misguided attempt to protect her brother once again, she had failed to trust her husband. She had failed to be the wife—and person—she had promised him to be.

"It doesn't say much for me," Claire admitted softly, hanging her head in shame. "You deserved better, Evan, and for that I am so verra sorry. Can you ever forgive me?"

"I think, this time, it'll take more than forgiveness. Where does your true loyalty lie, Claire? Once you finally figure that out, we can talk. But you need to decide if there's ever going to be any room in your heart for anyone but you and Ian. Only then, once you finally decide, can we see if there's anything left worth rebuilding."

With that, Evan turned and strode across the hall, into the parlor, and out the front door. He never looked back, and the rigid set of his shoulders and head held high were the most heart-wrenching thing Claire had ever seen. He walked as if he might well be walking out of her life forever. He walked like a man who held himself together by the slenderest of threads. He walked as if his heart was breaking.

And she was the cause of it all, yet another woman who had, at long last, betrayed him.

❧

Midnight came and went, and still Claire couldn't sleep. She tossed and turned, rose to pace her room until the cold wooden floors turned her feet numb, then staggered back to bed and the warmth of her quilts. She cried and cried until she could cry no more, her chest aching with the effort it took to muffle her body-wracking sobs so Ian, sleeping next door, wouldn't hear. And still there was no solace or answers to be found, neither by dint of her own desperate thoughts, or from God.

Moonlight streamed through the little room's single window, gilding the interior in a silver glow. Her clarsach's bright strings caught the beams, reflecting the light in shimmering lines on the walls. Claire watched the ethereal dance for a time, then rose once more from her bed.

Mayhap there was peace to be found in playing her harp, she thought. It had been some time since she had last taken up the beautiful instrument and made music. Not since the night of the Fall Festival, if the truth be told.

She took the clarsach down from the top of the chest of drawers, carried it to her bed, and sat. For a while, she lightly plucked the strings, waiting for the sweet, bright sounds to move her, carry her away to a happier place as it always had before. This time, though, all the music did was remind her repeatedly of the sad turn her life had taken. All it served to do was help her recall a simpler existence when she was in Scotland.

Life had been hard in Culdee, but she had never known such pain as she had endured here, especially in the past days. Just as she had feared, opening her heart too fully to others, allowing herself to trust and come to need them had ultimately resulted in sorrow. And it had only seemed to make things worse for Ian, too.

Claire clutched the harp, holding it close in a despairing embrace. Just like Evan and the MacKays, it deserved better than her. She had nothing left to give to the bogwood instrument. She had nothing left to give to Evan—and perhaps never had.

Still, Claire mused, stroking the timeworn wood, it was a beautiful thing, a work of art with its fine carvings and intricate scrollwork. She knew now what she must do. MacKay family heirloom that it was, the clarsach would serve her one last time. And when it was gone, the music would be over—for she would never play again.

⌀

She went to see Noah Starr that day with misgiving, desperate for any solution other than the one she had decided upon, hoping against hope that Noah would, as he always had before, have an answer. Even so, Claire knew it was a last-ditch effort. Still, something beckoned her to the rectory that cold, sunny day, just one week before Thanksgiving.

Millie answered the door promptly. At the sight of Claire, she smiled. "Well, well, what a pleasant surprise. We haven't had a nice visit together in a long while, have we?" She stepped back and motioned her in. "Come in. Come in."

Claire entered and, as soon as Millie had closed the door behind her, turned to the older woman. "Is Noah about? I-I need to talk with him."

At the somber tone of Claire's voice, Millie's expression grew serious. "You're in luck. He just returned from a visit to Jesse Herring's. That dear old man's been ailing of late, you know, with the rheumatism."

"I hadn't heard." Claire managed a wan smile. "What with all the excitement . . . well, I haven't been in town much."

Noah's aunt nodded in sympathy. "I understand, dear. How is Ian holding up?"

"As well as can be expected, I suppose." Claire sighed. "It's both Ian and Evan, though, I'm worried about. That's why I'd like to talk with Noah."

"Yes, of course. I'll go check right now." With that, she gathered her skirts and bustled off, so much like a mother hen that Claire had to smile.

What a good, kind woman Millie Starr was. She was blessed to call her a friend. And then, there was Noah . . .

Since she had left Culdee and Father MacLaren's wise tutelage, Claire knew her relationship with the Lord had waned. She was ashamed to admit she had let herself get caught up in the heady excitement of falling in love with Evan, journeying to a new land, and then struggling to adjust and fit into a new family. When Abby and Conor had left, the struggle had only gotten worse.

Yet part of that struggle—perhaps a very large part, if the truth be told—had been of her own doing, in allowing God to take an increasingly smaller place in her life. And now, when she needed Him the most, she almost didn't know how to approach Him anymore.

It was past time, however, that she try to at least set her life right again with God. If she didn't, Claire didn't know how she could endure the journey to come.

But Noah would surely know how to help her. He could guide her back to the path. He, after all, was her special gift from God in this new land.

"He'll see you now," Millie said, returning from his study. "He's just finishing up a few last thoughts for Sunday's sermon, or he would've come for you himself."

"It's no problem," Claire said, taking Millie's hand in hers. "I wouldn't be troubling him now, but it's verra important."

"Noah doesn't mind, child. Truly he doesn't." His aunt gave her hand a squeeze. "Afterward, if you've got the time, maybe we can have a spot of tea and visit a bit."

"Aye, mayhap."

Claire turned then and walked to Noah's study. The door was ajar. She peeked in. He was just putting away his papers, so she entered.

At the sight of her, the priest grinned broadly. "I'm so glad you came, Claire." He rose, came around his huge oak desk, and clasped both her hands in his. "Come, let's sit by the window and talk."

He led her past the two walls of bookshelves stuffed with books, across a blue, red, and green fringed Aubusson rug, to the room's only window. Two blue damask-covered wing chairs sat before the window's dark green, velvet drapes. Claire took her place in one chair, and Noah soon joined her in the other.

"So, what brings you to see me today?" he asked, leaning forward and clasping his hands between his knees. "Have all the problems with Ian and Evan finally been cleared up?"

"Nay, not yet," Claire said with a sigh. "Though no charges have been pressed against either of them, so far they're still considered suspects. It's all so ridiculous, though. You know Evan well enough to know he wouldn't kill a man in cold blood. And Ian's but a sixteen-year-old lad."

"I know that, Claire, and I suspect Sheriff Whitmore does, too. You must just be patient, though I'd imagine that's hard to do right now considering the circumstances."

"I've tried, Noah, but it doesn't seem to help. All I see is how it's tearing us all apart. And I feel caught in the middle, between Evan and Ian. And now, because of his concern for Beth, Evan wants to send Ian away."

"I wondered what would come of that night I found Beth and Ian together."

She dug her nails hard into her palms to keep from crying. "Ian's a troubled lad. It was bad enough when he caused problems back in Scotland. But now he threatens Evan and Beth, and the MacKays. I can't let my brother do that, yet if Evan sends him away, it might well destroy the lad."

"You also cannot sacrifice your own life and happiness for Ian, either. And, if you'll forgive my saying this,

I don't think you can help him on your own, Claire. Ian needs more than just you can give."

"Mayhap," she whispered, ducking her head to hide her tears, "but I won't send him away to some reformatory or special school. Since we were children, we've always pledged, one to the other, to be there for each other. *I'm* the one who first took him away from the safety of home and a family, because I couldn't stomach the woman my mither had become, or the man she had wed. It was *my* arrogance and selfishness that thrust my wee brother into the world he was ill prepared to endure. Yet he never once complained or accused me of ruining his life. And he has always been there for me, through good times and bad."

"Yet he cannot seem to allow you this happiness with Evan," Noah offered gently. "Why is that, do you think?"

She shook her head. "I don't know. Mayhap because he's a wee bit jealous of sharing the attention and affection. Mayhap because, save for Beth, he has no other friends and is lonely. And mayhap he doesn't know how to be happy, or doesn't feel he deserves it at any rate." Claire covered her face with her hands. "Och, I don't know what to think, or do for him anymore!"

"Well, for starters, how about placing your trust in the Lord?"

She looked up at him through tear-blurred eyes. "I'm trying, Noah. Truly I am, but God just seems so verra far away right now. I don't know if I can find Him again. Indeed, I don't even know what He wishes of me anymore."

"He's not as far away as you may think, Claire." The young priest's lips lifted in quiet understanding. "Ofttimes, when we feel farthest from the Lord, He is there, right beside us. As the Lord is with you, right now."

"I've put Him from my heart and mind for a long while. I don't deserve—"

"*None* of us, no matter how good we are, deserves the Lord's love," he was quick to counter. "But it's there for us nonetheless, without end, without measure. All it takes is for us to turn to Him, and ask."

Strangely, Noah's words made Claire think of Evan. She gave a shaky laugh. "Aye, as you say, God might well take me back, forgive me, and love me time and again. But I'm not so certain how many more times my husband will do the same. Not, leastwise, if he must also do the same for my brother."

"Times are hard for the two of you just now, but there's still hope you can weather the storm together."

There was such tender compassion in Noah Starr's eyes Claire wanted to weep. "I don't know what to do to help make peace between them. I pray to God every night that He'll help them, but He seems not to answer."

"Keep on praying. Don't give up. Both Evan and Ian are in pain right now, both struggling to find their way out of the darkness that surrounds them. You must be their light, Claire. A light of love and compassion to guide them through that darkness."

Strange, she mused, but Father MacLaren had once said similar words to her. It had been that day in the rectory, when he had first mentioned the growing affection between her and Evan, encouraging her to open herself more fully to life and love. But what had it gotten her in the end, she thought bitterly, this opening of her heart to Evan and others? Indeed, she hadn't been able to help anyone. All her efforts had been for naught.

"Och, I'm so verra weary!" she cried, a frustrated despair filling her. "I can barely find strength to keep myself going. I haven't aught left to give to anyone."

"You have more than you think left yet to give. And what you lack the Lord will supply, if only you turn to Him and place your trust in Him. The cup of compassion not shared is wasted, but the cup spilled out on others is continually refilled."

"Och, fine words," she muttered, her frustration mounting, "but I told you, I'm weary of trying. All I want is for the pain to end!"

This wasn't helping, Claire realized with a renewed rush of despair. This time, it seemed even Noah couldn't help her. Besides, there was no point in belaboring a subject she had already made up her mind about.

Claire climbed to her feet. "I must be going."

Noah stood, his gaze full of sorrow. "Just promise me one thing more."

Her eyes narrowed. "And what might that be?"

"Think on what I've said, and don't make any decisions about anything just yet." He took her hand in his. "You're the heart of your family, Claire. You're the love. And Evan needs you as much as your brother does."

"Och, a-aye." Her voice broke as she thought suddenly of the unborn child who might never know its father. Would she ultimately fail it, too, as she seemed to be failing everyone else? "If I'm the heart and love of my family, we're all in a verra bad way. And *that* frightens me most of all."

22

*For ye were sometimes darkness, but now are ye light in
the Lord: walk as children of the light.*

Ephesians 5:8

Evan rose early, then headed downstairs in the quiet house to start up the cookstove and put on a pot of water for coffee. Next, as was his routine, he left for his usual hour's worth of chores before breakfast. The sun barely peeked over the horizon by the time he finally made his way back to the house—a house he could no longer enter anymore with any real feeling of pleasure.

To his surprise, the kitchen was as he had left it, save that the fire in the cookstove was raging and the water in the coffeepot had all but boiled away. "Claire?" Evan called as he walked through the house, and then down the stairs into the cellar. "Are you there? Is something wrong? Why isn't breakfast started?"

She was nowhere to be found. With growing concern, Evan set out for the bunkhouse, where Claire and her brother had taken up what was beginning to seem permanent residence. He knocked on the door. No one answered. He knocked again, harder this time.

"Claire, Ian! Are you all right in there?"

Finally, fear beginning to lick at him, Evan tried the door handle, which opened easily. He walked into a silent house, the only sounds the dying fire popping and snapping in the little parlor's potbellied stove, and the incessant ticking of the table clock. A quick search revealed neither Claire nor Ian was present. Most of their clothing was also gone, as was Claire's harp.

Evan raced back into the parlor, glancing frantically around. His gaze fell on a white sheet of paper folded in two and propped on the table between the clock and a small pile of books. His heart pounding with dread, Evan picked up the note and read it.

His vision blurred. He threw back his head and groaned. Then, with a sudden, wild surge of fury, he crumpled the note in his hand and hurled it against the nearest wall.

Claire was gone, as was Ian. Apparently her love for her brother was far stronger and deeper than had ever been her love for him. Evan collapsed in one of the chairs by the table and buried his face in his hands. He felt on the verge of tears, but for some reason the tears wouldn't come. Myriad emotions roiled within him—confusion, anger, hurt, and a soul-deep sense of betrayal.

Claire was his wife. She had vowed to remain with him through good times and bad, until death parted them. How could she do this to him, to their marriage?

It was all that selfish, troublesome boy's fault! If it hadn't been for him, none of this would've happened. Yet, even as Evan heaped all the blame on Ian, he knew that he was as much at fault as was the boy. His own

312

actions, or lack of them, had driven Claire away just as surely as had Ian's.

He shook his head and groaned again, the sound little more than a mournful sough in the hushed, empty house. No matter what she might have done, in keeping secrets from him, in frequently putting her brother's needs over his, he still loved Claire with all his heart. What would he do without her? *What would he do?*

More than anything he had ever wanted, Evan wished his father was back home. His father would know what to do. His first wife—Evan's mother—had left him, too. His father would understand how it felt, could advise him.

"God, why?" Evan shouted suddenly, lifting a face ravaged with grief and anger. "We wed in *Your* church, before one of *Your* priests, in *Your* sight. How *could* You let this happen?"

But why wouldn't God let it happen? Evan asked himself bitterly. It wasn't as if he had ever particularly gone out of his way to follow the Lord. Oh, sure, he went to church every Sunday now that he was home, said all the prayers and sang all the hymns along with everyone else. And he tried to treat people decently. But when had he ever turned to God in times of trouble, thought to ask for His help? Or, more importantly still, when had he given Him thanks or thought of Him in the good times?

It didn't sit well with Evan now, to come whining and begging for God's help, when he couldn't ever be bothered before. His pride would've never allowed him to treat another person that way. He sure wasn't about to do that to God.

He'd just have to figure out what to do all by himself. That was what a man did, and he *had* been claiming that prerogative for a while now. He'd just have to figure this one out, come up with some way to get Claire back. He wasn't about to let some snot-nosed kid come between him and his wife. He wasn't about to give up on his marriage either.

Outside, he could hear the hands beginning to file onto the back porch and enter the kitchen for their breakfast. Evan shook his head. How was he going to explain where Claire was or why there wouldn't be much of a breakfast this morning, save maybe some jelly sandwiches and coffee?

Evan pushed to his feet. First things first, he resolved. He'd get Beth up to help with breakfast, pack for the journey ahead, and then go have a quick talk with Devlin. In his father's absence, his relationship with his cousin had grown into a surprising friendship. And, one way or another, Devlin needed to know what was going on.

There was no doubt in Evan's mind that he'd then head out after his wife. The problem lay in deciding what he'd say once he found Claire, and how he'd convince her to come home.

ê

Jake Whitmore and Noah Starr rode in just as Evan finished checking Culdee Gold's cinch one last time before mounting up. "Well, what's happened now?" he growled, knowing by the looks on their faces that this wasn't a social call.

Noah glanced at Jake, then Evan. "I need to talk with Claire."

Evan rubbed his beard-stubbled jaw, savagely tamping down a freshened swell of jealousy. "Well, she isn't here. She and Ian rode out some time last night, headed back to Scotland."

The priest drew in a sharp, shallow breath. "I was afraid of that. Claire came to see me yesterday. She was very upset, despairing over what to do, and something

314

just didn't seem right to me. I couldn't sleep much last night, worrying over it. So, first thing this morning, I headed out here to talk with her." His mouth quirked ruefully. "Seems, though, I got here too late."

Evan's gaze swung to the sheriff's. "And why are you here? Noah sure didn't need an escort."

Jake Whitmore shrugged and smiled. "Thought I'd ride along and bring you the good news. One of Sadie's girls finally broke down and confessed she was the one who shot Gerard. Seems she had a grudge against him that just wouldn't go away."

Evan knew he should feel some sense of relief that the cloud of suspicion hanging over him and Ian had finally lifted. But, somehow, in light of the imminent possibility of losing Claire, even a murder charge didn't seem all that important anymore. "Glad to hear that's all cleared up," he muttered. "Now, if you don't mind, I've got to hit the trail after my wife. No telling how much head start she's got on me."

"Evan, wait," Noah called out as he turned to his horse. The priest swung down from his own mount, tied it to the hitching post, and hurried over. "Before you leave, I think we should talk."

"And what would we have to talk about?"

"About Claire. There are some things you need to understand, if you're ever to have any hope of convincing her to come back home."

❧

Their trail was a lot easier to follow than he had first expected. But then, Evan thought, it wasn't as if Claire and Ian had had any experience tracking or being tracked. He should be grateful for that, he supposed.

From what he could tell from their trail, they had about a three- maybe four-hour lead on him. He'd have to do some mighty hard riding to close the distance before nightfall. Odds were, though, he wouldn't be able to catch up with them until tomorrow.

Their tracks headed north. Evan figured Claire meant to reach Denver, then take a train east from there. Lucky for him it was more than a day's horseback ride, or he might just miss them if they were able to catch a train leaving soon after they arrived. And, once they were on that train, he might never find them.

He urged Culdee Gold back into an easy, ground-eating lope. The big buckskin gelding was one of the ranch's fastest long-endurance horses. If any animal could catch up with Claire's and Ian's mounts, Culdee Gold could.

The hours passed with wearying regularity. Noon came and went. Save for a few stops to cool and water his horse, and the necessary times he had to allow for a fast walk to rest the buckskin, Evan kept up a blistering pace. He had no appetite anyway. His whole life had just walked out on him. The gnawing, ever-present fear he might lose Claire forever was enough to twist his gut in knots and make him sick to his stomach.

He had plenty of time to think long and hard on what Noah had told him. He had always known of Claire's deep commitment to her brother, and—now—what they had gone through all those years before he had come into the picture. But looking back, Evan realized he hadn't fully comprehended the guilt Claire carried, not only for her impulsive act that made both children homeless, but for Ian's emotional damage, for which she felt responsible.

It was that deep-seated sense of honor and loyalty, when Claire came to believe her and her brother's continued presence at Culdee Creek was beginning to irreparably harm the MacKays, that had been the catalyst for her decision to leave. She had finally felt boxed into a corner, caught between Evan and her brother.

Shame filled him. All he had been able to see was her lack of loyalty to him when she persisted in defending her brother, and when she withheld information. He had refused to allow that she saw both sides far more clearly then they had, and was battling ferociously to help the both of them open their eyes.

Not that the answers would've been simple or the problems easy to resolve. Ian wasn't going to settle down anytime soon. But then, Evan admitted with a twinge of guilt, neither had he. He imagined, if his father were here to talk to right about now, there would be an earful about all the frustration, anger, and heartache he had caused him.

He supposed no man could really, truly understand what it took to be a parent and husband until he was one. But even the finally knowing wasn't enough. It still took a day-in, day-out courage and determination that could tax any man's soul. Any woman's, too.

It scared him spitless, this knowledge. Responsibility, sticking it out when things got tough, and admitting to one's human limitations, always did. As much as Evan wanted to be the kind of man Claire could count on from here on out, he still secretly wondered if he had what it took.

That fear, though, didn't matter nearly as much anymore. Neither did his misdirected pride. They weren't half as important as the courage and determination needed to see things through. They didn't hold a candle to the strength and support the Lord could give a humble, caring, compassionate man. With the Lord's help, they weren't just gifts bestowed on some and withheld from others. They were brought to fruition by faith and dint of sheer hard work, each and every day of one's life.

One thing *was* certain. He wasn't alone in this, and never had been. He had a fine family and good friends to turn to, to help him learn. He had a magnificent woman who'd stick by him, if only he met her halfway. And then, there was always the Lord.

"When you made your wedding vows before God," Noah had offered in that kind, gentle, yet insightful way of his, "you didn't just make your promises to Claire. You made them to God, too. And, as Claire repeated those vows to you, promising the same, the Lord uttered them back to the both of you. After all," the priest had then said with a wry grin, "there's three in this marriage, not just two. Marriage is a living example of Christ's love-union with His Church, and one of the greatest ways of encountering Him and receiving His grace."

Though Evan had, on a simple level at least, understood the solemn importance of the marital union, he realized now he hadn't truly understood it as a sacred and holy call from God, a call as divine as that to the priesthood or unmarried life. For him and for Claire, marriage was the way in which they would fulfill God's will for them—and model the meaning of His love for His people.

"Lord, I know I'm a bit late in turning to You for help in this marriage," he said, raising his gaze to heaven as he rode along, "but I'm here now. Teach me what I need to know. Help me, when and if I find Claire, to say what she needs to hear, and say it right. And help me to be the man—the father—that Ian needs. I can't do this without You, so help me, please."

In the utterance of that prayer, a heavy weight lifted from Evan's shoulders. With a gladdened heart, he urged Culdee Gold back into another lope. Somehow, he knew the Lord would be with him when he needed

Him the most. Just as, from now on, he intended to keep the Lord ever at his side.

ℰ

"Are you going to sniffle and sob all the way to Denver, then?" Ian demanded finally, after several hours on the trail. "It's done, you know. We've put Culdee Creek behind us, and there's no going back."

"A-aye, I kn-know." Claire hiccuped, then reached into her jacket pocket to extract a handkerchief and blow her nose. "I just can't shake the feeling that we're making the biggest mistake of our lives."

"And how could it be a mistake? I was sure to end up in some reformatory, or worse, if Evan and that sheriff had their way. I left naught behind, save Elizabeth." He sighed. "If only she would've come with us, everything would've been perfect. But I couldn't trust her not to tell her brother of our plans."

"So, it would've then all been perfect for you," Claire muttered, inexplicably irritated, "but what about me? Have you ever once given any thought to *my* needs?"

"Well, I feel badly that you had to leave your husband. Not that," her brother added with a derisive snort, "he was much of a husband to you. Seems to me he took greater pleasure in tormenting me than in trying to please you."

"By mountain and sea!" The tension that had been building for the past few weeks exploded with a sudden, surprising force. With a tug on the reins, Claire halted her horse. "Don't ever again speak so against Evan, Ian Sutherland! He tried verra, verra hard to work things out with you. And, while we're on the subject, let me tell you that *I'm* getting sick and tired of all *your* moaning and whining, too. It's past time you stand up and be the man you seem to think you are. Until you destroyed his confidence in you, with your repeated refusal to have a care with Beth, Evan treated you well. But did you ever make much of an effort to meet him even halfway? Did you?"

His mouth agape, her brother stared at her in amazement. Gazing back at him, something clicked, finally fell into place, within Claire. Until this instant, she had never truly understood how much she had always catered to Ian, tried ceaselessly to smooth every rough bump in the road for him. Evan had spoken true, she realized with a pang of guilt. In the doing, she *had* all but crippled him.

She hadn't ever really trusted Ian, she realized, to make his own mistakes and learn what he needed from them. She hadn't even, if the truth were told, fully trusted Evan or his love for her.

It had always seemed the safer course to take matters into her own hands. After all, if she kept everything under control, nothing could ever hurt her again. It had been fear, pure and simple, that had gotten her to this sorry point. That fear, however, might now be the ruin of them all.

That fear of finally losing control was also why she was running now. Running away had always been a control of last resort.

This time, though, Claire saw the ultimate futility of her endless quest for control. Not only was she running from the man she loved, but the father of their unborn child, and that was wrong. What she had always really been seeking was the gift of trust—of others, herself, and, most of all, in God.

"What you lack the Lord will supply, if only you turn to Him, and place all your trust in Him," she recalled the words Noah Starr had spoken to her but yesterday. And those very words, that yesterday seemed not to hold any answers, suddenly assumed a clarity and meaning that took Claire's breath away.

Too many times before, Claire knew she had chosen to rely on her own counsel rather than on the Lord's. Too many times before, she could now look back and admit she had erred when she had done so. This time, however, she vowed, the stakes were far too high to rely solely on herself. This time, the prize was not only the rest of her life, but mayhap that of Ian and even Evan's, too.

Lord, Claire silently prayed, help me. I want to be Your light to others, but I don't know how. Please, lead me through the darkness. Lead me into the light.

"Well, Ian,"–Claire then turned back to her brother–"won't you answer me? Tell me true. Did *you* ever try and meet Evan halfway?"

"What does it matter now? We've left him far behind, never to return."

"It matters because we *must* work this out, or I fear it'll be the cause of a great, lasting pain for us all."

"You love him more than me." He ducked his head, refusing to meet her gaze. "I hate him for that most of all."

"Och, nay, brother." Claire nudged her horse closer to him. She leaned over and took his chin, lifting his tear-bright gaze to hers. In his eyes she saw fear, uncertainty, and pain. Yet, though it seemed a hard thing to do, this time Claire put all her trust in the Lord, and did what she knew she must.

"I don't love Evan more; I love him differently," she explained as gently as she could. "He's my husband. I've taken vows to love and cling fast to him all my life. Someday you'll make those same vows to a woman. Then you'll understand the difference. Brother and sister though we may be, sooner or later we must both go our separate ways."

"But you said we'd always be together, have each other. And we can, once we return to Scotland."

"While we were young and needed each other, aye, that was true. But, bit by wee bit, our lives are changing now. Others are beginning to claim an even more powerful place in our hearts, aren't they?" She released his chin and tenderly stroked a lock of hair from his eyes. "Though Beth is just the first of many lasses who'll win your heart, can't you see how strong a pull even she has had on you? So strong, indeed, that you were willing to risk hurting me and ruining your life here just to be with her."

"Aye, I suppose I can," he at last admitted grudgingly. "It won't change *his* opinion of me, though, no matter how hard I try to make amends. He's convinced I'm a liar and mayhap even a killer."

Claire bit her lip, at a sudden loss over how to reassure her brother to the contrary. Though Evan hadn't come right out and said it, the look in his eyes, the tone of his voice, most certainly had always betrayed his doubts as to Ian's innocence and moral fiber. Still, she couldn't blame him. Evan didn't know Ian like she did, and the evidence, however circumstantial it was, did seem to point an accusing finger at her brother. What mattered in the end, though, was that she trust in her husband and his ability to find some honorable way through it all. At the very least, he deserved the chance to try. And he deserved her love.

She straightened in her saddle. "You haven't made aught easy for anyone for a long while now. Can't you see that you must give—"

"Naught would change if we went back—and that's what you're now trying to talk me into doing, isn't it, Claire? If the sheriff came for me, or if Evan still eventually decided to send me away, I'd run off first. I swear I would!" her brother cried.

"Och, Ian, and what would that solve?" She shook her head, a sudden, strong certainty filling her. "It's long past time for running, for the both of us. I see that now. It's time to stand and fight for a good life, for home, for family. And Culdee Creek *is* now our home, the Mac-Kays our family."

Claire stretched out her hand to her brother. "We've always fought hard to survive before. Will you fight that battle one more time with me?"

Ian stared at her, his gaze hesitant and fearful. Then, he expelled a low, weary breath and nodded. "Aye, I'll try," he said, reaching out to give her hand a quick squeeze before releasing it. "But only for you, Claire. Only for you."

"Nay, brother," she whispered achingly. "Do it first and foremost for yourself. This life, with all its wondrous promise, is as important to you as it is to me. In Culdee we gained the right to begin anew. At Culdee Creek, we've finally found home."

With that, Claire turned her horse south. Not even glancing around to make sure Ian followed, she urged her mount back the way they had come, back to Culdee Creek, back home.

Epilogue

As if by God's own design, to welcome Abby, Conor, and little Sean MacKay home, the tenth of December dawned unseasonably warm and pleasant. The morning of their impending arrival was spent in a flurry of frenetic activity. Evan, Claire, and Ian hurriedly moved all their belongings back into the bunkhouse, while Beth cleaned her parents' bedroom and put fresh sheets on the bed. A huge slab of beef, complete with carrots, onions, and potatoes, was put in the oven to roast. A cake was made and iced, and bread was baked.

At long last, dressed in their Sunday best, they gathered to leave for Grand View's train depot. Claire settled in beside Evan in the buggy's front seat, cast a quick glance over her shoulder at Beth and Ian, and sighed in contentment. Her husband clucked to the horse, which immediately set out. Behind them, in their own buggy, came Devlin, Hannah, and their brood, followed by Frank Murphy driving the buckboard.

A gentle breeze blew, crisp but invigorating. Around Claire, the frost-browned landscape took on a soft, golden hue. Overhead, a red-tailed hawk soared on the air currents, his harsh, piercing cry filling the heavens.

Claire scooted close, slipping her arm beneath Evan's. He glanced at her, his face lighting in a loving smile. She didn't think she'd ever tire of looking at him. What woman would? He was so handsome, so good, so much a man among men.

The words Evan had spoken to her, that day he had ridden out after them, ran through Claire's mind now. She had seen him coming from far away and, even before she could truly recognize him, she had known it was Evan. As he galloped toward them, Claire had turned to Ian.

"Stay back a ways and wait. I need to talk to Evan first."

Her brother had shot her a nervous, uncertain glance, then nodded. "Aye. That'd be best, I'd wager."

Then, heart thudding with her own fearful uncertainty, Claire had ridden up to meet her husband. She watched Evan rein in before her, eye her warily, then remove his Stetson and wipe the sweat from his brow with the back of his sleeve.

"Get turned around in your trip to Denver?" he asked, a taut smile twitching one corner of his mouth, "or dare I hope you'd had a change of heart and were heading home?"

"We were coming home," Claire said. "That is, if you'll still have us."

Something flickered in his eyes, then was gone. Was it a flash of joy or relief? she wondered. Dear Lord, let it be so!

"You know I'll still have you," Evan replied hoarsely. "I love you, Claire. I don't want to lose you."

"And I don't want to lose you either. I just couldn't see through all the anger and pain until I finally turned my back on it and rode away." She inhaled a shuddering breath. "That's when I realized how unfair I had—"

He lifted his hand to silence her. "Don't. We've both made mistakes, but that doesn't matter anymore. What matters is our love, and the vows we made to each other. What matters is we have family and friends and God to help us. With all that, how can we fail, if only we keep on trying?"

"Aye, we have all that, and more." Tears filled Claire's eyes. "I'm carrying our child, Evan. It's yet another reason I came back. It was wrong of me to take our child from you."

His eyes widened. His glance lowered to her belly. "A child? I-I'm going to be a father?"

"Aye, that you are." Claire cocked her head, her apprehension flaring anew. "How do you feel about that?"

In reply, Evan swung his leg over the saddle horn and slid off his horse. With two quick strides, he was at her side. "How do I feel about it?" he repeated, gazing up at her and taking her hand. "Why, it's wonderful. Absolutely wonderful!"

"I-I wanted you to know. I don't ever want to keep any secrets from you again."

He squeezed her hand. "I know, Claire. I know."

Behind them, Ian's horse snorted and pawed at the ground. Evan's glance swung to the boy, then back to her.

"He came back willingly, too," Claire said. "Despite the charges that might still be made against him for Brody Gerard's death. Despite the way you still might feel about him. I just wanted you to know that."

Evan nodded. "I need to talk to him." He released her hand, stepped back, then turned and walked to Ian.

Her heart in her throat, Claire twisted in the saddle to watch them. Evan halted at Ian's side. Cautiously, her brother met his gaze.

"I'm sorry for how things have gone between us of late," she heard her husband say. "I know I took the news you killed your uncle pretty hard that day, but even in my anger, I never once imagined you a killer,

Ian. I'd already heard enough of that story from Claire, to know why you had to do what you did." He held out his hand to the boy. "I'd like to start fresh, if you can find it in your heart to forgive me."

For a long moment Ian stared down at it, his jaw working in an effort to contain his emotions. At last, though, he grasped Evan's hand. "I'd like that, too. To start fresh, I mean . . ."

Just then the buggy bounced over a rut in the road, jolting Claire's thoughts back to the present. Aye, she mused. Both Evan and Ian had shown commendable grace that day, and for that she'd be ever thankful.

There had been some equally tense moments between Ian and Evan since then. Still, both had worked hard to see each and every problem through to a satisfying end—even the problem of Ian and Beth.

With some help from Noah and Claire, both young-sters had finally come to the conclusion that things had indeed been progressing too rapidly between them. Both had agreed not to spend time alone with each other, and they *had* tried. Nonetheless, Claire was grate-ful Abby and Conor were finally returning. Their pres-ence and counsel could only improve the situation.

"It's a grand, grand day, wouldn't you say, husband?" Claire asked of a sudden, her heart near to bursting with joy. The babe, their babe, had just moved within, reminding her of even more to be thankful for.

"Yes, ma'am, it's indeed a grand day," he replied with a chuckle. "That sentiment, though, wouldn't have any-thing to do with the knowledge that you won't have to cook all those big meals anymore, would it?"

"Och, I suppose that would be a small part of it." Claire snuggled yet closer. "But I was also thinking of our new house, and hoping, with your father back, you'd now have time to finish it. We'll be needing it by the end of June, you know."

He angled his head in thought. "Well, with only the interior work left to do, I should easily meet that date. Just in time for our baby's arrival."

She took his free hand and placed it on her belly. "Can you feel our babe move? Can you, Evan?"

He swallowed convulsively, then proceeded to stare at her belly for so long, the horse began to veer toward the grass growing off to the side.

"Have a care, will you, Evan?" Ian shouted from the backseat. "You're going to run us off the road!" He gave a snort of disgust and turned to Beth. "They'll be wed six months just after the first of the year, and they still go on like they're courting. You'd think they'd have gotten all that lovey-dovey stuff out of their system by now."

"Don't count on it!" Evan shouted in reply, then threw back his head and laughed. "A father. I'm going to be a father!"

The next several minutes were a wild clamor of excited voices and happy exclamations. By the time they all settled down, they had entered Grand View's outskirts. To Claire the ride down Winona Street seemed like a triumphant procession.

The first time she had visited the train depot was that day they had arrived from Scotland. She had been scared, uncertain, and terribly homesick. So much, though, had happened to change her life since that day.

In the distance, she caught sight of the Episcopal Church. Claire thought of Noah and Millie Starr. The young priest had never let her forget how important the Lord was in her life. His aunt had served as confidante, friend, and frequently also as the mother Claire never really had. She thanked the Lord for them.

Gates' Mercantile came into view. Just then, Mary Sue Edgerton, her arms filled with packages, stepped out. Claire grasped the buggy's armrest, half-stood up, and waved. "Good day, Mary Sue," she called. "It's a pleasure to see you!"

The expression of utter surprise on the other girl's face was mirrored in Evan's eyes. "Whatever possessed you to greet her like that?" he asked. "After all she's done to try and hurt you . . ."

"Even as Christ forgave you, so also do you," she quoted from the third chapter of Colossians. "Never again will I hold rancor in my heart toward Mary Sue. Truly, she hasn't any power to hurt me in Christ's love. Besides, there's no room for aught but joy. A woman would have to be daft not to be happy with a husband as fine as you, and the fact she's to be a mither."

Evan laughed as he pulled up before the train depot. In the distance the locomotive whistled, and a black trail of smoke rose on the air. "Well, I've always thought you were a particularly bright woman. That statement of yours but confirms it."

He wrapped the reins around the buggy's brake arm, then turned to Claire. "Of course, I couldn't be happier with my bonnie wife, either," he said, taking her into his arms. "A baby," Evan breathed against her ear. "We're going to have a baby."

"Come on, Elizabeth," Ian muttered from the back-seat. "I can't bear to sit here a moment longer and watch these two. They're far, far too old to be carrying on this way."

"A lot he knows," Claire's husband whispered and, moving to her mouth, proceeded to kiss her fully and most possessively.

With a squeal of brakes and hiss of steam, the train pulled into the depot. Evan drew back, looked deep into Claire's eyes, and smiled. "Well, shall we join the others in welcoming my folks home?"

"Aye," she said, her heart full of a soul-deep satisfaction. "Let's welcome them home."

Discussion Questions for Lady of Light

1. Both Ian and Claire Sutherland carry secret pain, pain that keeps them from fully opening their hearts and submitting their lives and deepest needs to God. And until they do so, they will never awaken to their own unique purpose in the world or to God's plan for them. Has anything like that ever happened to you? How did you come to that realization? What did you do to overcome an impediment that kept you closed off not only from the Lord's healing love, but also from a humble submission to His will?

2. Pride and self-love can be some of the greatest stumbling blocks in our lives. The false belief that we know better than God, however, is not readily relinquished. Can you recall times in your life when your pride and self-love got in the way of your walk with God? What effect did it have on you—and others? How did you finally find your way out of that self-deception and back to the Lord?

3. Claire, which means "bright, illustrious, source of light," is the heroine of *Lady of Light*. Like all of us, she was born to manifest the glory of God that is within her. In what ways do you try each day to let your light shine and, in doing so, mirror the light of Christ to others? What are some specific incidents when you feel you've been successful? When do you think you failed? What could you have done differently in those cases?

4. Ian has a tendency to run from his problems rather than staying and facing them. In doing so, he rarely finds resolution or achieves personal growth. Can you recall a time you were tempted to run when you should have stayed and fought your way through a problem? Did you call on the Lord to guide you through the difficult time? If so, what was the outcome? Did you learn anything from the experience that has aided you in similar situations? How?

5. Claire carries a terrible guilt over what her youthful impulsiveness brought about for her and her brother. That guilt causes her to overcompensate in her efforts to protect Ian, and as a result, she takes away his opportunity to grow. Have there been times when you, through fear, have tried to control a person or situation when you should have trusted more in the Lord instead? What did you learn from that experience?

6. Were there any other characters that touched or inspired you in *Lady of Light*? If so, which ones and in what ways?

7. What story themes, besides being a light to inspire and lead others through the darkness, did you discover while reading this book? Was there one theme in particular that struck home more forcibly? Why?

8. If you could ask the author any question, what would it be?

Also check out
Book 4
in the
Brides of Culdee
Creek series

Child of Promise

by Kathleen Morgan

The Plains
East of Colorado Springs, Colorado
December 1903

Today was the worst day of her life. Today the world, as Beth MacKay had always known it and always expected it to be, had turned upside down and inside out. Today her heart would surely break, her romantic dreams would be permanently crushed, and her love at long last would shrivel and die.

Noah Starr was getting married. Dear, sweet, magnificently handsome Noah would plight his troth with another woman—another woman who would carry his name, bear his children, and be his lover and helpmate.

With a deep, despairing sigh, Beth turned over in bed and buried her face in her pillow. How in the world was she going to live through this miserable, heart-wrenching day?

Three perilous tales of love and betrayal

IN THE SCOTTISH HIGHLANDS

from KATHLEEN MORGAN

"Morgan's skilled pen transports readers to another time and place."
—*Library Journal*

℞ Revell
a division of Baker Publishing Group

Available wherever books are sold

Kathleen Morgan has authored numerous novels for the general market and now focuses her writing on inspirational books. She has won many awards for her romance writing, including the 2002 Rose Award for Best Inspirational Romance. If you wish you contact Kathleen, look her up online or write to her at P.O. Box 62365, Colorado Springs, CO 80962.